THE DOWER HOUSE

THE DOWER HOUSE

Malcolm Macdonald

This first world edition published 2011
in Great Britain and in the USA by
SEVERN HOUSE PUBLISHERS LTD of
9–15 High Street, Sutton, Surrey, England, SM1 1DF.
Trade paperback edition first published
in Great Britain and the USA 2011 by
SEVERN HOUSE PUBLISHERS LTD.

British Library Cataloguing in Publication Data

Macdonald, Malcolm, 1932–
  The Dower House.
  1. Holocaust survivors – Fiction. 2. Communal living –
  England – Hertfordshire – Fiction. 3. Great Britain –
  Social conditions – 1945– – Fiction. 4. Love stories.
  I. Title
  823.9'14–dc22

ISBN-13: 978-0-7278-8061-1   (cased)
ISBN-13: 978-1-84751-368-7   (trade paper)

All Severn House titles are printed on acid-free paper.

Severn House Publishers support The Forest Stewardship Council [FSC],
the leading international forest certification organisation. All our titles that
are printed on Greenpeace-approved FSC-certified paper carry the FSC logo.

Typeset by Palimpsest Book Production Ltd.,
Falkirk, Stirlingshire, Scotland.
Printed and bound in Great Britain by
MPG Books Ltd., Bodmin, Cornwall.

for Nathan
the Perl
among our family's many jewels

Life is not an orderly progression, self-contained like a musical scale or a quadratic equation . . . If one is to record . . . life truthfully, one must aim at getting into the record of it something of the disorderly discontinuity which makes it so absurd, unpredictable, bearable.

from *The Journey Not the Arrival Matters* – Leonard Woolf

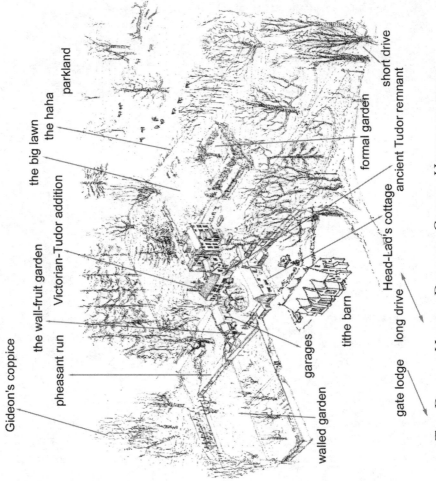

parkland

the haha

the big lawn

Victorian-Tudor addition

the wall-fruit garden

pheasant run

Gideon's coppice

walled garden

garages

tithe barn

Head-Lad's cottage

ancient Tudor remnant

formal garden

short drive

long drive

gate lodge

THE DOWER HOUSE, DORMER GREEN, HERTFORDSHIRE

Thursday, 15 April 1947

Willard A Johnson – the A stood for nothing (except, appropriately enough, itself) – emerged from the gloom of Hamburg's Hauptbahnhof with the feeling that he had somehow fallen into a time warp. The gap-toothed skyline was still as the firestorms of Operation Gomorrah had arranged it. There were the same piles of rubble, and between them the same makeshift carts threaded their way, drawn by men, dogs, even the occasional horse if it was strong enough to fetch a better price between the shafts than on the table. Nothing had changed.

A good omen?

Move! Stop distracting yourself. She'll say no, of course. And can you blame her? You can't treat a woman like that and expect anything else.

One taxi stood at the rank but it was waiting for a British colonel – or so the driver said.

He turned up the collar of his Burberry and triced himself into the drizzle-laden wind as he made his way down to the waterfront. April in Europe! People watched him with undisguised curiosity. A well-dressed, well-fed foreign civilian was not so common a sight on the Hamburg waterfront in that long cold spring of 1947.

What would she think, the moment she set eyes on him again?

How could you ever tell with Marianne?

What would she say? She might just stare at him and then maybe slam the door in his face.

Assume she would at least open the door. Yes, she'd do that, if only to leave him in no doubt that, when she slammed it again, she meant it.

An inch, then. If she gave him that inch . . . how, in two seconds, could you make your face say, 'I've traveled four thousand godawful miles and now I'm standing here before you because for almost six months I sat in my office, stateside, trying to work and all I could do was stare at the Mystic River and watch how the ripples turned into your face and because when

I tried to design houses the only shapes my pencil wanted to form were the letters of your name and because every female I saw on every street in Boston became you in the distance and not-you close up and because I was forever prepared for some magic to let me meet you around every corner'?

And that wasn't one thousandth part of it.

A seagull, made nervous by his sudden immobility, backed off to the edge of the quay, gave a single, plaintive mew, and launched itself into the rain. The port was busy. Big, ocean-going merchantmen, most still in camouflage, standing at the quays, being pillaged by cranes. Materiel for the new Germany. Or an age-old Germany?

The seagull was still wheeling overhead, waiting for him to move on. His eye soared with it, envying the creature its freedom.

Freedom! Two years ago he'd have been arrested by the Gestapo, just for walking along here like this – looking at ships, reading their names, guessing their cargoes. He'd have been shot, too, in these civilian clothes.

Beyond the fish market, where St-Pauli merges into Altona, he left the river bank and headed north toward the wasteland that had once been Kleine Freiheit and the Reeperbahn.

Here, too, nothing had changed. The buildings and punctured façades stood just as the firestorm had left them, five years back. Here and there a few householders had built shanty homes amid their own ruins, cleaning off the original bricks and reusing them with lime and sand. But the other kinds of premises, the bars, brothels, and nightclubs, which had made the name St-Pauli notorious around the world, stood roofless and hollow. The most dangerous of their shells had been levelled, reduced to neat, Teutonic stacks of brick, ready for the day when the wages of sin would be measured in something more bankable than coffee, butter, cigarettes, and nylons.

The occasional coincidence of such gaps, lining up across several blocks, revealed the wilderness that lies, buried but undead, beneath all the works of man. Great stretches of the city now bore the incongruous air of a park, a mighty, open space clothed in ragwort and fireweed as far as the eye could see – which, on a day like this was not so very far. Within half a mile the greens and yellows and magentas merged into an infinite, damp, unrelieved gray.

And somewhere out there, just beyond that near-horizon (just as she had been around every Boston corner) was Marianne.

Or perhaps she had patched it up with her parents and gone home to Sweden?

'Unfortunately, mein Herr, Fraülein von Ritter no longer lives here. I can give you her address in Gothenburg.'

Or worse: 'Fraülein von Ritter? Ach, die arme Marianne! Alas, you come too late, Herr Major . . .'

No – don't even think it!

Or worse yet – but very thinkable: 'Fraülein von Ritter? But she got married last week. It was the talk of Hamburg – surely you heard? She and the Baron are honeymooning in Austria right now.'

Anywhere near Mauthausen, I wonder?

Oh, for Christ's sake! That's why you're here now. That's why you've endured these months of misery – all because of stupid cracks like that. Mauthausen? She had nothing to do with Mauthausen.

Her last known address was in a narrow cul-de-sac off the square around the Brunnentor – a little oasis of old buildings that had survived the firestorm. He remembered a photograph Tony Palmer had shown him, taken the day after the last of the Gomorrah air raids. It showed the twisted, smouldering chassis of a fire-engine straddling a street. It had obviously been ignited by the flames; yet there, a hundred metres beyond it, stood trees in leaf and buildings that were not even scorched. A miracle.

'God is just a throw of the dice,' Tony had commented. 'At least this war has taught us that.'

Come to think of it, Tony must still be somewhere in this shell of a city, beavering away at its rebirth and teaching the Germans the veddy-veddy English art of losing gracefully.

The day was suddenly more cheerful. Perhaps, if it turned out that Marianne really had gone back to Sweden, or was married – or something – he'd look up his ol' buddy and they'd get drunk together like in the old days – like eighteen months back.

Like before they liberated Mauthausen.

He found himself facing her door. Still nothing had changed. The image that all Boston had not been able to efface slipped immaculately over the present reality. He raised his finger to the bell . . . but found himself paralysed. He stared at his hand in disbelief.

Move, he commanded.

It refused.

But the door opened anyway. Not a mere inch, but all the way, silently, on well-greased hinges.

A thin, starved-looking woman, mousey-haired and fortyish, stared belligerently up at him. '*Wass wollen Sie?*' she snapped – and then sneezed. She pretended not to notice what she left on Willard's raincoat.

'Ich suche Fräulein von Ritter,' he said.

'*Lincolnstrasse,*' she snapped, and slammed the door.

He turned, put his hands in his pockets, and thrust out his raincoat, hoping that the rain would wash it clean. But the name of the street left him with a sinking feeling, for Lincolnstrasse was one of the less-damaged side streets off the Reeperbahn. If she were truly there, he must have walked within a hundred metres of her.

A St-Pauli Girl? And not the buxom Bavarian blonde on the American beer bottle but a sad, semi-naked waif in a window. No – surely Marianne would rather swallow her pride and go back to her parents than . . . anything rather than that.

Lincolnstrasse was only five minutes' brisk walk away; he saw her immediately he entered it at the northern end – sitting under a café awning, on a folding camp stool, with a sketching easel before her and a young matelot, seated about a yard beyond at one of the café tables. She was sketching on-the-spot portraits for cash! It was, indeed, a kind of prostitution – the bartering of a talent that deserved so much more.

The sailor couldn't take his eyes off her. All her portraits of men must have that fixed stare, the gaze of men who cannot really believe their luck – to be licensed to gawp at such beauty for . . . how long? Four or five minutes? Ten? Short time, *Liebchen,* or long?

This particular session seemed to be nearing its end. Even from a distance Willard could see that most of the page was filled. He hastened toward her, unsure what he'd do when he got there but determined to let no one else take the sailor's place. And there he was in luck, for no one else was in line – though three lads across the street looked as if they were trying

to make up their minds. As he drew near he pulled his fedora
down as far as it would go and, lowering his head, took the
matelot's chair as soon as it fell vacant.

She did not look his way until the man had paid her – a few
coins, less than a mark – into her shaking hand. Then Willard
raised his head.

Their eyes met. He wanted to say something smart . . .
romantic . . . heartfelt . . . anything. But no words came. She
let out her breath in one long sigh. 'It's true,' she whispered.

'It's me, anyway.' He hardly recognized his own voice. 'I can't
live without you.'

She found her voice then. 'I watched you come all the way
down the street.' She tilted her head toward one of the café
tables where, he now saw, she had placed a GI shaving mirror.
'I said to me – myself – I said, "It's not true . . . it's not true
. . . it's not true . . ." all the way. Still I not can believe . . .'
She reached out and touched his face.

He clasped her hand to his cheek, her cold to his numbness.
'Fact is . . . I haven't known one single day's happiness since
. . . since I . . . I . . . was such a goddam fool, Marianne.
There!'

She reached out her thumb and massaged his lips. 'Will
. . . ard!'

'Think we can start over?' he asked.

'No!'

'No?'

'No – we start where we left off. Already enough time is
wasted.'

A waiter came out and began clearing a nearby table.

'Coffee?' Willard asked her.

She lowered her arm and nodded. 'Black – he knows. Anton's
his name.'

'Hey, Anton, ol' buddy! Black coffee for the lady and *café-au-lait*
for me – *with* milk!'

Marianne laughed. 'I'd forgotten that one! Oh, Willard!' She
reached out and this time gripped his arm. 'It's so good. *So*
good!'

He caught up her hand and kissed it fervently. 'The goodness
lies exclusively on the other side,' he said, paraphrasing a bit of
Swedish etiquette she had once taught him. 'I was ready for

you to turn away . . . hit me . . . shout at me . . . spit at me. Ha! Instead it was that lady . . . or that thing at the . . . where you live . . . she spat at me.' He tried to show her but the rain had done its work.

'Frau Becker? To spit at you? Tskoh!'

'She didn't mean to, I guess. She just sneezed but she saw where it went and she just did nothing.'

Anton returned with their coffees. 'And *Schwarzwälderkirsch torte*?' he asked.

'What else have you got?'

'Schwarzwälderkirsch torte.'

'Right – just leave the plate. You counted them, huh?'

The man merely smiled as he left them.

Willard picked up the mirror. 'I guess you have to watch behind you if you work around here.' He peered at the back of it. 'Hey! Whaddya know!'

She nodded as she bit hungrily on her torte. 'I still also have that packed bag,' she said through a mouthful of filo. 'Yours, too.'

He replaced his ex-mirror. 'That's good. You *should* eat. You don't look like you've been eating enough.'

'I knew you'd come back. So I never unpacked.'

'You really mean it? We head back to your lodging, pick up the bag, and . . . pffft? Hightail it out of town? Really?'

She looked up and down the street. 'I see nothing to keep us here.' Her hand reached out and took another slice.

He closed his eyes and shook his head.

'What?' she asked – inasmuch as any word could be articulated through such a mouthful.

'I'm just beginning to realize how . . . I mean, how little I . . . I dared to imagine how awful, how terrible it would have been if you'd just turned your back on me, here, now, and walked away. I . . . I don't know what I'd have done.'

'So!' She swallowed hard and cleared her mouth. 'We can sit here a bit and have a misery competition to see who was *most* miserable. Or . . .'

'Or?'

'Or you can tell me about where we shall live in America?'

'First things first. What say we head for Bielefeld and look up good-ol' Tony and good-ol' Adam?'

'But they are in London, working on that big plan.'

Willard laughed. 'Cute! So I'm not the only one to finagle an early discharge! So? Better still – a honeymoon in London!'

Tuesday, 22 April 1947

Felix Breit reached the cul-de-sac at the eastern end of Curzon Street and climbed the couple of steps into Fitzmaurice Place.

Steps. These of limestone, too.

The occasional car or taxi made its way around Berkeley Square but none entered this short dead-end of a street. At the door to the Lansdowne Club he paused, admiring its English modesty: 'Number Nine,' painted across the superport; there was no vulgar brass nameplate. He raised the simple knocker, hesitated, then let it fall once only. His imagination had worked on the words 'English Gentleman's Club' to paint an interior on the scale of the Paris Opera, so he expected to hear cavernous echoes. The knocker fell with a muted thud and without a rebound. After a pause, just as he was about to knock again, the door opened slowly, silently, to reveal a club porter. It opened inwards, which surprised Felix – a further reminder that he was no longer really in Europe. With one swift glance, the porter took in the caller's threadbare scruffiness and was on the point of directing him to the tradesmen's entrance when Felix said, 'Mister Wilson, please? Mister Adam Wilson?'

'Mister Wilson is not here at the moment, sir,' the man replied grudgingly. 'Perhaps you would care to leave a message?'

Felix produced a battered visiting card. 'Mister Wilson, you see. He gave me this card. And this place?' He pointed superfluously to the club's address, which was printed below Wilson's name: 9, Fitzmaurice Place. Scribbled on the back were the words: 'Breit – if you ever make it to London, look me up. A.W.!'

The porter tried to take the card but Felix clung to it as if it were a Nansen passport (which, in a sense, it was). 'You'd best come in and wait, Mister . . . er?'

'Breit. Felix Breit.' He spoke his name with a certain panache, as if the man should recognize it. He showed the back of the card again.

The porter let him in and took him up a short flight of steps past the reception desk.

Steps. These of marble. Another short flight led to the Crush Room, which was dominated by a large propellor on the far wall. 'If you wouldn't mind sitting there, Mister Breit?' he said. 'I can, as it happens, telephone Mister Wilson. Those are the morning papers.'

Left alone, Felix tried to read at least the headlines: DOLLAR-LOAN TALKS REACH NEW IMPASSE! But the text danced in a jumble before his eyes. It was partly exhaustion and partly the feverish excitement that had filled him ever since he had set foot on English soil, earlier that morning. He was *here* at last. He had finally, finally made it!

He rose and crossed the room to look at the propellor more closely, considering it as a piece of sculpture. An abstract. He was becoming more and more seduced by the abstract. The human form . . . well, it was difficult. Understandably.

Below the propellor was a framed pilot's licence, the first ever issued in Britain – to someone called Brabazon. What a magnificent name! After an ancient Aryan god, no doubt. Progenitor of countless petty gods, Celtic and Saxon. Felix could feel the sculpture itching in his palms already – Laocöon crossed with Mestrovic? No! Brabazon by Breit – pure Breit – of course!

He became aware that the porter was beckoning him to the phone. His heart sank. He had forgotten everything about Adam Wilson – and even the name of that other Englishman who had been with him the day they liberated Mauthausen. He could pass them in the street and never know it. Perhaps he had even done so, between Victoria and here. That whole period was turning into one merciful blur in his mind. Only the visiting card and its lifeline of promise, was sharp.

'Yes, hello, please?' he said. 'Mister Wilson?'

'Herr Breit? Is that really . . .'

'Please! *Mister* Breit.'

'Ah yes, of course. So it really is you! But how marvellous! I can hardly believe it.'

'Your card was all I had . . .'

'This is amazing. How are you now? Much better, I hope? Well, you could hardly be worse!'

Still no picture attached itself to that tinny voice. 'Yes, I am much better than when you saw me last, thank you.'

'Well, as I say, that wouldn't be difficult. Listen – there's no point in having a long conversation now. I can be with you in twenty minutes or so. Can you wait? I don't know what plans you—'

Felix laughed. 'I can wait, Mister Wilson. Believe me!'

'Silly question. When did you arrive in London?'

'Since two hours ago.'

'My goodness! A man who wastes no time, eh! Listen – be with you in no time, old man. And another thing – you won't believe this, but I have Tony Palmer with me at this moment – actually in my office! He was my oppo in AMGOT – the other English officer who was there that same day. I don't know if you remember much? But I'll bring him, too. He's grinning his head off here already. We'll both be over the moon to see you again.'

'I remember him well. Both of you.' Felix rummaged for his pocket sketchbook and scribbled the name: Tony Palmer.

'Good. Good. Let me have another word with McIver, the porter, eh?'

Wilson told the porter that Felix was his guest and was to be given whatever he wanted in the way of food or drink.

'He'd be some kind of DP, would he, sir?' The porter asked, anxious for some honourable explanation of Felix's scruffiness.

'Before the war, McIver, Felix Breit was probably the finest sculptor in Czechoslovakia. Or was it Hungary? One of those places, anyway. The only reason he's alive today . . . tell me, is he close enough to overhear this?'

'No, sir.'

'He spent part of the war in one of those concentration camps. The only reason he's here today is that the Nazis kept him alive for medical experiments. He's been very ill but now he's an honoured guest who deserves our every consideration. I'm sure you understand me?'

'Completely, Mister Wilson, sir. Leave it with me.' He cleared his throat. 'Just by chance, sir, Mister Corvo's in the Oval Room. The art critic, you know. I wonder . . . ?'

'Good idea, McIver. You're worth your weight in gold, man. Make the introductions for me, there's a good chap. Tell them I'll be along in two shakes.'

What finally reassured McIver as to the status of this down-at-heel European type was Corvo's response. 'Felix Breit?' he asked, springing to his feet. '*The* Felix Breit? My dear fellow – so you finally made it here! Wilson and I moved heaven and earth to find you after he came back to London, but you seemed to have vanished off the face of Europe. Where were you hiding?'

Felix observed Corvo closely throughout this speech. The man's name was vaguely familiar. 'In hospital in Salzburg,' he said. 'My papers went astray and for a long time I was delirious. Then TB. And then convalescence in Hamburg.

McIver cleared his throat. 'Mister Wilson said that if Mister Breit wanted anything in the way of refreshment . . . ?'

Corvo was all smiles. 'It would only be a spam sandwich at this hour – or might we rustle up an egg?'

Felix said, 'They wouldn't allow me scotch. I haven't tasted Scotch for three years. If you had even just a thimbleful?'

McIver thought he might be able to find a small sample of Scotch – and an egg and tomato sandwich, too.

Corvo took him into the Oval Room, saying, 'This is where George the Third was forced to sign away the American Colony, you know – in this actual room – when all this was Lord Lansdowne's private house. What a momentous bit of paper that was, eh! And now I sit here and scribble little jewelled articles for a living!'

Felix suddenly remembered where he had heard the name. 'Are you *William* Corvo, by chance?' he asked. 'The Corvo who wrote the British Council monograph on Kokoshka's English period?'

Corvo beamed. 'You know it?'

'One of the first things they put into my hands when I could read once more.'

'I'm flattered. Oscar still lives here, you know – down in Cornwall. Minus the famous doll! Martin Bloch is also here. I hope you'll be staying, too, Breit. So many of you brilliant Europeans are merely passing through on your way to America. I'm sure it's a great mistake. In the world of art America is *still* a colony – and likely to remain so. The post-war renaissance in art will be here in England. Art and Henry Ford are not compatible.' He raised his hands and gave a self-deprecatory smile, implying that he knew such talk was premature.

But Felix encouraged him with the lift of an eyebrow and a murmured, 'Interesting.'

Corvo needed no further invitation. It was a dreadful thing to say, but England had undoubtedly benefited from Hitler's loathing of 'modern' artists. Dozens of them had set up shop here: Bloch in Camberwell, Grose – teaching at Bedford but he'd come to London as soon as the theatres got into swing again – and Mestrovic, of course . . .

'My first hero,' Felix said. 'But for him I'd be an academic blacksmith today. Mestrovic, then Arp. And Brancusi, naturally.'

'Well, Paris isn't so far, either. The *Golden Arrow* is starting again soon. And when air travel gets going again, it'll only be an hour. London–Paris will be the new artistic axis of the world. And –' he glanced all about him and lowered his voice – 'strictly between ourselves, I think London will be the heavier end.'

Paris. His apartment on the Rue d'Argenteuil in the First Arrondissement, which was also the first arrondissement to be 'cleansed' by the Gestapo and their French collaborators. 'Paris is not a good memory for me.'

'Of course not.' Corvo was sympathetic. 'I heard about it from André Derain – when we were trying to trace you.'

'If he hadn't interceded for me, I'd have been taken to Łodz the following day. Sartre was no use at all.' He laughed coldly. 'I didn't even know I was Jewish until that day. *They* told *me*! I stood at my window watching the others being rounded up, thinking *poor bastards*! Can you believe that?'

'I can. But will we ever understand? It's so . . .' His long, slender hand groped for a word beyond his horizon. 'Your English is very good,' he concluded.

'I lived in America until I was seven.'

'Ah! Yes – I thought I detected a trace of American there.' He smiled apologetically and then added comfortingly, 'Only very slight, though.'

The sandwiches and whisky arrived – more than a mere sample. Corvo drank tea and declined all offers to share the food, though

Felix could see the man was peckish. *Enjoys self-sacrifice and deliv-ering commonplace opinions as if they were scandalous,* he noted. He could not break the habit of cold-classifying people; in Mauthausen it had spelled the difference between life and death.

Correction: between *survival* and death.

This was life, beginning again with nothing but a pre-war reputation, a DP pension, and a remote future claim against a reviving Germany – if it ever did revive. And meanwhile there was the heady whiff of grants – CEMA, UNRRA . . . Plus, of course, the seemingly boundless goodwill of all these splendid Englishmen. Oh yes, and the British Council.

'Talking of staying,' Corvo said, 'I trust you have somewhere organized for tonight? Otherwise . . .'

Felix waited as long as he decently could to see what that 'otherwise' might predicate – not realizing that in polite English usage the word had already delivered a bed and several breakfasts if he wanted them. 'I'm staying in Bloomsbury,' he said. 'A very nice man from CEMA has given me vouchers and a ration card. He says it's a small, private hotel. I haven't been there yet. My luggage is still at Victoria.' He dropped these personal details as people drop chips at roulette, with a public indifference that masks a churning gut. Would he ever accustom himself to yielding information freely, without the rubber hose, or the live wire an inch from his skin?

Corvo smiled. But so had the first caller from the Gestapo; he, too, had been a lover of art. What home in Germany now housed the largest single collection of Breits in the world? None, if the man had any sense of self-preservation. They'd be at the bottom of a lake somewhere.

'I expect you're longing to work again,' Corvo said.

Felix looked dispassionately at his fingertips. 'I did some clay modelling in hospital. I was surprised to discover how much these guys remembered.'

'Yes, your English really is excellent. It's so important to imbibe a language in one's boyhood.'

Felix stared into the middle distance and smiled as he echoed, 'Boyhood!'

The English were an enigma. In their heart of hearts, they knew that, although they had stood alone against 'the Hun' and battled him from Cairo to the Fatherland, those five gruelling years had still not taught them a thing. Europe was still a bewildering, far-off country where Hungary and Czechoslovakia were interchangeable. (Oh yes – his camp-honed ears had overheard that exchange!) From time to time he caught them off their guard, staring into his eyes, looking for answers.

Corvo said slowly, 'Of all those who survived the camps – I mean, of the few who survived – I believe the artists have the best chance of all. You are in touch with the means to comprehend it . . . convey it to the rest of baffled humanity. Oh dear! Is it patronizing of me to be saying such things to someone like you?'

The whisky burned pleasantly. A long-forgotten sensation, drowsy, fiery, massaged his muscles, slackened off his joints, enabled him to say, 'Not at all. I agree now, though it's only lately I've been able to think it.'

'And before?'

'I was too close to the experience. The idea of taking such an obscenity and somehow fashioning it into art seemed . . . well, an even greater obscenity.'

Corvo pulled a face. 'I hadn't considered it like that, but now you put it in such terms, I can't think of an answer.'

Felix watched him shrewdly. 'I could give you a comforting lie, Mister Corvo. Go back in history, for instance. Consider the starving eighteenth-century peasant, dying of consumption as he cuts the clay in the Austrian brickfields, and then the fine, brick-built concert hall where Mozart is heard nightly. It's too remote, isn't it, for the callous obscenity of the one to reach out and touch the sublime beauty of the other.'

'That's very good – and surely quite true?'

Felix shook his head, gently, because of the whisky. 'I know at least one man who managed it.'

Corvo leaned forward eagerly. 'A fellow artist?'

'An artist of a kind, anyway. Reinhard Heydrich – Himmler's deputy and the actual engineer of the *Vernichtung* of the Jews – there is no English word, I think.'

'Annihilation?'

'Too clinical. *Vernichtung* means "turning into nothing". Can one say "the *nothing*-ing of the Jews"?'

'One ought to be able to. I see what you mean.'

'Heydrich once shot a prisoner who dared to warn him that

the brake on a quarry wagon was defective. Yet that same Heydrich had his own quartet and was a superb violinist. Sublime, they said.' He shrugged his shoulders and smiled with an expansive, mid-European weariness.

'Impossible.' Corvo tried the same shrug but lacked the experiential referents. 'But to get back to art . . .'

'Ah, but we *were* actually talking about art. Art is *not* on the side of the angels. Nor of the devils, either. Art is on the side of itself. Only itself. I have survived. Mister Wilson and Mister Palmer will probably tell you it was because, for fourteen months, the doctors fed me nothing but peas and beans. But I know that is the least important part of the truth. I survived because Art wished it. Art needed me. For what purpose, Art will now reveal.' His hands gestured a mid-European hopelessness. He noted the effect of his words on Corvo and thought: *Metaphysics works here! I must remember this line.* 'I have no choice,' he concluded. 'Like the scorpion that stings the frog in the middle of the river . . .'

At that moment Wilson and Palmer entered.

The greetings were heartfelt but subdued – in a word: English. When they were done, the four men settled in a rough circle of chintz armchairs and Wilson sent McIver for a fresh pot of tea.

'I was just saying to Breit,' Corvo began, 'I hope he's not simply passing through on his way to America, like so many. I'm trying to persuade him of the advantages of staying.'

Wilson turned to Felix. 'It's up to you, old chap. Whatever you decide, we'll do our best to help. I know at least one American who'd sponsor you without hesitation – and he, in turn, would know hundreds more.' To Palmer he said, 'Willard A Johnson.'

'Snap!' Palmer said. To Felix he added: 'Johnson was our host on the day Mauthausen was liberated. Austria was American territory. We just happened to be on a courtesy visit that day.'

'There'll be a new renaissance in England,' Corvo explained to Palmer. 'We've obviously lost our empire. Our new role is to play Greece to America's Rome.'

'I hope you're right,' Palmer said. 'We're about to rent a Græco-Roman revival house in Hertfordshire – Adam and Sally, Nicole and me.' He smiled at Wilson. 'It will be the nucleus of *our* post-war renaissance.'

'May one ask where?' Corvo looked apologetically at Felix for turning the spotlight away from him for the moment. This was interesting. There might be a *Perspectives* article in it. Or *Country Life* at worst.

'It's the Dower House at Barwick Green. I don't suppose you know it?'

'Oh but I do!' Corvo placed complacent fingertips together. 'I wrote a piece on it for the AR. Between the wars.' He turned again to Breit, the catch of the week for him. '*Charming* place.'

'By Henry Holland,' Palmer said. 'With additions by Soane.'

Corvo winked at Felix. 'Architects and planners, eh! You can't beat them. Perhaps I should explain – Palmer and Wilson here are leading lights in the Greater London Plan, otherwise they'd still be waiting for their demob suits. Abercrombie pulled some strings and got them out. They sit in their offices all day, dishing out neat little prefabs for the proletariat, and then they down pencils and head for their country palace.'

Wilson said, 'Actually, old man, it's more of a commune – or a community . . . yes, more of a community.'

'Is it really a palace?' Felix asked.

'No – it's a pretty run-of-the-mill English country house, actually. Sixty rooms, three floors, Georgian, classical brickwork, pillared portico. There's a remnant of the original Tudor wing at the back, brickwork in English garden bond . . . plus stables, carriage houses, and so on. And five acres of garden.'

'*Ex*-garden,' Palmer said. 'But that's one of our communal projects.'

'It was a Catholic boys' school during the war, evacuated from the Channel Isles. Now it belongs to the South Herts Gravel Company, who, frankly, haven't the first idea what to do with it. However' – he winked – 'they *do* want to keep on the right side of a couple of 'leading architects in the Greater London Plan'!' He grinned at Corvo. 'Ta for the encomium, old boy.' Then back to Felix: 'But that's enough about us. It's *your* future that's important here.'

Felix bit a lip nervously. 'Sixty-odd rooms . . .' he mused. 'For just two families?'

'Ah! We hope there'll soon be more. There's room for eight or nine. Families, I mean.'

Wilson was on the point of asking Felix if he'd consider joining their budding community when he remembered the rule they had all agreed: No one should ever be invited to join; the first suggestion must always be theirs, so they could never say they were talked into it if things turned sour.

For his part, Felix was wondering how to work around to suggesting that if they had a small stable or outbuilding where he might set up his studio . . . He felt the invitation coming, saw Wilson's eyes dance in preparation. But then, with a brief flicker in Palmer's direction, they lowered again and the warmth fled. It reminded him of the despairing irony of the man from UNRRA as he surveyed that ocean of hopeful refugees, in the months after the liberation of Mauthausen: 'We offer them every assistance short of actual help.'

He understood that to get into this Dower House community he would have to beg. Well, he wasn't reduced to that, yet.

'You must come out and see the place,' Wilson said lamely.

That note he scribbled on the back of his card, Felix thought, and left pinned to my prison jacket – that was just the reflex shriek of an appalled conscience. It no longer translates into anything. Assistance, yes, but not actual help.

'Yes, that would be nice,' he said.

Where did one go in this city for a woman? Could one ask such a question in a club for gentlemen?

Friday, 25 April 1947

They emerged from the gloom of Hammersmith tube station, blinking at the bright autumnal sun, now in its evening arc.

Willard stabbed a finger toward the heart of its radiance. 'Over there!'

Marianne smiled; he always thought it so important to know his way around. For him, Hell must be a *new* foreign city for which he had no map. Arm in arm they walked down Queen Street toward the river. He asked her: 'When you said that – about Tony being taken from the Elbe and given to the Thames – did you know he actually lives in a houseboat?'

'No. That was pure . . . flux? Oh – *look* only! God, so beautiful!'

Above them now towered the northern abutment of Hammersmith Bridge, spiky, Gothic, crisp against the bleached sky – a contrast made even starker by the still-unwashed grime of the war years.

They both stopped, no longer man and wife, no longer lovers, but a pair of architects lost in the magical space defined and caged by its tracery. Willard echoed her, 'Will you just look at that!'

She took it as a gentle correction and stored away the phrase, a lover once again.

'Why do we respond like that?' he asked. 'Architecturally it's against all the values we ever learned. D'you suppose we could be in for a Victorian revival?'

They crossed the empty road, still gazing skyward, revelling in the dimensions now cradled between the swooping catenaries of the suspension chains, before they continued their stroll upriver, along the Lower Mall.

The sun burnished her fragile skin; every time he looked at her his love was renewed.

Where the Lower Mall joins the Chiswick Mall proper, they came in sight of the houseboat moorings, between the bank and the long, boat-shaped island of Chiswick Eyot.

'Heavens, so many!' Marianne exclaimed. 'It's a small town of boats.'

'But there's our man!' He pointed out a gray, oil-smeared hulk with the unmistakeable lines of a chine-hulled motor torpedo boat. It was moored to a barge, moored to an ex-pleasure boat, moored to . . . well, three or four other nautical mongrels that, finally, were moored to the bank. 'The only MTB in the pack. Tony always had a taste for the largest and grandest.'

There were perhaps half a dozen such columns of moored boats in all. Looking at them from this distance, Marianne was filled with a warm envy. In the evening sun, the little floating community looked so snug and secure. They must all lead the most wonderful lives. What more could people need than a few cabins, a galley, a mess room – and a huge, inviting city like London just a mile or two downriver? Threepence by Underground or bus. Tony's MTB had a new, civilian name painted on her bow in an architect's hand: LITTLE EXPECTATIONS. They stood on the bank and stared at her across the five intervening decks, wondering what to do next. Apart from the obvious ropes there were lengths of garden hose and some lethal-looking electricity cables, but nothing resembling a bell-push or even a line with a can of pebbles at the end of it. An RAF type with a Flying Officer Kite moustache poked his head out through a hatch on the second craft from shore, a squat tub of a thing with a sort of potting shed added to its deck. 'Need any help, old chap?' he asked.

Marianne wondered if he'd point out their directions with those luxuriant whiskers. Willard fought the impulse to ask if he could pick up the AFN on those things. 'Tony Palmer?' he said. 'I think he's in the MTB, but how do we get there?'

'Just stroll over all the decks between,' the man answered in a bewildered tone that implied, *What other way is there, for the love of Mike!*

His head remained poking out of the hatchway as he watched them picking an infinitely careful path among the mooring lines, pails, bicycles, boots, meat safes, and other junk that littered the decks. He chuckled at their caution. 'Beats any old temperance lecture, what!' he cried. 'When you get there, just stamp on the deck. I know they're aboard. TTFN!'

Marianne looked inquiringly at Willard. 'Ta Ta For Now,' he explained. And then he had to explain 'ta ta'.

She sighed. 'I'll never learn it. You must tell me when I say things wrong.'

'Sure. But don't worry. You'll pick it up in no time. English has no rules, really – not like German. There are just . . . well, different ways of saying things.'

The deck of the MTB was the height of a man above its neighbour. They had to climb a short ladder lashed to its rail. Somewhere in the bowels of the vessel a wind-up gramophone was playing a Debussy prelude. Willard, afraid that stamping on the deck might jerk the needle, took up a mop and tapped its handle on the chine of the hull. The music stopped. There were vibrations as someone ascended a stair. Moments later a young woman opened the deckhouse door. 'I'm sorry, I thought you were my 'usband,' she said, in accents more French than English.

Willard and Marianne glanced at each other. Husband?

'Mrs Palmer?' he asked the woman.

'Naturally.' She smiled.

'Mrs Tony Palmer? I didn't know Tony had married.' He turned to Marianne. 'Did you?'

She shook her head and stared at Tony's wife, a fine-looking woman with a no-nonsense face. Firm, determined jaw. Frank blue eyes, warily observant. And glossy, raven-black hair.

'Nicole?' Willard said suddenly, sure of his guess yet somehow not trusting it.

'Yes!' She laughed. 'And now I know *you*. Oh, forgive me, but you were much more . . . *élégant* in uniform. Major Johnson, no?'

'No – definitely not! It's *Mister* Johnson now. And this is my *Missiz* Johnson – Marianne. Honey, this is Nicole . . . er . . . oh, what kind of fool am I! – I was trying to remember your maiden name. Palmer, of course. Mrs Palmer.'

The two women shook hands. 'Come below, please,' Nicole said, though she made no immediate move from the door. 'Tony will be so 'appy to see you again, Willard. He talks about you often, you know. But he never says you are married?'

Willard grinned. 'He doesn't know. We only tied the knot last week. He's met Marianne, when we were with AMGOT, but he doesn't know we're married. We're on our honeymoon now, in fact – on our way back to the States. Are you expecting him home tonight – well, obviously, if you thought we were he.'

'He's only in the Dove, his favourite watering hole.' Nicole nodded toward the bank. Her eyes flashed with sudden merriment. 'Oh, let's go and give him a grand surprise!'

She grabbed a beret from a peg just inside the door and ushered them back down the ladder. A boisterous black Labrador leaped the gap, almost bowling Marianne over.

'Xupé!' Nicole scolded.

'What's that name?' Willard asked.

'It's really St-Exupéry. And this is Fifi.' She helped a small hairy terrier down to the lower level, where it skittered off in pursuit of Xupé.

'You must be very happy to live so,' Marianne said, gesturing toward the *Little Expectations*.

Nicole pulled a face. 'Last winter was the worst anyone could remember. I'm not spending another winter here.' She did not lock anything.

Conversation was difficult until they reached the bank.

'Going for a drink?' the RAF type called after them. 'Whacko!'

Nicole waved back at him. 'Don't walk near his hatch,' she warned Marianne. 'He only wants to peep up your skirt.'

'Your English has improved out of all recognition,' Willard said.

'Why not? I've nothing to do but listen to the wireless all day.'

He looked back at the boat and nodded. 'I guess it's not much of a challenge to you.' He turned to Marianne. 'During the war Nicole was a chef in her family restaurant in Trouville.'

'To be chef in the war must have required great art,' Marianne said.

'Oh, Nicole can make a gourmet feast of spam and rutabagas,' Willard said. Then, to Nicole: 'Marianne is an architect, too. But you – you'll take up your old profession now, surely? The English could sure do with it.'

'That's true.' She shook her head. 'But Tony has other ideas.'

'Such as?'

She chuckled. 'Oh, I'm certain he'll tell you, Willard. You especially. Be warned!'

These hints of an old, easy intimacy between them left Marianne feeling isolated.

They had reached the pub. He held open the door for the two women. Nicole put a finger to her lips and peeped inside. Then she looked back at them, nodded, and, imprisoning her two dogs, inclined her head toward the bar.

Tony was sitting on a stool scraping the ash and dottle from his pipe. He was dressed in the nondescript attire of an English gentleman at his ease, all sagging wool and leather patches; on his head, as a nautical concession, he wore a stocking cap topped out by an incongruously large woollen pompom that never settled.

Willard, now standing immediately behind Tony, his mouth just inches from his ear, said softly, 'I'd know the filthy stink of that secret weapon anywhere in the world.'

Tony turned round, not slowly, not quickly. 'Hello, Willard,' he said. 'I was just about to order another. What's yours?' Then he saw Marianne and – still without a great deal of surprise in his voice – added, 'Good God!'

Marianne laughed and threw her arms around his neck, giving him a mighty hug. 'Tony!' she scolded. 'You are so . . . so *typical!*'

Tony, in danger of overbalancing, slid round to face them, disentangling her arms in the process. He winked at her and looked Willard coolly up and down. 'Married?' he guessed. Willard nodded. 'Good-oh. Actually, not much point in asking what's yours. You can have stout or beer.'

'No Scotch?'

Several customers laughed, making Willard suddenly very conscious of being a bloody Yank.

They carried four half-pints of thin beer out to the river bank where they sat on the wall and luxuriated in the evening sun. 'Warm English beer!' Willard said. 'And easily three percent alcohol! How I have longed for this moment!'

Marianne sipped hers and, nodding at Nicole, said, '*Watering hole!*'

Willard had prepared himself for a flood of wartime reminiscences but none came. Nicole tried. She asked how Tony and Willard had met Marianne. Tony was vague. 'During our time with AMGOT,' he said, adding nothing to what Willard had already told her.

Simple loyalty impelled Willard to do no more than nod his confirmation, though he longed to tell Nicole everything, to make her and Marianne part of the same old-pals history. He tried to draw Tony out on his work with the Greater London Plan, but the man was equally laconic in his replies there.

The two wives started talking between themselves – again, not about the past but about the day-to-day difficulties of life in London and Hamburg. Mostly it was Nicole telling Marianne about rationing, and 'points' for everything, and 'Utility' furniture, and queues and permits and waiting lists.

Tony asked Willard if his civilian clothes meant he was out of the army, or was it some special dispensation the Americans allowed to honeymooning officers?

Willard told him, no, he was out for good.

Tony grinned. 'You old dog! How did you swing that one?'

'Don't ask,' Willard told him. 'I'm ashamed of it already. You're still working on this Greater London Plan?'

'Harder than ever, why? Want a desk?'

Willard laughed. 'It won't work, you know.'

'It's already working. Cheers! They've started with the Churchill Gardens Estate – go and have a look.'

'Cheers! Oh, sure, bits of it will get done. But you'll lose in the end. Impatience, inertia, greed, lack of vision – the same forces that scuppered Wren's plan after the Great Fire. But what the heck – I've said all this before. Abercrombie got you out good and early – and that's the most important thing.'

The talk drifted on to architecture in general – new styles, new materials, and the little matter of rebuilding the post-war world.

Finally, with a nod toward the MTB, Willard said, 'Somehow I don't connect that sort of thing with you.'

Nicole overheard him and broke off her conversation with Marianne at once. She stared at her husband, on tenterhooks for his reply.

Tony looked shrewdly at Willard, then at Marianne. 'Got anything on tomorrow?' he asked.

'Saturday?' Willard shrugged. 'Sightseeing, I guess. Why?'

'I'll show you a sight – a sight and a half! Care for a picnic?'

Willard looked at Marianne, then at the dead, turbid waters of the Thames.

'No, not here!' Tony laughed.

'Where, then?'

'Oh . . .' He was vague again. 'Near Hertford. Out in the country.' His eyes ranged from one to the other and for the first time since their reunion he was truly animated. 'What d'you say, eh? Adam Wilson will be there, too.'

Saturday, 26 April 1947

Felix left the train, as instructed, at Welwyn North. He watched as the tunnel swallowed it, watched the smoke obscure the daylight at the farther end. He lingered there on the down platform until it cleared again, from black through sepia to bright spring sunshine. Holes through solids held an increasing fascination for him. Not the moth-eaten mummies of Henry Moore's drawings but the pregnant-bellied granite and limestone of his own carvings.

'Barwick Green . . . the Dower House?' The words, spoken in an American accent, floated across the lines to him from the up platform. The man and the woman who had left the train with him and raced over the footbridge, were speaking to the porter. Felix drew breath to call out, to tell them he was headed that way, too, and that Mr Wilson was supposed to be coming to meet him; but a sudden violent shiver prevented him. Half of him warned that if he did not overcome this desire to shrink into cracks in the world, *they* would have won after all; the other half admitted the truth of it but pleaded that the time was not yet. He could not even make for the footbridge until the opposite platform was deserted.

While he dithered, Adam Wilson emerged from the ticket hall, saw him, and called out, 'Mister Breit!' Then his eyes fell on the man and the woman, too. 'And Willard and Marianne! Same train! Stroke of luck! Mister Breit! Sorry about this. Come over the bridge – or aren't you up to it?'

An express, bound for Kings Cross, came roaring out of the tunnel and severed their contact.

Steps. These of cast iron, pierced.

The guard's van rattled below Felix's feet as he crossed the bridge, whipping a tang of sulphur onto his tongue. The note changed as it clanged on over the viaduct but he did not linger now.

'Mister Breit! This, by the most extraordinary coincidence, is Willard Johnson. He was one of—'

'Willard *A* Johnson,' Marianne corrected him.

'Of course. Willard *A* Johnson, who was our colleague in AMGOT and our host at Mauthausen on the day you were liberated. And Willard, this is Felix Breit – *the* Felix Breit.'

Marianne saw her husband turn pale. 'Oh, my God! Feelicks Bryeet?' He pronounced it like a correction of Wilson's studiously correct German. To Adam he added, 'Tony didn't say.'

'He wasn't sure Breit would be coming.'

Felix was sure he and Palmer had forgotten the invitation altogether.

Johnson continued pumping his hand. 'Man! If it wasn't for

you, I'd probably be . . . I don't know – a Fuller Brush man.'
Seeing Adam's bewilderment he added, 'A door-to-door
salesman.'

'Why, please?'

'*Your* sculpture was *my* introduction to architecture. You . . .
Brancusi . . . the Bauhaus . . . architecture as an art form.
Eye-opening.'

Felix realized that Americans, too, inhabited that world where
Hungary and Czechoslovakia were vaguely interchangeable.
'Well!' he said, and smiled at the man's wife, who smiled
awkwardly back.

What was this awkwardness? Was she German? Did they
imagine he hated all Germans now? It was a German family in
Vichy France who sheltered him after his second arrest; he had
tried to look them up last month but was told they had died
in Ravensbrück and Theresienstadt. How to let these Saxons
know that Europe had become a little more complicated since
their tribe had last lived there?

'Forgive me,' Johnson apologized. 'Herr Bryeet, allow me
to . . .'

He was obviously going to introduce his wife. Swiftly Felix
took her hand and kissed the air an inch from her knuckles; it
would have offended him if *she* had been introduced to *him*
instead of the correct way round. '*Küss die Hand, gnädige Frau.*
Felix Breit.'

She gave a single laugh that was surely ironic and replied,
'Frau-Arkitekt Marianne Johnson.'

Their eyes dwelled in each other's and Felix experienced a
rapport that was purely European.

'Actually, Marianne is Swedish,' Wilson said. 'Or, I suppose,
American now.'

'She's also an architect in her own right,' Willard added.

She saw the surprise in Felix's eyes and realized he thought
she looked too young to be qualified. 'An apprentice,' she
added.

'It's not a bad profession to join these days, madame,' Felix
said.

'Listen!' Willard said. 'I can't take all this sir, madame, *gnädige
Frau,* stuff. It's Marianne, Willard . . . Felix – OK, Adam?'

Smiles all round.

'Well!' Adam rubbed his hands briskly. 'I don't think the pony can haul all four of us to the top of the hill so . . .'

'Pony?' Willard said.

'Petrol's rationed in case you didn't know.'

'Gee! I should've thought. I could have fixed you up with some.'

Adam threw back his head and laughed. 'Fix! Whenever I hear that word, I think of you, Willard.' To Felix he added, 'Whatever you want, Willard can "fix" it.'

Willard nodded. 'Be proud to,' he said as they wandered out to the station forecourt.

'I can walk,' Felix said. 'Let Mrs Johnson ride. Marianne.'

'I shall lead the pony,' she said, walking straight up to him. 'We can walk all the way and give this ol' fella a break.'

Adam could detect Willard's vowels in her speech.

'Tony told me you married Sally Beaumont?' Willard said. To Felix he explained, 'Another goddam architect! But she's special. She was his boss in AMGOT *and* the designer of the famous British army "spider" hut. She had the highest-ranking wartime commission in the women's services – acting-temporary brigadier. None of us made it above colonel.'

'Or even major,' Adam added. 'She's going into private practice when . . . well, you'll see.'

Marianne had meanwhile been appraising the pony. 'A creature like this should be worth a fortune in Hamburg,' she said. Then, to Felix: 'That's where I was living since the liberation, until we got married last month. D'you know it?'

The two men glanced in dismay at Felix, whose heart fell. How could he make them understand he didn't require their solicitude – or not in such small ways as that? If they wanted to pull strings to get him commissions, a free studio, a pension or two . . . fine. But not all this pussyfooting – as if he still had *feelings,* for heaven's sake.

'Hamburg!' he said. 'My favourite city – what's left of it! I suppose it had to be done. Ironic, though, that it was the most anti-Hitler city in all Germany. He got a very poor reception there.'

'You've seen it?' Willard asked.

'Several times. I went there for medical tests. And convalescence.'

'Not during . . .' Adam faltered.

'No.' He chuckled drily. 'Not *during*. Funnily enough, I, too, was there last week. We must *just* have missed each other.'

When they realized he was joking they laughed. Too much.

Adam cut in: 'As I was saying – Willard was with us the day you were liberated. In fact, Tony and I were present as guests of the American section of AMGOT.'

'I remember,' Felix said – which embarrassed them because, as Adam had been about to add, Willard had been on the far side of the camp at the moment when he and Tony had realized that the Felix Breit they were helping was *the* Felix Breit. And Felix had lapsed into a near-coma by the time Willard arrived.

'Liberated?' Marianne asked.

Adam explained. She reached across him, squeezed Felix's arm, and looked ahead, rather fixedly.

They reached the bottom of the slope below the forecourt and turned left, facing a reluctant pony up the hill. The watery sun cast shorter shadows on the slope ahead of them and soon their outlines were lost in the blunted, lacy penumbra of new, half-formed leaves on the overarching trees.

'So what's with this Great Secret out here in the boondocks?' Willard asked Adam. 'Tony was very cagey. It had better be good.'

'It'll be interesting, anyway,' he replied. 'Interesting to hear what you think of it.'

'And that's all you're going to tell us?'

'Until I can just say *voilà!* Tony and Nicole are there already, waiting for us – so I can promise you a wonderful high-tea, conjured out of nothing.'

'Yeah – that's another thing I meant to ask: She was back in Trouville, you two were in Hamburg – how did those two get together again?'

'He went back and found her. Couldn't face life without her.' He paused and asked Marianne, 'Why the grin?'

'When you said "went back and found her",' she replied, 'so was it with Willard and me.'

'All last winter,' Willard confirmed. 'I used to sit in my office staring at the Mystic River, seeing her face in every ripple.'

Adam levelled an accusing finger at him but said nothing.

Willard said it for him. 'I know, I know. You done tol' me!'

'What did he tell you?' Marianne asked.

'Never mind.'

'I told him he was a fool if he ever thought he could go back home and forget you.'

'Adam – how nice! When was that?'

'Right after . . .' he began and then fell silent.

Felix could feel the tension rise again.

'Oh, I get it,' she said flatly. 'Right after I was denazified.'

'Oh, Marianne!' Felix heard Willard murmur to his left. But he kept his gaze on the woman, who turned to face him at last.

'Now you know,' she said. 'I will understand perfectly if you should now wish to—'

'Her parents were the real Nazis,' Willard said. 'They deliberately sent her to Germany and—'

'Please!' Felix forced a laugh and then followed it with one that was more genuine. 'We draw a line, right? How old were you, Marianne? Eighteen?'

'Seventeen. Albert Speer was great friend to my father. We supplied steel. It should be smart for a steel maker to keep on the good books of Hitler's favourite architect – especially since he also was Minister for Armaments!'

'A bit like the gravel company with Tony Palmer and me,' Adam tried to say. 'As will soon be explained . . .'

Felix and Marianne ignored him; unspoken secrets were being passed behind their words. Besides, nothing that had happened in England this century could in any way equate with this.

'Who can answer for his or her opinions and actions at seventeen?' Felix asked. 'Not me, I do assure you! I had no love of the Jews, either – when I was seventeen and did not even know I *was* a Jew. For that I have *my* shame to carry. We draw a line, OK? The whole of Europe must draw a line. I have earned the right to say this, otherwise I am still not free. Sorry, Adam – the gravel company, you said? Were you telling Willard about this house that you and he—'

'Da-dee-da-dee-da . . .' Adam sang loudly. 'It's a secret until we get there – which will be in about five minutes.'

'Have you and Tony told Nicole of me?' Marianne asked Adam.

'Not yet,' he confessed awkwardly.

'Then I will – so soon as we meet. It's not fair on her – not after what has happened her.'

'Oh?' Felix asked.

'Willard was telling me yesterday night. Nicole worked as chef on her uncle's restaurant on Trouville during the war. It was much . . . I mean very popular with Germans and so the maquis asked her to pretend to collaborate to get information out of them – which she has done. Her secret was well kept – too much so that, after liberation they have done to her what they have done to all *collaborateuses*.' She mimed the shaving of her head.

Felix whistled. 'And she doesn't know . . . that you . . . ?'

'She shall. That's what I say.'

Having reached the hamlet of Harmer Green, at the top of the hill, they all mounted the gig and set off on the more or less level drive toward Dormer Green. The county councils were putting back the road signs all over England. The one at the hilltop said TEWIN and DORMER GREEN.

'Are we close now?' Willard asked.

'Close enough, maybe,' Adam replied. 'I'll end the suspense, anyway. Tell me – d'you remember a night we spent beside an overturned truck on Lüneburg Heath? We were headed for Bielefeld and left the road.'

'Vaguely . . . were we sober?'

'D'you remember what we talked about?'

He nodded. 'The destruction of Hamburg.'

'And of Europe generally. But especially about the chance it had given us to rebuild everything in a different way – a chance that we hoped would never come again but which we mustn't miss? Does that ring a bell?'

'I seem to remember a depressing conclusion – that people wouldn't take the chance. They'd play safe and go back to all the old ways – the old ideologies.'

Adam became slightly agitated; he wanted Willard to remember it exactly. 'We realized that we – the architects who would be needed in our thousands to rebuild this shattered continent – we could play our part. Surely you remember? Where three hundred slum houses had stood back-to-back in cramped little alleys we could *sweep* them all away – if the RAF or the Luftwaffe hadn't already done it for us. We're doing it now, in fact. We're turning the city green. And in each green oasis we're raising those three hundred families high into the sky in clean, modern, comfortable machines-for-living-in.'

'The things we say under the strain of war!' Willard laughed uncomfortably.

'OK, you played the cycnic then and—'

'Too damn right! My ol' grampappy had dreams like that. He used to say that if the working man was paid a decent wage and given good housing . . . education . . . health . . . all that, he and his family would divide their time between the library, the art gallery, and the concert hall. *Everyone* would be cultured and civilized!'

'But that's true – they would. Look at the thousands of ordinary people – men in the street – and women – who went to Dame Myra Hess's concerts at the National Gallery during the war.'

'There's a connection?' Adam could sense he was getting nowhere with the global argument. 'There was also the way *we* were going to live – putting our own ideals into practice. Can't you remember our list? Our no-no list, you called it?'

Willard gave a reluctant laugh. 'God, I'd forgotten that.' He scratched an ear. 'Let me see. We were against the nation-state and its chauvinism – all kinds of nationalism. We wanted—'

'Yes, but personally. For ourselves. What were the things we rejected for ourselves?'

'While we were still sober, you mean? I guess . . . the Victorian family and the old lines of authority. The tyranny, the cruelty, the economic dependence of woman on man . . .' He turned apologetically to Marianne. 'You know the sort of thing. It's hardly new.'

'You don't believe it any more?' she asked.

Adam grew impatient as he saw the discussion slipping away yet again. 'We wanted to take the next step beyond.'

'Maybe. I can't remember what it was, though.'

Adam sighed. 'You can – you just don't want to. In a little while now I'm going to show you a house – a large English country house, mainly Georgian with a Tudor remnant and a Victorian addition, and stables and outhouses . . . walled garden . . . five acres of wilderness that was once lawns, formal garden, fish pond, shrubbery . . . et cetera. I think *all that* is our "next step beyond the Victorian nuclear family".' He let the words sink in before he went on. 'Imagine eight or nine families living there. All like us. All about our age. We each have our own part of the house, of course. Not by virtue of title deeds or padlocks or anything like that, but just by common consent. I'd even say *communal* consent. But we have one kitchen where we cook one main meal each day and we all eat it together. And we play billiards or ping-pong or whatever we want in *our* communal playroom. And we have *our* music room. And *our* gardens. And this – *our* pony and trap in which *we* go shopping each Saturday. But the *our* and the *we* in all those things is not "Mum and Dad". It's *all* of us, including the children. We are the community of the future! It's the next stage of civilization. But even more than that, it's our only hope of moving forward from the tight, cloying, inward-looking, neurosis-breeding, festering, stultifying cocoon of the Victorian family.' He leaned triumphantly back and asked quietly. 'So what do you say? Tony and Nicole are already in, as I said. You'll see them when we get there. And Sally, naturally.'

Willard let out a deep breath he did not realize he had been holding. 'Gee, Adam, what the hell were we drinking that night? Are you sure it was *just* liquor?'

Marianne began speaking suddenly, almost intoning her words, 'An Englishman.' She nodded toward Adam: 'A Frenchwoman . . . an American with English, Italian, and Greek forefathers . . .'

'I didn't know that,' Adam said, staring at Willard as if he saw him in a new light.

'. . . and a Swede with German and Irish in the blood.'

'Nicole has Irish blood, too,' Adam said 'A little. And German cousins.'

'And Felix?' she asked. 'Is there room for him, too?'

'I was just about to say . . .' Adam began.

But Willard reached out and took Marianne's hand. 'Honey? Are you seriously considering this fantasy?'

'The same like you.'

'I am?' He shook his head in disbelief. 'You know – I have the craziest feeling.'

'Ideals aren't crazy,' Marianne said. 'If we can't succeed, what hope for the United Nations? What hope for the world? There must be *community!*' She turned to Adam as she said the word.

'Community among all peoples like us. Ordinary peoples. We do it now, the world does it tomorrow.'

Willard cleared his throat awkwardly. 'But you miss the point, sugar. I've never acted out of *idealism* in my life – not when there were good, solid reasons for doing the other thing.'

'You want good, solid reasons, too?' Adam said. 'I'll give you a good, solid reason for staying this side of the pond. Which country has suffered more war damage, England or America? Where will you find the more desperate need for architects?'

'Where will the architect be king?' Felix asked.

Willard had his eyes shut in a parody of pain. 'You're hitting me where it hurts,' he said.

'And where better than with a couple of fellow architects who are working on the Greater London Plan, eh?' Without waiting for an answer, Adam turned to Felix. 'Listen, old chap. When we met at the Lansdowne in the week, Tony and I desperately wanted to suggest that you join this little community. One of the old stables would make a wizard studio for you. But we had this absurd rule, you see, and, being English, we obeyed it.'

'Rule?' Felix echoed.

'It was Sally's idea, really, but we all agreed to it. She pointed out that if we overwhelmed people with our enthusiasm and they joined us against their better instincts and then regretted it later, it would cause a lot of ill feeling. So the rule was that would-be joiners had to ask directly; we would never be the first to suggest it.'

'It sounds like good sense,' Marianne said. 'Why are you breaking it now?'

'Because of the fickleness of women, if you must know. The minute I told Sally about it, she called me every sort of fool and said of *course* I should have broken the rule at once and asked Felix if he'd like to join us. Her own rule! Anyway, Felix, that has now become the point of your visit today. If you like us and like the house and think the stables would make a good studio . . . just say the word. When we're up to full ration strength, each rent will be about sixty quid a year including insurance. If you took one of the stables, it would be even less.' After a pause he added, 'Say?'

'I'll say yes now, please,' Felix replied. 'What is your English saying? A sculptor should never look three gift-architects in the mouth! Five if these two join as well.'

Adam had one more pearl to cast: 'I know we're all supposed to be working class now . . . certainly we're all workers. But we want some of the families – one or two – to be *real* working-class people. That's also part of the new order.'

'You English and your class system!' Willard began.

But Marianne cut in: 'It won't work! That bit of it won't work.'

'I don't mean the lumpenproletariat – the erks. But people in skilled trades – people who made sergeant in the skilled support corps – REME . . . the Service Corps – we all met them. We all got on with them pretty well. Anyway, Marianne – how d'you know until it's been tried?'

Marianne clearly had a stack of counter-arguments but all she did was smile and say, 'This beautiful, unspoiled countryside! Is America as cosy as this, darling?'

'This is very like New Jersey – Mercer County . . . the country round Princeton—' he began.

Felix interrupted, 'What happened there?' He pointed to a large patch of bare earth beside the road.

'Ammo dump,' Adam said.

'Please?'

'It was probably an ammunition dump. During the war they dispersed small piles of ammunition all over England, mostly in little roadside heaps – all secure in locked metal boxes and under cover, of course. Safer than keeping it all in one huge arsenal. There are thousands of them still, not yet dismantled – all over the countryside.'

Felix whistled in amazement. 'And they weren't afraid of revolutionaries?'

'Not really. We don't go in for that sort of thing. What revolutionaries, anyway? The communists? They were all on our side.'

'Not any more!' Willard said vehemently.

But Marianne had a different agenda. 'It would be so easy to forget the war here.' She smiled at Felix and added, 'To draw a line.'

'Talking of which' – Willard switched tracks effortlessly – 'you're right! I could draw a lot of lines right here in England.

There's something about all those hundreds of thousands of bomb-damaged acres that appeals to an architect's eye. How about work permits . . . stuff like that?'

Adam's only response was a withering look. 'You couldn't *fix* that?'

Willard shrugged. 'I still can't believe I'm taking it all seriously.'

'Try it for a year,' Adam suggested. 'What does that cost at our age? Just give it a year. It'll be an experience if nothing else. Something to tell your grandchildren.'

The road curved away to the left among coppiced trees that had run wild again. It increased the sense of enclosure and the snug, tunnel-like ambience. The curve proved to be the first half of an S-bend, with the road swinging back to the left again – toward Bull's Green, as another newly repainted fingerboard told them.

But it was what stood on the far side of this second bend that made Marianne and Willard catch their breath. 'What a little beauty,' he said.

She agreed. 'A jewel!'

The object of their wonder was a gatelodge. It stood inside and to the left of an impressive stone entrance way, which had once, no doubt, been furnished with equally impressive railings and gates in wrought iron; but, like most such ironwork, they had been melted down in 1940 for 'the war effort'. The lodge, however, was intact. The gable ends were concave, like those on a Chinese pagoda; the bargeboards were carved, not simply sawn; the windows were gothic; the chimneys were in fluted spirals and walls were of red brick.

The Johnsons dismounted and crossed the road, pressing against the sheep hurdles that had replaced the wrought-iron railings.

'D'you think we could?' Marianne asked hesitantly.

'What?'

'Have a peep inside?'

Adam laughed. 'You can live there if you like – unless Felix wants it, of course. He's got first refusal.'

'First choice?' Felix queried.

'First refusal, first choice – they mean the same.'

'Choice and refusal mean the same in England!' Felix glanced at Marianne and raised his hands in a gesture of hopelessness.

She laughed but was more interested in Adam's offer. 'You've rented this place, too?' she asked.

Adam jumped down and scrabbled aside some ivy near the top of one of the gate columns, revealing the barely legible word, cut in the stone: Dower. 'It's the gatelodge to . . . our future. The Dower House. It was originally called Dormer Hall, when it was a Tudor manor. Then the Grenfells of Panshanger bought it – before one of them was created the first Lord Desborough and turned it into a dower house, which is the Georgian mansion we're about to visit.'

Since they were all dismounted now, they walked up the avenue of limes, past open parkland on their right and woodland to the left. Carpets of bluebells stretched under the trees, pheasants rose from the undergrowth with a harsh clatter of feathery alarm, and every now and then the white scuts of stamping rabbits flashed in panic, too. The woods were choked with volunteer saplings of ash and beech, none more than ten years old and all struggling in the mighty shade of beeches, chestnuts, and firs that were hundreds of years older. The limes, Adam noticed for the first time, were riddled with mistletoe.

Here and there, deep in the shade, loomed the iridescent purple of bursting rhododendron buds. Other shade-tolerant shrubs abounded, too – Portugal laurel, *Acuba japonica*, bamboo, and many others he could not name. Yet.

'How I'd have loved to build dens and play games here as a boy!' he said apropos nothing.

After a furlong or so of twisting drive the random pattern of trees became more organized until, at last, the avenue, now straight, was flanked on both sides by matched pairs of limes – old limes, even older than the woodland all around, limes with elephantiasis, amputated and paraplegic from centuries of storms, yet still standing. One was actually hollow, being no more than a cylinder of living bark and sapwood, with yet more bark on the inside, too; even so, it supported three fairly solid branches that rose thirty feet or more.

However, they soon had no eye for trees, nor for anything other than the house itself, to which the ancient limes provided a living triumphal arch of an entrance.

'Wow-ee!' Willard exclaimed as they emerged from beneath the last branches of the final pair; even Marianne, who had grown up in an elegant château in south Sweden, was a little taken aback. She grabbed his arm as if she did not trust herself to stand unsupported. For there, a couple of hundred paces ahead of them, crowning a slight rise in the ground, stood one of the most elegant Georgian country houses they had ever seen. Larger than a rectory, smaller than a palace, modestly opulent, assertively reticent, there it stood in the afternoon sun, as confident of its ground as any mountain in the kingdom – and more sure of its place in history, too.

'Welcome to our country cottage!' Adam said as he unhitched the pony and turned it loose onto what had once been the main lawn.

They stood and analysed the house. It rose three floors on a semi-basement, the tops of whose windows could be seen over the ex-flower beds around the foot of the house. A flight of four shallow steps led up to a grand entrance, guarded by two pairs of simple Doric columns, which rose to support a large triangular pediment that formed the front wall of a balcony. The walls, of pale Hertfordshire brick, were symmetrical on either side. Each half had three large windows on the ground floor, echoed on the first floor above in lights of medium size. All were rectangular, though those on the ground floor were set back in shallow, semicircular arches of brick. At the moment they were blinded from inside by their once-white shutters. It made the house seem somehow fake, like a construction on a film lot waiting for the painters to darken the glazing and paint in the bars.

Felix wondered where the stables were. 'Which is your bit?' he asked Adam.

'See the Tudor gable just peeping out beyond? Well, the Victorian Desboroughs built a mock-Tudor annexe to it, to balance it. On the far side from here. We're in that.'

'And Tony and Nicole?' Willard asked.

'They have the back of the main house – three rooms on the ground floor and three above. You can just see one of their windows looking out on the lawn. And the bedrooms above that are theirs, too.'

'And who has the top floor?'

'Untenanted as yet. So is the genuine Tudor bit, and the

main-house ground floor on this front side, and the floor above
it. And the stables – with the cottage across the yard, which
you might consider, Felix.'

'And the gatelodge,' Marianne said. 'Seven family units, five
which not yet are uptaken.'

Felix noticed a tap set back a little from the drive. He turned
it on but no water emerged, only a spider, which abseiled to
the grass on one fine thread. There had been only one working
tap in the *Vélodrome d'Hiver* that day. One tap for more than a
thousand Jews.

Sally Wilson opened the high front doors and stepped out to
greet them. She was a tall, slender, platinum blonde; her features
were rosy, even babyish, but there was nothing babyish about
her manner.

'Where are Tony and Nicole?' Adam asked.

At the mention of Nicole, Marianne's heart skipped a beat.

'They went down the fields to inspect the septic tanks.
Apparently we have two for alternate months. You must be
Mister and Mrs Johnson – and Herr Breit?'

'Mister, please! Or just Felix.'

'Of course.'

When the introductions were over, and first-names agreed
on, Sally took Willard and Marianne to explore the main house
while Adam showed Felix over the coach houses and stables,
which would be ready-made studios or garages.

'Maybe the cottage across the yard would suit you better?'
he suggested, pointing out a two-storey red-brick building
beyond a huge weeping ash. 'The locals call it the gardener's
cottage but we think it must originally have been for the head
stable lad.'

'Lad?'

'Well . . . that's what they always called them, no matter how
old. Anyway, those big French windows are much later. Once
there were double doors there, to what was a coach house.' He
nudged Felix. 'Big enough for a sculptor's studio, I'd say. You
could get a Henry Moore in and out by that door.'

'I don't intend living alone,' Felix said as they crossed the
yard.

'Quick work!' Adam said admiringly.

'Oh, I've not found anyone *yet*.'

Adam pushed at the cottage door with his foot; the wood scraped the floor. 'Tell me to mind my own business, if you like,' he said, 'but are you really as . . . I don't want to say *indifferent* . . . forgiving, perhaps, about . . . you know . . .' He jerked his head vaguely toward the big house.

'*Indifferent* is good,' Felix said.

He saw at once that the big room Adam had mentioned would, indeed, make a fabulous studio. The French windows looked west, so the sunlight would steal inward each evening to caress his day's work and congratulate him. His fingers longed to begin working.

'It's odd.' Adam went to one of the windows and drew Euclidean shapes in the dust on one of the panes. 'I suppose we ought to stop trying to guess what your feelings and attitudes must be?'

'It would be best to assume that I have none.' After a pause he added, 'I had to learn certain techniques in order to survive. At least, I *hope* I learned them. I hope they weren't always there inside me, waiting to blossom, because they are not attractive.'

Adam said, 'I was amazed to see you eating peas at the club last week.'

'I know.'

'Sorry, did it show? I mean, you were eating with relish.'

'I owe my life to peas and beans. And lentils. Why should I dislike them?'

'I know. It's all very logical. But even so . . .'

'That's not what I mean. I'm talking about watching another prisoner being clubbed to death and thinking, *Gott sei dank* it's not me! Or stealing a crust from someone so close to death that it wouldn't help him anyway. Thinking only *me-me-me*! I had to learn to think like them – to think that the life of another human being was worth any sacrifice if it preserved my own.'

'I've tried to imagine it so often since that day . . . the unbelievable horrors of that day . . . wondering if I could have tolerated even one hour of it. Objectively, of course, I know I could have, probably – since so many obviously did.'

'They killed a hundred and eighty-five of us a day, every day – average – someone told me.'

'But thousands also survived – you among them, thank God.

Even so, I still can't imagine how. We must never let ourselves forget it.'

'That's your problem. You're right, of course – for *you*. For me, it's opposite. Art saved me for a purpose. When I first went into the camp they put me carrying quarry stones up those famous steps. One hundred eighty-six of them. Nobody ever lasted more than six weeks there. If you fell, they shot you. And they left your body there until sunset, *pour encourager les autres.* Then they needed skilled masons to shape the stones and the Kapo volunteered me. It was good of him. He was a communist and normally they only looked after their own. I'd done some stone carving but not much – only little things. Bagatelles. Clay modelling, metal welding – that was me. I had a one-hour apprenticeship between dawn and the time the head mason started work. He was an Austrian civilian. A Nazi, of course. By then I was rival to Bernini, believe me!'

'But that's admirable.'

'So? That's my point. And by the way, when it comes to Marianne Johnson . . . just assume . . .'

'Yes?'

Felix hesitated and then said, 'Just take it that I have every reason to sympathize with her predicament when her parents sent her to work in Germany at the age of seventeen.'

Adam sighed. 'In a way, much as I'm fond of Willard, I hope they decide to go back to Boston. I don't think Nicole will accept her in the same generous spirit. She spent all those years pretending to be nice to Nazis while she hated them from the bottom of her heart.'

'Well – that's what Marianne must always remember and Nicole must try to forget.'

'Easily said.'

'She must, though, for her *own* sake.'

'Maybe *you* can get her to do it.'

'Tell me something about *him* – Willard. Is he a good architect?'

Adam hesitated so long that Felix had to laugh.

'No, no!' Adam protested. 'He probably is quite good. It's just that you've made me realize I don't think of old Willard in either category – good or bad. He has a nose for what's impor-tant. For what's powerful. For the *movers,* as he calls them. I saw him once walk into a room full of two-star generals and yet he headed straight for a mere colonel. It seemed so out of character but afterwards we learned that the generals were all has-beens on their way out while the colonel was the rising star. *That's* Willard. So to ask if he's *good* misses the essential man. He's certainly going to be *successful*. I guarantee that within five years his office will contain at least a hundred drawing boards. Well!' He rubbed his hands and, looking about them, said, 'What d'you think? Will it do?'

'It will do very nicely. I will be grateful—'

'You will be no such thing! It's the very least we can do. When I told my father you were possibly coming here, it was all I could do to stop him coming down to meet you this afternoon. Yet until now he's had absolutely no sympathy with our project.'

'I was going to say I will be grateful if I could leave paying the rent until . . .' He saw no reason to be too specific.

The old servants' quarters and lumber rooms in the attics formed a square around the dome that gave light to the main stairwell of the house. Originally the parapet, which disguised the sloping roof and produced the architecturally correct Georgian box, had obscured the attic windows; but during the wartime occupation by the school, when the attic rooms had been converted to boys' dormitories, they had cut part of the parapet away in front of each window for fire escapes. It opened up views on all four sides that were spectacular – east to Bramfield, west to Bull's Green, north to Watton-at-Stone, and south across the Mimram Valley (which Cowper called the loveliest in all England) to Welwyn Garden City.

Sally left the Johnsons to talk it over in private.

'Lavender glass,' Willard said. 'Hand blown and flattened. They'd pay a fortune for just this one window back home.'

'Home?' Marianne took Willard's hand. 'Mmm?'

'Here?' he asked. 'Think so?'

'Don't you?' She squeezed his hand again. 'We could be very happy here – starting right now.'

'Eh?'

'There's a key in the door. Shall we test the floorboards for squeaks?'

*   *   *

Adam and Felix had rejoined Sally in the Victorian-Tudor annexe
to the genuine Tudor remnant.

'How much does Nicole know about . . . Marianne?' Sally
asked as soon as they came in. 'Don't look so surprised. She
told me when I was showing them over the attic rooms.' Then
to Felix: 'Can you really just shrug it off?'

'Felix thinks we must all draw a line across history,' Adam
said. 'Not just us – everyone in England.'

'Or even . . . dare I mention the word – *Europe*?' Felix
suggested.

'Yes, there too, of course.'

'I must say, Felix, that's very Christian of you . . .' Her voice
trailed off in dismay. 'I mean . . . of course . . . oh, dear!'

Adam sought to repair the damage. 'She just means you're a
real white man.'

Felix let her flounder until a small debt was created; dear
friends of his who had been unable to make such cold calcula-
tions were now dust and ashes in Austria. Then he laughed and
squeezed her arm reassuringly. 'Let's agree it's very humanist,
eh? From this point in history onwards, God must take lessons
from the humanists, I think, don't you?'

'Why not?' Still embarrassed, she turned to her husband. 'Has
Tony told Nicole? About Marianne?'

Adam bit his lip. 'Marianne wants to be the one.'

'So neither of you has told her!' Sally was shocked.

'Frankly, I saw no reason to. I thought they'd give this place
the once-over . . . maybe enjoy a few moments of pleasant
fantasy . . . then wake up to stern reality and take the next boat
to America. I still think they'll do that. Marianne certainly has
no ties to keep her on this side of the Atlantic.'

'Well, you can think again, my darling. They've fallen in love
with the attic unit. And how d'you think they'll get access to
it? What's the only staircase that leads up there?'

She turned to Felix to explain but he said, 'I imagine it'll be
through Tony and Nicole's unit?'

'You're quick!' She grinned. 'Anyway, we'll know soon
enough. I think you're playing with fire.'

Adam looked at his watch and said, 'They should be back
by now – unless they've fallen into one of the septic tanks.'

'Let's go and see.' Sally led the way through the communal

labyrinth to the front portico, where they arrived in time to see Tony and Nicole climbing out of the ha-ha that divided the front lawn from the parkland beyond. The lawn was flanked on either side by a rotting oak pergola, paved in red brick and so sunken in places that it would have been safer to walk on the lawn – if that wasn't a riot of weeds and volunteer saplings. Nicole stopped to pick a small bunch of bluebells. Tony halted, too, beneath the two overarching roses, where he tapped the ashes and dottle from his pipe against his upturned left heel.

'Ha!' Felix relished the complex arabesques of his silhouetted arms and legs.

'What?' Adam asked, startled.

'That day. In Mauthausen. He tapped his pipe on his heel just like that.'

'He set fire to some GS stores once,' Adam said. '"Just like that."'

'Felix!' Tony called out, having noticed them at last. To Adam he shouted, 'Is he going to take one of the flats?'

Nicole joined him and they trotted across the weed-littered carriage sweep; she had all the right attributes for a Mata Hari, Felix thought admiringly. Her hair had grown well again, lustrous, and raven-black – so black, indeed, that its highlights held a bluish sheen.

'Monsieur Breit?' Rather shyly she offered him the bunch of bluebells from several paces away.

'*Pour moi*, Madame Palmer?' He swiftly descended the steps to their level. '*Vous êtes vraiment charmante!*'

'Ongley, cherry,' Tony muttered.

She gave him a look that would have served for mustard and passed the bouquet to Felix.

'Do the septic tanks look as if they'll work?' Sally asked.

'Nothing's broken down above ground,' Tony said. 'It's the sort of engineering an Ancient Egyptian would understand.'

Nicole said, 'My husband has told me your story, Monsieur Felix. I heard your name back in the war, when I was visiting Paris. You were arrested and then released?'

'The first time, yes. *Tiens!*' He held the bluebells up beside her cheeks and said to the two men, 'The colour! It matches her eyes perfectly, see!'

An English girl might have blushed, but not Nicole; her gaze remained as cool as the blue of her eyes – even when he brought the bouquet to his lips and gave it a playful kiss. 'Sartre told me,' she added.

'You knew him well?' Felix asked, though he had never liked the man much.

'None of us knew him until *after* the Normandy landings,' she sneered. 'Then, *tout d'un coup*, we got to know many great artists and intellectuals who discovered overnight how anti-Nazi they had been all those comfortable, well-rewarded years.'

'Thank God it's all over and done with, eh!'

She sniffed. 'Is it?'

They drifted up the steps and indoors.

'I think I've found another interested couple,' Tony said. 'Name of Prentice, Arthur and May.'

'Not two more bloody architects, I hope,' Adam said.

'He's a cameraman with the BBC. They're going to expand television transmissions soon, so it's a good, secure thing. He worked for Pathé during the last show. Arthur's more Felix's age. When were you born, old chap?'

'Nineteen twelve,' Felix told him.

'Well, he's probably a couple of years younger. May is more our sort of age – mid-twenties. They've got two brats under the age of three. He obviously got home quite often in the war.'

'It would be good to have the patter of tiny feet about the place,' Adam said. Then – as well be hanged for a sheep as a lamb – he added, 'Actually, we have a bit of a surprise for you two . . .'

She stiffened. 'If you mean Fräulein von Ritter – the Nazi . . .' She turned on her husband. 'I still can't believe you let me *fraternize* with that . . . that . . .' A new thought struck her. 'And now you do the same with poor Monsieur Breit!'

'*Mais pas du tout, Madame!*' he said. 'I know all about *Mrs Johnson's* past. I also know my *own* past.'

She gave an expressive, Gallic shrug. '*Alors?*'

'And I say if the past will not set the present free, then we are still at war. You still seem to be at war with the Nazis. So you cannot yet claim victory. You keep the Nazis alive so you can go on fighting them.' He tapped his skull. 'And so you deny yourself this wonderful present – *doux present du présent!* It is just one handshake away!'

Nicole tossed her head but felt she could offer no rebuttal to this – especially to the one who made it. 'Another reason I'm angry is that I *liked* her. I thought we can have European nights here at the Dower House . . . Swedish cuisine, French cuisine, and . . .' She gazed uncertainly at Felix. 'Hungarian, of course. Goulash – *c'est au poile!*'

'The French never quite got the hang of rationing,' Tony said apologetically.

They crossed the hall, which was almost filled with the semi-spiral volute of the main staircase, a light, elegant structure that seemed too delicate to support even itself, much less the school-boys who must lately have charged up and down it.

Nicole turned to Felix. 'Why are you looking at me so . . . so . . .'

'Intensely?' he offered.

'Par example!'

He laughed. 'I was wondering if you would allow your husband to pose for me?'

'Good God!' Tony snorted.

'The pose you were in beside the lawn just now . .' Felix mimed his tapping his pipe on his heel. 'When I saw that I suddenly remembered you coming into Mauthausen. You did exactly the same thing then. I remember thinking at the time that if an Englishman can march into the camp and do that – so easily, so casually – then we really must be liberated. I think such a moment in my life should be immortalized, no?'

'I say, are you serious?' Tony asked.

'Not really,' Felix laughed again.

'The memory is true, though,' Adam said. 'He reminded me of it the minute he saw you.' He glanced at Felix as if expecting him to confirm it.

'Well,' Felix said. 'It's as true as anything can be these days.'

They started up the final stair, which led to the old servants' quarters, soon to be the Johnsons' flat.

Steps. These of pitch pine.

'Devil!' Marianne exclaimed.

It sounded like a whole delegation coming up.

'Well, we've finished,' Willard said complacently as he unlocked the door.

'*You* have. Look at my hair! Go and meet them – distract them!'

'How?'

'*Mm nnm mnh!*' Her mouth was stopped with two hairpins and a kirby grip.

'What about the dry rot?' Willard asked, meeting them halfway along the corridor. 'Hi, Tony . . . Nicole! Great to see you again.'

'Same here, old bean. You don't look a day older.'

'What dry rot?' Adam asked.

Willard led them to the room at the farther corner of the house. 'Can't you smell it? That's dry rot, surely?'

They fetched a bar and lifted a floorboard. Small frills of dry rot festooned the brick wall at one end.

'No fruiting body yet,' Willard said. 'It looks treatable to me.'

Adam glanced ruefully at Tony. 'A fine pair of surveyors we'd make!'

Marianne joined them, not a kirby grip out of place. 'We just are *loving* this whole attic,' she said.

There was an embarrassed silence, which Felix swiftly quashed. He tapped his chest. 'Me – Austro-Hungarian German . . .' Then pointing at the others as he went around: 'American . . . Swedish . . . French . . . English. It will be *good*. And we can have gourmet nights – Swedish cuisine, French cuisine, American cuisine, and –' he turned innocently toward Nicole – 'Hungarian, of course. Goulash – *c'est au poile, n'est ce pas, madame*? And just a handshake away!'

She flounced away to the stairhead, saying – without turning round – 'I must draw the arrangement of sewage tanks before I forget them.'

'She knows,' Marianne said.

''Fraid so, old thing,' Tony agreed. 'I let the cat out of the bag. I had no idea she'd react like that.'

Adam turned to Marianne: 'How d'you feel?'

She shrugged and looked at Willard. 'I'm willing to try.'

'Sure,' he said. 'Talking of rations – what's the nearest US Army base? I might know somebody there.'

'See!' Adam said, still to Marianne though his target was Willard. 'A community has strengths no nuclear family can match.'

'It's good so,' she agreed. 'But is it strong still after we get our first communal electricity bill?'

He frowned.

Sally explained, 'I told her – we have three electricity meters

– one for each phase – and eight fuse boards and no one knows which lights and sockets any of them serves.'

Tuesday, 6 May 1947

Felix noticed her at once – a tall, svelte, pugnacious young woman who advanced slowly along the gallery, peering suspiciously at each exhibit. Did she doubt their attributions, he wondered? Or did she think she could have arranged the whole gallery far better than this?

At last she approached the armour he had been admiring before he noticed her. She peered at it with the same distrustful gaze. Then, still without looking at him, she murmured, 'You'll know me next time, then.'

He took a chance. 'You want to fix that now?'

Fix! Willard's word.

It surprised her into facing him at last. 'Fix what?'

'"The next time", of course. I'm Felix Breit, by the way.' He offered his hand.

'Felix Breit!' The name surprised her so much that her handshake was quite perfunctory. It flattered him – until she added, 'Did you have an ancestor who was an artist? William Breit?'

He cringed as he admitted it. To think that this young woman knew of his appalling grandfather, painter of chocolate-box erotica for the rich Berlin bourgeoisie, but had not – apparently – heard of his much more famous and worthy grandson! 'You know his work?' he added.

'Not at all. Just the name – and the fact that he did paintings of some kind. D'you know anyone called Fogel?'

'Is that your name?'

'Me? No. Oh – sorry!' She held out her hand again. 'Faith Bullen-ffitch.'

'Will you join me for tea, Miss Bullen-ffitch? I saw a sign saying Tea Room.'

She accepted without coquetry – no gleam of *je-sais-quoi* in her eye. He decided she was a collector. Every artist gets to know them as his star rises. For himself he didn't mind. Collectors were often more willing to come across than cocottes – and they weren't limpets when it was time to move on.

The decor of the tea room at the V&A, once criticized by the Victorians for its incongruous modernity, was now a museum exhibit in its own right – a lofty, clattery, echoing hall, lined from skirting to apex in glazed tiles, unique to this particular tea room. Waitress service, suspended in 1939, had not returned; three skinny ladies dispensed almost sugarless tea, completely sugarless biscuits, and one slice of buttered bread per person. But customers could lard it with as much raspberry-flavoured turnip jam as they liked. The glass tabletop was cracked and the corner clips harboured samples of ancient snacks.

Miss Bullen-ffitch insisted on paying for herself – fourpence. 'Bread on ration!' she said disgustedly. 'Even in the darkest days of the war it was never rationed. Everything else was, but not bread. Mind you – when you think of the winter we've just kissed goodbye . . .'

'I wasn't here,' he said. 'I was in Germany. It was bad there, too. Trees hacked to bits in all the parks. People hammering the sides of coal wagons, just to collect the dust.'

She was unable to compete. Perhaps she thought they deserved it.

'Who is this Fogel?' he asked.

'Wolf Fogel, my boss. He's a publisher here in London. Well, he doesn't actually publish books himself. Not yet. He compiles them for other publishers. D'you know the King Penguins?'

'Birds?'

'Never mind. It's not important, really. The only reason I mentioned him is that *your* grandfather did a painting in a villa belonging to my Mister Fogel's grandfather – Julius. It overlooked a lake on the outskirts of Berlin. If he can find the painting, it might help prove his title.'

'The lake was the Wannsee, probably. I know it.'

'That's the name. *Am Grossen Wannsee.* So did your grandfather have a villa there, too?'

'I don't think so. Ours is not a communicating sort of family. Wannsee is one of Berlin's "lungs" – as architects like to say.'

'Don't they just! Anyway, although the communists have seized the villa, Fogel still wants to establish title because, apparently, he's the only one to survive out of the whole family. He got out just before the war. Wouldn't it be awful to be in that situation – all your family dead except . . .' She caught his expression and clapped her hand to her mouth. 'Oh, my God!'

'I agree.' He smiled. Later he realized that the smile had been uncharacteristic of him – to smile so immediately, anyway. He was so hungry these days for female company – and, be honest, female flesh – that, with any other young woman, he would have withheld it to make her feel a guilty little debt. What instinct assured him, so soon, that this one was different?

'You'd better tell me all about yourself,' she said. 'Otherwise I'll put my foot in my mouth every time I open it.'

'If you'll return the favour and tell me all about your Mister Fogel?' It occurred to him that a Jew who had escaped just before the war and had become prosperous during it, might have a conscience that could be played upon. And him a publisher, too.

'So you'd rather hear about him than me!' she teased.

'I think I already know quite a lot about you.'

Each audited the other for a moment before she said, 'Well? Go on.'

He told her as much of his story as he thought she could tolerate.

'You sum up people in the twinkling of an eye,' she said. 'Now I understand why. You must be very good at it, else you wouldn't be here. I wonder what you'll make of Fogel?'

'If we ever meet.'

'You'll meet.'

'So tell me about him. He's from Berlin?'

'Vienna – but he was at home in Berlin, too, I'm sure. Until he was nincteen. When he came here in 'thirty-nine he was Wolfgang Vogel – with a V, but after the English released all German Jewish refugees from detention, he changed it to Wolf Fogel – with an F, and pronouncing "Wolf" just like that – the English way. And he had a pretty good war, too. Can you imagine! The British locked up pro-Nazis and escaped Jews in the same camp together!'

'Naturally.' Felix shrugged. 'Why *should* they understand? How many British can swim twenty-two miles?'

She took his meaning at once and smiled ruefully. 'Quite so – we are dreadful.' But she spoke the word with a hint of pride.

And she went on to describe how Fogel was released and went straight into the ministry, working on leaflets to drop over the enemy. That was during the phoney war, when all the RAF ever dropped was leaflets.

And that led him into publishing – information books . . . keep-your-chin-up books . . . fight-for-our-heritage books – which allowed him to print in colour when others had to make do with black-and-white, and it also gave him entrée to intellectual and cultural circles – all of which he was now parleying into a profitable little peacetime business.

'But,' she added, 'the actual process of writing fills him with a sort of fidgety indignation. Words don't elude him – words on the air, words that can fade before the breath on them is dry, deniable words. But real words on real paper are like a contract with the truth. They can return to haunt him. Written words, for him, reek with the stench of costly litigation.'

Felix chuckled. 'But not for you, I think?'

'That's why we complement each other perfectly,' she replied. 'He always gets others to do the writing for him. And as for editing, subbing, and problems of layout . . . in between the occasional flashes of his undoubted genius, they just bore him. In short,' she laughed, 'Wolf Fogel is a born publisher – not an editor but a born *éditeur* – he can see the bigger picture that often eludes those who dot eyes and cross tees.'

'And what is he working on now?' Felix asked.

'It's a project he's lusted after for the whole of the past year – just waiting for the paper situation to ease – an encyclopedia of European modern art.' She smiled. 'Actually, d'you mind if I say no more about it, just for the moment? Meeting you has given me a brilliant idea. Where can I get in touch with you if I need to?'

'D'you think you might need to? We all have needs, Miss Bullen-ffitch.'

She took his meaning but not the bait. 'No promises, mind,' she said.

He had applied for a telephone at the Dower House but they had told him it would be at least a six-month wait. He gave her Wilson's number at the Greater London Plan offices and they arranged to meet, again at the V&A, the following Saturday.

What had brought their conversation to its sudden conclusion on her part was a memory of a recent conversation with Fogel about the projected encyclopedia of European modern art. The first dummies promised chapters on Cubism, Fauvism, *Der Blaue Reiter,* Surrealism, Dada . . . and so on. The obvious thing to do was to take a key work of art from each school or movement and use it full-page, facing the introduction to each chapter. But Fogel occasionally hated the obvious.

'Better,' he had told her, 'would be something plastic, change-able . . . an object . . . an art *thing* that we could adapt in some significant, thought-provoking way for each chapter. Maybe light it differently . . . shoot it from a different angle each time. Something. I don't know. We need a unity here.'

'You mean get a sculptor to do something like that?' she asked. 'A big name?'

'Yes, but not so big he's also expensive.'

'Who?'

'I'll think,' he said.

The thinking stopped the moment Miss Bullen-ffitch told him of her meeting with Felix Breit. He could provide just the thing – a sensuous piece of sculpture, sensuously lighted, printed in the most sensuous Swiss photogravure – but at British-gravure prices . . .

Mentally he added a nought at the end of his projected print run.

Felix and Miss Bullen-ffitch met the following Saturday in the graphics room of the museum, where he had requisitioned the folders of Impressionists and Post-Impressionists – etchings, litho-graphs, monotypes, and a few Expressionist woodcuts, all higgledy-piggledy in display portfolios, much as a private collector or even the artists themselves might have kept them.

'You could practically do the whole book from this one collection,' he said, turning over a Bonnard monotype of two slightly comical dogs chasing a third along a Montmartre alleyway.

'Learn to say "we" rather than "you",' she advised. 'I mean – Fogel is on tenterhooks to meet you. Could you spare a day a week?'

'One day this week?'

'No, a day *every* week. He wants you to become design consultant for the whole project. I told you how he works – a

big name on every book. Or, in this case, series of books. I'm
sorry, I didn't realize what a big name yours is.'

'But I'm a sculptor. I don't know the first thing about book
design.'

'You do. Everyone does. You just don't know it. Listen – you
can be a sculptor six days a week and a book designer on the
seventh.' She eyed him cautiously. 'D'you mind if I coach you
a little?'

He laughed. '*Someone* will have to.'

'When we have tea. Meanwhile, you tell me about these
artists. I'm obviously going to have to bone up on them a bit.
Bonnard – you mentioned him last week, when you described
being arrested in Paris. Did you ever meet Manet?'

'Manet died thirty years before I was *born*, for heaven's sake!
My grandfather was friends with Monet – he's the only
Impressionist I ever saw in the flesh. But I know many Post-
Impressionists – Picasso, Matisse, Braque, Vlaminck, Derain,
Chagall . . . friends and acquaintances. Rouault. I can get many
private informations, if you are interested.'

They beguiled the next couple of hours with the V&A's prints
and his reminiscences. At one point Faith said, 'The two I really
don't understand are Picasso and Braque. They did their paintings . . . what? Thirty . . . forty years ago. I really ought to
understand them by now. But I don't!'

Felix thought awhile; at length he said, 'Go and look at back-
numbers of *Vogue* from the time of the Great War. Did it exist
then? Well, any fashion magazine from that time. In fact – any
magazine, any newspaper. And then look at the equivalent today.
What's the difference? I'll tell you what the difference is – Picasso!
Today's magazines . . . newspapers . . . advertising . . . they would
look completely different without the Cubists and the Surrealists.
And Picasso was prominent . . . pre-eminent? . . . in both. I
never liked the man but I can't deny him that. He's the giant.'

From that moment on, he sensed a certain shift in their
relationship, in her estimation of him. Every now and then he
caught her looking at him as if to say, 'I need to know you a
lot better than I do.' Behind it, perhaps, was the thought that
he could be very *useful* to her. He relaxed even more in her
company then; '*You* could be useful to *me*' was the motto of his
homeland.

And it cuts both ways, of course.

After fifteen minutes or so the Curator of Prints himself asked if he might join them and he, too, listened to Felix's tales in fascination. Before they left he asked if he would return some other day and repeat the stories to a shorthand note taker.

'You should charge them for it,' Faith told him as they made their way down to the tea room.

'Don't tell me what to charge for.' He gave her arm a friendly squeeze. 'I'll suggest an intimate dinner to which he might also invite the Curator of the Tate and the head of the sculpture school at the Slade. Or the Royal College.'

She laughed. 'I'm sorry, Mister Breit. I shouldn't have . . .'

'We're from the same mould, Miss Bullen-ffitch. You needn't worry.'

'But I do. You have such an unworldly air. You seem so vulnerable.'

'I'm vulnerable when it comes to book design – I make no secret of that!'

They brought their tea and biscuits to one of the tables and she began: 'You are only vulnerable, if you try to get too technical. Don't! Fogel has first-rate book designers in the house – people who know all about typefaces and ems and points and serifs and stuff like that. He doesn't expect anything like that from you. From you he wants an artistic –' her hands began to shape huge, airy spheres – 'overall view.'

'From the depths of my ignorance!'

'From the profound depths of your artistic sensibility! Listen! You know the difference between an artist and a designer? A designer *always* has logical reasons for whatever he does. He can always say, "I chose these four tints because we can get them with only one colour separation and black." Even if he really chose them because they're pretty. See? The blighters always have a logical reason. But that's what keeps them down at the level of mere *tactics*. They're just lieutenants and captains – fortunately for *you*, General Breit! Because you can step in with the grand, overall strategy.'

The tutorial continued for another half-hour, until Felix's head was so stuffed with typographical arcana that it almost made a coherent whole.

'I'm just putting together snippets I've picked up since going to work at Manutius,' she warned him

'Which is how long?'

'Two months – a lifetime. Two months *is* a lifetime with Wolf Fogel, believe me. It won't be a sinecure, Mister Breit. It'll be one frantic day each week.'

'You mean I should ask a lot of money?'

'Of course.' Her eyes narrowed. 'What d'you call a lot of money?'

He shrugged. 'Four hundred?'

She slumped in her chair and asked the cracked glass tabletop, 'Am I wasting my time with this man?'

'More?' he asked.

'*Much* more! Ask for two thousand and stick firmly at sixteen hundred – and that's per volume, mind.'

'My God!' His hands began to tremble. 'That's four times what I'm getting in—'

'Listen – when Fogel meets other publishers he boasts about two things: how *little* he pays his slaves and how *much* he pays his consultants. You ask for four hundred and he'll want you to come in every day. For sixteen hundred he'll be so grateful you can spare us one day a week. This is not the *real* world, you know – it's the world of publishing.'

He liked that 'us'! 'Whose side are you on?' he asked.

'Need you ask? D'you know the secret of success, Mister Breit? Never acquire any skill that might detain you at the bottom. I actually learned shorthand-typing before I realized my mistake – and I'll kill you if you ever tell Fogel I can do it.'

Wednesday, 14 May 1947

The Manutius Press occupied the entire first floor of a nondescript, three-storey, 1930s glass-and-concrete box in Rathbone Mews, not quite two hundred yards from the Saint Giles's Circus end of Oxford Street. The ground floor was a cross between a warehouse and a shop, where all kinds of war surplus was for sale. The commissionaire, a one-armed ex-soldier, showed Felix to the lift. 'If it doesn't work, sir,' he said, 'the stairway's down the end there.'

It worked; no steps today.

Faith Bullen-ffitch was waiting for him in the vestibule; the man must have buzzed her. 'Fogel has booked us for lunch at Schmidt's,' she said as she led him along the corridor. 'Sorry about the lino. We can't get a requisition to replace it.'

The walls were all of light steel framing filled in up to waist height with asbestos board, painted and repainted many times, the latest coat being cream; above it, frosted wired glass rose to the ceiling – all paper-thin. As they progressed she said, over her shoulder: 'Editorial, editorial, typing pool, design, Ozalid room, copy, editorial . . .'

Almost all the doors were open, allowing Felix (when he wasn't admiring the way Faith walked) a composite of Utility office desks, none tidy, young men in shirt sleeves, ties loosened, jackets draped over chair-backs, sucking pencils as they read, drumming fingers as they read, typing two-fingered, closing their eyes as they waited for telephone connections. Where she indicated *design,* men and some women stood hunched over machines that looked like some kind of camera obscura, with lights below and a hooded canopy above.

'Production's in the other corridor,' she concluded. 'And here's the nerve-centre. Me, Mister Wiggs of accounts – Hans Dreyer, who . . . does all sort of useful things – and—'

'What's on the top floor?' he asked.

'Nothing but ghosts.' She opened a door with a flourish. 'Fogel!'

Fogel leaped out of his chair and pirouetted round his desk with extraordinary grace for so large a man. 'Breit!' He advanced on Felix, right hand fully extended. His left, holding a large cigar, hovered nearby. He had large, slightly watery eyes of a penetrating blue; their lower lids hung a little slackly, forming cisterns which maintained that watery sheen. His hair was so minutely wavy that it would have been impossible to caricature it, especially with so much brilliantine. His lips were never still – nor were his eyes. 'I've been looking forward to this meeting ever since Bullen-ffitch told me about crossing you at the V&A,' he said. 'Sit down. Ve go for lunch soon. A sherry? Anything? You smoke a cigar?'

Felix declined all offers. '*Bei mir ist es ganz überaschend . . .*' he began.

'English!' Fogel looked both pained and apologetic. 'It's politic in these times. You speak English, no? America? You were a boy in America?'

'Sure. But I get so little chance to speak German.'

'Oh you get used to that.' He grinned. 'Where you live now? They speak German there? Sit, please.' He waved a hand toward a sofa, facing his desk.

'There's a Swedish girl . . . woman . . . married to an American. She speaks perfect German.'

On the sofa he was a good thirty centimetres beneath Fogel, now back at his desk – which was certainly not from the Utility range.

'You live in their house?' Fogel asked.

He explained about the Dower House.

'A kibbutz.' Fogel chuckled. 'A kibbutz of capitalists! That should be interesting.'

The conversation skated briefly over a number of topics – Fogel's grandfather, Felix's grandfather, the villa on the Wannsee, artists Fogel had known in Vienna, artists Felix had known in Paris and Berlin . . . shame . . . blame . . . survival.

When the cigar was ready for mashing to shreds, Fogel stood abruptly. 'Vee lunch,' he said. 'You can speak German to the vaiters. Fritz is very good. He knows all from Schiller. Can you believe – all in the war a German restaurant stays open in London, very popular with BBC people, and nobody breaks the vindow glass even! Come – ve go!'

It was barely a quarter of a mile but they took a taxi up Rathbone place and into Charlotte Street, where Schmidt's was to be found. Fogel enlivened the journey with a joke about a diner who tells the waiter that his sauerkraut is not very sour. And the waiter tells him that's because it's actually spaghetti! And the customer laughs and says, 'Ach so! No, no! You can leave the plate because – for spaghetti – *it's already quite zauer enough!*'

When they were seated at *his* table in Schmidt's, he returned to the joke and said, 'This is precisely our problem vith modern art, Breit – our series. Ve cannot simply look at a piece of modern art and say it's good, it's bad, it's zo-zo. First ve must ask what it's set out to be – is it Surrealist-Sauerkraut or

Symbolist-Spaghetti? Every act of criticism begins with the question: *Papiere bitte, Herr Künstler!* And this, dear Breit, is where you and your artworks will be zo absolutely crucial. They *are* that framevork. You can do it, yes?'

Felix, who hadn't the first notion of what was really wanted of him, even now, played for time. He said he would prefer to look at whatever work had already gone into planning and outlining the series.

But Fogel would have none of it. 'In that case all you make is an illustration of *our* vork. All you do then is follow us. But you are not our follower – you are our *Führer!* Ve flounder with labels – Dada . . . *Fauves* . . . Abstract Expressionist. Ve shuffle cards. But you – you come crashing in with just one *zupreme* flash of genius and you pull it all togezzer. You make the grand synthesis in *one* sculpture! Ve light it in many different ways. Ve put it in different backgrounds. Ve combine it vith uzzer material. No?'

Throughout this and several other inspiring monologues Fogel's hands gestured dynamic but unhelpful shapes, neither grace notes toward any kind of sculpture nor rhetorical flourishes to guide Felix through the vehemently sincere opacity of the man's thoughts. The entire meal was shrouded in that same rich fog of allusion and cajolery. Fogel's restless gaze quartered the room as often as it settled on Felix, who now realized that he was going to see nothing of the restaurant and its other clientele – whom both Fogel and Faith Bullen-ffitch seemed to find every bit as interesting as they found him. So, after the Bratwürst and Sauerkraut (both of which he could eat without surrendering any ration coupons), he made an excuse and went to the gents. Most of the other customers, he now saw, were men in city suits but there was a more bohemian group at a cluster of tables at the farther end of the restaurant. BBC types, he guessed. Among them was a young woman in a long-sleeved floral-print dress who looked rather interesting. On his return he hung back in the dark of the passage and studied her as long as he dared.

She was statuesque and blonde, with short, tight curls that clung around her head. The one word that occurred to him, watching her every move, was 'dignified'. She held her head high and spoke without animation to her two companions, both men and both clearly somewhat in awe of her. Her face had a sculptural quality, like a de Lempicka. All her gestures were precise and unhurried. When she spoke, they listened; when they spoke she had no hesitation in cutting in once or twice. As he re-entered the restaurant she broke off what she was saying and stared at him. Their eyes met and, for some reason, Felix found himself responding with the faintest of smiles and the smallest nod of his head before threading his path back to Fogel.

'Someone you know?' Faith asked.

'Who?'

'Never mind.' She gazed pointedly over his shoulder.

He turned and followed her gaze. The de Lempicka woman was talking to Fritz, their waiter.

At the coffee-and-brandy stage Fogel began to bargain over the fee for his work on the series. Remembering what Faith had told him at the V&A, he parleyed his way up to a sum that seemed dizzyingly unreal. Curiously, the harder he pushed, the more delighted Fogel appeared.

Fritz came with the bill. '*Hat es Ihnen gut geschmäkt?*' he asked, addressing Felix in particular.

He replied, in German, that he had enjoyed the meal immensely. Fogel told the waiter that Herr Breit was a distin-guished artist and that he, Fritz, would probably be seeing quite a bit of him because he was going to direct an important project at Manutius. Faith tried to interrupt this exchange, squeezing Fogel's arm rather hard and reminding him of an afternoon appointment.

'*Ja-ja-jaaa,*' he said, shaking her off. He simply signed the bill and handed it back.

As they left, Felix paused in the doorway and took one last look at the BBC blonde. Once again she was talking earnestly to Fritz.

Back at the Manutius office, after his farewells with his new employer, Faith showed him back to the lift. This time she took his arm and held it tight all the way. 'You'd never have dared push him that high without my coaching,' she told him.

'Could I have gone higher?'

'Not a penny. Aren't you glad we met, though? When are you going to show me this capitalist kibbutz?'

★   ★   ★

Felix gently pushed open the door to the Palmers' part of the house and tiptoed along the corridor to the stairs that led up to Willard and Marianne's flat. Nicole heard him nonetheless. 'I think they went out,' she said, appearing at the half-landing as if by magic.

'I saw their lights as I crossed the yard,' he assured her.

When he drew level she hissed, 'How can you?'

He shrugged.

'She didn't just *work* in Germany, you know. We all worked for the Germans in one way or another. We had no choice. But she had a choice – and she choiced to join the Nazi Party. She worked for *Speer!*'

'I wish I'd been so lucky.'

'How can you say such things? You of all people? I don't understand you.'

'I'll tell you then. Speer called all his officers and sergeants together one day and asked them what they'd do to a machine operator who didn't oil his machine so that it broke. And they said they'd beat him into the middle of next week. So then he told them that his slave labourers were the finest machines they were ever likely to come across. He wanted the maximum output from each and every one of them, and he wasn't likely to get it if they were starved and beaten black and blue – was that understood? In Mauthausen, the harder you worked, the quicker you died. So, Nicole, you wish to ask me once more why I would have been lucky to work for Speer – me of all people?'

'*Alors!*' She turned on her heel in disgust. 'You people can make black white and white black. Well, *I* will never fraternize with that one. *Jamais, jamais, jamais!*'

'The loss is yours,' he called after her as he started on the last flight.

Steps . . . pitch pine.

Her remark – *you people* – had not slipped by him. An unconscious anti-Semitism from an all-too-conscious anti-Nazi. Not at all uncommon in France.

Nicole turned again and followed him. 'You know that new electric cooker they have – the monster he got from the US base?'

'That's one of the things I want to see now.'

'She heats their apartment with it – it's true. She turns it on full and leaves the oven door open. We're going to have a horrid electricity bill all because of her.'

'You've seen her doing it?'

'Not me. I won't set foot in the place. But just go and look at the meter if you don't believe me. The wheel spins faster than you can watch. It must be her. Who else?'

He opened the Johnsons' door and called out, 'Anyone home?'

'Felix!' Willard called back.

'We're in the south room,' Marianne added.

'See – lights on everywhere!' Nicole shouted as she went back downstairs.

'Nicole!' he called after her. 'Don't you know what sort of scars you get if you keep up picking at the wounds?'

She slammed a door.

Willard and Marianne had turned their largest room into a temporary workshop, full of American power tools running off a 110-volt transformer. The other families had each lashed up some kind of kitchen in their portions of the house but for most of them it was still a matter of carrying large enamel bowls of used washing-up water to the nearest lavatory for emptying. The Johnsons, however, were making the kitchen to end all kitchens – a combination of American gadgetry and Scandinavian design. In fact, the way they planned it, the entire apartment was to become a lived-in advertisement for their architecture-and-design partnership. When they had finished, this temporary workshop would become their studio, where clients could see for themselves the sort of quality they could expect.

Willard was lighting a log fire and cursing the short chimney for not drawing very well. 'What can we do for you, Felix?' he asked between puffs.

Marianne was laying out tongue-and-groove matchboarding, all cut to size and sanded to a fine satin finish; she was swapping boards around, trying to get an even scattering of the cinnamon-red knots, each of which she had carefully blinded with French polish.

'Or should I try to make random groupings of them?' she asked Felix when she had got them perfectly distributed.

'Are you a designer or an artist?' he asked in reply.

'What's the difference?'

He told her.

Nonplussed, she said, 'I guess I'm an artist pretending to be a designer, then.'

'Just like me. I'm a sculptor who's going to have to pretend to be a typographer.'

'Eh?'

'Say again?' Willard added.

'I got hired today by a publisher in London to make the specifications for a series of books – a five-volume encyclopedia of modern Western art.'

'Hey man . . . wizard . . . well done!' The congratulations rained upon him.

Willard gave up on the fire and said, 'This calls for a celebration. Did you eat yet, Felix? Let's see if anywhere's open for dinner.'

'No, honey,' Marianne insisted. 'We've got to stick to our quota. Sorry, Felix. I'll cook us a dinner here. Say you'll stay for that.'

Willard said, 'I'll go get a bottle of wine from our cellar.' Over his shoulder he added, 'She should never have gone to Germany. That Teutonic sense of duty has ruined her.'

Left alone, Marianne smiled apologetically as she and Felix drifted toward the half-finished kitchen. 'He thinks if he makes enough jokes about it, Nicole might even laugh one day.'

'Can I peel potatoes or something?'

'We peel them *after* they're cooked, don't you? The English throw away the best bits.' She set half a dozen to boil. The stove was not being used as a room heater.

'Shell peas, then?' He saw a basket of them behind the door.

'Peas? You don't mind?'

He shook his head. 'I call them lifesavers.'

She tipped out a heap of pods on the plain deal table and put a large, broken-handled saucepan beside it. 'We'll save the empties in that for the chickens.'

'Pods, they're called.'

Occasionally their hands touched as they reached for the same pod. Their eyes met and they smiled. On the third or fourth occasion she squeezed his hand deliberately and said, 'I am really grateful to you, though, Felix.'

'For?'

'You know what for. You give us hope that Nicole will one day be reconciled with me. If you were not here – and if you were not so . . . what's the word? *supportable* to me – we should never have taken this apartment, though we love it so dearly.'

He continued shelling the peas.

'D'you know what's so wonderful now?' she went on. 'To wake up in the small hours and just listen to the silence. And to know it's not the silence you get before a raid. To look up at the moon and clouds and not even think of bombers up there. And if you hear a lorry, it's only for milk or cattle or something.'

'To know it's safe to make babies?' he suggested.

She smirked.

'That's the usual consequence of waking in the small hours. In Vienna they used to call them "children of the night watch".'

'You should get married, Felix,' she said.

'Maybe one day,' he told her. He thought of Faith Bullen-ffitch and then thought no. Faith was a collector, not a marrier. He wondered about the BBC woman, too – though he knew that was just fantasy.

'That's enough peas,' she said, adding after a brief silence: 'You must be psychic or something.'

'Me?'

'What you said just now – about making babies?' She spread both hands across her belly, a protective gesture.

'Oh! That's marvellous! When?'

'Sometime in July.'

'Golly! You're not showing?'

'I know. To do with rationing . . . I hope! Willard and I started it last November, still in Hamburg . . .'

'So *that's* why he came back!'

'No. He didn't know until I told him that day – Thursday the fifteenth April. But his . . . *Unterbewusstsein* – what's that?'

'Subconscious?'

'Yes. It must have told him. And now you're the first I've told – in the community. Willard doesn't want me to tell anyone until it shows – which it must any day now.'

'So why tell me?'

'I don't know. I feel I sort of owe you . . . sort of more than most.'

They heard Willard talking to Tony on the stair.

'So, Felix,' he said when he joined them, 'tell us about this publishing thing.'

Marianne stripped the parboiled potatoes and diced them into a pan of hot lard, adding chunks of carrot, spam, and sausage. 'We call this *pytt-i-panna*,' she said, though it wasn't strictly true; it was the nearest the English rationing system would allow.

'It's a crazy world,' Felix said. 'The people who actually design the books and edit them and so on get six hundred a year . . .'

'Hey!' Marianne was impressed.

'All I do is make some vague specifications and do one abstract sculpture, which we can colour and light in different ways for each chapter opening . . . and just look at things generally . . . "consultant", they call it . . . one day a week . . .'

'And?'

He was afraid to go on, after Marianne's response.

'They pay you double?' Willard guessed.

'More. Sixteen hundred.'

'Felix!' Marianne shrieked. 'You're going to be rich! Will you be godfather?'

Willard darted her a glance.

'I told *him*,' she said. 'He won't tell anyone else.'

Willard glanced from one to the other. Felix had seen that same uneasy light in Adam's eyes when he found Sally and him having tea together the other day. He was beginning to realize he'd have to get some sort of partner soon; what Adam called the 'dynamics of the community' demanded it. Especially if he was no longer the poor DP who roused that community's impulse to charity.

'Actually,' Willard said, 'it's no more than your due, Felix. I assume the publisher . . . what's his name?'

'Wolf Fogel. The Manutius Press.'

'I guess this Wolf guy gets to keep your piece of sculpture, eh? So he's getting your consultancy services cheap.'

'It's sixteen hundred per volume. And five are planned.'

Willard whistled. 'Seven and a half grand! That's more like it.' He laughed. 'So how's about the godfather thing?'

'Marxfather?' Felix suggested. 'God never did too much for me.'

'Marx? Are you crazy?' Willard was genuinely shocked.

Felix backed out of the minefield. 'Humanist father?'

'That's good!' Marianne put in hastily.

Willard yielded. 'Oh . . . I guess so. It won't play too well in Peoria, but what the hell.'

Willard was right, Felix realized. 'The Wolf guy' would end up with a new, post-war Felix Breit to grace his Hampstead home, and all paid for by his firm. He realized he needed an agent – fast. Perhaps Corvo could suggest one.

Thursday, 15 May 1947

Sam Prentice, 3½, disappeared when he got bored with being shown over the Dower House. Arthur Prentice said he probably couldn't come to any harm and went on asking about the price of season tickets on buses to Welwyn North and trains between there and London; May, his wife, who could not decide whether she liked the ground-floor front or the first-floor front better, went in search of the boy. Hannah, 2, toddled at her side, talking scribble.

She hunted through all eight cellars without success. Ditto the rest of the house, all the way up to the Johnsons' top-floor flat. They were away – in Hertford, buying paint.

'Look at these,' May said to her daughter, walking among Marianne's nylons, which were strung along the passage to dry. She let them brush lightly across her face. 'Eight pairs! Just make sure you marry an American when you grow up, pet! I wonder what her frocks are like? D'you think we dare? D'you think Sam's hiding in one of those wardrobes? I do.'

But Marianne's wardrobe was a disappointment after the promise of those nylons.

'Well, pet, we start off a bit more level,' she sighed.

'Sam!' Hannah murmured, staring out of the window.

'He's not here. That's definite.'

'Sam.'

May went to join her and saw him at once – wrestling with a piece of timber twice his own length out in some sort of chicken run built against the outside of the walled garden. That foreign sculptor man was there, too. Mr Breit. He was also waving a bit of wood about. 'Let's go and see what they've found,' she said.

It wasn't that she distrusted Mr Breit – well, she did, really
. . . a bit, anyway, or maybe not distrust. The thing was she
couldn't quite fathom him. The way he'd looked at her when
they were introduced – if an Englishman had looked like that,
she'd have been tempted to slap him. But with foreigners it was
different. She'd learned that in the war, after Italy capitulated
and they'd let the Eyetie POWs out to work on farms and places.
Foreigners didn't mean any harm by it; it was just their way. So
she felt no distrust of *him*, just of his strangeness.

They were funny sort of chicken runs because there were no
nesting boxes or places for laying eggs or anything. They ran
the full length of the garden wall, about a hundred yards. They
were roofed in corrugated iron, about ten foot high where it
butted the wall, sloping down to about seven foot in the front,
which was ten foot out from the wall. The front was of wire-
netting down to knee height, then corrugated iron down to the
ground. The floor was all sawdust, brown with age. At least,
May hoped it was age. Someone had put up washing lines near
the entrance. Two off-white sheets were hanging there, bone
dry. May saw that they had been turned sides-to-middle, not
very expertly in her view.

They stepped out from behind those sheets and saw at last
what they were doing with those planks. An old car chassis had
been pushed into these chicken runs at one time and Mr Breit
was showing Sam how to get it moving, using them as levers.

'Don't you!' Sam was pushing the man away. 'I can do it.
You watch.'

Felix rested on his length of wood like a warrior on his spear.

Sam inserted his lever under one of the flat tyres and, crouching
beneath it, heaved mightily. Nothing moved.

May was about to cry out that he would hurt himself when
he gave a shriek of triumph and rested. 'It moved!' he shouted.
'You saw it.'

'I saw it,' Felix said, 'but . . .'

'I did it. On my own. I did it, didn't I?'

'You did, Sam. But that only makes me wonder – are you
sure you want to come and live here? Is this the *right* place for
you?'

'Yes!' the boy shouted, again at the top of his voice. 'This is
the bestest place.'

'The bestest place,' Hannah called out, slipping from her mother's hand and running to join him. 'Me! Me!'

May, knowing a fight was about to occur, ran to separate them. But the girl had barely begun to tug at her brother's lever when Felix offered her his own. It was much too heavy for her but he let her wrestle a bit before he stepped behind her to help. Together, while May looked on, the three of them got the chassis to move several inches more.

'What is this place?' she asked when they tired of it.

'We use it for hanging up laundry now. It *was* a pheasant run. They grew hundreds of pheasants here – fed them, admired them, smiled at their plumpness. Then shoo! Shoo!' He flapped his hands toward the coppice beyond the walled garden. 'And . . . bang-bang!'

May knew his story and was embarrassed. 'The Wilsons and the Palmers . . .' she asked. 'Are they serious – all this community talk?'

'It's all still theoretical. We've already given up the idea of a communal kitchen and one communal meal a day.'

"Cos that Palmer woman can't abide that Johnson woman?'

'No flies on you!'

'It stood out a mile. I asked Mister Wilson if I could take a bit of the walled garden to grow our vegetables in, like an allotment, you know?'

'We will have a community vegetable garden,' Felix said. 'All contribute – all take. As you see, it's already dug and manured.'

'Where?' She stared through the wooden rails of the ornamental oak gate that led into the walled garden. 'I can't see it.'

'Precisely,' Felix replied. 'We have been here a month. The weeds are soon shoulder-high. The potatoes are like forests in all the fields around. And we have not dug a single . . . what d'you call it? A spade's-worth?'

'A spit.' She laughed. 'Don't ask me why.'

'I don't think our "community spirit" will weigh too heavily. On any of us.'

'We all learned to muck in together during the war,' she said vaguely. 'I doubt Arthur and me need any lessons.' She turned away from the walled garden and stared out across the fields. 'Where exactly is the boundary?'

'The iron railing beyond the line of pine trees. We're allowed to walk wherever we want though. And we can gather wood in the coppice and cut up any of these fallen trees. There's a path to Dormer Green between that line of lindens – you'll probably get to know it well.'

She looked at him sharply.

'That'll be your childrens' way to school.'

She scanned the landscape with new eyes. 'I'd like to see that.' She looked dubiously at the ploughed field. 'Can we?'

'I'll show you the way. There's a gate somewhere in all that undergrowth.'

May took Hannah on her shoulders. Sam toughed it out for several dozen increasingly arduous paces and then yielded; once on Felix's shoulders he kicked him hard and cried, 'Giddyup!'

Felix obliged until a hidden vine nearly brought him low; it frightened Sam into behaving sensibly after that.

May complimented him on his English; she now felt much more comfortable in his company.

He explained about living in America until he was seven.

'Fortunately you didn't pick up the accent,' she commented, adding hastily, 'you've got a nice *foreign* accent, instead.'

They negotiated a patch of brambles and calf-high nettles in silence.

'You were in one of those camps,' she said.

'Yes. Mauthausen.'

'My Arthur filmed one of those places on the day they liberated it.'

'Belsen, probably. That was in the British sector.'

'Wouldn't it be weird if it was the same one, though!'

'Doesn't he say?'

'He won't talk about it. Or can't. I don't . . . I mean I wouldn't press it.'

They arrived at the gate, which was, in fact, a swing-stile that would pass one person at a time.

'D'you think that's right?' she asked when they were all through.

They were into parkland now, where the grass was cropped by sheep, who gazed at them with placid wariness, and rabbits, whose white scuts and panic-stamping filled the panorama.

'Everyone must find their own way,' Felix said. 'If you mean do I refuse to talk about it, no. It's hard to think it was real now – except in dreams. This is the path. It must once have been the family's way to church.'

'Dreams!' May said. 'That must be terrible – not being able to wake up from it.'

'Waking up is like a new liberation, though.' Felix stared across the fields and coppices ahead of them. 'Dormer Green church,' he said, pointing out the spire. He put Sam down and let him run free. Hannah struggled to be let down and then tottered after him.

May said, 'It'll be quite a walk in the rain. You don't want to talk about it. I understand.'

'It's not that,' he assured her. 'It's trying to explain why it *isn't* terrible. Why it stops being terrible after a few days . . .'

'This tree's empty!' Sam cried from a little way ahead of them along the path.

'Hollow,' May said when she came up to it. 'D'you want to go inside it?'

Felix lifted the boy and set him down inside the trunk, which was, in fact, a cylinder of living wood, about three inches thick and furnished with bark on both sides. Her mother did the same for Hannah.

They stood inside, jostling and giggling until Felix went round the far side and put his lips near a hole where a branch had once sprouted. 'I'm so old!' he moaned, putting on the quavers and wheezes of an old man.

Hannah screamed in happy fright and cried, 'Again!'

Sam stared up uncertainly at his mother.

'It's the tree talking,' she said. 'Didn't you know some hollow trees can talk.'

'And I'm bored!' Felix added in the same geriatric tones. 'Five hundred years! Day and night . . . wind and rain . . . sun and snow . . . I'm so *old*!'

Fascinated, May watched him assume the part, saw him shrivel into himself, saw his knuckles become gnarled and rheumatic . . . and she wanted to fling her arms round him and mother him – or something.

Saturday, 17 May 1947

It was a local train to Hemel Hempstead, fussy, self-important on skirts of steam, and slow. The coaches must have been built back in the twenties – no corridors, just six-a-side compartments, each with its own slammer of a door. The wartime years had left them battered and smutty. Through its grimy window Felix could just make out Faith in the last compartment of the last carriage – Ladies Only, No Smoking.

He whistled and waved.

She sat up with a jolt, grabbed her bag, and made it to the platform just as the guard blew his whistle and leaped aboard the caboose – no . . . the guard's van – at the tail. She laughed across the five or six yards that separated them. 'That was a bit of luck – spotting you!'

She was wearing a white lace bolero over a pale floral print dress – couture, he felt certain – a cutely angled white beret, and white kid gloves that matched her white leather shoes. No jewelry . . . oh, except for a little brooch above her left breast pocket. She seemed to float up the stairs and across the footbridge; he wondered if she had been schooled as a mannequin before she took that secretarial course.

'Were you expecting the train on *this* platform?' she asked as she joined him.

'Steps,' he said, knowing he ought to say more.

'Oh. Heart . . . or something?'

'That sort of thing. The pony and trap's just outside.' The porter tore off half her ticket and tipped Felix a wink. 'Hope this weather holds, sir,' he said.

The brooch was a silver lozenge, set about with small diamonds framing a round glass window behind which a decorative letter F was embroidered, in what was surely human hair, on a pale blue silk. 'F for Felix,' she said, following his eyes. 'That's why I chose it for today. Actually, it was my Great-Aunt Frederika's.'

He helped her up into the trap and said he'd walk with the pony to the top of the hill. 'I can't imagine having a great-aunt,' he said. 'My father had a brother — Tony Bright, b, r, i, g, h, t — born Anton but he Americanized it. We lived near him in New Jersey, when I was about four.'

After a pause she said, 'One hesitates to ask any European DP about their family. Have you tried getting in touch with him over there?'

'Like — Hey Uncle Tony . . . remember me? Here I am — penniless and in need of some pretty expensive hunks of stone . . .'

'Penniless!' she sneered. 'Anyway, he might be a millionaire. Aren't you even curious about him?'

How to explain? Explain that his grandfather, an anti-Semitic Jew-turned-Protestant, to whom Hitler had been a god, was dead . . . that his mother was dead and his father was almost certainly dead, too . . . that he, Felix, had walked out on his father — his only known relative in the whole of Europe — in 1937 and had completely and wilfully lost touch with him from that day on? He said, 'We are not . . . or I probably should say *were not* a loving family. My father quarrelled with my grandfather and I, in turn, fell out with him. Hitler did the rest.'

'I'm sorry. I shouldn't pry. But I do want to know a lot more about you than I know now. God, I'm gasping for a fag — will that pony mind if I smoke?'

He laughed. 'Feel free.'

'You don't?'

'I used to — before I got TB.'

'You've had TB?' she asked excitedly as she extracted a Balkan Sobranie from a gold cigarette case lacquered coral red. 'Are you cured?'

'They said yes, but it leaves its mark behind. Why the sudden interest?'

'Well!' She took out a red-lacquered lighter and puffed her cigarette into life. 'They're bringing in a new law saying that every employer of a certain size must also employ a cripple or someone with a handicap. We're close to that limit now. Fogel's already got his eye on a sweet little dwarf who could be put on the switchboard but if your TB would count, we could postpone the evil day at least until the Modern Art Series is over.'

'It would be doubly nice to be *doubly* useful,' Felix said solemnly.

'You're not useful at all yet. Have you come up with an idea for your sculpture?'

'Is he getting impatient, then?' They had reached the top of the hill and Felix swung himself up beside her. 'Keep the reins if you like – you obviously know what you're doing. Why d'you smile?'

'I've had ponies since before I could walk. I have a magnificent hunter now – Jupiter – who's getting fed up with Rotten Row.'

'How often d'you ride him there?'

'Every morning before breakfast, every evening after work. I used to hunt him with the Badminton . . . still do on the odd weekend in the season. But he wants more. He deserves more.' She gazed right and left. 'This country looks very promising. What's the local hunt like?'

'I haven't the foggiest. You must be quite well off.'

'Ha!' The note was half-angry, half-resigned. 'You haven't made a single inquiry about me at all, have you!'

'I've wondered about you,' he replied calmly. 'And I have a stack of questions I'm going to ask of my future colleagues at Manutius – whenever I dare show my face there again . . . when I have my sculpture planned.'

She was instantly placated. 'Well, we can short-circuit all *that* here and now.'

'This is Barwick Green,' he said.

'Yes, it's lovely, I'm sure! Fire away.'

'What d'you really want out of life? Surely not to play Crito to Fogel's Socrates for ever?'

'*Whoooew!* Ask me an easier one first. Like – why don't I bring Jupiter out to the Dower House occasionally and ride around our park?'

'Riding . . .' he murmured. 'Riding is good.'

Their eyes dwelled in each other's for one long moment of full-scale audit, after which he knew that his most urgent question of the day (and, he suspected, her most urgent question, too) had been satisfactorily answered. Her eyes danced and a new glow seemed to suffuse her skin. 'What do I really-really-really want to do in life?' she mused. 'I want to shape something. I want to *make* something . . . and I want to control it. If I stay in publishing, I want to start something absolutely new, something no one has ever thought of before but which, when they see it being done, they'll say, "Why didn't I think of that?"'

'And if you don't stay in publishing?'

'I used to think *movies!* But the great experiments have all been done. Maybe television is now the thing, the virgin thing. When they make it national, I think I might be near the head of the queue. And if you ever breathe a word of this, or even hint it, to another living soul . . . no, you won't. I can tell. God knows how many secrets are locked away inside your head but I'm sure every last one of them is safe. Does anything ever shake you?'

'Not any more. Very little, anyway.'

'Was it really so bad − all-the-time bad? Never-letting-up bad?'

He wanted to answer her. Nobody else ever asked these questions so directly; and they *should* be answered − not least because he would quite like to hear the answers himself. 'What would constitute a loud noise in a shipyard?' he asked. 'In the rivetting section, say?'

She drew on her cigarette and inhaled deeply, letting it out in a long, tight plume that hung raggedly on the motionless air behind them. 'Right,' she said.

'No,' he went on, 'that's too easy. I'll tell you one thing about life in that camp. The worse it got − the harsher the treatment − the easier it became in one small but important way: the need to survive. When life gets that bad, all choices get narrowed down to just once choice − which, of course, is no choice at all. But I didn't realize it until I was free again − when the men with the choices arrived. And that filled me with panic, you know? Suddenly I must decide . . . a thousand things. But I've lost the ability to do that. I'm talking about then − just after the liberation. Now it's slowly coming back.'

She gave a baffled sort of laugh. 'You're amazing, you really are. You describe the darkest nightmare anyone could imagine and you say, "But I'll tell you one good thing about it." Now at least I know how you survived when so many didn't.'

Along the lane to the Dower House gatelodge she clucked the pony to a trot. 'He knows he's going home,' she said. 'Does it feel like home to you now?'

'I suppose it does. Though what makes it like home for me
. . . no, this is going to sound ungrateful.'

'That doesn't matter. Ingratitude is my middle name. Go on.'

'It's not all English people. Willard Johnson is an American
– married to Marianne, née von Ritter, Swedish. And Tony
Palmer is married to Nicole, née Trocquemé, French. And—'

'Quite a miniature United Nations! Do they fight? What do
they all *do*, anyway?'

'They're all architects or interior designers – so far. But there's
a TV cameraman – I mean, he's retraining at the BBC at Alley
Pally – he's probably going to take one of the apartments.'
Casually he added, 'And there are two others yet to be filled.'

She did not take the bait. 'What a superb little gatelodge!'
she said. 'Not so little, actually. Is that going, too?'

'Probably not. There's an economist from LSE looking at it.
I haven't met him yet. You asked if we fight, all us Europeans.
Slow down! I ought to explain one or two things before you
meet them.'

With the lightest tug of her fingertips she slowed the pony
to a walk and then a slow walk. 'I'm all ears.'

He explained about Marianne and her steel-baron father and
Rudolf Speer and how she became involved with the three
AMGOT officers and the liberation of Mauthausen . . . only
breaking off when they came in sight of the lawn. 'Good God!'
he cried. 'Someone's *mowing* it! That's Willard. Hi Willard!'

They waved. He waved back. The mowing machine was a
large Atco with a four-foot cylinder blade – and a powerful
motor to judge by its roar. It was heavy enough to roll as well
as cut.

'I wonder where he "liberated" that? He's a great one for
liberating useful things for the community. Oh! And that's his
wife Marianne standing on the balcony on the top floor there.'

'Whew! She looks like all those blonde gymnasts we saw in
those German propaganda films before the war. *Kraft durch Freude.*
Do we give her the Hitler salute?'

'Don't!'

And he went on to describe Nicole's war and how it had
poisoned her relations with the Johnsons.

Willard, having finished the leg that ended near the drive,
cut the motor back to tickover and parked the machine at the

lawn edge. 'Felix, you old son-of-a-gun! So at last we get to meet the beautiful and talented Miss Bullen-ffitch. Hi!'

Faith turned on Felix. 'Who is this talented beauty? Have you been seeing Another Woman?'

Willard laughed, unfazed. 'Good one, lady!' He turned his hand into a Colt 45 and shot her. 'Felix told us he was meeting you at the station. In fact, he's spoken of nothing else for days now. Well . . . back to the rockpile! I'll see you at teatime – with clean hands.' Halfway back to the mower he turned and added, 'Good to know he wasn't lying about you, Miss Bullen-ffitch.'

'Did you tell them I was beautiful?' she asked archly.

'Not was. Are. What he said about teatime, by the way . . . well, it's a sort of tradition in the community that when anyone visits us for the first time, they visit *all* of us. Someone makes tea, someone brings milk, someone brings sandwiches or scones – all very simple – and we meet in someone's house for tea . . . which will be –' he checked his watch – 'in a couple of hours.'

They turned the pony loose in the paddock and refilled his water trough. Then he showed her where she could stable her horse, and she said, 'Yes.' And after that they strolled around the grounds. The walled garden was still an acre of weeds but now there were a few strips tamed into producing salads, potatoes, and next year's soft fruits. Faith said that with a bit of horsedung and some fertilizer the community could probably live off the produce of this one garden. 'We just need to get rid of all these weeds and put up some rabbitproof fencing across the two entrances and fit a new spring to keep that gate closed at all times.'

'*Jawohl!*' he barked.

She laughed at herself and took his arm. And then held it. She ran her eye over a couple of dozen fruit trees – apple, pear, plum, and damson – which had not been pruned since before the war. 'We'd lose a season in getting those back into shape but after that they'd crop quite heavily,' she said. 'You have to open out the centre – the heart.'

'Ah – *that's* the difficult bit,' he told her.

'Oh Felix, darling!' She leaned her head on his shoulder. 'You are so self-sufficient and yet so . . .'

'So . . . ?'

'I can't find the word. Not exactly "vulnerable" but . . . well, you're about to enter a new sort of world. Or *re*-enter a world you once knew very well but a world that has changed out of all recognition while you were away. It's much more brutal. The war killed the idea of patience. Everybody realized that death was just round the corner, potentially, so we had to pack in as much as we could *now*! It was almost a sort of madness. With some of us it actually *was* madness. And then there were people who made their fortune out of it, even doing good things, patriotic things.'

'Like Fogel?'

'Just like Fogel. His *Illustrated Britain* series was a wonderful thing in the war – and, of course, it's still continuing, still neces-sary. It reminded people of everything British that was worth fighting for. It took a foreigner to see it and to inspire British writers to write it. And don't forget his maps. Mundane as they were, they helped Adams and Palmer and Willard Johnson to find their way to you the day after VE day. But the thing you should realize *now* is that all those people – the ones who had "a bloody good war" – they are the new Medici, and they are *hard* men who don't give second chances.' Then, without a change in tone or pace, she added, 'Shall I take off my skirt? Here?'

'I will be a gentleman,' he promised.

They lay in the uncut grass and out-of-control comfrey and consummated the ambiguous and unspoken bargain that seemed to have developed between them ever since their first meeting at the V&A. And, to confirm its ambiguity, she said, as she slipped back into her dress, 'This does not imply any *commitment,* you realize?'

They had set up a couple of trestle tables in an L-shape on the back lawn. *Two* tables were not strictly necessary but they allowed Nicole to keep her vow that she would never sit at the same table as Marianne. The smell of new-mown grass hung on the late-afternoon air.

Felix and Faith sauntered hand-in-hand around the Wilsons' end of the house – the Victorian-Tudor extension. 'Felix has suggested I should share his cottage across the yard there,' she announced. 'Does anybody mind? Also I have a horse who needs a good stable.'

While the others were trying to remember how many bedrooms the cottage had, Arthur asked, 'Have you got a car? The transport situation is getting pretty desperate. The bus doesn't always get to Welwyn North in time for the eight-ten to Kings Cross.'

The two of them sat across the outside corner of the L. 'I'll drive Faith to the station every morning in the trap,' Felix started to say, but Adam cut across him: 'I'll be getting transport next month – a van, quite a big one, a Jowett. We can bung a couple of old sofas in the back and travel in style. But we'll all be able to catch the eight-ten. And we can all go shopping in it to Hertford or Garden City on Saturdays.'

Willard said, 'I was going to liberate a jeep, but that sounds a whole lot better. How did you wangle it? Last time I asked, the waiting list for any new vehicle was about a year.'

Tony mimed the pulling of a string. 'The Greater London Plan. Open sesame!'

'But I still have to sign a covenant not to resell it within twelve months,' Adam added.

Willard shook his head. 'What did we fight the war *for*, huh? How dare any government try to tell me what I can and can't do with my own goddam property! The communists—'

'We fought the war,' Nicole said, 'to beat the Nazis.' Even had she added, 'Not to marry them!' her meaning could not have been clearer.

Willard clamped his jaw tight. Marianne, taciturn as ever, shook her head almost imperceptibly.

'Did you say you have a horse?' Sally asked Faith.

'Yes – Jupiter. Four-year old gelding, half thoroughbred, half Connemara. His grandsire won the Grand National back in the thirties. He'll fly anything you point him at. Why? Do you ride?'

'I used to. I hunted with the Cottesmore.'

'Wonderful! You should get a horse yourself and we could ride to hounds together. What's the local hunt like?'

'The Herts. Slightly battered by the war, I'm told. But it's good hunting country. I might take you up. Who d'you hunt with now?'

'My people live near Hawkesbury so I go down and hunt with the Beaufort. My father's joint-master this year.'

Nicole saw Marianne draw breath and then hesitate; 'I can ride, too,' she said quickly – thinking of the donkeys on the sands at Deauville.

Marianne smiled wanly at Felix.

'I'm told you have some very good hunts in Normandy,' Sally said. 'Did you belong to any?'

'No, but I can ride and, how you say? Leap?'

'Jump.'

'Yes – jump.' She dug herself in deeper with every word.

Felix said, 'Any thought that Faith's attraction to this place has anything to do with *me* has long since . . . *pfff*!' He mimed a small explosion with his fingers.

'Oh . . . diddums!' She leaned across the table corner and kissed him – and all doubts about what she meant by 'sharing the cottage' evaporated.

'What did you do in the war?' May asked. Without even looking she reached behind her and slapped Sam's hand as he reached for another biscuit.

'Not fair!' he protested. 'Hannah had two and I only had one.'

'Who says it's got to be fair?' she asked him. 'Why don't the pair of you push off and play on the lawn or something.' As they raced away she turned to the company and said, 'Will some of you others please have a baby soon, because I can tell you—'

Nicole and Marianne spoke simultaneously. Nicole said, 'I am . . .' and stopped, while Marianne said, 'I can tell you . . .' and stopped. They stared at each other, abashed.

Nicole turned to Willard. 'When?'

It was Marianne who answered, 'We think July.'

Nicole tossed her head in annoyance.

'Same here with us,' Tony said. 'July – August . . .'

Sally asked Marianne, 'Are you sure? It's not really showing.'

Marianne rose. 'If I pull in this smock at the waist . . . ?'

'Me, too.' Nicole, who was wearing a Regency-mode dress, did the same.

'You can count me *out*!' Faith assured them. 'As far as I'm concerned, a baby is a benign tumour. I assisted at many births during the war – to answer your question, Mrs Prentice . . .'

'May – please.'

'May. I've seen enough little bags of bone and jelly come

howling into this life to dampen the slightest craving for mother-hood.' She smiled all around to a sea of none-too-sympathetic faces. 'Well – I suppose that's me blackballed.' She shrugged apologetically at Felix.

'Not at all!' Adam's assurance was joined by the others with varying degrees of enthusiasm.

'It'll be useful to have someone who knows the ropes,' Tony added.

'No – ropes are for calves and foals,' Faith assured him solemnly. 'I've done that, too.'

'What about you, Sally?' Arthur asked. 'You're the only one who hasn't . . .'

'I've been waiting to say it. I think I'll be due just after – well, a bit later this summer. That's the prediction.'

Shrieks of laughter from Sam and Hannah on the lawn turned their heads that way.

After a short silence Willard said, 'Won't it be just great – this place teeming with kids!'

Felix raised an eyebrow at Faith.

No! she mouthed.

Tuesday, 27 May 1947

A week had gone by and Felix had still not hit upon an idea for Fogel. In some obscure way he felt his failure had to do with a growing obsession with Angela Wirth – the de Lempicka lady from the BBC. He had learned her name from the waiter, Fritz, of course – and Fritz had told him that she, too, had been asking questions about him. But that only seemed to make it more difficult for him to approach her – or, apparently, for her to approach him. But perhaps it was also because he had learned that she was a survivor of the Ravensbrück KL – the one for women, north of Berlin; and she must have learned of his imprisonment at Mauthausen, too.

One lunchtime he was sitting at what had now become *his* table when she passed by on her way to what had always been hers. She half-turned and said, '*Pea* soup?'

He glanced down at his plate. 'Yes. Why not?'

Now she was flustered. 'I'm sorry. It was just so—'

'Not at all. I do understand.' He rose, wiping his lips. 'Won't you join me?'

She hesitated.

He said, 'You have a more agreeable table, I admit.'

'No – it's not that.' She came back, suddenly very nervous.

He slipped the chair smoothly beneath her, looking down on her silky, blonde hair, the tweed shelf of her breasts, her scarred hands, older than her years. 'Felix Breit,' he said as he returned to his side of the table.

'I know. Angela Worth.' She pronounced both names as if they were English. She was panting slightly.

They shook hands over the table as he sat down. 'I know that, too. Fritz is a handy chap, eh? Well . . . *Mahlzeit!*'

'No! No German! I will never speak German again.'

'Oh?' He hesitated. 'Do you not think it, too – that beautiful language of Goethe and Schiller and Thomas Mann – do you not think it, too, was a victim of the Nazis?'

'*Gnädiges Fräulein?*' Fritz set the menu down before her and a sideplate with a small slice of bread. No butter or marge.

'Just a salami and salad,' she said. Then, to Felix: 'He's incorrigible.' She was recovering her composure quickly.

'He knows his Schiller. About the peas – I expect Fritz told you? They kept me alive, you know. Peas, beans, lentils . . . I'd be dead but for them.' He stretched his arm until his tattoo just became visible.

She nodded. Her fingers toyed with her bread. He could see the last digit of her prisoner number, 7, lurking inside her sleeve.

'Of course I feel guilty now it's all over,' he said. 'The best fed inmate . . .'

'Is it "all over"? Do we talk about all that?'

He shrugged. 'Perhaps not now. You work at the BBC, Fritz tells me?'

She nodded. 'My father was a sound recordist at UFA, before the war. When BASF brought out the first commercial tape, he was the first to learn how to get the best from it. He corresponded with von Braunmühl and Weber about introducing high-frequency bias.'

'That was *him*?' Felix asked in mock surprise. 'I've often wondered.'

She pulled a face and grinned. 'It was a huge improvement – all right? Anyway . . . my mother died when I was nine, so I spent a lot of time with him, on the set and in the sound studios. By the time I was fifteen, I was as good as any of them, but, of course, I couldn't get a union card. Until the war.'

She hesitated and he guessed that wasn't quite true, or *all* the truth.

'After the liberation, BFN hired me to "show them the ropes", because they only had the old wire recorders. Or those little four-minute wax discs, of course. Then the BBC invited me over. HMV wanted me, too, so –' she shrugged – 'that was quite good. These days I'm getting more into electronics . . . using valves and capacitors and things to make sounds. Avant garde music. Did you ever hear of a Frenchman called Fourier?'

'The philosopher? Charles Fourier?'

'No. Joseph. It doesn't matter – it's too complicated. Actually, the reason I moved into this field is I can see the writing on the wall. I was very popular when I was one of the few engineers who knew how to get the best out of tape recordings. Now it's more common at the BBC, they're beginning to notice I'm a woman and I really—'

'I noticed it straight away!'

'Why, thank yew!' She pretended to simper. 'Anyway, they also noticed that I really shouldn't be paid as much as those gentlemen-engineers. So I went to a crammer – you know what that is?'

He nodded.

'A maths crammer and made him teach me enough to understand Fourier's transforms, as they call them. And so now, once again, I'm *the queen bee*!' She giggled. 'That's what someone introduced me as yesterday – queen bee of the Experimental Audiophonic Unit. English is a funny language, don't you think? It's all saying one thing when you mean another. Raining cats and dogs. Changing horses in midstream. Hitting someone into the middle of next week. Lord, love a duck! Pulling the wool over someone's eyes . . .'

'Except Betty Grable,' he pointed out straight-faced. 'She pulls everyone's eyes over her wool.'

'Tskoh!' She laughed and punched his arm. 'But what about you? Oh! I know what I wanted to ask.' She swallowed hard and took a deep breath. 'Did your grandfather ever own a house on Am Grossen Wannsee? You know the Wannsee – the lake south of Berlin?'

He stared at her.

'What?' she asked.

'Sorry – it's just that someone else asked me that identical question, only a few weeks ago.' He nudged his soup plate away and went on to explain about Fogel's grandfather. Fritz scooped it up in one continuous movement, after laying down her salad.

'So old Fogel thinks he owns it?' she mused. 'There's an irony!'

'Why?'

'Oh . . .' She stared about her like one trapped. 'It's too complicated to explain now.'

'D'you know "old Fogel"?' he asked.

'I've only met him here, at Schmidt's, just to exchange a few words. Who is that young woman who's usually with him. You know the one I mean?'

'Miss Bullen-ffitch. She's the one who introduced me to Fogel. I met her at the v&a once. Now I work for him – one day a week.'

'She seems very . . . nice. Very . . . strong.' After a silence she asked, 'What are you thinking?'

'Remembering. The Wannsee. A boat. Expensive waterside villas with weeping trees over manicured lawns . . . a pretty girl . . .'

'Yes?' She leaned forward. 'What was *her* name?'

He shook his head. 'Gone . . . long gone. She was an ardent Nazi and we didn't really hit it off . . . very short hair, cut like a boy's. Very Berlin – you'd be too young to remember all that, I suppose. But I can see her arms still – sturdy as she rowed. Arms as Maillol would have carved them. Why did you ask about that villa?'

She breathed out, leaned back, and smiled. 'Oh . . . nothing really . . . I was there once – during the war – and I saw a painting of your grandfather's on one of the walls. Large. A view over the lake from that same villa. It would have taken him quite a while to paint, so I wondered if he lived there once. Billy Breit – that was his name, wasn't it?'

Felix nodded. 'He was born Solomon Breit – though I didn't know that until . . . well, it was . . .'

'Until January the twentieth, nineteen forty-two.'

Again he stared at her . . . long enough this time to realize that he was holding his breath. 'Yes,' he said. 'But how did you know that?'

Her face was unreadable. 'It's a long story. Have you anything planned for this afternoon? Could we go for a walk, a long walk, in Regent's Park? Not near the zoo. Perhaps you'd rather not?'

He smiled. 'And then again – perhaps I'd rather.'

Fritz brought his meatballs and cabbage – another dish that did not require the surrender of points from his ration book.

'Ever since that day,' she went on, 'when I was in that villa – I was a recording engineer then, *with* a union card, and the villa was Interpol HQ – I overheard two Nazi officials discussing your grandfather's painting and one of them said that you – his grandson – were an up-and-coming artist, a sculptor, and he gave your name, Felix Breit. And the other said he knew the name was familiar because you were on a list of Jews to be arrested in Paris that same day – January the twentieth. Often since that day, I wondered about you. The other officer said you probably didn't even know you were a Jew. He said you'd be in for a shock and they both laughed.'

Felix nodded. 'They were right. I had no idea my grandfather was a Jew until then. I stood at my window in Paris, watching the round-up and thinking "poor bastards!" And then they came for me! I protested, of course, but they showed me his birth certificate and there it was: Solomon Breit. He must have adopted the name William, or Billy, when he converted to the Protestants. I know nothing about that. But I do know – everybody knows – that he was viciously anti-Semitic. He adored Hitler. He died just before Kristallnacht but he would have approved of all that, too.' He gave a single, sour laugh. 'He would have been outraged to have died among all those vile *Jews*!'

With a deft twist of her fork she curled a slice of salami into a fragment of lettuce. 'And your father – did he know?' She popped it into her mouth, which was deep red – not cadmium red but carmine. The colour of jeweler's rouge.

Immediately he thought of carnivores but a moment later he

realized it was probably Gordon Moore's toothpaste. 'They got him, too – or so I assume. He must have known our ancestors were Jewish, though he kept it from me. He was an atheist.'

'You mean, you don't know what happened to him?'

He shrugged. 'I don't even know where he was living when the war started. We fell out. He didn't want me to be an artist because . . . well, he fell out with *his* father, too. We're each a one-generation family.'

'And your mother? Sorry – I'm being nosey . . .'

'No. Not at all.' A thought struck him. 'D'you know, there's no one I know – here in England – no one I can talk to about these things. I mean people who I absolutely *know* will under-stand. They listen . . . sort of. But to them it just seems like European politics . . . European history . . . Too complicated and also . . . too unimportant.'

'Yes!' Her face suddenly came alive. 'That's exactly it! They fought their way across the map, they put in their military governments – very efficient governments – and yet they have no *idea*, no . . .' She could not find the word. 'They know more about Africa, India, America . . . Europe's twenty-two miles from Dover yet it might as well be half the world. But you were saying – about your mother?'

'Yes. She and my grandfather both drowned, sailing between Kiel and Denmark.'

She picked up the last speck of lettuce with her fingers and licked it into her mouth. She had good teeth in those Gordon Moore gums. 'One of those Nazis said your name was starred. On the list of Jews to be rounded up that day – your name had a star beside it. He said it meant there'd probably be a public outcry among—'

'There was! Derain led a deputation to Gestapo HQ to demand my release. They had a cable from Matisse in Marseille, too, which carried a lot of weight. The same artists had also protested to the French government back in 'thirty-nine, when I was arrested by the French, along with all the other Germans. Back then it took three weeks to get me out. But for some reason, in 'forty-two, the Gestapo gave in at once and released me in a few hours. It was a weird time.'

She made an awkward gesture, an apologetic shrug.

'What?'

'It was planned that way,' she said. 'They knew there'd be a big protest, so they'd make a gesture . . . get good headlines in the papers . . . meanwhile, all the others would be safely deported with the minimum of public fuss. They knew they could get you anytime. Actually, when *did* they finally get you?'

'In Vichy France, March the fifteenth, nineteen forty-four. The Ides of March. I fled to Vichy the day they let me go. By then, of course, all those Americans who helped artists and intellectuals get away – Peggy Guggenheim . . . Varian Fry – they'd all gone. I had a forged exit visa and a forged transit visa to Mexico via Martinique, which might have worked. Excellent forgeries. But I arrived too late. I actually saw the ship sailing out of the harbour.'

'That must have been dreadful.'

'Then I was on the run for the best part of two years. I almost made it to the end of the war.'

'You joined the Resistance then, I suppose?'

He shook his head. 'It wouldn't have worked. I was too well known – and *already* a wanted man.'

'So what are you doing *these* days?'

'Fogel has asked me to be the *Führer* of a five-volume history of modern art – the Post-Impressionists, *Les Fauves, der blaue Reiter, die Brücke* . . . Cubism . . . Surrealism . . .' He stopped in mid-flow and stared at the salt cellar.

'And?' she prompted.

'An egg!' he exclaimed. 'Look! It's like the top half of an egg. That's *it*!'

'What is? I'm sorry . . .'

'No!' He laughed as he picked the salt cellar up and turned it round and round in his hand. 'I'm the one who's sorry. I've just . . . I found the answer to a problem. It's perfect.' He placed the salt cellar back on its stand. 'But we were talking about modern art. Did those names mean something to you?'

She gave a slight shrug. 'A bit.'

'I'm trying to build a bridge back to them. The war . . . the whole Nazi . . . *abomination* . . . is like a vast sterile desert that divides the century. Before it we had absurd hopes and monstrous naïveté . . . but the art was great. If we can build a bridge – not just me but all of us – a bridge back across the Nazi desert, and let the power of all that pre-war greatness put down new roots on this side of it, where the hopes are despairing and only the cynicism is monstrous, then there's a chance.'

While speaking he had watched her lick a fingertip and mop up every last crumb – dab, lick, dab, lick, dab, lick . . . with compulsive monotony. 'Are you going to have any pudding?' he asked.

She shook her head.

'I don't think I will, either. What luxury – to say no to food! Let's take that walk?'

On the way up Charlotte Street, beyond where he had ever walked before, he noted an art shop – Tiranti – worth a visit perhaps. On through Fitzroy Square and into the Euston Road they commented on the architecture, the bomb damage, the post-war scruffiness, the static water tanks; in their minds lay images of the total devastation they had left behind in Germany – all façades, and the blind windows thronged with ghosts. Here, even the most recent bombsites were greened over with rosebay willowherb and London pride, for no V-bomb had fallen in this part of town.

Narrow little Euston Road, lined on both sides with closed or rundown shops and greasy cafés, was a surprise after the relative opulence of Fitzroy Square, where just one building had been destroyed.

'I miss Paris,' he said. 'The Paris that has gone forever. They tell me London will be the new art capital of the world but it can't hold a candle to the Paris that was.'

'Hold a candle?'

'Sorry. Can't hope to equal. You've no idea—'

'Hold a candle!' she repeated approvingly. 'I like these things in English.'

'You've no idea how vibrant . . . alive . . . *gay* . . . Paris was in the thirties. That's why I stayed on, even after my first arrest – which is when I should have got out.'

'I have digs just across there in Robert Street,' she said.

He told her about the Dower House but did not mention Faith.

They entered Regent's Park, past one of the two vast static water tanks that flanked the road.

'EWS?' she asked, looking at the huge, now-faded letters.

'Emergency Water Supply?' he guessed. 'You were going to

tell me about that villa in Wannsee – Interpol HQ? Were you employed to record proceedings there?'

There was a long pause before she replied, 'I was an officer in the SS.'

He was too stunned to make any response. Then it dawned on him that he had been rather naïve. She'd been a recording engineer at Interpol HQ. They'd never have trusted that work to a civilian. But then . . . that Ravensbrück tattoo on her arm . . .

'D'you still want to hear?' she asked.

'Of course.' He recovered swiftly. 'You ended the war in Ravensbrück. Of course I want to hear. More than ever, now.'

Did she have a prisoner's tattoo added after the liberation? Many SS guards had done that.

The buzz of traffic receded as they penetrated farther into the park.

She drew breath and took the plunge. 'Have you heard of Heydrich? Reinhard Heydrich – he was Number Two in the SS.'

'Assassinated in—'

'Yes. May the seven-and-twentieth – I mean twenty-seventh – nineteen forty-two. In Prague. They liquidated Lidice in reprisal. The whole village. He was also head of the German branch of Interpol. He was one of the most evil men I ever met but it was the sort of evil a young girl might take many years to understand, because he was also most charming. And to see him with his wife and children – as I did, many times – was . . .'

'But he was also one of the architects of the *Vernichtung*. Pardon my German.'

'I met him through recording, of course. He was – you may find this hard to believe – he was a virtuoso on the violin. If the war—'

'No, I knew that.'

'It was true. If the war had never been, I think we might now be buying Heydrich playing the Beethoven violin concerto with the Berlin Philharmonic – truly. Anyway . . . he formed a string quartet of fellow SS officers and . . . they weren't up to his standard, of course, but they weren't bad. And he came down to UFA with Goebbels one day to borrow some recording equipment and my father wouldn't let it out of his sight so he went with them to manage the recording. And that happened many times. But then, one day, he was too busy doing some editing and so he sent me along. And –' she swallowed heavily – 'I fell completely under his spell. I thought he must have the most sensitive soul because he played so exquisitely . . .'

'You could say the same about Picasso – draws and paints like an angel but in private life he's a bastard.' Felix wondered if she had ever slept with Heydrich.

Meanwhile she was saying, 'We knew they were doing unpleasant things to the Jews, of course – and this was even before they had to wear the yellow star – but we knew about all the race laws. And then there were bloody beatings-up. But I thought that had to be the work of the lower ranks of the SS – the dregs – and that such sensitive men as Heydrich and those senior officers would never lower themselves to behave like that.' She gave a mirthless laugh. 'You were right to speak of our "monstrous naïveté" back in those days. And of course they cultivated it, that façade of civilization. Anyway, after that first time, Heydrich always asked for me to record their music. I don't know what happened to all those tapes and disks. Probably Bormann had them destroyed after the assassination. Bormann had no charm and Heydrich had too much. Ersatz, of course, like everything else in our lives back then. Shall we sit on this bench? I don't think it's good to walk too strenuously after a meal.'

'Especially a heavy salad like that.'

She dug him with her elbow as they sat down. Ducks paddled expectantly toward them but a little boy, out with his nanny, soon diverted them with a bag of crusts.

Watching them fight for each morsel, Felix was reminded of scenes from Mauthausen. He said, 'Takes you back, eh?'

She reached a hand across the void between them and squeezed his arm.

'Those recordings,' he said. 'Did they take place at the Interpol HQ?'

She shook her head. 'No. I first became *officially* involved with the SS in 'thirty-nine, when they set up the Gestapo brothel – Kitty's, in Giesebrechtstrasse. I supervised the technical work – setting up the recorders . . . hiding the mikes. That's a story in itself. I never *believed* all that Mata-Hari stuff where aged generals would cry out in their ecstasy, "The forty-fifth cavalry will be

moved to Passchendaele at dawn on the twenty-third . . ." but it
happened. Anyway, that's when I had to take the SS oath – as
Heydrich's personal recording engineer, more or less. I mean not
officially. Women didn't officially join the SS until 'forty-two, of
course. That's when I also joined – officially. But Heydrich told
everyone, already back in 'thirty-nine, to treat me as if I had the
authority of an SS-Führerin. He was obsessed with knowing what
people might be saying behind his back, you see. There was a
rumour that he was a half-Jew, a *Mischling,* because his mother
married a Jew – but that was her second marriage, a long time
after he was born. So he was fanatical about secretly recording
even his closest associates – *especially* them. But by nineteen forty-
two he was dead and certain people who resented his patronage
of me were after my blood. So by joining the SS and taking the
oath I had walked into a trap.'

'Is that why they sent you to Ravensbrück?'

'No. I'll tell you about that. Heydrich organized a conference
at the Interpol villa in forty-two – the twentieth of January, that
dreaded date for you. And for me! It was just a few months
before he was assassinated. And after he was dead they accused
me of recording it, that conference.'

'And did you?'

'Yes, of course. It was Heydrich's orders. I had two tape
recorders there and four wax-disc machines, to record everything
– conversations in the anteroom . . . the lavatories . . . the
hallway . . . everywhere. And he also ordered me never to tell
anyone – because of his obsession. So I never admitted it – at
least, not until after they tortured me for days and days.'

'Why didn't you admit it at once? They always get it out of
you in the end.'

'That's why. That's exactly why. They already knew I had
recorded it. Because Eichmann came back that night . . . he had
confiscated everyone's notes. No one was allowed to take anything
away from that meeting. And he came back to stir the ashes so
the burned papers could not be put back together.'

'He got away, you know. They never caught him.'

'I know. But he certainly caught me! I was dismantling the
microphones and cables when he turned up and I had to pretend
I was actually installing them for an Interpol meeting the
following week. But I could see he didn't believe me.'

'So why didn't you admit it at once?'

'Because I had to make them think my confession was their triumph. I had a much worse crime – in their eyes, I mean – to conceal. I not only *recorded* that meeting, I also made a *transcript* – a private transcript for myself. They would have shot me for that. In fact, I made two transcripts. One I recovered from where I had hidden it and I gave it to British army Intelligence – after the war, of course – and now they claim it's "gone missing" – which I don't believe.'

'And the other copy?'

The boy, the nanny, and the ducks had moved away; only a ragged breeze stirred the lake with illusions of fish shoals beneath its surface. She did not answer and he did not press her. At length she sighed and rose to her feet. 'We must keep moving,' she said, as if it were winter. They started to walk again, around the lake, toward the rose garden. 'One of the difficulties in trying to explain what happened in the KLs – to people who weren't there, I mean – is that none of it makes sense unless you know *all* of it.'

He agreed. 'It makes sense in a shallow sort of way – *sensational* sense, you could say – but it doesn't connect. It's like describing a rainbow to someone who was born colourblind. They can see the outline of the thing but not the thing itself. I don't try. But with other survivors – with you – there's no need. And no point.'

Now she took his arm and shook it urgently in time with her words: 'But I have the same problem in trying to tell you what happened at that conference . . . and why I made two transcripts . . . and why I joined the communist party – Yes! In nineteen forty-two, I – an officer in the SS – joined the communist party. And all because of what I heard at that conference. No!' She closed her eyes and stamped her feet. 'I heard *nothing* at that conference. That's the most awful thing of all. There they were – all the top people in the SS except Himmler telling second-rank men from all of the Reich's Ministeriums – ministries, I mean – telling them that the SS had worked out the most efficient way to kill millions of Jews and Romanies and poofs and . . . anyone they didn't like . . . and they were now going to start doing it on a big, *big* scale . . . and when they'd finished, there wouldn't be a single one of those inferiors left in Europe, nor in England if the Reich won the war . . . judenrein, they called it. The entire Europe will be judenrein and if you civilians argue against it or obstruct us or even just fail to cooperate, you could end up being liquidated alongside them . . .'

'*Um Gotteswillen!*' Felix felt the day shivering into something less than real.

'Yes!' she insisted. 'And *I didn't hear a word*! I was so busy checking recording levels . . . worrying about . . . I don't know . . . bias in the valves or . . . grid feedback . . . decibels and overload . . . anything except what they were actually saying. It was only when I played it back − just to check that nothing had dropped out − that's when I actually *heard* what they were saying, those fine ss gentlemen, one of which had been my hero. That's when I made those transcripts and that's when I put out seeking . . . how d'you say it?'

'Put out feelers? You put out feelers toward the communists?'

'Yes. Put out feelers − another strange expression.'

'And obviously you succeeded, since you joined.'

'Well . . . I never actually *joined*. I mean I didn't ever have a party card, not then. I do now, of course. I still believe in communism. The communists saved my life in Ravensbrück. But back then she said I was too valuable, being inside the ss. It would be idiotisk to have any incriminating bits of paper. And she was my only contact. The only one I ever saw. She's the one I gave that other transcript to. The Party must have it somewhere. They'll bring it out in the war-crimes trials, I expect.'

'Did you know her name?'

'Only . . . she called herself Maria but I'm sure it wasn't her real name. I gave my name as Edit. She spoke perfect German but I think her accent was Danish. Or not even accent, but intonation.' She spoke a few random words, putting a rising intonation on the final syllable − *diese Zeite . . . die Elbe . . . Querstrasse.*

Her ear was perfect − as one might expect from someone who devoted her life to analysing and recording sound. Felix could tell as much because the words were exactly as Marianne would have spoken them in her Scandinavian accent.

'Extraordinary!' he said.

'What d'you mean?' she asked suspiciously. 'That's how she spoke.'

'Oh I believe you. Your imitation is perfect. There's a Swedish woman at the Dower House – pretty close to Danish, I think. She's now married to Willard Johnson, that American architect I told you about – she speaks German exactly like that. She was in Germany during the war.'

'A Nazi! Married to an American . . . living free here in England? I bet she's very pretty, yes?'

'She was very young – and she's paid heavily for it since, believe me.'

He broke off a rose – a bourbon – and handed it to her like a peace offering, which she accepted with a smile. He moved her hand to place the rose beside her cheek. 'No,' he said. 'You still win.'

'Oh!' She laughed, a strange staccato laugh, as if he had punched her and she was trying to show it didn't hurt. Tears simultaneously started in her eyes.

As she wiped one away she said, 'The first time I cried after liberation was when I saw flowers – the first time I realized I still could cry.'

It was undoubtedly true, but he knew that was not what brought tears to her eyes now, and he regretted his thoughtless *jeu d'ésprit*. Why had he done it, anyway? Whatever had driven him to become an artist had enabled him to survive as an artist, emerge as an artist, and continue living as an artist. But whatever had driven her to become the personal recording engineer to one of the truly great monsters of this entire century had withered and died in one single, eye-opening recording session. She had been left to reinvent herself from the inside while maintaining every outward appearance of a self that she now loathed. Their paths could not have been more different. For as long as she lived she would be compelled to play the Flying Dutchman to her own unsalvaged conscience, never finding haven, never again being able to settle ashore.

'All fantasies of what might have been are pointless,' he said, forcing a wan smile to her lips.

'Perhaps we need them all the same,' she replied. 'To defend us from the guilt of having survived when so many more worthy people, wonderful people, outstanding people . . . died. I often think of Milena Jesenská, one of the most wonderful people . . . I mean – can you imagine someone whose soul was so great that when she died, almost the entire camp, the prisoners, I mean, went into mourning? I don't mean we wore *black* – my God, that was the SS colour! But mentally we mourned. Can you imagine someone like that in a place where *hundreds* were murdered every day? And when I remember her I think how dare I survive when someone like her did not. She was Franz Kafka's lover. Have you heard of him? He died back in the twenties. The most gruesome thing – she told me once – is that he wrote a short story in nineteen-fourteen called *In der Strafkolonie* which exactly describes the Nazi KLs – *exactly*. We can't say it came without warning, can we.'

Monday, 9 June 1947

It was a lump of pure white Carrara marble, eighteen inches square at the base and some thirty inches high. It came to the Dower House on the flatbed of an LNER delivery lorry from Welwyn Garden City.

'All yours, mate,' the driver said as he part-slid part-walked it to the edge. 'Can you manage? Just lift it down.'

Felix trumped him, embracing the stone and drawing breath as if for a mighty lift.

'Christ no!' the man yelled.

Willard emerged from the back door of the main house and ran to join them. 'You're out of practice at this sort of thing,' he said, winking as he pulled Felix's arms away. 'Tell you what – I'll get those old floor joists we dumped in the pheasant run.'

'No need,' the driver said. 'I was jokin.' He lifted two stout planks from the flatbed, which he passed to them; there were steel hooks at one end, which he manoeuvred over a bar at the tail of the lorry, making a long ramp. While Willard jumped up, ready to help him, he unstrapped a porter's trolley from the back of the cab and handed it down to Felix.

'Now we're cooking with gas,' Willard said.

There were a couple of heart-in-mouth moments as they manhandled the marble down the ramp but it arrived safely at the bottom and, with the help of the trolley, was swiftly taken into the cottage and set squarely upon the braked turntable Felix had installed the previous week.

'I'd offer you a cup of tea,' Felix told the driver, 'but I don't have any. All I've got is beer . . . sorry.' And he turned away as if it was all over.

Willard let the man dangle briefly before saying, 'Revenge is sweet. Come on – I could force myself to swallow a beer, too.'

He put his arm around the man's shoulders and steered him toward the kitchen, where Felix was laying out three glasses before fetching the beer from the larder.

'Yeah, I asked for that,' the man said. 'You almost give me a heart attack when I thought you was goin' to lift it down. Todd's the name – Todd Ferguson.'

They introduced themselves, said 'Cheers', took deep gulps, and let out male-solidarity gasps of satisfaction.

'What is this place, then?' Todd asked. 'Last time we had a delivery 'ere it was a school. The driver told me he delivered a bale of cloth for makin' choirboys' cassocks. Catholics, they was, from Jersey. You an artist, then, Mister Breit, sir?'

'No "sir", please – for God's sake. We all use first names here – Todd. And yes, I'm a sculptor.'

Todd laughed. 'Gonna carve one of them naked women, eh? I've seen 'em! What a life!'

'Something very feminine, anyway,' Felix agreed.

'You asked what this place is now, Todd,' Willard said. 'It's a community of people who got used to the sort of communal life we all – or most of us – shared in the war and who don't want to go back to living in separate little boxes of brick and mortar. But we don't want the completely communal life we had in the war, either, so we're trying to build something in between.'

'Blimey!' Todd's truculence vanished.

'You think we're mad?' Felix asked.

'No! Blimey no. I was sayin' to the missus only yesterday – we're already losin' that old wartime spirit. "Little boxes of bricks and mortar" – that just about says it. I wish I'd a thought of that. Says it perfectly.'

'Have you been married long?' Willard asked.

'Gracie and me got spliced in nineteen-forty. I was in the fire brigade she was a dispatcher. Got bombed out a foo months later. Lost everyfink. Come out to Garden City – still in the fire brigade, the local one. Bin 'ere ever since. Got free kids – a gel, a boy, and a noo little baby gel – Betty, Charlie, and we can't agree on no name for the noo one. I want Vera, cos of Vera Lynn. She wants Sheila, cos she likes readin' Sheila Kaye Smith. What abaht you blokes?' He looked at Faith's nylons hanging over the curtain rail above the sink, and then at Felix. 'Married, then?'

'Next best thing.'

'Ooo-err!' Todd belly-laughed.

Felix wondered who Betty and Charlie were named after – Grable? Chaplin? Chan? Chester?

Marianne joined them at that moment. 'I take it the stone has arrived? Can I see it?'

Todd leaped to his feet, almost upsetting the beer; rather sheepishly the other two followed suit.

She laughed. 'For heaven's sake sit down!' She peeped into the studio. 'Oh – that shall keep you busy, Felix!'

'Todd,' Willard began while Felix went to the pantry for a fresh glass and more beer, 'this is—'

'No!' Felix shouted. 'You Americans are barbarians! Marianne – this is Todd Ferguson, delivery driver for the LNER. Todd, this is Marianne Johnson – Willard's better half – his much better half.'

They shook hands. Marianne took the beer bottle and poured her own.

'Smatterer fact,' Todd said diffidently, 'I'm the goods depot *manager* in Garden City. I'm just drivin today cos we was short.' After a pause he added, 'I tell a lie. We are short but I could of sent someone else. I picked meself cos I wanted to see this place and I wanted to know what you was goin' to do wiv that marble.'

'Well, you'll have to wait to see the sculpture but we could show you over the place if you like.' To Willard he added, 'I think we can show him around, don't you?'

'I had that thought,' Willard agreed. Marianne nodded, too.

The men had finished their beers; Marianne took hers with

her on the tour, during which she extracted his life history in greater detail. 'So,' she said, 'you've just turned twenty-eight and you're already manager of quite a large goods depot.'

'Yeah,' he agreed. 'I was deputy fire chief out 'ere in the war, and actin' fire chief at the end. I like organizing fings. I like to get everyfink runnin' . . . like well-oiled.'

Behind his back, Willard held out crossed fingers to Felix, who nodded vigorous agreement.

They took him to Nicole, who showed them over her and Tony's flat. Marianne tactfully withdrew 'to prepare her place', which came next. Then Sally joined them and showed him over their place and the rest of the house, including the Prentices' flat – they being out for the morning. When they came to the empty front flat – the largest in the house – Felix warned him that Faith thought she had found someone who might want to take it.

The significance of the warning was not lost on Todd, suggesting as it did that if Faith had not found such potential tenants, the apartments were open to offer.

'Who?' Sally asked. 'I haven't heard this.'

'A couple called Brandon. Isabella and Eric. She's something to do with fashion. He's a book illustrator – mainly for children. Does the odd spot of writing, too. They're coming at the weekend – I meant to tell you.'

Todd glanced at his watch.

'Yes – sorry,' Felix said. 'There's only one more to look at.'

They took him to the upstairs flat in the old Tudor part of the house.

'We refer to this as the smallest flat,' Willard said, 'but, in fact, it has the same number of rooms as Tony and Nicole's, and Adam and Sally's . . .'

'And more than my cottage,' Felix added.

They showed him the hallway, which was long enough and easily wide enough for a generous kitchen; then the sitting room, which was quite large, and the two bedrooms, small by Dower House standards but as big as any in a modern suburban house.

'And we could make a third bedroom if we took out that old slate water tank, which is huge – come see.'

The tank, bone dry and filled with cobwebs, measured some six foot by five by almost five foot high.

Todd gauged it with a knowing eye; the slate floor and walls were almost two inches thick. 'Take some shiftin that would,' he said.

'It would need some organizing,' Willard agreed.

'It'd suit a man who's fond of organizing, though,' Marianne added.

Todd looked from one to another. 'You blokes serious?' he asked.

'Never more so.'

Felix nodded, Sally nodded; they turned to Nicole, who said, 'Of course.'

'Blimey! Stone the crows!'

They arranged for him to bring his wife, Betty, out that same evening.

Felix knew he should have started on the carving at once; instead, he went out to the walled garden and dug a whole barrow-load of comfrey roots. With every thrust of the spade he could almost hear Faith saying, 'What on *earth* d'you think you're doing, man? You know how impatient Fogel is getting.' He dithered over lunch – he even washed up his plate, cup, and fork. But at last he could postpone the long-awaited moment no further. He opened the box from Tiranti of Charlotte Street and took out his new mallet and his set of new carving tools – with tungsten-carbide tips – and laid them out on the whatnot (as Faith called it) beside his carving stand. And only then did he dare even look at the block of marble.

He had imagined this moment so many times over the past three days but now that it had come he was completely at a loss. He knew why, of course, but was loath to admit it, even to himself. His last effort at stonecarving had been in the sheds at Mauthausen – just before the guard had dug him in the back with his rifle barrel – '*Du! Jude! Kom!*' – and led him to where they did the medical experiments. Now came the leap from *that* to *this*.

He spun the stone gently round, watching the interplay of light and reflected light. Soon it began to seduce him. Marble is chalk that has been to hell and back. Tempered and purified by Vulcan, it has gained an inner luminescence that gives its surface a depth no other stone can equal. Let the merriest sunlight fall upon granite and it immediately sobers down and returns to the eye, all dour and forbidding; it moans grim sermons at you from every granite chapel in the land. But let the merest shaft of that same light play upon the gentle face of marble . . . and back it dances, full of invitations to touch, to caress, to behave like an Italian.

He caressed it with the lightest touch of his widest chisel. Feather-gentle, it nonetheless left a mark; there would be no room for mistakes here. But what would constitute a 'mistake'? He certainly didn't want to produce an egg-shape that looked as if it had simply been turned on a mechanical wheel; it had to be *carved*. And yet, when the viewer saw it first – that *premier coup de l'oeil,* as Bonnard always called it – he must think that that was how it *was* made: mechanically perfect upon a turner's wheel.

But close-to, after, say, half a minute's inspection, its subtlest of imperfections must reveal that a human hand had made it so. A perfect circle drawn with the aid of a compass has a dead sort of beauty; a perfect circle drawn by a Leonardo has the same beauty but is vibrant and passionate as well.

He laid the tools down again, took up his drawing board, and pinned a half-imperial sheet of conté paper to it – Barcham & Green's best quality, hand made. Then with charcoal, 6B pencil, and conté crayon he covered it with egg-shaped spheroids – eggs inside eggs . . . eggs overlapping eggs . . . eggs correcting eggs . . . and in this way he arrived at last at the perfect – no, the only *possible* or *permissible* shape for this particular block of marble. And with that he picked up his mallet and chisel once more and whacked off one of the square corners with some panache. Then the kitty corner.

Then the other two corners. And so he continued until, within the hour, he had the intimation toward which he had been groping ever since he began – the conviction that *his* egg, the one he was going to carve, had actually taken form already, just beneath the surface where his chisel was presently making its bites – so that he was not so much carving it as liberating it from an encrustation of stone.

By the time Faith returned that evening he had the upper half of the egg roughly formed. The ringing tap-tap of mallet and chisel told her he was working at last, so the sight of him standing there, carving away, came as no surprise. But as for the object itself . . . 'Ah!' she cried. And then, 'Oh!' And finally, 'Well!'

'I've changed my mind,' he said.

'Meaning?'

'I was going to carve it into a perfect egg-shape. If I cheated slightly and cut a flat surface at the very bottom – no more than a penny in size – I'm sure it would stand without props, if it was completely symmetrical all round. But then I got to thinking of Michelangelo . . .'

'As one does.'

'As anyone carving marble does, and I remembered his *Slave*. Do you know it?'

'Only in photographs. God – we must start visiting in Europe again now they've lifted the ban. Florence! The Uffizi! Rome! Venice! This bloody socialist government with its five-quid limit! What about the *Slave*? It's the one he never finished, no?'

'Yes – and no. He thought each one of his sculptures already existed inside the marble. All he did was liberate them – or half-liberate in the case of the Slave. I think I'll do that with this egg – only in a more advanced state of liberation. It will be a perfect egg except for this corner, at the bottom. I'll leave it so that that bit of the egg still must be liberated.'

'Why?'

'Because if I make the work complete, then it is just another work of art among thousands in the series – and probably inferior to most of them. And because it is repeated, again and again at the start of every chapter, it would soon begin to intrude. So instead it will take one step back from completion. It will say, "Over-to-you, Señor Picasso, Monsieur Derain, Herr Klee . . ." all the artists whose *finished* work will fill the pages around.'

She started to laugh.

'What?' he asked.

'Remember what I told you about the difference between artists and designers? You began this morning as an artist – but you end the day as a designer!'

He thought it prudent to let her think so. In fact, a cheap

unfinished Felix Breit would have no *cachet* in Fogel's Hampstead circles. Not while the artist himself was alive and well and working in London.

Wednesday, 11 June 1947

Eric and Isabella Brandon's Morris Ten wove a careful path among the potholes along the drive. It drew up, dead centre, in front of the house. The engine died and the cooling exhaust pinged in the silence – or what would have been silence if Isabella had not said, 'Didn't I ask you to get that spider out of the speedometer window?'

Her voice, fruity and penetrating, carried across the carriage sweep in front of the house to the welcoming delegation of Adam, Tony and Nicole, and Faith; it was Faith who had suggested to Eric that he and Isabella might like to join the Dower House community. She had run across him at several launch parties and other publishing haunts in Soho, for he was the author and illustrator of a string of successful children's books; his wife, Isabella, was . . . well, that remained to be discovered. 'In the rag trade,' was all Eric had told her when she met the couple casually in the Hay Hill Bookshop in Curzon Street, near where they lived.

And now his flatter London tones proved quite as penetrating as his wife's. He wound down the window and stuck out his head. 'How d'you call spiders – anyone? It's not "kitty-kitty", is it?' He retreated inside the car again. 'No, my pet, we are adrift in a sea of ignorance.'

She closed her eyes and said, 'It's a simple question, darling. Did I ask you or didn't I? A yes or no will suffice.'

'You undoubtedly did. A-a-and if you will tell me how to seduce spiders out from behind immovable glass, I shall evict him forthwith. Or her. Dead flies don't work, by the way. Nor worms.'

'Worms?'

'Well, they work with fish.'

To the waiting delegation their voices were clearer than their images, cowering in the dark tomb of the car and part-obscured by wipers that seemed to be stuck at half-quadrant. Isabella's face loomed forward until her nose almost touched the windscreen. 'Oh, hello!' she cried, apparently seeing the welcome party for the first time; they were dwarfed by the Ionic pillars that flanked them. 'I say! How grand!' She retreated back into the gloom and they heard her say, 'Which one is Miss Manningham-Buller?'

'It's Bullen-ffitch – and she hasn't changed much since we met her in Curzon Street.' Eric leaped from the car, shooting his cuffs and straightening his tie. 'Good afternoon to you all.'

As he slammed the door the trafficator hoisted itself out of its pocket in the door pillar, almost hitting him in the neck. 'Not tonight, Josephine!' he said, pushing it back into place.

'Aren't you going to open *my* door?' his wife asked.

'If I could achieve it from the driver's side,' he said as he strode around the car, 'I would. But this –' he arrived on her side to open her door and assist her out – 'is quite a bit easier.'

Like Aphrodite rising from her seashell, Isabella Brandon rose from the tiny car on a cloud of Chanel bouclé. As she smoothed her white lace gloves her eyes took in – in fact, *possessed* – the grandeur of the portico and the restrained elegance of the pale brick façade; almost as an afterthought she turned her attention once again to the quartet who waited to greet her. And to greet her husband, of course. She wobbled slightly on ultra-high heels as she negotiated the gravel between them. 'Isabella Brandon,' she said, extending her right arm along a ballistic trajectory toward them; then, with a sidelong glance, she added, '. . . and my husband, Eric.'

'What a splendid place,' he remarked when they had all introduced themselves. To Faith he added, 'Your description didn't really do it justice.'

Faith was too engrossed in studying Mrs Brandon to reply that her parents' home in the Cotswolds was a good deal more grand than this.

'Is that American person here?' Isabella asked.

'Willard Johnson?' Faith was surprised. 'You know him?'

'He called on us last week,' she replied but did not elaborate.

'Country air!' Eric said, inhaling deeply through his nose.

'Well *there's* a surprise!' his wife exclaimed.

'The place has seen better days,' Adam said. 'Er . . . I'm afraid I'll have to ask you to slip out of your shoes. The pine floors in this part of the house are a hundred and sixty years old and . . . ah . . . haha . . . your heels, you know. I don't think I've ever seen heels so . . . sharp.'

She corrected him, '*Delicate*. They are next year's fashion so I sincerely hope *you* won't have seen any such thing as yet.' She looked daggers at Eric. 'You never mentioned the floor. You can get my gumboots out of the car.'

As he walked back to it, he said, in a kind of sing-song, 'So *many* things I forgot to ask before we came . . .' On his return, bearing a pair of lavender-coloured gumboots, he began to enumerate, 'Are the interior walls of plaster or gesso? Are the pillars Doric or Ionic? Is the soil acid or alkaline? What is the prevailing wind? To tell the truth, I thought it more important to get the right directions.' Handing the boots to his wife, he said to the others, 'Just try getting a map of *any part* of England nowadays. Stanford's offered me the entire Hindu Kush at six inches to the mile but Hertfordshire? Not a hope. The Ordnance Survey seems to think there's a war on.' Then, noticing how violently the lavender boots clashed with Chanel's pastel, he added, 'How delightful, my darling! It's utterly you!'

Their bickering almost ceased and they were almost well behaved while the four residents showed them over the apartment that was on offer. 'This entrance hall is communal,' Adam explained. 'But yours would be these two rooms—'

Isabella interrupted him, 'Why is it communal?'

'Because this is the only access from the front of the house to the main staircase – which leads up to the Prentices' flat.'

'And to our flat,' Tony added. 'Unless you walk right round the back.'

'You mean there's no back door to this entire house?'

'The entrance is communal because we make it so,' Nicole said.

Adam resumed his usher's role: 'Yours would be these two big rooms on either side. Each of them is actually big enough on its own to accommodate the average council house.'

He flung open a door and let them marvel.

'The fireplace is by Barry,' Tony said.

Sally added, 'And the plasterwork is Italian – by the same people who did the plastering in Sir John Soanes's house in Lincolns Inn Fields. It's very fine.'

'The house was taken over by a Catholic boys' school evacuated from Jersey during the war,' Adam told them. 'They put in lots of extra lavatories, which suits us perfectly, of course. *And* they treated the place pretty well.'

Isabella shot him a glance, taking this as a veiled comment on her heels. 'Does the central heating work?' she asked, running a glove lightly over a painted cast-iron radiator of Edwardian vintage.

'We were told it takes a ton of coke every twenty-four hours, so we haven't tried it. Most of us have paraffin heaters.'

'Except that one in the attic,' Nicole insisted.

'Now, now!' Tony warned her.

Faith saw that Isabella's eyes darted eagerly between Nicole and her Tony, eager for more.

'Has anyone lit a fire here?' Eric was prodding a heap of twigs in the grate.

'It's what fireplaces are *for*,' Isabella told him.

'There's a crow's nest up there,' Tony admitted, 'but we'll get some rods and fetch it down.'

'This was the butler's pantry.' Adam moved them on toward the back of the apartment. 'That's the door to the silver safe – which is big enough for a child's bedroom. Have you got any children?'

'Isabella has a delicate throat,' Eric explained.

'Oh, cork it!' she snapped. To the others she added, 'It's the punchline of an extremely tasteless *joke* – so-called.'

Tony, remembering the joke from his army days, suddenly vanished into the silver safe. 'Yes, quite big enough,' he managed to say without corpsing.

'We shall be starting a family very soon now,' Isabella went on.

'How interesting!' Eric said.

Nicole suddenly noticed that his shirt was buttoned up askew, leaving a bulge of cloth and an unused buttonhole at his throat, mostly hidden by his tie. Isabella had just noticed it, too; she drew breath to tick her husband off, thought better of it, and, saying loudly, 'What's at the bottom here, then?' pushed him ahead of her down a short flight of stone steps. At the foot of it she thrust him round the corner, out of sight of the others.

Adam, still at the top, complained that they'd missed the room that could be turned into a kitchen, but Nicole tripped lightly down after them. Isabella was jerking and tugging at Eric's shirt and tie, getting each button in the right hole. But, most unexpectedly, the look in her eyes was one of pure love – angry, yes . . . exasperated, yes, but love for all that. 'Do *you* have such trouble?' she asked Nicole.

'Since the Garden of Eden, I think,' she replied.

'Talking of which,' Eric said affably, 'd'you know the first animal Adam took as a pet, *after* they were expelled from the Garden?'

Nicole shrugged.

'The serpent.' He raised his voice and called out to Faith, 'Does any room in this apartment have a north light? I need a north light for painting.'

'Did you say *kitchen?*' Isabella asked suddenly. 'Where?'

Adam took her back; most of the others followed. 'It was the staff dining room when the school was here,' he said.

Isabella turned to her husband. 'What colour curtains should we have, d'you think?'

'Blue,' he said at once. 'Flies can't abide blue. And chromium-plated taps.'

'Why?'

'Because they'll reflect the blue.'

She turned to Adam. 'I'm sure you give more sensible answers to your wife than that!'

Adam smiled feebly and, avoiding Sally's eye, said, 'North light, old chap?'

'This way!' Tony was still at the foot of the steps. 'Just follow me. You're now entering the ground floor of the original Tudor Hall. One room of it goes with this apartment. It's the only one with a north light.'

'And very little else,' Isabella said. 'What's above?'

'The smallest flat of all – in terms of room size, anyway. It's been taken by the manager of the LNER depot in Garden City – Todd Ferguson and his wife Gracie. They've not moved in yet because they're building a new kitchen in their hallway.'

Nicole added, 'They have two small children and a new baby.'

'And the rent?' Isabella asked. 'On this flat?'

'A hundred,' Nicole replied.

'What?'

'Per *year*,' Tony added with a grin. 'And that includes insurance on the fabric of the house, by the way. Especially all the lead on the roof. Anyway, we'll leave you to look over the place and see whether it would suit you. You'd also get the room immediately below this one, down in the basement – for a box room, workshop . . . whatever you want. When you've finished looking, go round the back of the house and up the stone steps there – that's our front steps – Nicole and me. You're welcome to tea and you can meet all the rest of us. After which, we'll show you the grounds and talk about buses, shops, train services, doctors . . . all the pukka gen.'

For the next twenty minutes, while the rest of the community assembled and Nicole set out the tea she and Tony had prepared, they heard the Brandons argue their way from room to room, back and forth several times. They could not make out every word but the gist of it was that Isabella made every conceivable objection while Eric advanced arguments at the extreme opposite end of the spectrum. For instance, when she feared that the people in the flat above might hear every word they said, he pointed out, 'That'll be handy when I finally blow a fuse and murder you, darling. You can die knowing that your cries for help did not go unheeded. *Unanswered* – if they have any finer feelings – but not unheeded.' The community listened eagerly, part in fascination, part in disbelief.

'It's like fights in cartoons,' Felix said. 'They hammer each other into the ground, slice each other like salami . . . and *hux-flux* they're entire again and carry on slicing like before!'

'But they do love each other,' Nicole said.

'Funny sort of love!'

Nobody disagreed.

The Brandons joined them at last and were introduced all round. Willard apparently knew them already.

'A question,' Eric said. 'What colour would you say these trousers are?'

Xupé and Fifi sniffed around his turn-ups, liking what they sensed there.

'Grey?' several voices replied. 'Sort of bluey grey?'

'Not green?' he asked. 'No one here in their right mind would call them green?'

'Definitely not green . . . could be a faint hint of it . . . against crimson it might *look* green . . .' The opinions were varied.

Glancing triumphantly at his wife, he continued, 'Next question – what about the garden? Is it communal or can one have one's own strip?'

'You?' Isabella laughed scornfully. 'Gardening?'

'Not exactly, darling. I just want a little patch of my own where I can keep bees – or wasps – or whatever countryfolk do keep these days. I expect the war has changed a lot of hobbies.'

'Hens would be more practical,' she pointed out as she settled between Sally and Faith.

'Only if they can live peaceably with my wasps.' He sat on a Victorian chair that might have been made for Barbarossa. 'This is rather grand.'

'You live in Mayfair?' Sally asked.

Isabella ignored the question. 'Rather too grand,' she told her husband. 'You look lost in it.'

'No such luck, my dear.' He turned to Sally, 'Some might still think of Curzon Street as Mayfair, but it has gawn down aawwfully, dontcher know. We even get *Americans* hoping to live there.' He grinned at Willard. 'And we're deafened by the heel-clacking of *les filles de joie* – pardon my French, Mrs Palmer – on the pavements outside. The damage they must be doing to all those Georgian floorboards does not bear thinking about. Still – they lift them soon enough.'

'The floorboards?' Marianne asked.

'No – the heels. I say! I don't think I've seen so much butter all in one bowl since nineteen thirty-nine!'

'It's not butter,' Tony said proudly. 'Nicole has a way of mixing all our butter rations and all our margarine rations with gelatine and water, and the result –' he gestured at the bowl – 'no one can tell it from butter. French people just have a way with food.'

'D'you hear that, darling?' Eric asked excitedly. 'All the things you're going to learn if we take this apartment! Really *practical* things!'

She stared icily at him and said, 'We'd lose our Mayfair

telephone number. We couldn't bring it out here to Hertfordshire. Have you thought of that?'

Eric said, 'Therefore . . . ?'

'What d'you mean "therefore"?'

'I mean, why bring it up now – at this particular juncture?'

'It's a fact.'

'Therefore . . . ?'

'Don't keep saying "therefore"? A fact is a fact. It's just a fact.'

'Oh! A *fact*! I see-ee. Look, if this is going to become a habit – dropping in the odd *fact* to clog the stream of an otherwise smooth conversation – perhaps we should get a little notebook to jot down these *facts* as they arise. It would be a shame to overlook them merely because they happened to be utterly irrelevant. We could even clasify them on the spot. You know: Facts that are interesting but not relevant . . . Facts that are relevant but not interesting . . . Facts that are so bleeding obvious it's not worth mentioning them . . . that sort of thing. Eh?'

Isabella turned wearily to the rest of the company. 'We waited God knows how many months – or years – to be connected. And Eric absolutely depends on the phone.'

They all looked at Eric, who shrugged and said, 'Apparently.'

'You do!' she insisted.

He, aware now that their conversation had embarrassed some of the others, put on an apologetic smile and murmured, 'So I do.'

'It never stops ringing,' Isabella added.

But that was too much for Eric. 'OK, let's just consider the last five calls – all of which I had to take – that is, I had to put down my brushes and cross the room to open the cupboard and extract the phone.' He counted them off on his fingers. 'A query from a weaving firm in Lancashire; a mannequin asking if some show in Kingston was still on; an incomprehensibly middle-European woman from Aquascutum confirming an appointment for next week (as far as I could make her out at all) ... .' He broke off, aware that everyone was looking at Felix. 'Sorry, chum,' he continued, 'Nothing personal. Someone from Kangol Berets wanting you to OK an ad they're about to place; the butcher – reminding us yet again that you haven't brought in the coupons you promised him; and the secretary at the Central asking if you'd come and give a series of three talks to their costume department.'

'That's six, darling.' Isabella pointed out.

'*A fortiori*, my dear!'

'You keep your telephone in a cupboard?' Sally asked.

'They sent the wrong colour,' he explained.

Isabella corrected him, '*Someone* ordered the wrong colour.'

'Colored phones in this land of socialist conformity?' Willard asked.

'Oh there's a little man in South Audley Street who paints them,' Isabella explained. 'Or coats them with some sort of *plahstic* skin. He's awfully good.'

'And is six foot tall,' Eric murmured to no one in particular.

'People know what I mean when I say he's a "little" man, darling.' She beamed all round. 'Don't you?'

'In England,' Marianne said, 'it seems to mean you don't have to pay them very much.'

'I suppose that's one way of looking at it,' Isabella conceded. 'It also means they're not some ghastly great anonymous corporation.'

'I don't think telephones – of whatever colour – will be a problem for us much longer,' Willard said.

Stirrings of surprise all round. 'You don't?' Adam asked.

'I think we'll all be getting them in a few weeks – anyone who wants one. Coming back from Garden City today, I saw a guy up a pole, fixing a line into that big, white mansion down in the valley. I chewed the fat with him a while and he said they had four lines into this house during the war, when it was a school. They're disconnected in the exchange now but they're still there. And they'd be happy to string up four more, especially if we have important business.' He looked directly at Isabella. 'D'you have any big-name clients, ma'am?'

'Well . . .!' She gazed around in embarrassment.

'I know,' Willard said sympathetically. 'I hate name-dropping, myself, too – as I was saying to Winston Churchill only yesterday. But sometimes we simply have to bite the bullet.'

'Would Marks and Spencer do?' she asked. 'Or Harrods?'

'Well, they'll just *have* to do,' Willard said to general laughter. 'A letter on their office notepaper explaining that there are priority business reasons for your needing a phone would be a great help. It doesn't matter if it's only signed by the janitor. The important letterhead is what counts.' To the others he added,

'We'll be on the Hertford exchange so I'll go light a fuse there tomorrow.'

After a tour of the grounds, the Brandons set off for home. 'I know the French are all a bit weird,' Isabella said before the house was even out of sight, 'but I'm surprised at *him*, Tony. He's supposed to be a top-class architect. But look how they've arranged the furniture! I mean – what's the *first* thing you see when you come through the door?'

'That rather fine landscape hanging between the two big windows?' Eric guessed – knowing it was the last thing on her mind.

'Oh, well, *you would*. Any normal person . . . Look! There's that bloody spider again. You *must* get him out the minute we get home. Just look at it!'

'I think it's a she-spider.'

'How can you possibly know that?'

'There were two of them when we left London – and now there's no sign of the other and she's looking suspiciously gorged. It happens even in spiderland.'

'For God's sake keep your eyes on the road! Anyway, the first thing you see when you enter that drawing room is the back of the sofa.'

'Good heavens – you're absolutely right,' he told her. 'That's *awful*. In fact, I think you should do a little sketch for them – show them how they could get the *front* of the sofa to face the fire *without* the back of it facing the door. In fact, I'd quite like to see that myself.'

'And I thought French women were supposed to have a certain flair with clothes? You'd never believe it – looking at *her*. Even the Swedish one – Marianne – was more stylish. D'you think she's expecting? I'm sure of it. And Nicole. It's a good omen.'

'Damn! I didn't ask either of them. I'm so sorry, pet. We *must* get that notebook, you know. And we'll have a page where you list all the questions I should ask a woman on first meeting her: Are you preggers? And so on.'

'Yes, darling, very funny. Anyway, I think there's no love lost between Nicole and the Swede, don't you? And I must say, I'm not at all sure about that couple with the children. Living right above us. Arthur and May Prentice. They're not quite our class, d'you think? Not that I'd hold that against them, of course. He's in television, so we wouldn't want to fall out with them.'

'But . . . ?'

'Well, the whole place is rather bohemian, you must admit. They do need someone to raise it a little.'

'Like you? And me?'

'These things are important. It's a wonderful place to bring up children – *our* children, too. But there must be some sense of order.'

'If we took the gatelodge we could work our benign influence from a distance. When the Dower House children get tired of chaos they'll know they can find a haven of peace and order *chez nous*. And we'll inspect their fingernails and behind the ears before we let them in.'

After a frosty silence she said, 'Did you really take all those phone calls for me?'

'No.' He gave a self-satisfied grin. 'You *know* I didn't – or else I would have passed them on to you. I thought you played along jolly well.'

'But why did you say you did?'

'You have to admit – they are the sort of calls I might very easily take and pass on to you. I just wanted them to know that my wonderful wife is, in fact, a woman of some consequence – contrary to all appearances.'

She reached across and hugged his arm. 'Darling! You do have your uses.' Then: 'What d'you mean – "contrary to all appearances"?'

'Hang on – tricky corner, this.'

'Perhaps they're drinkers – Willard and Marianne,' she went on. 'I thought he had a bit of a beer belly, didn't you? A lot of Yanks were like that, in the war. Maybe that's her trouble, too. And I wonder if Adam and Sally's marriage is going to last. She's obviously a super organizer he hasn't a clue. Did you see his work desk as we passed their window? She's out of the top drawer. So is that Faith Manningham-Buller.'

'They need to iron out this bit of road,' he said. 'I think we'll try going back via Hendon. And it's Bullen-ffitch.'

'Well, I know she's a friend of yours and she's the one who

put this mad idea in your head, but I wouldn't trust her too far – whatever her name is . . .'

'I said – Bullen-ffitch. And she's not exactly a friend, she's just someone I meet occasionally at launch parties and all those little Soho bistros that publishers love.'

'Yes – quite. Wouldn't trust her as far as I could throw her.'

'And as for Felix Breit—' Eric began.

She cut across him. 'Well now, don't say a word against *him*! He'll be a *useful* connection – if we move out there.'

'That's a big "if". Look! Another old Morris Ten!' He hooted and exchanged salutations with the driver.

'D'you think so? I've already decided: Mad idea or not – we'll take it. And we'll move in next quarter-day.' After a silence she said, 'Say?'

'Me? Oh, gosh, I'm actually being asked my opinion! Well, I decided we'd move there the minute I was told that the floorboards wouldn't tolerate next year's fashion in heels.'

'Done, then,' she said.

Back at the Dower House, Adam was summing up, 'So Sally thinks they're useful. Faith thinks they're just about solvent enough for us. Willard thinks their *other* car, the Lagonda, will look just swell outside the front portico. But – most important of all – does anybody actually *like* them?'

The eager chorus of yesses surprised everyone.

'Done, then,' he concluded.

Friday, 13 June 1947

Faith's throwaway remark that Felix had started his carving as an artist but had soon turned into a designer was so apt that Felix stopped work on the sculpture as soon as he had a dozen or so square inches of its final form 'liberated' from its marble shroud. He got a photographer to come out from Hertford, take a few quarter-plates of it from various angles under different lighting, and develop and print by that evening. Next day he laid the results out on Fogel's desk, saying, 'I know you've been impatient for me to finish, Wolf, but the truth is I was stopping myself. Something inside me *knew* from the beginning that to make a *finished* sculpture would be wrong. Absolutely wrong.'

The words had the desired effect on Fogel. Happy, Felix continued, 'I had the concept weeks ago – my sculpture will be an egg – a giant marble egg, twice as big as an ostrich egg. It's a symbol of the creation of life . . . well, you understand perfectly, I'm sure. But to have this symbol . . . the same symbol – finished, completed, unchanging – at the beginning of *every* section . . . don't you see, it would be a song with no verses, only one chorus repeated again and again and again. Very boring.'

Fogel nodded unhappily. He saw the force of the argument and – simultaneously – 'his' precious Felix Breit sculpture was vanishing under a publishing imperative he could not gainsay.

'So,' Felix continued blithely, 'have you decided? Is it certain that Arthur Taylor is the chief in-house designer for this series?'

Fogel shrugged – awkwardly, as he always shrugged when cornered for a binding commitment. 'For the foundation volume . . . sure.'

'OK – so we have six opening spreads for that volume – text on the left verso, image on the right recto. Then we create a setting – a *mise en scène* – for the opener, which is *Intimations of the Modern*, and we photograph the sculpture *in this exact condition* –' he tapped the photographs – 'in that setting. Then for the next chapter – *The Salon of the Rejected* – we make another *mise en scène* and I carve it a *leetle* bit more and we photograph that . . . and so on through the book – through all five volumes. The egg becomes a *leitmotiv* to permeate the book but never competes with the art. And there is a tiny bit more revelation for each new *mise en scène*, to suggest the progress of art.'

'Ah!' Fogel perked up. 'So it will be finished for the last chapter of Volume Five, no?'

Felix pulled a dubious face. 'Maybe not. My instinct – the thing you are paying me so much for – says we need a *big shock* at the end – because all new art must shock. All through the series the egg will be shown nearer and nearer to the moment of hatching – its liberated perfection. But in the last picture we *smash it to bits*! The egg has *already* given birth! Now its offspring stands on the threshold of an unknown future. Also it shows that art progresses by destroying art.'

'I have a better idea,' Fogel said at once. 'You finish the sculpture. We make a copy in porcelain. No glaze. We smash the porcelain – who can tell? And your sculpture is saved for posterity!'

'Did you really think you could get the better of him?' Faith asked as they left the building for lunch at Schmidt's. 'You'd have to get up three days early to do that.'

'I just resent it that he'll be getting the first post-war Felix Breit sculpture *and* my best efforts over these five volumes.'

'Even if you *gave* it to him, it might do no harm. One of the directors of the Home and Colonial told me that if only the law allowed it, they would sometimes sell sugar, flour, milk, etcetera at a loss.'

'That would be crazy.'

'No. Everyone has to buy those things so the word would spread like a bush fire. And then the shop assistant would say "We have Bath chaps in peak condition, moddom – off-ration, of course . . . And long spaghetti at last . . . shall I just slip a packet in with your delivery?" . . . and so on. And the sixpence profit on these choice items would easily cover the penny loss on the staples. If they ever abolish resale-price maintenance, that's what will happen.'

'Thank God I'm not in trade.'

'But you *are*, my pet. As Fogel says, "Vee are all prostitoots nowadays." He's one of the greatest party-givers in Hampstead. Within three months your sculpture will be seen by every important man and woman in London's artistic and literary circles – not to mention bankers . . . captains of industry. How can that be bad?'

As they rounded the corner, where Rathbone Place wiggles into Charlotte Street, Felix caught sight of Angela just as she was entering Schmidt's. 'Tell you what,' he said to Faith. 'Why don't we try that little working-class Greek café just off Goodge Street?'

'Oh but I've set my heart on Schmidt's,' she pleaded – but her smile told him that she, too, had spotted Angela up ahead. She giggled and took his arm. 'I think it's about time I met her, don't you?'

'There's nothing between us,' he assured her.

'Yes . . . well . . . I was watching you that day when you first set eyes on her! Tell me what you know about her – anything – in the next hundred yards. And walk slower.'

'I'll tell you something odd. Maybe shameful. Don't ever breathe a word about it to her – but she and I *did* meet once, before the war. We had a date – just one afternoon together, in a rowing boat on the Wannsee. She did the rowing. I was quite a chubby little chap then. Lazy, too. And I mentioned the occasion to her a couple of weeks ago and she clearly did remember it and then I panicked and pretended I'd forgotten all the details. And later, when I wanted to admit I hadn't been quite honest . . . the moment had passed. How do I undo all that? The longer I leave it, the harder it gets.'

Several other diners entered and left the restaurant before Faith answered, 'I think you'll be the best judge of that – knowing when the time is right.'

Inside, he made a good show of surprise at seeing her. 'Hallo, Angela! I've missed you – where have you been? Sorry – may I present Miss Faith Bullen-ffitch? Faith . . . Miss Angela Worth.'

They shook hands. 'Please to join me,' Angela said. 'Felix has told me much of you, Miss Bullen-ffitch.' She gestured to Fritz to reorganize her table for three.

'You have the advantage of me, Miss Worth. He has told me very little of you – but all of it very interesting. You work at the BBC, I understand? At Broadcasting House?'

Angela shook her head and turned to Felix. 'That's the answer to your question. I've been up at Ally Pally, as we BBC types call it. For the last three weeks.'

'Alexandra Palace!' Faith interpreted for Felix. 'I've pointed it out to you on the train.' She turned back to Angela. 'Television? When are they going to make it a *national* thing? It's ridiculous that only London can get it. The audience is so small there's no budget – so the programmes are appalling – so nobody wants to lash out on a set. It's absurd.'

Angela nodded. 'Are you interested in television, Miss Bullen-ffitch? It'll be less than a year now before the service goes national.'

Fritz planted water-filled tumblers on the table, one before each. '*Das Menu.*' He started to proffer it but then tucked it firmly under his arm. '*Das kennen Sie, ja,*' he said.

'*Menu!*' Felix mocked, thinking the word far too grand for Schmidt's limited, austerity offering.

Angela asked for her usual salami and salad; the other two

went for a *Wienerschnitzel* and surrendered their ration books for clipping.

'I work in publishing, as you probably know,' Faith said. 'But every time I hear the word *television* something inside me leaps up at it. "Less than a year" might suit me down to the ground. D'you know an illustrated magazine called *Forward!* Miss Worth? My present boss is its publisher.'

'Mister Fogel. Yes, I see copies lying around editorial desks at Broadcasting House.'

'But do you ever look at the contents? It's a mixture of a fairly academic text, slightly popularized, but made highly accessible by brilliant graphics. I feel in my bones that some such thing could also be done in television, too. Graphics.'

This final statement was so abstract, and so unlike Faith – who always cut to the heart of the matter – that Felix suddenly realized how serious she must be. These ideas were miser's gold to her. Angela must have caught something of it, too, for she said, 'One day – and quite soon I think . . . five or six years – we can record TV like we now record sound – on tape. Commercially. Then . . . well, so many things will become possible.'

Unspecified 'graphics'. . . unspecified 'so many things'! They were *both* doing it! Like dogs (and unlike bitches) they were scent-marking their respective territories. Felix almost laughed aloud.

'I *adore* your dress!' Faith said. 'Especially the pattern. Not English, surely? Did you run it up yourself?'

'It's my own print.' Angela tried to sound modest. 'A discharge print on self-coloured cloth. I do evening classes in textile printing at the Camden Town Working Men's Institute. Two nights a week. You can't just work-work all the time.'

'I totally agree,' Faith began.

'She kills foxes,' Felix put in.

'I ride to hounds,' she said wearily. 'I don't care two hoots if they put up a fox or not.' Her eyes narrowed. 'D'you know what I *really* enjoy? I love to see three gentlemen riders refuse a fence, just before Jupiter and I go thundering between them and simply *fly* it for a gold medal! No, it's better than any old gold medal.'

Angela laughed. Her eyes were shining. 'Oh, *yes!*' she exclaimed.

'So how does the BBC work?' Faith spoke as if the question followed on quite naturally. 'Is it all Civil-Servicey or would I need a friend to dig a hole on the inside and pull me through?'

'Are you now jumping *ship* for a gold medal?' Felix asked.

'Of course not,' she replied impatiently. 'But one should never get into anything without knowing where all the exits are.' She turned again to Angela. 'How did *you* get in, for example?'

'I was invited. Have you heard of *tape* recording?'

'I think so.'

'It was invented in Germany by BASF. We used it at the UFA film studios in the war so I knew more about it than anyone at the BBC.'

'Yes but how did *they* know that? Who put *you* and *them* in touch? I like to know how these things *work*.'

Angela, aware that Felix was about to protest, said, 'I don't mind. I was a political prisoner and all political prisoners were seen by Allied intelligence people before they resettled us.'

'You scratched their back – they scratched yours, eh?'

Angela laughed. 'What a language! Do you ever say anything straight?'

'I mean you each helped the other.'

'Yes, I understood. They soon realized that what I knew about tape-recording was still *years* ahead of the BBC.'

'And what made them think of the BBC?'

'Intelligence people? Perhaps because a lot of them work there.' She shrugged. 'I don't know.'

'Work there? Intelligence people? At the BBC?'

'They filled a whole floor of Broadcasting House in the war – and they're still there, most of them.' After a pause she added, 'You don't think the government dares leave the BBC in the hands of *itself*, surely?'

'I suppose not.' Faith grimaced.

'Changing your mind about working there?' Felix asked. He admired Angela's performance. These 'intelligence people' were the ones who had lost – or *claimed* to have lost – her transcript of that meeting at the Interpol HQ – the minutes that sent her to a KL for years. But she gave no hint of it in her voice or manner. He knew precisely where, when, and why she had acquired such skill, but it still left him filled with admiration.

Their meals arrived.

'What would you like to do at the BBC?' Angela asked.

'I don't know so much about radio – but television when it's truly national . . . that could be very exciting. You remember the way . . .' She suddenly recalled how Felix and Angela had spent the war. 'Well . . . newsreels – the way they were filmed, the way they did interviews . . . every aspect – they changed enormously between the start of the war and the end. And they're still changing – newsreels and documentaries. And I've often thought it would be wonderful to do that on little screens in people's drawing rooms. Or "lounges" as they probably call them. Making a documentary for four or five people round the fireside would have to be very different from the way we present it to a single audience of several hundred in a cinema. Don't you think? We'd have to invent a new visual language.' She turned to Felix. 'That's one of the exciting things about what we're doing at Manutius. We're inventing a new graphic language for presenting information in print. On the page. Wouldn't it be exciting to do that same sort of thing in an utterly *new* medium? On that tiny screen?'

'I can see the logic,' Felix told her. 'But I still don't get a concrete picture in my mind. What d'you think I will actually *see* on this little screen?'

'A face, of course – exactly what you'd expect to see around your own fireside. A friendly face. And the friendly face will tell you something . . . and then you can have a bit of the documentary or travelogue or newsreel . . . anything. But it will always come back to the friendly face.'

'Did you *just* think this up?' Angela asked.

Faith shrugged. 'Well, it's not new really. I was listening to Christopher Stone the other night, playing those simple melodies on *These You Have Loved* on the wireless, and I suddenly thought, Why are you listening to this . . . this awful kitsch? And it's because he's such a lovely old man with such a mellow voice and so relaxed. And then I started thinking, What sort of man or woman would I choose to play hot jazz records or some heavy classical stuff? And they'd each be different, of course, but they'd each be utterly right for the job. And then, when I started thinking about television, that all came back to me and I thought, I know exactly who should present a television programme on . . . I don't know, "modern housing" or "chaos in the docks" or "the last days of the Music Hall" . . . that sort of thing.'

'Who?'

'Oh − I don't know any actual names but I absolutely know the *sort* of person to go looking for. There's only one problem.' She smiled at Angela. 'D'you think I'm arrogant enough for the job?'

Saturday, 14 June 1947

```
There will be a Communal Meeting at the
Palmers' tonight, immediately after our
meal together.
Agenda:
  1. Sharing out of electricity bill
     (£12.7s.4d.)
  2. Establishment of a Communal Fund.
  3. Essential rewiring?
  4. Central heating and hot water supply?
  5. Possible purchase of items of
     communal equipment.
  6. Deliveries of post and milk - where
     to make a central point?
  7. Suggested new arrangements for
     communal meals.
  8. Broad ideas for the vegetable
     garden.
  9. Provisional plans for other flats.
 10. Preliminary structural survey.
 11. Special arrangements for Christmas
 12. A. O. B.
```

Willard glanced through the list. 'See how the civil service is eating into his soul − everything is "possible, provisional, broad . . . suggested". And when he runs out of those words, he just tacks on a question mark at the end.'

'Well, he can strike out "suggested" in item seven. We girls have decided already. We shall have one last try for communal meals. Just weekends.' She raised her eyes ecstatically. 'Oh, and never more shall we eat off plates licked clean by Xupé and Fifi and then washed in half-warm water and called "good enough" by Nicole!'

'I still don't like this *communal* stuff. Communal . . . commun*ist* . . .'

'Nicole shall do all the cooking, which she loves. Sally to do all the marketing, which she's good at. And I to do all the washing-up, which I don't mind.'

Willard shook his head. 'Tony won't like it.'

'Nicole will just remind him of the last two meals Sally cooked.'

'Just those last two? I guess they were pretty spectacular, though. But it's a shame you should get all the coarse work, honey. I thought you liked cooking, too?'

'I like cooking for you and me – and for our guests when we're ready.'

'Well, it won't last long. Just wait till we've all got families here. And kids. It'll fall apart.'

That evening Nicole celebrated her new appointment as effective chef de cuisine to the community with a superb ragout of a roadkill pheasant. Their apartment had been greatly improved – in an artistic sense – since the day of the Brandon's first visit. Nicole had acquired a whole parachute from somewhere, an item that most women used for making blouses, knickers, slips, and nighties. But Nicole had turned it into a dramatic feature, with a pre-war tailor's dummy, based on Leslie Howard, and several *objets trouvés*. It broke up the view of the back of the sofa that had so upset Isabella Brandon.

As this was their first, formal Communal Meeting, they opened a couple of bottles of wine, too. But the resulting goodwill did not last ten minutes into item one.

Willard was astounded. The trifling little electricity bill seemed such a cut-and-dried business that he had not even bothered to discuss it with Marianne. Obviously he and she had used the most electricity – with all their power tools. Felix, who only had a few lights and one electric ring, had obviously used the least. Willard therefore proposed a simple division: Johnsons, £5; Wilsons and Palmers, £3 each; the Prentices £1; and Felix the small change. No one else had been there long enough to have used a meaningful amount. Next item.

'Not so fast please!' Nicole had ideas of her own. 'I think

Johnsons *six* quid, Wilsons and Palmers *two-fifty*.' She turned
on Marianne. 'You have that beeeg American oven. Ours is
small.'

Marianne disagreed. 'But it's summer. I cook very little.'

'I don't mean only cooking.' Nicole addressed the meeting,
'She heats the whole upstairs with it.'

'Not true!' Marianne objected. '*Vous n'êtes pas honnête!* I have
seen you dry Fifi with *your* oven when her furs get wetted.'

Tony turned aghast to Nicole, who had covered her ears to
blot out Marianne. 'Fifi in the oven?'

'I open the oven door and hold her over it,' she admitted
crossly. 'But only a few minutes. It's a tiny oven, anyway. Not
like that big American—'

'*And* you heated the bathroom with it. You carried it in there
and opened the oven door, too.'

'Just twice! It's a little portable oven. How much can it use?'

'Funny – I was only in that part of your flat twice, and both
times you had it in the bathroom, open and . . . I could feel
the radiation even just walking past.'

'Anyway,' Felix said, 'I don't think Faith and I should only
pay the loose change. I think we should split it four ways evenly.'

Tony said, 'I don't think you should pay at all until you've
got an oven. They're the big users. But I think perhaps Marianne
has a point. I suggest we and the Johnsons go fifty-fifty and
leave Felix out this time.'

'That's so *bloody* patronizing!' Faith blurted out to Felix. She'd
already put away a few snifters before they came over for the
meal. 'Are you going to let them patronize you like that? Pay
the fucking lot yourself. You can afford it easily. Stuff them!'

'Faith, dear,' Tony said mildly. 'There is a matter of principle
involved here.'

'Oh, sod your principles!' she sneered. 'This bickering is just
so petty bourgeois. *I'll* pay it if Felix won't – so there! God –
how I *hate* democracy.'

Then everyone began talking at once.

'For Christ's sake!' Willard shouted above it all. 'I mean, what
the hell are we talking about here? A lousy twelve quid and a
few odd pence!'

They fell to silence.

'Anyway,' Marianne said, 'we don't know how much should

be communal electricity. The hall light often gets left on all night. That's communal.'

'You mean *I* leave it on?' Nicole accused.

'It doesn't matter who leaves it on. It's just a fact. The hall light should be communal – paid for communally.'

'Which brings us on to item two,' Faith said. 'For Christ's sake let's get on or we'll be up all night.'

'We must finish item one first,' Tony insisted.

'*You'll* be up all night anyway,' Nicole sneered at Faith. 'Your light's always on over there.'

'I don't believe this,' Willard said. 'Why don't we draw lots for who pays and how much?'

'It would be equally as fair as anything else,' Marianne said. 'How can we know who owes more than anyone another?'

Eric Brandon spoke. 'I think we should chip in with at least a quid. I know we're not living here full time yet, but we have—'

Marianne interrupted, 'And besides – Willard has got the front lawn looking like grass again—'

'So?' Nicole challenged.

'So – he has done more for this community than *some* other people. No one else bothers.'

'Did you speak, my darling?' Isabella Brandon asked her husband.

He brought the flat of his hand down on the table and raised it again to reveal a pound note. 'Actions speak louder than words,' he said.

'As the Irishman said, "Is this a private fight or can anyone join in?"' Sally asked. 'I suggest that, as we have the best part of three months until the next meter reading, we use that time to investigate the actual wiring circuits and see if they are sufficiently separate to allow us to install individual private meters to help us divide the *next* bill with less . . . what can I call it?'

'Democracy?' Faith offered. 'Communism?'

'This argument is not about electricity, anyway,' Marianne muttered.

'What then?' Nicole challenged.

'We all know what it's really about.'

'Sit up straight, precious,' Isabella snapped at Eric. 'No wonder your back hurts – the way you sit.'

'Ah!' he replied wistfully. 'I see you have not grasped my

purpose, my dear. I was seeking to make myself as small and inconspicuous as possible – just while these torrents of unbridled abuse and contumely pass overhead. You and I are so utterly unused to this bickering sort of atmosphere.'

When the laughter died, neither Marianne nor Nicole could find the way back to the battleground.

'Item two!' Willard barked at Tony.

Most of the remaining agenda went through smoothly.

A Communal Fund would be levied at the rate of one pound per family per month.

The rewiring done in the days of the evacuated school would probably last another ten years; meanwhile a certain amount of extending and patching was all they need do. And private meters could intercept most if not all of the electricity they used.

Willard would look into restoring the old central-heating system at least to the flats in the main house.

Everyone should look out for a good second-hand Rotavator – to take the pain out of digging the vegetable garden. Also a flame gun to keep down the weeds. And individual families would be responsible for their own barrows, forks, spades, etc.

The Johnsons volunteered to make and fit a broad shelf in the passage, just inside the old Tudor back door, with seven divisions – six for the families and one for A.N. Other – where deliveries of milk, letters, newspapers, etc. should be left.

'Item seven,' Tony snapped.

'Eight!' the three women said in unison.

He looked hurt at each in turn; then at Willard, who held up both hands à la Pontius Pilate.

'The communal meals work very well when Nicole is the chef,' Marianne said. 'Too badly when I am chef.' [murmurs of dissent] 'And so-so in-between. So now – until the babies are coming – Nicole is chef, Sally and Faith are shopping ladies. I am washer-upper. And everybody is host and hostess in turn.'

'Can't *we* contribute more?' May Prentice asked.

'Somewhere else?' Sally suggested. 'Sweeping the communal area? Weeding? Pruning? When the babies are coming – as Marianne says – everything will change, anyway.'

Tony conceded with a sigh. 'Item eight.'

They decided that the vegetable garden was so large that, if they got a good rotary tiller, they could devote half an acre to some communal project – potatoes for sale, say – and in the remaining enclosure people could take as much as they liked for individual vegetable and flower gardens.

Tony reported he had completed only half the structural survey and had found one possible piece of dry rot which the landlord would tackle. Adam had mortared glass telltales into the brickwork over several small cracks, which were probably ancient and harmless.

Nicole said she and Tony were planning a midsummer party – actually on the 21st of June when there was a full moon – to be held on their lawn for 'some people from the village'. Everyone in the house was welcome, of course. They were so vague as to who these 'people' might be that Willard's suspicions were alerted at once. The community had no leader, it was true; but he felt that if anyone was to represent it to the wider world, the mantle should fall on him.

When Nicole said she hoped everyone would make a special effort to keep the communal areas clean and tidy for the occasion, Marianne almost had a fit. She wasn't the only one. The stunned silence seemed a good note on which to finish. Tony said, 'Any Other Business?' in a tone that clearly expected none.

Willard raised a finger. 'They're talking about us in Barwick Green and Dormer Green.'

'Only natural—' Adam began.

'They're saying that we're running some sort of temple of free love here. Or worse.'

'A brothel?' Eric asked. 'That would certainly count as "any other business".'

'It's no laughing matter, Eric. That's where our kids will be going to school.'

'Oh, they'll surely know the truth by *then*,' Sally said.

Willard shook his head. 'Can't wait for that, honey. We have to kill it stone dead – PDQ.'

'We?' Adam said.

'Sure. If Nicole and Tony don't mind, I'd like to suggest that we – the Dower House community – invite the people from the village – in fact, *all* the people we know from round here – to a *big* midsummer party on the big lawn. Really go to town.'

'To Hertford?' Nicole asked.

'No – it's a saying. Like . . . really . . . you know . . .'

'Really "make a meal of it",' Eric suggested. '"Tear the place up . . . go overboard . . . have a gilhooley . . . give it socks".'

'Enough!' Sally said, turning to Nicole. 'Do you *mind* if we make it a communal invitation?'

Nicole shrugged.

'Wizard idea,' Tony said.

'People we know in London, too,' Felix suggested. 'Fogel is longing to see this place – a capitalist kibbutz, he calls it.'

'Now that I *like!*' Willard crowed. 'Capitalist kibbutz! We should hang that as our shingle on the gate.'

On their way home across the back yard Faith said, 'We must ask Angela as well.'

'We? You mean whichever one of us gets to her first.'

'No – you ask her. She might not come if I do the inviting.'

Saturday, 21 June 1947

Each family arranged for one or two rooms to be available for people who wanted to stay at least until dawn – which, they thought, would be most of the London and more distant guests. Willard fixed palliasses and sleeping bags through friends at the US depot near Wheathamstead. He and Tony flushed out the old cast-iron central-heating system and refilled it with water and some kind of rust inhibitor, also courtesy of Uncle Sam. The communal fund paid for a ton of coke to fire the boiler. Nicole went around the butchers in Hertford and got all the bones and off-ration offal they could spare, from which she made a stock, using herbs she gathered in the countryside around and saddle-fungus from a big beech near the pheasant runs – the only edible fungus she could find in June. Its bouquet filled and tantalized the house all week.

'I'm not going to let her flaunt herself around as the solo caterer,' Marianne told Felix.

He told her about Fortnum and Mason's.

Every woman sewed the old blackout curtains into loose covers to protect the furniture they were lending for the communal party.

To floodlight the main lawn, Willard acquired a perimeter light from the Yanks and almost started a fire when he plugged it in. When they went to take out the fuse, they found it had been replaced by a two-inch coach-bolt – another Jersey legacy; and when they lifted the floorboards in the Prentices' flat to inspect for damage to the wiring, they saw that the conduits there were the original bare copper rods, set into the floor joists – a legacy from Edwardian times. So a complete survey of the wiring of the entire house was no longer item 3 on the community agenda, and there was no maybe about the rewiring. Arthur Prentice liberated some new sheathed cable and they ran it directly from the fuseboard to the lamp.

Felix invited Corvo and his current friend, Julian Buller; also Fogel and Peter Murdoch who was the new editor-in-chief of the Modern Art series at Manutius; he had been seconded from Macdonald's, who were to publish the English edition and wanted their own man on the inside.

The Wilsons and the Palmers invited several colleagues from the Greater London Plan, including the great Sir Patrick Abercrombie, himself; also friends from architectural college and their schooldays.

Willard's list included the local doctor, neighbouring farmers, handyman Bob Ambrose, and Mrs Tawney of the local War Agricultural Executive Committee, the Herts County Council, the Watch Committee, the Workers Educational Association Committee, a justice of the peace, a parish councillor, and Brown Owl of the Dormer Green Brownie troupe.

'His instinct has not deserted him,' Adam commented.

Arthur and May Prentice asked several colleagues from Alexandra Palace. Todd and Betty Ferguson asked his mates at the Welwyn Garden goods depot and hers in the hair stylists at Welwyn Department Store. The Brandons, whose Bentley-designed Lagonda stood dead centre in front of the main portico for the day, brought along important buyers from Aquascutum and Selincourt.

The community as a whole invited John Gordon, the land agent for the Hatfield Sand and Gravel Company, their landlords. He, in turn, said that Sir Waldron Bligh, the chairman, would not turn down an invitation – especially when he learned that Sir Patrick would be briefly present.

'Surely this is what we meant by *community*?' Adam said to Willard as they surveyed the gathering crowd upon the big lawn – a mix of the Royal Enclosure at Ascot and the Chelsea Arts Ball. 'None of us, if we were sole occupiers of the house, could have done all this. And just think what it'll be like when we all have our own families – a dozen of our own children here all the time!'

'Adam!' Willard patted his arm. 'You should have married that woman called Eve. That was the first and last time every living human was a true communist.'

Adam checked his watch and laughed. 'Funny you should say that, old chap. As a matter of fact I've invited a girl called Eve. She was my first ever girlfriend at school.'

'What does Sally say to that?'

Adam winked.

The guests had arrived in ones and twos – by train and bus, by bicycle and motorbike, by taxi, and even a few by car. Sally ran a shuttle with her horse Copenhagen and her gig between the house and the bus stop at Barwick Green. It was a fine evening with only the mildest breeze under an almost cloudless sky. The early arrivals lent a hand with the tables and chairs. Nicole took two tables to one side of the lawn and set out her contributions to the fare – the mouthwatering broth, the profiteroles, and the tartes tatines. Marianne's table, on the opposite side, was laden with smörgåsar of egg and anchovies, prawns in mayonnaise, and soft cheese dotted with lumpfish roe.

It was the sort of feast that, since 1938, most English people had seen only in Hollywood costume epics. Many of those who had come out of curiosity, feeling more than sceptical about this experiment in communal living, were given food for thought as well. As Sally said later, 'They came to scoff and they scoffed the lot.'

And the chatter was unending. If words had been visible, there would have been a haze drifting over the whole of south Hertfordshire.

Faith went up to town early and came back by taxi with Wolf Fogel and – Felix was surprised to see – Angela Worth. He ran toward them but Fogel leaped out and, grasping him by the arm, asked, 'Which is your bit of this kibbutz?'

'But . . .' Felix glanced toward the two women.

'Ignore it,' Fogel said. 'That's business.'

'What business?'

'Faith thinks television and publishing can get in bed together. Ritchie Calder calls it *synergy*. She wants Miss Worth to introduce her to a Mister Hugh Wellington, from television, who should be somewhere in these crowds.'

Reluctantly, Felix took him to the cottage – where Fogel only had eyes for 'his' sculpture. When showing the man upstairs (these of pine, numbering twelve), Felix was surprised to discover that Faith had written out two cards, one saying *Faith*, the other *Felix*, and had pinned them to separate bedroom doors. 'It would be embarrassing if your lovers – or hers – made a mistake, eh?' Fogel suggested. 'Life in *any* kibbutz must be complicated, no?'

'*My* life is simple enough, Wolf. I suspect this is for Miss Worth's benefit – not yours.'

At that moment Faith was saying to Hugh Wellington, 'Yes, but just suppose Richard Dimbleby or Wynford Vaughan Thomas had been able to shoot *thirty minutes* of a report – not just three . . . I mean, the war we saw in the newsreels was like salvaging five pieces out of a two-hundred-piece jigsaw puzzle. What if they'd been able to show us the whole damn thing?'

'My dear young lady,' he responded. 'The top brass would have had a fit!'

'And would they have deserved it?'

'Well . . .' He gazed over her shoulder, seeking someone less demanding to chat with. 'A lot of water must flow under the bridge before we get there.'

'Oh!' she responded briskly. 'Somehow I imagined we were talking about the very reservoir from which all that water must one day flow.'

She introduced Felix and Fogel, who had just joined them. Fogel took Wellington by the arm, saying, 'I have champagne in the taxi.' As they strolled away, he was saying, 'You know vot ze scientists call *synergy*, yes?'

'Where's Angela?' Felix asked. 'I thought I would be meeting her at Harmer Green.'

'It seemed only a kindness to offer her a lift. And Robert Street was only a couple of miles out of our way. So many people!' Faith stared toward the back lawn, where Nicole and Marianne had set out their tables. 'She said she saw someone she thought she knew. She went off that way.'

They didn't find her – she found them at the head of the big lawn, by the ballroom steps, and in some agitation. 'You know Marianne Johnson?' she said to Felix, gripping his arm almost painfully. 'I'm sure she's the one I told you about – Maria – in Berlin.'

'You . . . what . . . ?' He understood the words but . . .

'My contact with the communists! And she recognized me, too. The moment she saw me . . . *pfft!* Up the steps and into the house. Can we go in there?'

'Er . . .' Felix's mind was racing.

'Is that her husband – Willard?'

'Did you speak to him . . . tell him anything about—?'

'No! Of course not. She's the Swedish girl you told me about?'

'Yes. The thing about him and Marianne . . . I meant to explain all this when . . . I mean, if I'd collected you off the bus. The thing is . . . Willard is . . . well, he's a wonderful fellow in many ways . . . done wonderful things for this community . . . but he has an absolutely fanatical hatred of communism. That's why Marianne took fright and bolted. Nothing to do with you.' He chewed his lip. 'What do we do now?'

'Can you take me up to see her?'

Faith put her oar in: 'If Marianne really is Angela's communist contact, then it's not fair to leave Nicole in ignorance. My God! And Marianne has accepted Nicole's taunts all this time rather than risk Willard's finding out she was a heroine all along! A heroine who happened to be a communist!'

'*Gott in Himmel!*' Angela exclaimed. 'I'm going to give that Willard a bit of my mind!'

'No!' Felix spoke loud enough to turn several heads. More quietly he added, 'Do that and you'll smash a good marriage.'

'How *can* it be good with such a man?'

'That's not for you to judge, Angela. Take it from me – it's a good marriage—'

'Not for *me* to judge? Not for you, either, I think.'

'I know more about this than—'

'We have lived in Hell for years. Never again can we make judgements on –' she waved a hand at the entire garden party – 'the *normal*.'

'All the more reason not to interfere,' he said calmly.

'Except,' Faith put in, 'how much did Willard see? I'll bet those little brain-cogs are already going clicketty-click!'

Felix nodded glumly.

Faith had not finished. 'And *we* can't let Nicole go on digging herself deeper and deeper in a hole. These things always come out in the end . . . and if she discovers that *we* knew the truth all along . . .'

'Also,' Angela said, 'Maria, or Marianne, has – or had – the only remaining copy of the protocol I made of that conference at Interpol HQ in 'forty-two . . .'

'Should I have heard about this?' Faith asked.

Felix told her. 'It was a conference where the SS told the rest of the Nazi bureaucracy they were going to murder all the Jews, gypsies, and queers they could find.'

'And,' Angela added, 'I gave a copy to British Intelligence when I was debriefed. And now they say they can't find it. I hoped they'd use it in the war-crimes trials because everything is there. It's like fifteen signed confessions – the things they said. But they've lost it!'

'Here's what we'll do,' Felix said.

'Well, *we* had a John Logie Baird set before the war,' Isabella was telling Arthur Prentice. 'And if *that's* what your television is going to look like when it returns for all the nation, you can jolly well keep it.'

Arthur assured her that the BBC had ended the Baird experiment in 1937 and the apes would quit Gibraltar before the BBC would agree to let Baird and his wretched excuse for a television system come within ten miles of any TV studio. It would be exclusively Schoenberg's electronic system from EMI.

'And who is that extraordinary man talking to the Continental-looking person who came in a taxi with Faith Bullen-ffitch. Where on earth did he learn to speak like that?'

'Schtumm!' he warned. 'That's Hugh Wellington – my boss.'

'Oh! Poor *you*!'

'Dylan Thomas says the man speaks as if he had the Elgin Marbles in his mouth. He says it's the standard BBC accent.'

'You know Dylan Thomas?' Isabella said, taking a step back and looking him up and down.

'I run across him now and then at Mother Redcaps in Camden Town. He does poetry, they say.'

'Very good poetry, too.'

'If he writes as well as he puts away a pint . . . I can believe it.'

They drifted off toward the Palmers' lawn and the two buffets. 'Is it too early to light the boiler?' she asked.

'Give it another half hour,' he advised.

Todd Ferguson explained to a woman from Adam and Tony's office that they ought to light a fire under their union organizer. The nationalization of the railways was going to double the wages of all its workers . . . or *someone* was going to get lynched. 'They can afford it now they're not paying dividends to all those idle-rich shareholders,' he explained.

Faith – who overheard him in passing and who also knew that her parents held shares in several British railway companies and were looking forward immensely to being bought out by the Labour government, since none of them had paid a dividend since 1923 – almost stopped to enlighten him. But her mission – hers and Angela's – was too important for that.

'Her real name was Angela Wirth,' Felix told Marianne, up in her kitchen. 'I kick myself now that it never crossed my mind. When she told me about "Maria", she imitated the way you speak German perfectly.'

Marianne stood well back from the window, at the farthest point from which she could still see Faith talking with Willard – and Angela sitting at a table a little way off. 'It is she,' she murmured. 'Hardly has she changed. Yet never for one moment I imagined she should have lived.' She closed her eyes tight. 'Listen to my English! I believe I dream only. She won't say anything to Willard?'

'That's the one thing you can be quite sure of. Nor will Faith. The problem is Nicole.'

'Nicole?' Marianne was aghast. 'But she must never know. Never.'

'It's not fair to leave her in ignorance.'

'No!' She gripped his arm and shook it. 'No! Please – never! Never must that one know. She is too . . . feeling?'

'Emotional. But the way she treats you . . .'

'That plays no part. I don't mind. I admire her indeed. For what she believes, she is perfectly right. Please, now – no one must ever tell her. Not you. Not . . . Fräulein Wirth . . .'

'Angela Worth. She's made it English.'

'Not her. And absolutely not Faith. You must make them to swear it.'

'Angela's worried . . .'

'Promise you make them swear it!'

'OK. Angela's worried about the transcript she gave you. The one of—'

'I know the one. I never read it all through – just enough to make me spew.'

'You have it still?'

'I know where it is – or should be.'

'And?'

'I gave it to . . . well, it ended up with a comrade. In Hamburg. He was still living there when I left. But he has it. He works in the docks. Never I thought she'd come back for it.'

'Unless he's handed it over to the Russians.'

'I don't think so. He was quite . . . what's the word? Like out-of-love?'

'Disillusioned – with the communists?'

She nodded. 'Same with me. With the *Soviet-style* communism. Disillusioned.' She tucked the word away.

'And can't you just explain all that to Willard?'

She stared at him a long moment and said, 'I want a father to my baby. Not a memory. Those things Nicole says . . . the things she does . . . I hardly notice them by now.'

'So?' Felix shrugged helplessly. 'We have no right to tell you what to do. But can I suggest this – I'll go down now and explain your wishes to Angela—'

Marianne interrupted, 'She's not your girlfriend now? Faith's not moving out?'

'Why?' He was taken aback. 'What have you heard?'

'Nothing!' Marianne assured him – a little too earnestly, he thought.

'OK. As I say – I'll explain your wishes to Angela and you'll recover from your "migraine" in about ten minutes from now . . . or discover it was just a passing headache or something. And then you'll come back downstairs. And meanwhile, Angela will say confidentially to Willard something like "Did your wife ever work in an office in Berlin . . . in a very important office . . . an architectural design office . . . ?" Sort of edging toward the question rather than coming straight out with it. And at some stage Willard will ask why all the probing. And Angela will explain that she was a technician in Goebbels's documentary-film department and they once did an interview with Speer in his office . . . and there was this ravishingly beautiful Danish girl . . . And Willard will say, "Swedish!" and then all is explained – including your "migraine".'

'How does that help?'

'Well, I would think the last thing you'd want would be some ex-employee of Goebbels turning up today and recognizing you – not with Nicole standing just three or four yards away.'

Marianne stared at him, slack-jawed. 'I can imagine how you survived,' she said. 'But can Angela can carry it off? Carry it off – that's right?'

'A simple deception like this?' He smiled condescendingly. 'Never wonder if any survivor of the KLS can carry off a deception.'

'Oh no!' Sally had her eyes on a battered pre-war Austin Ten that had reached the start of the lime-tree avenue and come to a halt. 'I think that's Terence Lanyon's car.'

'Did he say they were moving in today?' Tony asked.

'No – definitely not until next week. The thing is, I don't have the gatelodge key. Have you seen Bob Ambrose? I gave it to him to clean out that old wasps' nest.' She ran out into the drive and waved for Terence to come on up to the house.

'A garden party!' he exclaimed as he got out of the car and half-lifted half-slammed the door shut. 'We *are* going up in the world.'

'No Hilary?' Tony asked, joining them.

'She's still packing up in Manchester. I'm on my way back so I thought I'd cry in in the passing.'

'On your way back from the LSE?'

'No. The Fabian Society have asked me to chair a symposium on welfare economics. Who's here?' All the while he spoke his eyes quartered the crowd.

Tony was reminded at once of Willard, who had the same habit. 'Have you eaten?' he asked. 'You should come and try some of Nicole's offerings before they're all gone.'

When Sally told him how many useful people were at the party he said, 'I think I'll stay the night – if someone can kindly put me up?'

'So let me get this straight,' Bob said. 'You've got to move a hundred-thousand people out of London – the ones Hitler never shifted – and you're going to build copies of Welwyn Garden City sort-of dotted all around London, and in-between it's all kept green and no one's allowed to build nothing. Strewth!'

Sir Patrick chuckled despite himself – for the last thing he wanted to talk about today was *The Abercrombie Plan for Greater London,* which had consumed his life for the past decade. 'I wish, young man, that you could teach our politicians and civil servants to put things as concisely and as accurately as you. The only item you missed is our plan for the roads. We shall build a ring of roads around London, roads for motor vehicles *only*. All the other roads will either go over them or under them. So all traffic in London will be local traffic. All the rest will whizz around the outside on great highways that carry no local traffic whatever.' His smile and his beetling brows invoiced a bright-bright future to Bob and his generation. 'And now – if you'll excuse me – I see a gentleman I very much wish to buttonhole.'

'Nutty as a fruitcake!' Bob said admiringly after he'd gone. 'But you gotta hand it to him for conviction. You can't deny that.'

'It's more sinister than that, matey,' Eric said. 'Did you hear the language? *We* will move *them* . . . *We* will give *them* houses, streets, parks to be proud of . . . *We* will give *them* light and air and sunshine . . .'

'What's wrong with that?'

'I wouldn't have minded just *one* sentence beginning with *they* – as in "They may choose . . ."'

★   ★   ★

'Fogel is talking to Sir Patrick Abercrombie,' Faith said to Felix as he rejoined them. 'I'd better go and see if he wants me there.'

He caught her arm. 'Just before you go. I've spoken with Marianne and she is absolutely, utterly determined that Nicole must *not* be told.' Faith opened her mouth to object but he went on. 'I agree with you. It's wrong to let Nicole carry on the way she does. But today is not the day. We'll have to work on it.'

She looked as if she would still argue her point, but the urge to join Fogel was stronger.

Still Felix held her back. 'You should also hear this.' He turned to Angela. 'Marianne and I think that you should go to Willard and tell him how you were a recordist with a Propaganda Ministry film crew that visited Speer's office. Tell him how Marianne stood out . . . the only woman on the top floor – and so beautiful – so, of course, you remembered her. And say she was Danish. Not Swedish. Let *him* make the connection. He'll understand that the last thing she wanted was for someone with that sort of memory turning up and blurting it all out. Especially with Nicole so close. You can do this?'

Angela nodded. 'Did she say anything about the transcript?'

Faith escaped and went in search of Fogel.

'As far as she knows, it's safe. She left it with a fellow communist in Hamburg. It's best if you go and beard Willard in his den by yourself. *Danish*, remember. It'll stop him thinking your association was anything more than that one day. I'm going to find Arthur and help him light the boiler.'

'Beard? Den?' Angela muttered as she walked away.

Fogel didn't notice Faith until she was a mere twenty paces away; then he gave her a surreptitious *not-yet* sort of sign. She paused, marooned in mid-lawn, and, to her dismay, found herself being approached by Hugh Wellington. 'Miss Bullen-ffitch!' he called out. 'I knew I had seen you somewhere before. Do please forgive me for not recognizing you at once. You used to ride in Hyde Park, I think?'

She could not place him in that context. 'You rode, too?' she asked.

'Me? No! I couldn't afford that. No, I go for a bit of a jogtrot round the Serpentine every morning before brekker, don't you know. But I used to see you in Rotten Row on a magnificent chestnut.'

'He's here now – loose in the field beside the drive.'

'Well, I'm glad I wasn't mistaken. But what I really wished to talk to you about was Mister Breit. I gather from Mister Fogel that you're the one who recruited him for this arts encyclopedia?'

'Yes, I suppose I was.'

'Just so. Just so. And that is why I'd welcome your advice, dear young lady. I think that a sculpture by him would also add lustre – as you put it – to our new quarters at Alexandra Palace. In the reception area. Not outside. It's not the most salubrious part of London. And we'd want to take it with us if we ever moved to a more central location.' He eyed her diffidently. 'Could you . . . sort of . . . sound out the ground and – if favourable – introduce me sometime this evening?'

He held his breath and only let it out when she replied, 'You'll need to talk first to *me* about that, Mister Wellington. I'm now his agent, you see.'

And why not? she thought. God knows he needs one.

'One great thing about the war,' Bob Ambrose said to Mrs Tawney, 'was that all the voluntary work – you know – like running canteens for bombed-out folk and the tea-and-a-wad service for the armed forces at the railway stations – things like that – it was all done by ordinary people . . . women in the wvs.'

'*I* was in the wvs,' Mrs Tawney complained.

'Yeah – that's what I'm on about. It brought you down to the level of being ordinary – like the rest of us. You and Lady Hunter. And very good at it you was, too, if you don't mind me saying so. I take me hat off to you and her 'cos it can't have been easy.'

Mrs Tawney was desperate to have three rotten windows at the back of Monkswood – her ancestral home – replaced; and this awful common little man seemed to have the knack of getting building materials when no one else for miles around could manage it. What made it so galling was that her family had employed the Ambroses for generations.

'I wouldn't exactly call it difficult,' she said. She longed to add, 'After all, *my* ancestors have carried nourishing broth and uplifting pamphlets to *your* hard-up ancestors since time immemorial.'

'No! You shouldn't run yourself down, Mrs Tawney – making out like it was nothing. In the war, you come down toward our level and we come up toward yours – and we was all British and proud of it together. And we can't go back now. That's all gone forever. And I'll tell you anuvver thing, I pity all these Europeans – and the Yanks – 'cos it never happened to them. Look at all these foreigners here today – they live among us and, fair's fair, they pull their weight. And they'll all get British passports, too, I shouldn't wonder. But they'll never really understand us like what you and me understand one another. And isn't that the truth.'

Reluctantly she had to admit that she could hardly have expressed it more trenchantly herself; more elegantly, certainly. 'Talking of understanding one another,' she said, 'you know those heavy teak frames your grandfather made for the windows overlooking the back lawn at Monkswood?'

'Willard Johnson?' Angela asked. '*The* Willard Johnson?'

'The one and only, lady. Try one of these egg-and-caviar smörgåsar? They're almost gone.'

'Thank you, yes. I'm Angela Worth, by the way – a friend of Felix.'

'Lucky guy!' He handed her the open sandwich on a waxed cardboard plate with a GI stamp.

She took a bite and made appreciative noises. Then she said, 'That lady who was here just now . . .'

'My wife? Yeah – she got some kind of migraine, which she never—'

'I think not,' Angela said quietly.

The smile left his face. 'Tell me.'

She leaned forward. 'Did she work in Germany in the war?'

After a pause he said, 'Listen lady – we've all passed a lot of water under the bridge since then – as Sam Goldwyn said. So why don't we—'

'No! I worked in Germany, too. For Goebbels' propaganda ministry. I was recording engineer on a film they made in a certain office? A very *high* office of a very important architect?

And there was only one woman there – on that floor, anyway, a beautiful Danish—'

'OK, Miss Worth. That's a hit. A home run.' He turned and gazed up at their kitchen window. 'Migraine!' He gave a brief, dry laugh. 'No wonder she bolted.'

'Well, you can tell her I had absolutely no intention to speak of it with her, except in private if the chance came. I am not so unsensitive. Unsensible?'

'Either, I think. Or both. I doubt she'd want to talk about those days, anyway.' He sized her up. 'I guess you had to be a party member to work in that outfit?'

Angela had not intended to answer as she did, but when she found the words on the tip of her tongue she did nothing to prevent them. 'I was a communist – working secretly inside the Nazi party. And communist I still am.'

His eyes dwelled coolly in hers an uncomfortably long time. 'You know,' he said at last, 'I reckon that if I had been born a German, living in Germany back then, I just might have become a secret communist myself. Did the Gestapo ever catch you?'

She stretched her arm until a few digits of her prisoner-tattoo showed.

He smiled at last. 'Well, you're personally welcome here today, Miss Worth, despite your politics – they'd play better *that* side of the lawn.'

She turned and saw Nicole, who was doling out small pieces of French bread on each of which she was spreading some sort of pâté.

'That's right,' Willard said. 'You're very quick. You'd be welcome on that side all right. Her name's Nicole Palmer, châtelaine of the apartment behind her and a fellow commie – but she's also the finest cook you or I are ever likely to meet. And in these dark days we can forgive her almost anything for that. You really ought to go across and try that pâté.'

As Angela thanked him again and turned to go, he added, laughing, 'Tell her you were a Nazi party member . . . and *then* add that you were also an undercover communist. I'd just *love* to see her face!'

Faith said, 'Don't stray too far, Mister Wellington. There's someone I'd like you to meet.' And she slipped away to find

Corvo. But Corvo proved reluctant to leave his friend Julian with a young woman from the GLP office, who was obviously taken with him.

'She might not realize about him,' he complained as she dragged him away, 'and he might forget himself, too. I suspect he can tack to port *and* starboard. Do I shock you, young lady?'

'Not in the least, Corvo – may I call you Corvo? I have many friends who are queers.'

'Really?' He took her arm and stepped out. 'Call me whatever you like, darling – but do call! Miss . . . ?'

'Bullen-ffitch. But Faith will do. I'm going to introduce you to the man who lords it over the BBC's junior branch at Ally Pally, so you—'

'Television?' He wrinkled his nose and slowed down again. 'I saw it before the war – quite ghastly. Must I?'

'I think so. There's still space on the ground floor – and from there you can only go in one direction, you know.'

He still dragged his heels but now it was in a more thoughtful mood.

'I think you should challenge him from the start,' she said. 'Ask him a challenging question. He's a man of forthright opinions.'

'Black and white, eh? Well, it suits the medium – which is what I don't like about it, the lack of subtlety.'

'I think he'll respond well to a challenge.' She all but nudged him in the back as they joined the listening circle around the great man.

'I'm Corvo,' he said, offering his hand. 'Tell me – what are you people going to do for the arts?'

'Dear fellow!' Wellington beamed at him. '*You* tell *me*! And if we like it, we'll do it.'

Corvo was taken aback. He had expected a torrent of plans and wishful thinking from the man – something that would let him find a small niche for himself. Instead, he, who had never thought of television as having the remotest connection with serious art, was being forced to extemporize.

Faith, seeing him about to flounder, inclined her head toward the Dower House behind them.

'Stately homes,' he said. 'Yes, of course. The military are starting to hand them all back now. I *personally* know scores of

places . . . written them up for *Country Life* – including the
Dower House here, indeed. You could do a splendid series of
documentaries on restoring them, reviving the gardens, getting
the treasures back out of storage . . .'

'And,' Faith added, 'apart from being a feast for the eye –
which is surely another definition of television? – it would also
be an elegant reminder of the things we fought for in the war.'

'Fought for the stately homes of England?' Bob Ambrose
picked up the fag-end of the conversation as he approached
them. 'I'd have signed on as a conshie if I'd o' known that.
You're the boss of television, right?'

Reluctantly, Faith introduced them.

'What I want to know is are you going to put your cameras
actually on the racecourses and football pitches and cricket
grounds . . . places like that?'

'Live broadcasting, we call it. Yes, indeed, young man, we
certainly shall. We're working on all the systems now. And the
Oxford and Cambridge Boat Race, of course. There are a few
technical problems still to solve about getting the signal back to
the studio – but we'll master them before too long.' He turned
back to Corvo. 'Mister Ambrose here has voiced an objection
to your sort of programme that would find quite a bit of support
at the BBC, I fear.'

Felix joined the group.

'Ah! Mister Breit!' Wellington welcomed him and pointed to
Faith. 'I'm talking with your agent here – as you see.'

'Pay no attention to Mister Bob Ambrose and his prejudices.'
Faith distracted Wellington to allow Felix time to adjust to
the news. 'He'd simply adore to sit in front of his television
set, shouting insults at poor Corvo as he shows us around the
glories of Blenheim or Hatfield House or Castle Howard.
Besides, Corvo's tour wouldn't be all interiors. There are our
glorious landscape gardens, too. His programme would
combine the English love of gardening with gloating over
antiques and the lure of inaccessible places, to say nothing of
fantasies of wealth and noble birth. It has everything to make
the Ambroses of this world cancel their pub-crawl and stay
home to watch.' She winked at Bob, hoping he'd have the
sense to shut up.

Wellington looked her shrewdly up and down. 'Yes,' he said

at last. 'You are very persuasive, Miss Bullen-ffitch. One begins to see *all sorts* of possibilities.'

'You were talking to Wolf Fogel, the publisher, earlier,' she said. 'He's produced dozens of books with a British heritage theme. Did he mention them to you?'

He shook his head. 'He told me about this encyclopedia of modern art and Mister Breit.'

'Oh! He should have mentioned the heritage books, too. I'll go and get him.' She smiled at Felix, who pretended to shoot her with his finger.

As she turned to go Wellington asked, 'Are you by any chance this Mister Fogel's agent, too?'

'You could say that.'

'Who *is* she?' he asked Corvo after she'd gone.

Felix said, 'I think she's using us – all of us – to find the answer to that very question.'

Evening was drawing on into night. Marianne, having recovered from her 'migraine', had put together a final plate of smörgåsar – home-made cheese and off-points anchovies, this time. She took a small selection of them over to Nicole's table and left them with a smile – which Nicole did not return. Later she saw Tony offering them around. He brought the plate back to her with a rueful smile. 'Give it time,' he murmured.

Alexander Griffith, one of the architects who did occasional work for the gravel company, approached her. 'I hear your father's a steel maker,' he said. 'Does he know any wheezes for getting round import controls? This damn socialist government is so dead set on building council houses for the masses that we in the private-building business can hardly get a bag of nails.'

Angela rose from her seat and, drawing a deep breath, started toward her.

May Prentice put Sam and his younger sister, Hannah, to bed – knowing very well they'd fall asleep with their heads on the window sill – and went to look for Arthur, to remind him it was his turn to stoke the boiler. She went down bravely enough though she hated the musty dark of those subterranean corridors and cubby-holes. She was sure they were all overrun with ghosts – which was why she went on tiptoe. Which, in turn, was how she came to hear the unmistakeable sounds of a man and a woman rising to the climax of an act that would have been singularly inappropriate, not to say impossible, for a pair of ghosts.

'Eve! Oh Eve!' the man cried in a loud, hoarse whisper.

As she backed off she heard Eve say, 'Hurry up! This coal is bloody uncomfortable.'

She found her husband washing the coke dust from his hands. 'It's going to burn a ton before the night is out,' he said. 'We'll never afford it for the whole house – unless we can cut down half a forest somewhere.'

She told him what she'd just heard.

'I believe you, pet,' he replied. 'He'd shag anything in knickers, would our Adam.'

'Oh dear! D'you think we did the right thing – coming to live here?'

'It's going to be what we used to call a bomber's moon,' Angela said.

'I remember,' Marianne replied. 'Let me show you round the place before the light completely goes. Or is that something Felix was looking forward to doing?'

'Oh . . . never mind him.'

'I'll just tell my husband, so. He worries – because of . . .' She patted her stomach and turned toward Willard, who was now clearing up at their buffet table.

But Angela did not move. 'When is it due?'

'Not long now. Sooner than we calculated.'

'Your first?'

Marianne darted her a look of surprise. 'Yes!'

'In the war . . . so many things happened. Anyway, I told your husband I was in that film crew for the Speer propaganda film – and, of course, noticed you. Nothing about meeting you after that.'

'You didn't mention . . . you know – the party?'

'I said you were Danish but he didn't correct me.'

'He wouldn't see any reason to, but that's good. You said nothing about the party?'

'I told him *I* was a member – and that I was—'

'But why?' Marianne cried.

'To see his reaction – which *was* a surprise. He said that if he'd been a German, in Germany, during the war, he'd probably have been a secret communist, too – a communist inside the Nazi party.'

For a moment Marianne could only stare. 'That can I hardly believe,' she said at last. 'Just so? He said that, just so?'

'Honey?' Willard, who had been watching them closely, called out.

'I must go. He's calling. Shall you come too? Please?'

Angela followed her some way behind.

'Old times, eh?' Willard said.

'Hardly.' Marianne laughed briefly. 'I was a fool to run away. Just panic. You know she's a friend to Felix?'

'So she said.'

'She's asked me to show her around the place. Can you manage here? Shall I ask Sally to help?'

'She's gone hunting for Adam. If I were her, I'd go loaded for bear. Sure I can manage here. Off you go!'

Marianne linked arms with Angela and steered her around the end of the Wilsons' annexe and into the narrow lane that led into the back yard. 'D'you want to talk in German?'

'Never!'

'OK, OK! I have to say I got a shock to see you. Never I thought you would have survived.'

'Felix and Miss Bullen-ffitch have told me about Nicole Palmer – you and Nicole . . .'

Marianne halted and hung her head theatrically. 'Too many people know. It's not good. It's not good.'

'Are you now wishing I *didn't* survive?'

'No!' She hugged Angela's arm to her. 'No – I'm absolutely delighted. I started to make an inquiry – after the liberation – except I didn't know your real name. And then I thought it might stir trouble for you if you had survived – me asking for a communist who was also an ex-SS officer . . . if you hadn't told them . . .'

'And I just wanted to get out of Germany and come to the BBC as fast as possible.'

They were now strolling through the back yard, in front of Felix's cottage. The old car chassis, liberated from the pheasant run, had been pushed onto the grass beneath the weeping ash and people were sitting on it, pushing it gently back and forth

as they drank beer and chattered. Everything was silvered by
the rising moon.

'It is extraordinary,' Angela murmured. 'You and I, we share
an experience that we could never begin to describe to any of
these English – even the ones who fought the war from
Normandy to Berlin. It was like a tourist war for them.'

'All English wars for the last nine hundred years have been
"tourist wars". Always they have fought on other people's lands.
That's why they will never understand Europe. They will never
be European. I have discussed this with Felix.'

'Me, too. And I agree. But I feel safe here, too – which I
never felt in Germany, not once in all my life. London is my
Heimat! Not *Vaterland* but *Heimat*. You have the same difference
in Sweden?'

'In Sweden we say *hembygden*. Not our motherland but our
native –' she pointed at the ground beneath their feet – 'earth?
Soil? It's true. I feel more safer here, also, than anywhere and
any time before. Poor old Europe is a million miles away.'

They meandered up the side drive to the front gate and then
turned back toward the house along the main drive. 'Those
transcripts you left with me,' Marianne said. 'I think they're safe.
In fact, I'm rather sure they're safe. The embassy didn't want
them hanging around – obviously – so they entrusted them to
the embassy's German chauffeur, Hermann Treite, a communist
who works in the docks. He lives in Reiherstieg now. I can
give you his phone number.'

'Is he still in the party?'

Marianne shrugged. 'Like me – still a believer, but disillusioned
with the Russians. It's a difficult time for us – head going one
way, heart the other.' After a pause she added, 'And you?'

'The same, I suppose.' She shook her head impatiently. 'Enough
of all that! Tell me about Faith.'

Coming up to midnight Marianne lit a bonfire she had assembled in the basin of the dried-up fountain. In Sweden, the
midsummer bonfires reached fingers up among the stars; this
was the feeblest imitation – but still bright enough for one wag
to parody the wartime cry of 'Put that light out!' Marianne
and others of the community linked hands and danced around
it – sedately because of her condition. After a couple of circuits

she dropped out and sang the old Swedish Midsummer songs for them to dance by. Soon, however, they switched to 'The Lambeth Walk', 'Knees Up Mother Brown', and 'The Hokey Cokey'. And as the flames died they formed a conger line and retreated toward the house to the strains of 'I kissed her on the lips, 'ow ashamed I was . . .'

'Have you ever heard the songs they sang in the war?' Marianne asked as Angela left the line and the others dispersed.

'All about marching against Germany?' Angela guessed, fanning the opening of her blouse.

'No! Exactly the opposite. "The Quartermaster's Stores" and "You'd be Far Better Off in a Hole". They're all about mocking the army, the officers . . . the government. And the BBC used to broadcast them, too!'

'Germany isn't even a hundred years old yet,' Angela mused. 'Maybe you need to be an old country to be relaxed and mock yourself like that.'

Come one o'clock, there were people lying on the lawn like silvered logs, staring up at the sky, remembering how many more stars they had been able to see during the blackout.

'If you could shrink the entire solar system, right out to Pluto, down to the size of your wedding ring,' Eric said to Betty Ferguson, 'the next nearest star to us would be somewhere in Ware – about four miles away. And the centre of our galaxy would be up there on the moon.'

She considered this a moment in silence and then said, 'Funny – I didn't want to move here when Todd come home that night and told me he thought we should up sticks. But tonight I see what it's all about. True, we do get all Sally Palmer's cooking smells up through our bathroom – especially the fried onions – and I know if Isabella comes down to your studio and you two start on at each other, we get the benefit of your opinions, too . . . but still and all, this *is* better than everyone living in their own little boxes.'

'It's a form of love, you know – the way Isabella goes on at me.'

Betty laughed quietly. 'It's gotta be, hasn't it – otherwise you'd never still be together. Also she admires your painting.'

'How d'you know that?'

''Cos she never says a dickey bird about them – which she surely would if she *didn't* like them.'

'Hmmm. The truth is she knows I'm not a *real* artist – like Felix Breit.'

She turned over and propped herself up on her elbows, to see if he were serious. 'You reckon he's an artist? I think your paintings are . . . well, they're *real*. Anyone could carve a bleedin' egg out of a block of marble if they was careful enough about it. What's the art in that?'

'You've put your finger on it there, Betty. We must all try our best to pity today's artists. They're in a terrible fix. Everything that can possibly be done with line, colour, shape, and what have you – either on a flat surface or in three dimensions *has already been done.* The sort of painting I do was done more than a century ago by a man called Samuel Palmer. He'd have absolutely revelled in this moonlight, by the way. And the sort of sculpture Felix is doing was done before the war by sculptors like Arp and Brancusi. It's just not possible now to imagine anything new. From now on, all art is like copying – call it pastiche for a few quid more.'

'You could stand with your back to the canvas and just chuck the paint over your shoulder,' she suggested with a giggle.

'*Sshhh!* Someone'll hear you – and then they'll go and do it. And they'll give it some fancy name like random-structured painting and Corvo and his crowd will wet their knickers in ecstasy and American millionaires will fall over each other to buy it up. I'll make you a prediction, Betty – and you can hold me to this – are you listening?'

'Yeah. I'm also wondering what your wife is saying to Felix Breit over there.'

'Probably about fashion in Paris before the war. She's doing a feature on Schiaparelli for *Marie Claire*. Anyway – my prediction is this: Sometime in the next ten years someone calling himself a painter is going to exhibit a gallery full of blank canvases and call it art.' A refinement occurred to him. 'And he'll refuse to sign them because it would spoil the purity of the canvas. And – this is the point now – *the exhibition will be a sell-out.*'

Betty laughed – a melodious, silvery laugh that carried across the lawn.

Isabella broke off her conversation with Felix. 'What nonsense is he talking now?' she called out.

'Just the usual, my pet,' Eric assured her before continuing in a lower key to Betty, 'The interesting question is – will it happen in Paris or London or New York? Because that will determine which city will become the new art-capital of the world.'

'So you knew Schiaparelli *before* she moved to the place Vendôme?' Isabella asked excitedly.

'Not really,' Felix assured her. 'But I used to pass her place in the rue de la Paix. I met Dali on the street outside once.'

'When he was designing that outrageous costume, all covered with lobsters, for the Duchess of Windsor – actually before she became the duchess? That must have been a *wonderful* time to be in Paris.'

Felix drew breath to reply but, in the end, said nothing.

'No?' she prompted.

'Superficially, yes. They used to tell me it was even gayer in the twenties, before the Depression, before all the rich Americans became poor and had to leave. But it was still pretty dazzling when I arrived in the thirties.'

'Only superficially?'

Felix wondered if it was worth the effort – trying to explain to yet another uncomprehending English person what had happened between the wars, a million miles away over the Channel. 'There were . . . undercurrents,' he said. 'The Great War didn't end in peace – just exhaustion. And you could see it clearly in Paris at that time.'

'Paris?' Nicole turned aside from the gravel path at the word and glided across the lawn to join them. 'What about Paris?'

'You must be exhausted,' Felix told her. 'Shouldn't you be in bed?'

She laid her hand on her stomach. 'This beast wakes when I sleep and sleeps when I wake. This is good. I relax now. You spoke about Paris?'

'I was talking about her in the thirties, when I moved there from Berlin after a quarrel with my father. I missed the big riots of nineteen thirty-four but you could feel the aftermath. The right wing and the royalists just smouldering with hatred and waiting their chance for revenge – which they got soon enough.'

He turned to Isabella. 'Didn't the English ever wonder why France fell so swiftly in nineteen-forty?'

'I was a bit young . . .' she began. 'But wasn't there something about the Germans simply walking around the top of the Maginot Line?'

'But why did it collapse so quickly *after* that? I'll tell you – because the right wing and the royalists *wanted* the Nazis to win. They thought they could all be fascists together, standing shoulder to shoulder, cleaning out the liberal-socialist-communist-deca-dent-homosexual-Jewish filth. And by the time they learned what the Germans meant by *Übermensch*, it was too late. Then they had to collaborate or be cleaned out themselves.' He looked at Nicole. 'Right?'

'Completely,' she agreed and drew breath to add some analysis of her own.

But Isabella wanted to bring him back to more important topics. 'So! When you met Dali that time,' she said, 'did he take you inside Schiaparelli's salon? Did you *ever* go inside?'

Willard, who had been looking for Nicole, wandered across the lawn to join them.

'How's Marianne?' Felix called out as he drew near.

'She's gone to bed. It's been quite a day.'

'Well, you both did a wonderful job,' Isabella said.

'And Nicole and Tony,' Felix added.

'I was coming to that,' Willard said. 'Nicole – I think you and Marianne deserve to sleep late tomorrow. Tony says you got some off-points sausages – or what the English fondly *believe* are sausages – I got four or five pounds of bacon rashers and a few dozen eggs from some old pals who owed me one. So he and I will take care of breakfast for the masses. OK?' When she started to protest he added, 'Have it out with your husband, honey – I'm only passing on the orders here.'

He sat down next to her and – in the brilliance of that full moon – turned into one of Henry Moore's reclining figures. 'What's the scuttlebutt?' he asked.

'Paris in the Thirties.'

'And,' Nicole added, 'the traitory? Treechery? *Trahison* of the royalists and the right, who capitulated France to the *Boches*.'

Willard understood she was trying to provoke him. 'Heap

big moon!' he said, now rearranging himself in the pose of a Plains Indian.

'Fortunately,' Nicole continued, 'the right is being obliterated all across Europe. Soon it will be socialism from Liverpool to Vladivostock. And then – let America look east or west, she will see socialists on either side.' She turned to Felix, picking up on his earlier comment. 'And now the Great War really *is* finished. You agree?'

Felix shrugged.

'You do!' she insisted.

He spoke as if musing aloud, not specifically answering her. 'I had so many socialist friends who went to fight in Spain and some were very critical of Stalin – we all remarked on it at the time – it was odd how the socialists who criticized him were the ones who got "killed in action" in Spain. Stalin's admirers somehow survived. And then again I remember the Paris Writers' Conference of 1935, when Maxim Gorky was supposed to be the star of the Soviet delegation, but he didn't appear. And from that moment on, by the way, not a single Soviet newspaper – not a single *communist* newspaper *anywhere* – mentioned his name again until Stalin had him murdered in 'thirty-six. In his place they sent some minor novelist called Pasternak, who gave a speech of such embarrassing banality that everyone could *see* he was scared of saying anything – *anything* – that might upset dear old Uncle Joe. "Poetry will always exist down there in the grass," he said. It was all empty platitudes like that.' He smiled at Nicole and, as if it were a concession to her, added, 'Of course, none of that mattered down on the factory floor and out in the fields of the collective farm.'

'Yes!' Nicole agreed. 'That's where the future is being made now.'

'Heap big bull . . . er . . . bullshine,' Willard said. 'But it's too fine a night to argue. Tell us, Nicole – what do you call that group of stars in French . . . The Big Dipper . . . and those . . . The Seven Sisters?'

He went on pointing them out until that other fierce pride of her life – her native tongue – got the better of her politics.

'Willard calls it the Eagle's Nest,' Marianne told Angela. 'He honestly wasn't aware that's what Hitler called his place in the mountains. The Americans and the British didn't fight *our* war.'

They were standing on the balcony that topped the semicircular bow on the south front, overlooking the lawn; the moon was now halfway down the sky to their right, silvering their faces and staining their lips deep purple.

'It must be wonderful to belong to a nation that carries no such baggage,' Angela remarked.

After a silence, Marianne said, 'I've dreamed of you rather much. Perhaps it will stop now. I hope so.'

Angela just stared, uncertain how to respond.

'The strange thing was – the dreams were all *about* you but you never appeared in them.'

'How?'

'The typical sort of thing, I'd go into a shop – a dress shop, say – and while I'm looking at dresses one of the assistants comes up to me, very quietly, and hands me a packet. It could be a packet of fish or a brick . . . anything. But it's a secret. I know she has risked much to pass it to me. And she says, "Get this to her somehow. Don't fail." And then I spend the rest of the dream looking for you. And never can I find you. I can be on a platform at Hauptbahnhof and there are all these other strange platforms – new platforms – up in the air over my head and I just know you're on one of *them* but I can't find a way to get up there. And even when I find a stairway going up, I end in the cellars. Or I find an elevator but it goes all the way to the roof, not to stop at the platforms where you are. I have had many such dreams.'

'Why fish?' Angela asked. 'Did we meet once in a fish shop?'

'No. It was only fish once. Another time it was a brick . . . and a tiny violin . . . and a big brass key, like for a church . . . it can be anything, but always is it dangerous for me and urgent I should carry it to you. And always they give it me in a strange shop – the brick in a baker's . . . the violin in an auto-dealer . . . like that.'

'Perhaps now we have met again, that, too, will happen in the dream. I think if you find me in the next dream like that . . . how often, by the way?'

'Once or twice every month – less since I'm waiting for this baby.'

'If you find me at last, it will stop.'

Angela half-turned to go back indoors but Marianne said, 'Do you think Felix has dreams?'

'Everyone who was in a KL has dreams.'

'I thought so. Sometimes, in the morning, quite early, I see him out in the walled garden – the kitchen garden, they call it – and he's not gardening. He's just walking around touching things – touching the apple trees, the wooden posts that Sally has put up for her beans, the artichokes Nicole is growing . . . as if he needs to touch them to be sure of them. And I think, *Poor man – you had a bad night!* D'you think I'm right?'

Angela shrugged. 'I'm surprised to hear that.'

'Why?'

'Because Felix is different from most other prisoners. He went in as an artist, remained an artist, and came out as an artist. I think he is the least-damaged man I know. But hardly anyone else ever came out being the same *sort* of person as they went in. I was a sound technician before and a sound technician after, but when I was *in* Ravensbrück – not. In there I was . . . a penitential. I didn't *welcome* the punishment – no one could welcome what happened inside there – but I made myself accept it because . . . well, because of what I had been before. In fact . . .' She hesitated.

'What?'

'Perhaps we should get back to the party. They've all gone indoors for something.'

'I bet I know exactly what's happening – they're talking *Art*. Corvo is saying Art is now for the people and Eric is explaining that means committees of artists are telling each other "you itch my back and I'll itch yours".'

Angela was about to correct her but then thought, No, actually, that's right! 'You should go back to bed at least,' she said.

'I will. Just tell me what you were going to say.'

Angela thought a while before responding. 'I've never told anyone this. Certainly anyone who was in a KL would think me mad. There were two camp personnel who took special delight in hurting and humiliating me. One was an absolute beast – SS-*Aufseherin* Heugel. The other was her superior, SS-*Oberaufseherin* Völkenrath. She wasn't *too* harsh – because then my endurance would be seen as heroic and that was the last thing she wanted. It was little pinpricks all the time. Until one day she got me all alone and said, "You enjoy this, don't you! You don't feel the slightest guilt at betraying your SS oath and your old SS comrades. In fact, you're ashamed of both – and you accept humiliation as a way of purging your guilt. Well, madam, I'm not going to play your game any more." So then I had to do things to *provoke* her to punish me – which was dangerous because they'd shoot you or hang you for the smallest thing. But I had to do it.'

'Why? I would have been—'

'Otherwise the other prisoners would start to think I was still in the SS and sent to spy on them. I was like a . . . a *Seiltänzerin*, whatever that is in English – up on a high wire. High-wire dancer?' After a pause she said, 'There's something else. There was a lunatic sort of excitement in provoking her . . . steering that narrowest line between life and death. And then, after the liberation, I went to Berlin Zoo one day and, wandering around among the big cats and the bears and wolves and things – carnivores – I felt an almost irresistible urge to reach a hand into their cages and pet them. You can't actually do it, of course. You'd have to climb over the barriers. But I wanted to do it. And then I realized – I was trying to recapture that deadly excitement. I won't go near a zoo now, because one day I just might do it.'

'What about that *Oberaufseherin?* Have you ever . . .?'

'I gave the British a deposition. Hundreds of us must have done the same – about all of them. They let die Heugel off with prison. She's the one I really wanted to see hanged. But they hanged Völkenrath. Albert Pierrepoint, England's top hangman, he did it. One of the first – the thirteenth of December nineteen forty-five!' After a pause she added, 'There's a colleague at the BBC who thinks he can get me a copy of the film. They filmed all the executions, you know.'

'D'you have somewhere to sleep tonight?' Felix asked.

Angela told him that Marianne had offered one of their bedrooms – and the bed. Beds were more at a premium than rooms tonight.

'I still think it's pretty amazing,' Faith said. 'The story about you and her in the war.'

'You do understand that none of us must ever let Willard know the truth about it?'

'Of course,' Faith assured her. 'Completely.'

'And that includes telling Nicole.'

Faith was still less positive at that. 'I just hope she'll understand when the truth finally comes out.'

'Isn't that something we all have to learn?' Felix asked. 'That we *never* know the full truth about anything, so we must be careful to judge. She's doing to Marianne what those barbarians with the hair-clippers did to her – jumping to conclusions.'

'I think Marianne's wrong, mind,' Angela continued. 'Willard would be more tolerant of her past than she imagines.'

'It isn't that,' Felix said. 'You have to remember that Willard has deserted her once already. She was deeply in love with him and she thought he felt the same about her – which he *did*. But he had to go back home to Boston and try to live without her before he realized it. And during that time her life was . . . nothing. Worse than nothing. People wouldn't help her because her parents are stinking rich and they thought she should go back to them. Especially as she was under twenty-one. But she would rather starve to death than do that. So if there's only a one-in-a-million chance that Willard would desert her again, she still won't risk it.'

Angela considered this a moment and then said, 'So! *He's* the one who must be careful, then.'

'Who's left?' Tony asked Adam.

'The chief went back with Fogel in his taxi – mid-evening. The village people have all gone, I think. Most of the others came by train or bus, so they're stuck here until tomorrow – or later today, I mean. Corvo and chum have a bed in our place – next to our bedroom. I don't really want to go to bed until I'm sure they're fast asleep.'

'And – talking of which . . . your little friend Eve?'

'Why d'you say it like that?'

'Don't come all innocent! But you've got a bloody nerve . . . shitting on your own doorstep like that.'

'Like what?'

'The war's over. We've no excuse for carrying on like that now.'

'Oh, come on! She's getting married next month – to someone she calls "Trev". She just wants a bit of a fling before she walks into the trap and hears it slam shut behind her. Now where's the harm in that?'

'In an anonymous box in a no-name street in London . . . none. But . . .' Tony hesitated and then blurted it out: 'It's different – being in a community.'

'I don't see that. I think we're a pretty liberal lot here.'

'Not in that way. How d'you think Arthur's going to feel. I mean, if you're prepared to be unfaithful to Sally – right here where we all live – and with the whole community and God knows how many guests here – Arthur's going to wonder if there's anything you'd stop at. And not just Arthur.'

'You?'

'No! I bloody know you, mate. That's why I'm taking the trouble to tell you this. I think you should draw a five-mile *cordon sanitaire* around the Dower House and enjoy all your extramaritals *outside* it. Just don't shit on our dream – OK?'

Sunday, 22 June 1947

Deeply hung-over, Felix lay in a shop doorway. A *book*shop doorway – though he couldn't say how he knew that. And he couldn't bear to open his eyes, so painful was the light, even of early dawn.

He knew it was early dawn because a water cart went by, darkening the sky and sprinkling the dust. Some of it even wet his face.

But the water was warm – almost hot?

He opened his eyes and discovered it was not a water cart but a dog – one dark Z of a leg cocked up over his face.

He woke with a merciful jolt – and was less perturbed than he might otherwise have been, for it was not the first time that particular dream had jerked him awake and he had the vaguest memory of its happening to him for real, in student days in Berlin.

'I know you're awake.'

Faye . . . voice husky today.

'How d'you know I'm awake?' He still did not open his eyes
– the real ones, not the ones in the dream.

'It was the fly, crawling over your face – and, of course, the
way you cried out *"Juden raus!"*.'

'Liar!' He opened his eyes at last.

Her hair was dishevelled but her face was immaculate; makeup
could not have improved it. Objectively, he ought to be in love
with her. If this face had appeared in his waking dreams in
Mauthausen, he would have adored her beyond the point of
folly.

So why not now?

'Perhaps I dreamed it,' she said. 'What were *you* dreaming
about?'

'I couldn't possibly tell you.'

'Ooooh! Like that, was it?' She reached a delicate finger across
the small gulf between them and stroked his arm seductively.

He laughed, carefully. 'All right! I'll say this much. I was lying
asleep in a shop doorway and a dog came along and – to put
it delicately – marked his territory, which included my face.'

'Oh . . . God!' She shrank from him and curled up. 'Are all
your dreams like that?'

'I don't know. I'm sure I do dream but every bit of it usually
vanishes the moment I wake up. I don't have nightmares, if
that's what you're asking. Lots of the KL people do, but I don't.'

'Is that good or bad?'

He shrugged. 'Time will tell. But I'm certainly not going to
lie on a couch to find out.'

'You've been talking to Eric Brandon.'

'Not about that.'

'He's so scornful about psychiatry and analysis and stuff . . .
I found myself wondering if Isabella doesn't perhaps have a
weekly lie-down in some clinic in Swiss Cottage. By the way
– d'you know if Willard has taken over the Brandons' lease on
their flat in Curzon Street?'

He nodded and then winced. 'Last month, but he won't be
doing anything there – adapting it as a drawing office, I mean
– until after the baby.'

'A West End address and a Mayfair phone number . . . he's
cottoned on to the vulnerabilities of the British pretty swiftly.'

Felix sat up gingerly, favouring his head. 'I'm going to make several litres of tea. You?'

She rose from the bed, trailing an accidental sheet that fell away to reveal a living Canova – one of the Three Graces. His heart thumped an extra systole; it might or might not be love but it was just as thrilling. 'I'll wander over and patronize Willard and Tony's breakfast effort.' Deliberately prissy, she added, 'We should aawl suppaawt voluntary effaawt.'

She stood in the bath and ladled pan after pan of cold water over herself; Felix sat in the doorway and sketched swift notes on the tumbling, tossing restlessness of lithe flesh. Then, because she had left the plug in, he lay in the bath and rolled over and over in the fractionally warmer water while she, towelling herself, said, 'I can see – and I mean literally *see* – why the public schools go in for all those cold baths.'

A short while later, as Felix waited for the electric kettle to boil, she crossed the yard and, happening to glance up, saw Marianne and Angela at one of the top-floor windows. She flapped an exhausted hand at them and they waved back.

'D'you think she suits Felix?' Angela asked.

'I don't think anyone suits Felix,' Marianne replied. 'He's a beset – beseiged? – artist. He'll offer himself to his work . . .'

'Sacrifice himself.'

'Yes, sacrifice. So he wouldn't understand why his lover should come before.'

'But,' Angela objected, 'Faith is "beset" too – a fanatic. She's fanatic about Faith. Felix is dedicated to his art and Faith is dedicated to Faith's career. Perhaps they are ideal for each other?'

Marianne took a step back and eyed her shrewdly. 'But that's not what *you* hope?'

Angela smiled slightly and gazed at a floating tealeaf in her mug. 'I don't think love is ever possible for me again. And I suspect it may not be possible for Felix, either. So – in a completely different way – maybe I'm as ideal for him as Faith?'

'Were you ever in love – really deep? Really hot?'

'I had a schoolgirl passion – I mean, I was twenty but it was very schoolgirlish – a passion for Heydrich. That shows how good *my* judgement was!'

Marianne shrugged. 'I was the same for Speer – at eighteen. They could be very charming, those high-up Nazis. Very imponering.'

'Impressive. Yes. But there was a young man, a lighting technician at UFA, who . . .' She fell into a brief reverie, which ended with a shrug. 'What the hell – he died at Stalingrad. What about you?'

'Nobody in Germany, but there was a boy at . . . Konstfackskolan? Art and technical school? Had he come to Germany after the war, looking for me, maybe if Willard had not found me that time he came back . . .'

'Have you heard about him since? D'you know what he's doing now?'

Marianne shook her head. 'You choose *this* door, you never find out what lies behind *that* door.' After a pause she added, 'And perhaps it's best. Since the fifteenth of April, all is changed for me.'

Angela darted her a surprised glance . . . then twigged what she meant. 'Oh!' she said with a mildly embarrassed laugh. 'Yes, of course.'

'Why? Does the date mean something to you, too?'

Angela was silent a long moment before saying, quietly, 'It was the day they indicted SS-*Aufseherin* Ruth Neudeck who was head of the extermination camp at Ravensbrück. The British sentenced her to death and they'll hang her in Hameln any day now. My God, you and Willard were getting together again not half a dozen miles from where she was standing trial!'

'You don't . . . let be? Can one say "let be"?'

'I could tell you the day and the hour when each of them was caught – the ones who didn't kill themselves – their trials, the verdicts . . . everything. Don't tell this to Felix. He wants all that to be over and done for. It isn't, of course, but he needs to over-live it in his own way.'

Marianne pressed her: 'You don't think his way might be better?'

'For him, yes. For me . . . what I'd really like is . . . no. Some other time.'

'More tea?'

Angela tilted her head toward the window. 'Talking of Felix – can you keep a secret? Oh! What a stupid question! The thing is

– Felix and I met before the war. And we *almost* fell in love. In fact, I think I did. He's forgotten it, thank heavens.'

'Why?'

She pulled a face. 'I was a bit of a Nazi in those days. More than a bit – a *Lumpen-Nazi*. He hasn't actually forgotten the occasion, but he doesn't remember it was me. My hair was cropped very short then. We went rowing on the Wannsee. That's how I pricked up my ears when they talked about arresting him. He was the "boyfriend" – if you can call him that after only one day – he was the one I thought most about in the KL. I nearly had a heart attack when he walked into Schmidt's that day.' She sighed. 'Anyway – he's out there in the garden. And he's doing what you said – touching everything. I think I'll go and find out about all that.'

Halfway to the door she paused. 'You know that moment – when you think you may be falling in love? You look at him and you're thinking, I want to see a lot more of you, or even something so trivial like, The way your beard curls round just below your ear . . . it gives me gooseflesh of pleasure! You know that feeling?'

Marianne nodded.

'I think the first time Felix and I met again, since the war – or the first time we actually talked to each other – we went for a walk into Regents Park and he picked me a rose and held it here, beside my face, and he said, "No – you still win".' She laughed. 'And then he was so embarrassed! But he did it without thinking, you see. And what *I* think is that he had that first falling-in-love moment and it *horrified* him!'

'Horrified? Why?'

'I don't know. Did he think love – the capacity for love – was dead inside him and this was the horror of seeing the dead come to life? Or did he think *I* couldn't manage . . . couldn't respond? Because . . . I mean, we both know hundreds of KL survivors who honestly couldn't. No matter how loving the other person was or how much their . . . their intellect persuaded them to try. Love is still years away for them. Did he think I'm like that?'

'And are you?'

'No!'

'That's very positive!'

'Until that moment I wasn't sure. But when he did that thing

with the rose and when I felt my own response . . . then I
knew!'

Felix closed his eyes and ran his fingertips over the boughs of
the apple tree – a Ribstone Pippin, Sally had told him. He
murmured the name syllable by slow syllable. Pippin was a good
name for a girl. If ever he had a daughter, that's what he'd call
her – Pippin Breit. His fingers sensed the different textures of
the top of the bough, where the wood was in tension and the
fibres were knotted in the king of all tangles, and then the under-
side, where it was in compression and the fibres had a long
wavy form you could feel but not actually see. He had met
these fibres before – in seasoned wood, ready for carving. It
was a thrill to feel them here in their making.

And the new scars where children had climbed. And old scars
where skilled gardeners had opened out the heart of each tree
to light and air – scars that begged the community to repeat
the therapy before the wood went wild and gave nothing but
little crabs.

Some sixth sense made him open his eyes at last.

Angela – gazing at him from the path, three or four paces
away. 'Do you see something different when you close your
eyes and use your fingers?' she asked.

'It's as immobile as any sculpture, but there's a life inside it
– a living quality . . . a *livingness* – that sculpture can never
achieve. Do you know Bernini's *Portrait of Mister Baker* in the
V&A? Old Bernini could make marble look like flesh in ecstasy,
but even so, it still *feels* like marble.'

'If they heated it?' she suggested.

'That's a thought!' He laughed and, returning to the path,
linked arms with her. 'You are a very practical lady. How are
you feeling this morning?'

'*Fragile*.' She pronounced it the French way – *frah-zheel*.

'Too *frahzheel* for a gentle stroll around this wilderness?'

'I can probably manage that.'

They set off at a funereal pace to circle the semi-cleared half
of the walled garden.

'How's Marianne?' he asked. 'A little less nervous about your
reunion, I hope?'

'I hope so, too.'

'You haven't talked about it?'

He felt her arm lift as she shrugged. 'There's too much else to talk about. We're both women, after all.' The shrug turned into a laugh. 'Perhaps you've noticed?'

'*Touché*,' he said.

'Do you think she misses her family? She likes to give an impression that she's calm and relaxed but every now and then I feel a —' she clenched her fist — 'a sort of . . . like knots inside her.'

'Well, it can't be easy — being married to Willard. She absolutely adores him — I'm not saying otherwise — but that doesn't make it easy.'

'I don't know him, obviously. Yesterday he seemed very . . . American. Easy . . . casual . . .'

'Try ruthless . . . driven . . . focussed . . . unsleeping . . . Tony and Adam saw him in action in the war — and I don't mean with a gun. He carved out a Europe-wide empire of favours done and favours owed. Nothing illegal. Just a good ol' boy doing well by doing good. And now he's doing exactly the same thing among the architectural elite and the planning elite and the business elite here in England. Twenty years from now we'll be able to walk around London, looking at all the grand new towers of steel and glass growing out of old bombsites, and we'll say Willard . . . Willard . . . Willard . . .'

'Oooiiy!'

'Ask Adam. Ask Tony. When you know them better, they'll tell you more.'

After a pause she asked, 'How will I get to know them better?'

He was silent a moment, too. Then he said, 'Time. Give it time.' They were approaching an area where comfrey had completely ousted every other plant. Bindweed, cleaver, hairy bittercress, brambles — all the invasive scourges of the average garden had here met their match. 'I must do something about this,' he said glumly.

'Why just you?'

He hung his head. 'It's my fault, that's why. I chopped the roots all up with a cultivator we bought in the spring. I thought it would kill them, but . . .' He waved a hand to complete the confession.

'It's interesting about Marianne,' Angela said. 'D'you think she's right about Nicole Palmer? If Nicole knew the truth about her?'

'How can anyone know things like that for certain? Nicole is very warm . . . very passionate . . . and completely honest. But honest like a child. You know how a child can try to deceive you, and be convinced it's working, but their very honesty gives them away? If we told her the truth about Marianne's war and asked her not to change all of a sudden, only gradually, she would try to go on sniping at Marianne – I mean, she'd see why Marianne thinks it would be necessary – and she'd really try her best. But everyone else would see through it. Her honesty would give her away. So Marianne doesn't want to take the chance of letting Willard know the truth.' After a pause he added, 'And I can see her point.'

'And yet Nicole spied for the French Resistance. Throughout the war. And she was never found out – in fact, she fooled her own people so well that they cut her hair off!'

'I know. I was thinking the very same when I was saying those things. But, you see, I don't believe she ever pretended to *like* the Germans. She just saw it was necessary to cooperate with them in order to survive . . . and they accepted that as a businesslike arrangement. She was efficient, impersonal . . . she hid all feelings . . . didn't criticize or complain. And they accepted her at her own valuation. She didn't need to pretend *emotionally*, you see. But that's exactly what she'd have to do if she learned the truth about what Marianne really did in the war and the risks she took.' He sighed. 'Standing here isn't going to clear this comfrey.'

The resumed their slow perambulation.

'Pigs!' Angela said suddenly.

'Eh?'

'If you could fence this off . . . we made a film at UFA in the first year of the war – how to clear land when you couldn't get petrol for the tractor. You fence the land all round and you put pigs inside it. You'd have to find out if they like comfrey roots and if they're not poisonous . . .'

'We are thinking of getting a pig, in fact – to feed off the scraps we throw away.'

'A couple of pigs would clear that patch inside a week – and leave it better than ploughing.'

As they closed the gate behind them and turned toward the big house, they saw Tony coming toward them. 'Is Nicole there?' he called out, still twenty paces off. 'She came out to gather some herbs. She usually starts there.' He halted and faced more toward the west. 'Damn! She must be down in the coppice. Bloody naughty – she knows she's near her time.' And he set off at a smart trot.

'Shall we come and help look for her?' Angela called after him.

'No – we have a special family whistle. Thanks all the same.'

A moment later they heard it as he stood at the woodland edge – six piercing notes to the rhythm of diddy-diddy-diddy.

'She can't possibly miss *that*!' Felix said.

'E-flat, E-flat, C, C, E-flat, E-flat.'

He threw back his head and laughed – without wincing now. 'I see a white shirt, grey trousers, a touch of red in his hair, all against the deep blue shadow of the woodland, hatched with the pale brown of the coppiced trees – all notes of colour. And you hear notes of music. We live in different worlds, eh?'

This time she slipped her arm through his. 'Complementary worlds?' she offered.

Thursday, 17 July 1947

Willard took the steps down into the Palmers' flat three at a time. 'Hey-hey – buddy-boy!' he called to Tony, who was wrestling with a tape measure on the first-floor landing. 'Could you dash through to the Prentices and tell May that Marianne thinks her time has come?' Over his shoulder he added, 'I've called Mrs Harpur and I'll meet her in the yard because she'll never remember her way up in the dark.'

The last of his explanation was more inferred than heard over the thud of his shoes as he raced for the ground floor.

Nicole emerged from their bedroom. 'I heard,' she said. And, passing him, she started up the stairs.

'What d'you think you're doing?' Tony asked. 'Go back to bed. Everything's all right. It's all in hand.'

Nicole turned at the entrance to the Johnsons' flat. 'Someone must be with her till May comes. You get May – go on, go on, go on!' And she was gone.

She found Marianne lying on the bed, wearing only a parachute-silk slip. The sheets were kicked away onto the floor. She was forcing herself to breathe deeply and slowly – until, that is, she saw who her visitor was. 'What?' she panted. 'Willard said . . .' She struggled to sit up.

'Lie down! Tony has gone for May but it's best you not are alone. She comes soon. But I have delivered two babies myself.' Seeing Marianne's wide-eyed response to this, she added, 'Not mine! But girls in the Maquis who could not risk . . . you understand?'

Marianne nodded – and relaxed slightly.

'*Ah oui*,' Nicole said as she jerked the creases out of the undersheet. 'The risk! You also understand, I think. The risk . . . the war . . . the Nazis . . . secrets . . . the risk. You understand!'

Marianne half-whimpered, half-laughed. 'Nicole! Dear, dear Nicole! This is not the time . . .'

Nicole ploughed on: 'This Angela – the friend of Felix. She is from a concentration camp in the war, yes?' She broke off suddenly. 'How often are the . . .' She mimed the idea of contractions by clenching and unclenching her fist.

But Marianne took it for the communist salute and slumped in abject disappointment.

'So bad?' Nicole asked. She suddenly remembered the word from her pre-natal talk with Mrs Harpur. 'The contractions! How . . . *souvent*? Often?'

Marianne was gripped by one at that very moment. Nicole clasped her hand and, recalling how long she had been in the room, said, 'OK – it's not near yet. It's lots of time. Just relax. Breathe like she told us. Just relax.'

The spasm passed. Marianne stretched out and, closing her eyes, said, 'No more talk of the war, eh? Nor the Nazis? Nor risk?' She even managed a yawn.

'You were not Nazi,' Nicole murmured. 'That Angela would never have been so close with you. I know I am . . . they say "emotional" but not a fool. One day you will tell me all of it, but already I know – from Angela behaving at you – I know you were not Nazi! Sssshh! Rest now. It's good. It's all right.'

The relief from the pain of that minor contraction was like a narcotic. She felt her mind go spiralling down into . . . but no! Nicole's words penetrated at that moment. 'What?' she asked as she struggled once again to sit up. 'What did . . . I mean, has Angela . . . or . . . ?'

'Shhh! It's no matter now.'

'But Felix was friendly with me from the beginning, too. Didn't that make you think?'

Nicole gave a huge, Gallic shrug and said, 'Oh . . . Feeelix!'

'What's that mean?'

'If Himmler himself would stand before Felix and give him his coat and said, "Brush that for me, please?" Felix will do it. He is a saint. Besides, he is a man and you are . . . quite . . . beautiful.'

'There was nothing like *that*, I can promise you!'

Another shrug. 'There is always *something* "like that". Shall I comb your hairs? It always relaxes me.'

And that was the scene which greeted Willard on his return. 'Well, fan my brow and part my hair!' he exclaimed from the doorway.

'You must go!' Nicole was shocked. 'Your part is long over – and your next part will soon begin. But not now.'

'He can stay,' Marianne murmured, stroking Nicole's arm cajolingly.

'Here?'

'In Sweden many men assist at the birth – and I mean *assister à* as well.'

'Tskoh!' Nicole raised her eyes but made no outright objection.

Willard crossed to the far side of the bed and half-lay half-sat beside Marianne. 'How is it, honey? May is out for the evening. Tony's down waiting for Mrs Harpur.'

Nicole answered for her, 'She has have . . . has *had* one twinge. But the water is not broken. Oh, this barbarian's tongue!' She glanced up at Willard and asked, truculently, 'What are you thinking, then?'

'I'm just thinking, Nicole, how profoundly grateful I am – to *you*.'

'*Moi?*'

'To you, that when it counts – when it really, really counts – you can turn round like this.'

'Tony says "bury the hatchet". If we cannot bury the hatchet and make a different . . . *avenir* . . .'

'Future,' Marianne offered.

'Vous pouvez parler français?' she asked in surprise.

'Mais bien sûr!'

'Tiens! Tu n'as pas dit . . .'

'Et quant à vous? Vous n'avez pas demandé!'

Willard cleared his throat delicately

'Ha!' Nicole reached the comb across Marianne and tapped Willard on the wrist with it. 'You see! Your wife has the English, German, French . . . and *naturellement* Swedish. *Moi* – I have English, German, French, and a little Spanish. We are European. You Americans and English, you are . . . *isolés.*'

Willard winked at her. 'When de Gaulle asked Ike to get the Yanks out of France by New Year's, Ike said, "Including the ones we buried here?"'

And Marianne just lay there wondering whether that switch from *vous* to *tu* meant anything other than that Nicole was more than a little 'thoughtspread' – as the Swedish word has it.

Just before midnight Marianne was delivered, with no complications, of a healthy, placid, elfin-faced baby girl. Mrs Harpur laid the gory little bundle on her newly deflated belly and said, 'Ten fingers, ten toes. We'll just wait for the afterbirth. D'you think you could manage one more small push, there's a dear?'

When it came, she held it up and massaged the cord down toward the baby. 'This is something I can never get the doctors to do,' she said. 'There's a fair bit of blood in that and I don't see why the babies shouldn't get it. There now! She'll thrive the better for that. *And* – do you notice? No crying! They hardly ever cry if they get that extra bit of blood.' She clamped the cord and severed it. 'I'll just weigh the mite.'

'Right!' Willard stopped mopping Marianne's forehead. 'Roedean it is. I'll get her name down tomorrow.' He checked his watch. 'Later today.'

'You'd be more use bringing in that warm water,' Mrs Harpur told him. 'Seven pounds two ounces. A good weight for a firstborn – I'm surprised you didn't show more. Test it with your elbow.' She carried the baby back to the bed. 'Hold her till the hot water comes.'

The baby, half-wrapped in a towel, fitted snugly into the arc of Marianne's arm. All those hours spent savouring this moment in her imagination had not prepared her for this intensity of pleasure; her eyes filled with tears.

'Her head will change shape to more normal soon enough. Have you got a name for her?'

'Siri. She looks lovely though, doesn't she – even squashed like this? Look at those eyes.'

Mrs Harpur laughed. 'All their eyes have that intense colour. It won't last forever.'

'I want four,' Marianne said. 'Three more.'

Willard returned with the water, singing, as he barged the door with his butt: '*Mairzy doats and dozy doats and liddle lamzy divey . . .*' The baby did a three-stage yawn.

'Shh!' Marianne warned him. 'You'll wake up the Palmers and the Prentices.'

The midwife took the baby, tested the water, and started to wash away the gore.

'As a matter of fact,' Willard said, 'one reason I was so long was that Tony came up to say Nicole wouldn't let him sleep until we had some news. Then he heard the Prentices returning, so they had to come up, too. May says she's very sorry. It would happen the night they were out. I told her all's well. May I hold her?' Willard took his daughter and, demonstratively careful to support her head, cradled her in his right arm. 'Aintcha gonna open your eyes, li'l darlin'?' he asked. 'I wouldn't blame you, mind – keepin' 'em shut. Oh! You heard me! My-oh-my – but you're gonna break a l-o-t o' hearts with them peepers. Oh yes – you surely are.'

She gave a shivery little sigh and closed her eyes again. He passed her down to Marianne. 'D'you feed her now?'

'Tomorrow.'

Mrs Harpur said, 'Siri – where's that name from, then?'

Willard answered, 'Marianne had a Cousin Siri who died in the war. She used to ferry Danish Jews across to Sweden and . . . the boat capsized one night. It's a name to carry with pride.'

Shrewdly Mrs Harpur detected an edge to his tone. 'You'd have preferred something more American?'

He shook his head. 'Not once I heard that story.'

The woman nodded. 'I'll take the placenta, then. Unless . . . ?'

'Unless what?'

'Unless someone's got dogs here?'

'Oh – thank you for that!' Willard shut his eyes tight.

'My dog thrives on them.'

'Nicole!' Marianne said. 'Xupé and Fifi can share it. Put it in the fridge, honey.'

'Honestly?' He stared at her, still not entirely believing.

'Honestly. It's good.'

He laughed feebly and turned to the midwife. 'Well! I've heard of some peace offerings in my time but this beats the band. We haven't always seen eye-to-eye with Mrs Palmer, below, but tonight she was magnificent.'

'Good – that's what I like to hear.' She turned to Marianne. 'I'll pop back tomorrow sometime. And I should warn you – they don't always enter this world so easy and so quick as that.'

Willard took her back to the yard door and watched her wobble away on her bicycle, a mere silhouette against the feeble yellow circle of her front lamp. When he returned to the bedroom he fished out a key, and went to unlock one of the cupboards. 'Shall we put her in her crib?' he asked airily.

'What crib?'

He pulled out a modernistic affair, all bent out of a single sheet of laminated wood.

Marianne propped herself up on one elbow and stared. 'It's beautiful! Have you made that?'

'Designed it. I got Len to make it up – the guy we met at the Haymarket Theatre? He's pretty good. This could be a prototype. We've had ten pounds of potatoes in it and we couldn't rock it to overturn. Wanna try it?'

'That bedding – it's aired?'

'It's bone-dry in there. Feel it.'

'Well – OK. She's deep asleep. It must be hell – what she went through.'

'It wasn't exactly paradise for you, either, honey.'

They laid her in the crib and Willard went to take a shower. 'All's well?' he asked when he returned.

Marianne nodded slowly, in time to rocking the crib.

He put his hand to the dimmer – a 6kW monster liberated

from a voltage regulator for an entire Quonset hut. 'Sleep?' he asked. 'You've been through a lot, honey. I was so proud of you.'

'Well, thanks-you kind, sir. I'm glad you were there. Actually, I don't feel very tired. Let's just lie back and look at the moon and talk.'

'About Nicole?' He dimmed the lights.

'Yes. I must explain to you about Nicole.'

But Willard already had a theory of his own. 'When you took – remember at the midsummer party, when you took a plate of smörgåsar over to her stand . . .'

'And she looked . . . knives?'

'Daggers.'

'She looked daggers at me.'

'Yeah, but when you walked away – I was watching her – and she raised her hand like this and opened her mouth, as if she was going to call you back. But then she caught sight of me watching her and she all clammed up again. I think she was going to make it up there and then. And now, this evening, or yesterday evening – the birth and all – it gave her the best chance ever and she took it.' Only then did he ask, 'Has she explained it to you?'

'She said it was seeing me and Angela Worth together . . . knowing that Angela was in a concentration camp, and being so friendly with me . . .'

'What does she know about Angela – apart from that?'

'I don't know. It was hardly the occasion when one could—'

'No – of course not. But what do *we* know about her, come to that. She told me she was a communist.'

Marianne felt there would never be a better time than this. 'She secretly recorded an important Nazi conference – on the orders of Heydrich. It was all about *die Endlösung der Judenfrage.* The *Vernichtung.*'

'My God – is that what they called it!'

'After Heydrich was assassinated they said she should have told them. And for that they sent her to Ravensbrück.' She drew a deep breath before she continued. 'If they had known she also made a transcript, they would have shot her instead. In fact, she made two transcripts. When she knew it was only a matter of days before they arrested her, she gave one to a friend in Berlin.'

'And the other?'

'The other she gave to me to pass on to the Swedish embassy.'

Willard whistled, almost silently. 'You go way back,' he said quietly. 'This is something you never told me, honey?'

'There's a lot you did in the war you never told me, either. Not that I *want* to know, mind. It's over. That's all over. And there are many things we never mention because – for some – it's *not* over, and life is still cheap in Germany.'

'I guess that's right. So . . . why did she give a copy to *you*?'

'If I tell you, will you keep it secret? It must never be told to anyone else. Not your family. Not our children. Otherwise I won't tell you.'

He thought it over. 'Boy – this had better be worth it!' he said at last.

'Angela gave me many documents. That conference so shocked her that she joined the Resistance – or she became a one-woman resistance. And why me? Because we were friends after that day in Speer's office and because I had legitimate reasons to call on the Swedish embassy. I took copies of many secret Nazi documents there, including that transcript . . .'

'You were a spy? Hey – you were an anti-Nazi spy!'

Marianne shook her head. 'I was a go-between. That was all.'

'Did you take stuff from Speer's office – or only what Angela Worth gave you?'

She shrugged. 'Both.'

'Then you were, too, a *spy*! You should get a medal. Why didn't you ever say anything about this?'

'That's why it's so secret. It must never come out that the Swedish embassy – the *neutral* Swedish embassy – carried out espionage in an alien—'

'Oh, oh, oh!' Willard's cry would have been a lot louder but for little Siri. 'Honey! Honey-*chile*! *Every* embassy of *every* nation in *every* capital engages in espionage and *every*body knows it.'

'I'm not a complete fool, Willard. But it's one thing for people to know it generally and quite different to have exact details – names, years, particular embassies. Those diplomats I met – they are real individuals with real names. And they may be working in Washington now. Or London. Or India . . . Persia . . . Moscow! How can they do their work properly if every foreign ministry in the world has stark facts on file that they are spies. If you should know that an American diplomat is a spy . . . if you have names, places, dates . . . do you tell the world? Do you tell *anyone*? I don't think so. I *hope* not. Well, I am a patriotic Swede, too. And if it was the price to pay that I not prove to Nicole that I, too, was anti-Nazi . . . *alors* – so it had to be.'

Chastened, he said, 'OK, OK. I guess you're right. By God, I didn't think it was possible for me to be more proud of you than I already was. But for me, you'll always wear a purple heart – even if I'm the only one to see it.'

She gave his arm a squeeze.

He lay back and watched the first blush of the false dawn suffuse the southern sky.

Ten days later Xupé and Fifi had another treat when their mistress had a six-and-a-half-pound baby boy, whom they named Andrew Mercier Palmer; Nicole felt that her Uncle Pierre Mercier was wealthy enough to deserve having her firstborn named after him.

Monday, 25 August 1947

That autumn Willard moved his office to the Brandons' old flat in Curzon Street. He bought a little Bedford van, put an old Victorian sofa and a milking stool in the back, and drove to and from Welwyn North with Tony, Adam, and Faith to share the petrol. Adam's Jowett stayed at the Dower House for emergencies, visits to the post-natal clinic, and so on. If any of the wage slaves wanted to get home earlier, they could usually rely on a lift from Garden City with Todd, who worked shorter hours than Willard. Everyone worked shorter hours than Willard.

One evening, when Faith had done just that, she turned to Todd, as he lifted the bonnet to drain the radiator, and said, 'Look at him!' She pointed to the studio window, where Felix was just sitting and staring at something in the room 'I don't know what to do with him. Guess what he's doing.'

'Having trouble with the sculpture?' Todd guessed.

'No. With a bloody letter. It came two days ago and he's done nothing but stare at it ever since.'

'Two solid days?'

'No. I mean he's done nothing *with the letter* but stare at it. Nothing can stop him sculpting.'

'Maybe he already knows what's in it? Who's it from?'

'From a neighbour of his father's. When they lived in Berlin. Before the war. And he thinks he knows what's in it.'

'He was in one of them concentration camps, wasn't he, poor sod. I look at him sometimes and try to imagine, but it's impossible, isn't it. I mean – to live somewhere where the police can just walk in and take your life away. Without any law. It's never been like that here, has it. What's he think is in this letter, anyway?'

'It's quite bulky and you can feel other papers . . . documents . . . maybe even other letters inside. He thinks they may be from his father. So if it means his father's still alive – they quarrelled, you know, quite badly – then that's one sort of problem. But if it means his father's dead, then that's a different sort of problem. But it's a problem either way. And he just doesn't want to face it.'

Todd hesitated before saying, 'You don't know whether to push him or not, eh?'

She sighed. 'It's not the sort of problem that gets easier by being left to fester, is it. I try not to go on and on . . . anyway, he's only listening half the time.'

'And you don't speak German yourself?'

She saw his drift and, for a moment, it seemed like the answer; but the hope faded as quickly as it had risen. 'Not nearly well enough.'

'What about Marianne? Or Nicole? They all seem to speak each other's lingos – beats me how they do it.'

'Todd! Darling Todd!' In a fit of exuberance she flung her arms about him and kissed his ear. 'You've hit it!'

'And you've found the way to get your Felix to take an interest in us at last.'

She released him, snatched up her briefcase, and ran across the yard to the cottage. 'Don't worry,' she shouted to Felix as she slammed the front door. 'It's just a little fling Todd and I are having. It doesn't mean a thing.'

He chuckled as he came from the studio to take her coat. 'What were you talking about?'

'That!' She pointed at the still-unopened letter.

'You discussed our . . . no, *my* personal affairs with him?'

'Yes! Yes! Yes! Because I can't discuss it with *you* . . . and it's eating you out with worry . . . and it's wearing me down, too. But Todd – wonderful, man-managing Todd, who knows more about human nature than you or I will ever fathom – he has come up with the answer.'

She held her breath, forcing him to ask, 'Which is?'

'It's obvious once you put your mind to it. We give it to Marianne, or Nicole – or, come to think of it, both – and ask them to read it and then either break whatever news there is gently to you or urge you to read it yourself. And there are no two people better – in all the world, I'd say – to do you that service. But I'm not going to push it on you. I'll say no more. You can pour us a cocktail and I'll . . . open a tin of baked beans or something.'

In fact, she produced a tasty dinner of leek, bacon, and potato pie and bread-and-butter pudding. After which they went across the yard to the Wilsons and finished a game of Monopoly they had started four nights earlier. And then they went to bed and made pleasant, rather dreamy love for quite a while.

Ten minutes after that, when normally they would both have been fast asleep, he said, 'OK . . . but tell them it's a favour to you – not to me!'

And she answered at once and not at all sleepily, 'You think it *wouldn't* be a favour to me? My God – where have you been these past two days?'

When Nicole returned the letter – or letters, in fact – she handed them to Felix but spoke to Faith. 'He used to call her Tante Uschi.'

'I know that,' Felix said. 'What does she say?' He reached for the letters.

'You have to read them. They are from your father and very beautiful. You will be proud. It's nothing to hurt you.'

'Cup of tea?' Faith asked.

Nicole laughed. 'You English! Cup of tea! Crisis? Cup of tea! Yes please.' She sat down and let out a great sigh. 'Babies! Andrew is *just* sleeping through the night, but now he's more awake by day, of course! It's no peace.'

'I'll go and read these upstairs,' Felix said.

There were two letters from Frau Schneider – Tante Uschi to him. One of them was marked 'Read this first':

> My precious little Felix!
> I have learned from the Americans that you survived the war, and the KL at Mauthausen, they say, and so this is the happiest Week in my life for many Years. And you are safely in England, too, which makes me happier still. Let us all hope that Europe has now lost its Appetite for Wars for ever. After so much Suffering we deserve it, and you most certainly deserve Prosperity and a good Life in England.
>
> But now I must risk making more Unhappiness for you, though when you read these Letters from your Father you will understand why it must be so. And later, perhaps, when you take in Everything he has to tell you, you will feel as proud of him as any Son could be. But first I must explain why there are two Letters from me, both with the same date. This one is to tell you Everything you need to know before you read the first Letter from your Father. The second is to explain certain Things to you after you have read all he has to say. His Letters were certainly not written on the same Day – not even in the same Decade. He did not date them, which was typical, but the first was written in Berlin, in your old Apartment there, shortly before the War broke out; the second was written quite a long Time after we moved to Kiel, which we did in February, 1942.
>
> To me it will always be just Yesterday that he went away, and the Pain of it is as sharp as ever it was. For you, I hope it may have something of an opposite Effect. Your last Parting with your Father was full of Anger and Bitterness, but you were in the Right and he in the Wrong. I tell you that now. But I think I know my dear little Felix well enough to be sure that all those awful Things that have happened to you since have softened your Judgement – also that these Letters, one of them the last your Father ever

wrote, will bring you all the Way back to the Love and
Admiration you would surely feel if he were here at my
right Hand and you at my left. Oh, if only I could make
that Bridge right now! To take each of you by your Hands
and join them. I would give those few Years that now
remain to me – all of them I'd give – to be able to do that.

Well, if I can't do it in this Life, I'll do it in the next.
And this Letter and its Contents are a Preparation for such
a wonderful Moment. I know you don't believe in all that,
but you will see. I shall have the last Laugh.

Now you'll see there is another Letter from me in this
Packet. Please read the Letters from your Father before
opening that one. I'll say no more now. Open your Father's
letters and read them.

All my Love
Tante Uschi.

There were two letters from his father, as well, marked only 1
and 2, each numeral circled in red. Perversely, Felix saw his
hands move toward the one marked 2, as if, even now, he could
not obey his father in the smallest detail.

Grow up! he told himself and unfolded the first letter.

My dear Son,

It is now three years since you left Berlin. News reaches
me now and then – you are in Prague . . . in Vienna
. . . in Paris. Perhaps you are in all three – and more?
Back with my brother in America? Otto tells me you are
on Goebbels' list of decadent artists – the ones they
threaten to liquidate. Willi agrees you are on the list but
very low down. Does this, I wonder, mean you are not
a very good decadent artist? Maybe you have a base in
England from which you make these visits? I hope so.
But where shall I send this letter? Would 'Felix Breit,
Paris' find you? If you are that famous, then I must eat
every word I spoke to you when we parted for what is
now, probably, the final time. Anyway, I write in the hope
that this will one day, somehow, reach you. The minute
I hear of a reliable address for you, I will send it. All
Germany's finest are now scattered to the winds. Europe

is quite simply not possible with this Third Reich at its heart.

If it reaches you – and where it reaches you – will depend mostly, I'm afraid, on how efficient the Nazis are with their racial genealogies. My father was such a Jew-hater that I always suspected we were of Jewish descent, but, for the sake of peace, I never raised the question with him and I never passed on my doubts to you. I was an agnostic with tendencies toward Buddhism; you – when I last knew you – were an ardent atheist. ('God is a cancer on the face of Reason' remember?) Why upset ourselves with a past that had no bearing?

Well, now it most certainly has a bearing. Old Billy Breit's anti-Semitism was so fierce and so public that all the world (except us) suspected he had been born a Jew. He didn't look Jewish. Nor do I. Nor do you. But these Nazis are bound to have recorded that suspicion (to put it at its weakest) somewhere. They miss nothing and they follow up everything. They have even persuaded the Catholics to hand over all records of Jews who converted. If there is a war, I hope they will lose it not because of bad generals but because they will be too busy hunting down Jews, communists, poofs, and other subhumans to fight properly. If my suspicions are true, then I am only what these new 'Nuremberg Laws' call a Mischling – a half-Jew. I would be permitted to keep a caged bird but not to walk in the state forests and I could only sit out on a balcony over a main street after dark. (I'm inventing these rules but it will be something like that.) Perhaps they will expel all full-Jews before they start on the half-ones. And you would only be a quarter-Jew.

And I'm certain they mean to expel every last Jew from the Fatherland. They talk of Madagascar as a new Jewish homeland, but if war comes before that gets going, they'll deport them to the East, among the Slavs, whom they also classify as less than human. Jews and Slavs as neighbours? What does history teach about that! Maybe they mean the Slavs to finish the Jews off this time – which they will do willingly before the Master Race turns on them.

It's all our own fault, of course, for voting for the Nazi

Ermächtigungsgesetz in '33 – carte blanche for them. When the Allies took away our colonies after 1918 we smarted. Then the Nazis gave us this vision of becoming the colonial master-race of Europe and, like all colonial masters – the English, the French, the Americans are no different – we liberals believed in democracy and freedom and equality but not for our colonial subjects.

The one great hopeful sign for me personally is that I'm still a member of the Reichschriftumskammer and so can still continue to write and be published. They've expelled all the Jews, who can now only write and sell their work abroad, for a fraction of what they used to earn here in Germany. But what do we write? Tales of Jacob – Mann; something historical about Austria-Hungary – Roth; Nero – Feuchtwanger; Erasmus – Zweig . . . old history. Who dares to write anything about modern Germany?

All these thoughts of mine can be boiled down to one sentence: Do not even consider coming home. If you are in France, go to England. If in England, then America. You cannot get far enough away from these swine. I see them every day in the streets – here in our beautiful Berlin where, just a few years ago, life was so vital, so rich – I see them humiliating the Jews, making their lives a misery. Last week an old Jewess – she must have been eighty if not more – she dropped a glass jar of Sauerkraut and it smashed on the pavement, and two of this new breed of policemen made her go down on her hands and knees and eat it up – while they made noises snorting like pigs. And laughing, of course. Even when she cut her tongue on the glass they did not let her stop. And I did nothing! Well, I came back home and I drew their faces, quite good likenesses, and I wrote a full statement and perhaps one day, with a different regime, something will be done. One brave Lutheran pastor told them the old woman had had enough and they should stop; they just took his name and address and went on tormenting her (in the language of Goethe and Schiller, too). Next week, next month, his congregation will be told their pastor has gone for 're-education'. And when he comes back, he will no longer obstruct the police.

When things like this happen – and they happen often – the people just stand and watch, as if it were an opera – yes, something very familiar by Wagner. I'm surprised they don't bring opera glasses.

I would leave this miserable country myself except that I cannot desert Tante Uschi. But I'll explain that later. First, I want to tell you where I believe everything went wrong between us, you and me. It started when your mother drowned in that dreadful accident with Opa; all I wanted for myself was to be dead, too. I know we argued a lot, and quite bitterly, but it was a kind of love, you know. I cannot say I actually hated you but I resented your being there, needing me to take care of you, feed you, buy your clothes, schoolbooks, take you on holidays – I didn't know your mother did so many things for your welfare and upbringing until she was no longer there. And, like every adolescent boy, you were too absorbed in the rages and passions and miseries of growing up even to notice what sacrifices I was making. (These are the thoughts and feelings of me-then, not me-now.) You grieved for your mother, you grieved often, but you never grieved for very long each time. Grief was something you fitted in between going down to the park with your pals, and bantering with the girls, and doing stunts on your bicycle, and all those other things that took you out of the house while I did the household accounts and answered letters from your teachers and tried to find out from your friends' mothers where to buy clothes for you and what to do for acne and . . . on and on like that. My grief was day-long and night-long and yours came in such short bursts. Intense, yes, but soon spent. We were as different as Day and Night in our grieving.

I don't believe that our father-son friendship – and son-father friendship, too – ever recovered from the absence between us of your mother. What made it worse was that I never spoke of it to you and so you had no way of opening the subject with me. I understand that so clearly now, but back then, since something within me refused to broach the subject, I – what is that word the psychologists use? Transferred? Projected? Displaced? No matter – I did all of that in criticizing, opposing, mocking, belittling you.

Sometimes nowadays I go off to sleep very quickly and then, quite soon, wake up again, filled with a great unease. And then I know what's coming next. I will recall, word for word, angry look for angry look, some argument we had in those awful years. But even more shaming to me than the perfect re-enacting of the words and tones of our voices, is the bitterness it brings flooding back into my heart, almost like a taste on my tongue, and the precise texture of my feelings, like a rasp inside my brain. But now there is another self there, too, overlaying all of this. And he, or I, for it is me as I am now, I want to shout, 'Stop! For the satisfaction of overwhelming your son with clever, bitter words' – and I could always do that, alas! – 'you are storing up miseries that will haunt you for the rest of your life!'

If I were truly clever with words, instead of just smart, I would write a play or a novel about it, and it would be in two parts. In the first part someone would say something quite trivial and no one would pick up on it and life would go on and at the end of the first act – so, OK, it's going to be a play – the audience would wonder where it's going. Then the second act would open in precisely the same situation, same dialogue, as the first. And those quite trivial words would be spoken again but this time someone would pick up on them, and so there's discussion, and argument, and shouting and . . . murder? Divorce? Father and son who part, never to see each other again?

And so I would use an art that, sadly, I do not have, to sublimate . . . that's the word! Sublimate! I would sublimate the guilt I feel and the unhappiness it gives me by producing a work of art. And so that – my own dear son – is what I truly hope for you, now: that my parting words to you – 'You are not an artist and never will be anything but a pasticheur and you are just hoodwinking yourself into the free life' – I hope I was never more wrong in all my life. Indeed, I hope you are truly the artist you thought you were and that you have managed what I can not – to sublimate all that bitterness and bad blood into works of art that are pure and serene.

Half of me wants you to read these words tomorrow

and, heedless of my advice, to come post-haste back here and allow us to indulge in an orgy of reconciliation and a healing of so many old wounds. The other half hopes that will never happen – so that I can chastise myself and heap miseries upon my head in endless atonement. So it's true – you can take the man out of Jewry but not the Jew out of the man!

At least I may truly sign myself . . .

Your ever-loving

Vati

PS: It was Tante Uschi, your second mother, who rescued both of us from total collapse into barbarism. I know I should take my own advice and get out of Germany as fast as I can but she needs me and, as she did not desert us, even when we were at our worst, so I cannot leave her now. I must take my chance and sing the old song quietly: 'Berlin – halt ein! Dein Tänzer ist der Tod!'

PPS: Someone in the Konditorei down on the corner left this on one of the tables yesterday. I thought it quite clever:

MUSSOLINI

HITLER

FRANCO

DALADIER

BRITANNIA

MENSCHHEIT

Cui bono?

(To discover who wins, look at the third letter in each name, starting at the top. It's right, too, I fear.)

Felix opened the folds of the second letter but instead of reading it from the top he let his eyes wander down the page, picking words and phrases at random, among them: 'Gestapo . . . Vichy . . . living in the shadows . . . hundreds of thousands of corpses . . .'

He could not face it.

'That was quick,' Faith said when he came back downstairs.

Nicole, forewarned by her own reading, was more perceptive. 'I thought you might read just one and then stop.'

'Does it show whether your father survived?' Faith asked.

He spread empty hands; Nicole shook her head.

'For sure?' Faith persisted.

Felix held his breath.

Nicole shrugged. 'It would be a miracle. I'm sorry, Felix. Of course, you know him better than anyone. When you read the second letter, maybe you will think it's a chance and I am pessimist.'

Faith realized that if Nicole was merely pessimistic, Felix would opt for triple-proof denial. 'I'll just go and say night-night to Jupiter,' she said.

'You want me to tell you?' Nicole asked when they were alone.

'That's why she's popped out, I'm sure. She won't speak of it unless I do but she will fret and fret until she knows everything.'

Nicole shook her head in wonder. 'You think only of her!'

'Not *only* but a lot.'

So she told him as much as she thought he should know, but to certain of his questions she answered that he should read that for himself.

'So?' Faith asked after she had gone home.

'I'll read the other letter tomorrow. You can look at the first one if you like. I need to . . . to readjust to him. It's on my bedside table.'

He thought she would go upstairs immediately but instead she asked, 'What about that transcript business – the transcript Angela made of that conference? Is she going to go back to Germany to try to find it?'

'She's been in touch with the man who had it from Marianne – Herr Hermann Treite – and he *still* has it. And he's still living in Hamburg. So that's one big worry lifted. She doesn't want him to send it by ordinary post, though. She says the BBC is still riddled with Secret Service people.'

'Do you believe that?'

'I believe it's possible. I'm going to have a Scotch. You?'

'Yes, why not!'

He continued as he poured their drinks, 'I believe it's possible but I also know how easy it is for us ex-citizens of the Third Reich to see agents of the state under every stone.' He splashed a little soda in hers and brought it to her. 'Doesn't it put you off wanting to work there?'

'Television won't be in Broadcasting House. A little dicky bird told me that when they go nationwide they'll—'

'What's that?'

'It's BBC-speak for achieving full national coverage, except for a million or so people who will insist on living in valleys. Anyway, they're close to it now and this little bird also tells me they're negotiating to take over the old film studios in Lime Grove, near Shepherds Bush. But I didn't want to talk about television. The thing is—'

'These "little birds",' he said. 'You have lots of them?'

'No more than I need. The thing is – will Angela go over and collect this transcript?'

'Why?'

'I just wondered. Does your Tante Uschi live near Hamburg?'

He sat beside her and hugged an arm around her. 'Are you worried I might go over there with her? Is that what all this is about?'

She handed him her empty glass. 'A bird never flew on one wing – as the Irishman said.'

He gave her the refill. She went on, 'I think it would be a *good* thing if you and she went over there together.'

Monday, 29 September 1947

Thanks to some nifty work by Corvo and an intervention by the Arts Council, Felix had a princely allowance of thirty pounds to take him to Hamburg, Kiel, and back. He had no intention of spending it all but he had had enough experience of being stranded and penniless in post-war Germany for one lifetime. He and Angela had arranged to meet at Victoria and take the Southern Railway's *Golden Arrow* service to Paris. There they would spend one or two nights with relations of Nicole's at Ville d'Avray, and, on the Thursday night, catch a through sleeper to Cologne via Brussels. A connection from there would get them to Hamburg around five on the Friday afternoon. Fortunately for their travel allowance, they had been able to pay the fares for the entire journey, including Felix's onward trip to Kiel, in sterling and in advance.

There had been a delicate moment when it came to agreeing the night-sleeper portion of the journey; each had hung back, waiting for the other to say, 'Look, we're both grown up . . . not awkward teenagers . . . should be perfectly possible . . . share . . . without . . . you know . . .' but then Felix had said, 'Dammit! We're neither of us paupers now. Don't we deserve a little luxury? I don't want to share with some *petit bourgeois* travelling salesman. Let's go first class and have a compartment each to ourselves!' And so it was.

But that long, delicate moment had been interesting, all the same.

His train to Kings Cross had been delayed, so she was at Victoria well before him. He saw her first, standing just inside the ticket barrier, looking toward the arch that opened into the concourse directly from the Tube exit – whereas he had deviated via the newspaper kiosk to buy *The Economist* – something meaty and magisterial to while away the hours. He paused a moment, set down his suitcase, and considered her.

She had fleshed out since he first saw her and was even more like a de Lempicka. When he saw the Dower House babies growing at the speed of light, and felt a strong desire for some of his own – a feeling he had never had before – he always pictured them in the strong embrace of de Lempicka arms, not Faith's.

He hefted his suitcase, resettled his trenchcoat over his shoulder, and stepped out into the concourse where she would be bound to see him. The radiant excitement of her recognition took his breath away.

The concourse beneath his feet was tired and stained, another war victim, still convalescent. He had a vision of khaki trousers, green-blancoed gaiters, once-shiny boots tramping . . . to the trains, from the trains . . . singing 'Bless 'em All'. The chummy, carry-on-smoking-chaps war that Europe had not known. It faded like a cliché from the silent cinema.

'Coach C is up near the front,' she said. 'Oh – I was getting so worried.'

'Your bags?'

'I put them over our seats. It really is a de-luxe carriage. The porter said it wouldn't be too crowded but there's only one non-smoking Pullman in the whole train. Eee – aren't you excited?'

'Paris, yes. Germany?' He seesawed his free hand.

'Oh, it's not so bad there now. Even before the Marshall Plan, everything was a lot better already.'

They passed a solo engine, parked by the adjoining platform, hissing and pinging like a kettle rising to the boil.

'The heat off those things!' he said. 'You're going to have to speak German over there.'

'Of course – when I have to. There's no need to start now. Anyway, I've been thinking about what you said – the language of Goethe and Schiller . . . all that.'

'That was a good day,' he said.

'Yes, it was! Here we are. I do like the way English platforms are the same level as the floors of the carriages, almost.'

One step – this one of wood.

'Down the far end,' she told him. 'Table for two.'

When they reached it he hoisted their bags up to the luggage rack and they settled in the two window seats, facing each other. Looking about the carriage he said, 'I like the pictures in our carriages on the LNER out to Welwyn – those coloured linocuts of *Fountains Abbey* and *The Vale of Evesham*. A world of permanence.' He leaned back and closed his eyes. 'It *was* a good day – the twenty-seventh of May.'

'How's Faith?'

He shrugged. 'She was out riding when I left. Half-past six every day, rain or shine. Willard drove me to the station so she'll have to go in with Todd this morning.'

There was a shrill whistle but it must have been for some other train because the *Golden Arrow* did not move. The waiter took their order – coffee and Kunzle cakes, which Felix called 'the nearest thing in England to *Sachertorte*'.

He continued, 'It'll be interesting – Germany. Post-war. Terence – our economics brain who lives down in the gatelodge – says that England's limping along with out-of-date equipment that wasn't destroyed in the war while Germany thrusts ahead with brand-new industrial machinery everywhere. It's the Versailles of nineteen twenty-two stood on its head.'

She drew breath to speak . . . then thought better of it.

'What?' he asked.

'It's something I think about often. Sometimes I want Germany to suffer for what they did – we did – in the war. Then, other times, I know that would only be a repeat of the suffering after the nineteen-fourteen war . . . and all the horrors that led to.'

While she was speaking the waiter put down their coffee and cakes; Felix initialled the chit. There was a new, more distant shrill of a whistle, and this time the train started to move – smoothly, without a jolt. The coffee did not even tilt in their cups.

'Those horrors couldn't possibly be repeated,' Felix said.

'We're an inventive lot,' she countered. 'We'd think of something.'

They emerged into the full light of day, into a south-London townscape so drab and tired that, for a long moment, it deprived them of speech. At last she asked, 'Did you bring something to read? I saw a magazine in your raincoat pocket.'

'Why? Actually, I have something Eric Brandon asked me to read . . . part of some book he's writing – about state patronage.'

'I think it's very relaxing to sit and read on a train. We can talk again when there's some nice country scenery to look at. This is so . . . *schäbig*.'

'Drab.' He picked up a Kunzle cake – a small cake in which the traditional crinkle-paper cup was replaced with one of crinkle-chocolate and filled with a dense, frothy-choclatey-chewy-nougaty cream. 'Don't let me eat more than one of these,' he begged her before taking the smallest, make-it-last bite.

'I suppose I could force myself to eat just one,' she replied, biting off a regular mouthful and closing her eyes in ecstasy.

He wondered how many fellow prisoners he would have killed just to be able to get one of these into his hands. Was that on her mind, too? He could just make out the title of her book: *The Woman of Rome*.

'Good?' he asked.

'Unpleasant,' she said, 'but you have to keep on reading. Fascinatingly unpleasant. I was going to bring *The Diary of Anne Frank*, but then I thought . . . no.'

'No,' he murmured, absent-mindedly fingering the second Kunzle cake, and opening Eric's folder of loose leaves, 'perhaps not.'

From time to time she broke her communion with Adriana and her existentially inevitable drift into prostitution to watch Felix as he grappled with Eric's complex but constipated effort to reconcile artistic freedom with the patronage offered by the modern state. 'Any good?' she asked as he laid the final sheet back in its folder. 'It certainly held your attention.'

'Wyndham Lewis did it better,' he said. 'The free-ranging artist who accepts handouts from the state must ever after accept that he is now confined to a paddock. Didn't some scientists prove recently that the bumblebee cannot possibly fly?'

She laughed. 'I read that somewhere.'

'Well, I think Eric's saying that culture has come to a dead end. Art can no longer fly.'

'And he's asking for *your* opinion? What are you going to tell him?'

'I shall say I feel very like a bumblebee.'

'The White Cliffs?' Angela murmured. 'More like gray, don't you think?'

'And the "bluebirds" turn out to be seagulls. Promises are so easy to make in wartime.'

'But you can see why they haven't been invaded for almost a thousand years – and not for lack of trying. Do you get seasick?'

He leaned over the rail, staring directly down into the sea, enchanted by the flickering interplay of black and gray-green, offset by white streaks of foam. 'Only when asked,' he replied.

'I think I'm going inside.'

'Below,' he told her. 'On a ship it's called going below. Would you like to read my father's second letter? Or later, perhaps?'

She held out her hand. 'I'd be honoured to be allowed to read it.' She found a seat that would allow her to glance up at the horizon from time to time; someone at work had told her it was the cure for seasickness. She unfolded the letter and smoothed it carefully on the cut moquette of the empty seat next to her. The pattern, self-consciously avant-garde in the Thirties, now seemed merely trite. She read:

My dearest son,
My earlier letter to you is still not sent. And now this one
will join it and who knows if either of them will ever be

read by you? When we heard of your arrest in Paris and the petition to the Gestapo by so many famous artists, we were so thrilled and so proud, Tante Uschi and I. Even more so when it led to your release. But, for that same reason, I knew then that I could not risk sending you anything whatsoever. For one thing I hoped you had gone into hiding somewhere in Vichy France. For another, they would know how to trace the letter back to me, no matter what care I took, and I could not risk putting others in such danger. So many people helped me put my life back together after your mother drowned and I would rather endure a hundred deaths than put them in harm's way.

After that, things became so bad that I and others were forced to move here to Kiel, where the mother of one of us has become too feeble to manage on her own – though, fortunately, she still has her wits about her and knows how to keep a secret. I know at least half a dozen Jews living 'in the shadows' in Berlin and they tell me they know of dozens more; altogether there must be more than a thousand. But I have not the temperament or the skills needed to survive in that way. Here I simply hide and make no noise.

But what would even a thousand Jews on the run be against the hundreds of thousands who once lived in that beautiful city! They took them away in comfortable passenger trains but once they were out of the city they pushed them into a siding and packed them like sardines into cattle trucks and continued in that way to the east. To where? We don't know. All we do know is that no one ever hears from them again. So this is not 'resettlement', which is what we once feared above all. Above all? No. It was the limit of our fears because no one could believe they would actually murder every Jew and other 'undesirable' they could get their hands on.

How are they doing it? With typical German efficiency – of course – but how? With bullets? Surely they cannot spare that much ammunition, especially with things going so badly for them on every front? So do they put them inside rings of electrified barbed wire and simply starve them to death? Or let them die of exposure? But they would still have to dig pits to bury the bodies. Perhaps the new arrivals have to do that before they, in turn, are left to die? But how many soldiers would it take to guard thousands of people, armed with picks and shovels, who have just had the most vivid demonstration that they have no hope of surviving? That cannot be it, either. So how are these devils managing an industry whose raw material is hundreds of thousands of living people and whose product is hundreds of thousands of corpses?

Such thoughts plague my mind these days because now, in the summer of 1943, I have decided I can no longer expose my friends to the risks of harbouring me here. In other words I have decided to try to make my way to Denmark. The border is only a day or two away on foot. And then I shall try to make my way onward to Sweden before autumn is too far advanced. The Danes are not surrendering their Jews to the Nazis, so I have a better chance there than here. And in Sweden, of course, I shall live in perfect safety.

If I get there.

If you receive these letters from any other hand than mine, you will know that I almost certainly failed to make it. If so, I shall, I fear, discover the answer to the question of the killing factories. And, by the same token, you will have escaped them or you will have survived them. I can imagine you doing either.

And what can I say to you in what may be my last communication with my own dearest son? That I bitterly regret the words on which we parted – certainly. You are an artist whose talent I not only failed to recognize . . . I actually mocked you for thinking you possessed it: 'hood-winking yourself into the free life'! I was jealous of you, to be sure. I started out with ambitions to become the Grand Old Man of German Literature, a latter-day Schiller, the sun to Thomas Mann's moon. I ended up, at my very pinnacle, a penny-a-liner, scribbling in cafés for pin money and hanging on the coat-tails of men and women with real talent. Do not think this is false modesty – a great artist once assured me of its truth!

Why did it happen so? I think because I never got out

from under your grandfather's shadow. His brand of
Protestant hatred made my flesh crawl. And he robbed me
of our family's Jewish heritage, which I did not realize
until it was too late to try to recover it. Jews have to grow
from the cradle; even a Jewish atheist is more Jewish than
the most ardent convert. That man harried me from the
pulpit of his own evangelical self-righteousness and I never
managed to escape him. 'Yea, though I scale the highest
mountain or hide myself in the deepest deep of ocean,
there also willt Thou find me!' – one of his favourite texts.
For him that 'Thou' was God. For me it was him.

It would not have mattered so much if I had not also
loved him. You, at least, did not make that same mistake
with me. That sounds bitter but I do not mean it so. If
this really is the last communication we share this side of
the grave, we cannot afford those comforting half-truths
that lubricate our ordinary lives. Whatever you may have
felt for me – love, at times, I'm sure, and ennui, and distaste,
and bewilderment – the entire gamut – you never let it
come between you and your art. And nor must you do so
now unless you wish to become the third wreckage of a
Breit in three generations. Your grandfather – for all his
commercial success – went whoring after his Protestant
God and failed to understand what was happening all around
him in the world of Art. Your father – notwithstanding the
comfortable living he made in journalism and on the
foothills of belles lettres – wasted himself in futile justi-
fication of his ways to God and That Man. And you? Well,
if you think of either of us more than fleetingly, once a
month, perhaps, it will be to your detriment as an artist,
which is what you first and foremost are.

If you survive this vile bloodbath, please do what you
can to see that those who helped me do not fall upon hard
times. Love has no comparitive. I cannot say I have come
to love one of them more than I loved your mother or
less, but love her I do, and with all my heart, for she is
one of the noblest women I have ever known.

I will close with some lines you will remember well.
You spoke them to 'Brutus' in the person of Kurt
Zuckermann in your last year at the Gymnasium: 'Farewell!

Forever and forever farewell! If we meet again, we shall smile indeed. If not, why then this parting were well made.'

Your loving Vati

She had not glanced even once at the horizon – and she did not feel the least bit queasy, either. She re-folded the letter and went back to join Felix on deck. 'Tummy OK?' he asked.

'For God's sake! Shut up about it!'

'Sorry. You know the cure, don't you.'

'I can hardly wait,' she replied wearily.

'Sit under a tree for ten minutes.'

She burst into laughter and, helped by a heave from the deck, launched herself at him. 'Oh, Felix!' she cried, steadying herself with a firm grip on his arm. 'You've been trying to tell me that since we came on board – haven't you! And I never gave the right answer. I'm s-o-r-r-y!'

'Forgiven,' he said crisply. 'By the way – before you ask – the "great artist" my father mentions was me.'

'Well, funnily enough, I did manage to work that out for myself. Also that his deliberately vague talk of "others" is really just about your Tante Uschi. He obviously feared the Gestapo might get their hands on the letter. Do you think he *really* tried to reach Sweden through Denmark?'

Felix was surprised. 'But surely it was his best hope – his only hope?'

'That's exactly why I question it. If I had been in his situation and really intended going back to Berlin – the one city I knew inside-out – and if I feared the letter might fall into the hands of the Gestapo, I'd say what he said about living in the shadows in Berlin. And then I'd go into some detail about escaping in exactly the opposite direction. So I think this letter tells you nothing about what really happened to him. But that's the least important part. The rest of it is very moving.'

She did not point out – she did not *need* to point out – that if he had made it to Berlin and had managed to evade the Nazis, then the fact that he had not surfaced after the liberation probably meant that he had been taken to God knows where by the Russians.

No one was coming back from there, either.

★   ★   ★

At Calais the *Golden Arrow* became the *Flêche d'Or,* whisking them in faded pre-war luxury across the flat autumnal plains of northern France to the Gare du Nord.

'Does the *Orient Express* still run?' Angela asked.

'I don't know. Why?'

'One of the things we used to do in the KL was to talk about our dream journeys. One girl swore the first thing she'd do if we ever got free was take a cruise from Narvik in Norway all the way round the top of the world to Archangel and back – in the time of the midnight sun, of course. It was wonderful to think of standing in freedom in endless sunshine.'

'And your dream?'

'Mine was to take the *Orient Express* from Paris to Constantinople. I didn't even know if it still ran – I still don't – but that was my dream journey.' Impetuously she took his hands across the table. 'Except now I'll have this one instead. Truly – I don't think I could have faced going back to Germany without you.'

Mildly embarrassed by her outburst, she made to draw her hands away. But he held them in a tight grip. 'I don't know,' he said. 'I . . . I . . . that is . . . I don't know.' He released her then and looked away.

After a longish silence, while they each stared out at the passing landscape, she said, 'What are you thinking?'

'About forests,' he told her – they had just passed through a stretch of dense and decaying woodland. 'I was wondering why they are places of terror in so many old folk tales and the Brothers Grimm and so on. All dark and gloomy and only half-seen – I was thinking it must have been like a KL to our earliest ancestors – a place in which they felt powerless and full of terrors. And they had no alternative they could dream about.' He gazed once more at the darkling landscape. 'Actually, I don't think I'd have embarked on this journey . . . alone, either. I've been wondering how to ask you if you'd consider coming all the way to Kiel with me. I mean – if it was *fair* to ask you.'

'I'd love that,' she said. 'I mean – to meet your Aunt Uschi.'

The house had once belonged to Alfred de Musset. It stood in its own extensive grounds in Ville d'Avray, about halfway between Paris and Versailles. Now it belonged to Nicole's cousins – their hosts for the next few days – Amy and Roger Trocquemé.

'It's good you have come just in this moment,' she said as she led them up to the attic. 'Tomorrow . . .' She took them over to a window and showed them that the house was L-shaped, which was not at all apparent from the road. 'Over there, tomorrow, we have the first French-German conference since before the war. French and German Christians will sit down together and discuss practical ways how we can make sure it's no more war in Europe – *ever*. And you are German, no? Both? And living in England. Perhaps you can join us just for a little while? To give your experiments? Experiences! It could be a much valuable addition.'

They had now climbed three flights of stairs – and, Felix suddenly realized, he had not faced them with his obsessive categorizing of every flight he ever attempted. Mme Trocquemé paused before a door at the head of the last flight. 'It is possible you can sleep over in the conference wing, but this is nicer.' She waved toward the paintings and prints that lined the passageway and stairs. 'Especially for the artists. You are artists, yes? You, Herr Breit, especially. I remember the petition for your release from the Gestapo in nineteen forty-two. *Tiens!* Only five and a half years ago – but what years they have been! So much killing. But you were free.'

'We must all work to see it can never happen again, madame,' Felix said.

'And we will be honoured to attend your conference,' Angela added. 'It's very good of you, madame, even to *think* of putting us up when you must be so busy.'

'Ah! Pfff!' Amy waved away the thought.

'And, of course,' Felix added, 'we require no entertainment. I just want to show Miss Worth to Paris before we leave.'

'The conference, it's only one day,' she assured them. 'So –' she threw open the door – 'I leave you to unpack and settle. We have a very simple dinner in half an hour.'

And she was gone before it dawned on them that she somehow expected them to share the room.

From the bottom of the first flight down she called back an afterthought, 'I'm sorry it's two beds but you are young, *hein!*'

'Well!' Felix said as he set down his suitcase and hers. His heart was now racing from more than the climb to this attic.

'Nicole!' Angela said. She looked at her watch. 'Bloody Nicole!'

I'll bet she is bathing little Andrew Mercier exactly now and giggling over this trick she has played.'

Felix turned back toward the door. 'I'll go and explain.'

'She'll feel so embarrassed,' Angela said, adding, 'We're not going to be able to wash in this handbasin without bumping our heads.'

'You think we can . . . ?' Felix hesitated.

'We are completely grown up, Felix. Not kids who see the teacher's back is turned.'

But later, at the 'very simple dinner', Roger took a phone call in the hall and then called Amy out there, saying, 'Nicole,' in a slightly sepulchral tone.

The conversation was brief and, at the Paris end, rather heated. The moment Amy returned, Angela got in first, 'We *guessed* it was her! We weren't going to make a fuss about it because of tomorrow's conference.'

'And – as Nicole may have told you, madame,' Felix said, 'we have both lived in circumstances where personal privacy was not, so to speak, uppermost in our minds. We can manage very well.'

'Circumstances?'

Nicole had obviously *not* told her.

'Mauthausen.' Felix pointed at himself. 'And . . .'

'Ravensbrück,' Angela said.

'Oooh!' She sat heavily in a chair just inside the door. 'Oh!' She shook her head slowly. 'Oh!'

Roger was watching her closely, wiping his lips on his napkin – mechanically.

The thought suddenly struck Felix. 'Perhaps we should not take part in your conference tomorrow, madame? It might embarrass your German delegates? Though I should tell you that neither of us bears any individual Germans ill will.'

'Certainly not,' Angela put in.

'It must be faced,' Roger told his wife.

'Of course.' She combined a shrug and a sigh – in which Felix clearly saw Nicole's dramatic sort of mime. 'Perhaps *le bon Dieu* always intended this for our first conference for peace and understanding.'

'Then you must know *all* the truth about me,' Angela said.

'No!' Felix cried.

'Yes,' she insisted. 'Until January the twentieth, in nineteen forty-two, I was a technical officer in the *Schutzstaffel*. In my work as a sound-recording engineer I answered directly to Reinhard Heydrich.'

'The twentieth of January?' Amy looked at her husband, then at Felix. 'I was in Paris that day. I can never forget it. It was when they . . .' She turned to Felix. 'But they let you go.'

He nodded. 'And rearrested me in Vichy, with no publicity, two years later.'

She turned again to Angela. 'So did you know each other even then?'

She shook her head and went on to explain why the conference was held (to implicate the entire party in the *Vernichtung*) and her own role in recording it, which ended in her defecting to the Resistance and her imprisonment. And how she came to know of Felix's arrest in Paris on that same day. 'They said there would certainly be a big protest from the artistic cliques in Paris and it was already decided to release Felix again to make good headlines in the papers. The idea was from Goebbels, of course.'

Amy glanced sorrowfully at her husband. 'Oh, Roger – do you hear? It's true! The Parisians would not mind too much the rounding-up of the Jews . . . but *an artist*! *Tiens*! That's something different. Ooooooh –' her sigh was like a swiftly deflating tyre – 'where do we even begin?'

And now she was so wrapped up in the alterations she felt obliged to make to the following day's agenda that she completely forgot the other change she ought to make.

And the last thing Felix and Angela wanted was to make a fuss.

'You go first,' Felix said. 'I want to have a good look at these pictures.'

'You won't see much in this light,' she warned him. 'You know what the richest man in France does? I'm sure he manufactures fifteen-watt lamps.'

She closed the door, leaving him in the pasage. He wondered whether he would, in fact, be able to speak to this conference tomorrow.

The picture at the stairhead was a crude but probably valuable woodcut of the St Bartholomew's Day Massacre of French Protestants. Dress the perpetrators in SS uniforms and it would be a gruesomely familiar scene. It struck him then that the Trocquemés must both be Protestants – no papal portraits, Sacred Hearts, ecstatic images of the Virgin . . . how quickly life at the Dower House had stripped him of his old European habits.

Could he talk about 'The New Europe' without invoking his particular experience of the old, which seemed too petty to connect with such vast ideas?

Next was a sepia photograph of Alfred de Musset himself, sitting beneath a parasol on the lawn behind the house; the woodland beyond him had since been thinned to a few specimen trees – prudent gardening or wartime necessity?

And talk to committed Christians? Tell them God must now take lessons from the Humanists?

Click!

Darkness.

He cleared his throat to alert whoever had turned the light off . . . and then remembered it was one of those pneumatic switches that slowly refill with air after you push them in. He thought he remembered where it was and so felt his way gingerly down the flight to where it . . . *wasn't.* He tried a fingertip search for it along the passage but soon gave up. Not even the dimmest light penetrated the windows overlooking the street. He had forgotten that all French villages seemed to have a terror of light – outdoor light – after sunset. Even before the war, playing surrealist games with André Breton in country villages near Fontainebleau, they had walked through one pitch-black and seemingly deserted village after another.

Give them the existentialist answer – tell them they're on a journey to nowhere? The road is a cul-de-sac. There is nothing beyond that door – open it and see for yourselves. The men with the darkness have arrived, disguised as God. Why was he standing here in the dark?

Oh yes!

Forgetting he had descended one flight, he began working his way along the wall, feeling for their door, looking under them for a sliver of light and whispering Angela's name urgently. There was a sudden flood of light overhead and she startled him by almost shouting his name.

'Er . . . ah . . . yes,' he replied. 'Don't shut the door. I've got to find the light whadyoumaycallit.'

'Don't bother,' she said impatiently. 'Surely this is light enough.'

Stairs. These of wood. Thirteen steps. Lucky for him?

Halfway up he was transfixed at the sight of her, standing in the doorway with the light behind her – and it certainly was more than fifteen watts. It was only her silhouette, her shadow, against the translucent silk of her nightdress, but . . .

'Pity you haven't got your sketchbook!' she taunted, doing a coquettish little twirl before skipping out of sight. Her bed played a spring symphony.

As he shut their door behind him she let out a small, quiet fart. 'Oh dear!' she said. 'I didn't quite mean that . . . but it does at least answer one unspoken question between us – in this situation.'

'Well, speaking as a man who once lived on nothing but beans, you're up against an expert here.' He undressed to wash behind the screen.

'I accept your word for it,' she said. 'Proof will not be required.'

She was lying on her side, facing away from him, when he at last came out again. 'Goodnight, my dear,' she said without turning round.

But for that he would have switched out the light and gone directly to his bed. Instead, on an impulse, he went to sit precariously on the edge of her bed. She spun round and stared up at him with great, searching eyes.

'A little goodnight ritual,' he explained. 'Something Willard taught Marianne.' He stretched his hand toward her face. 'Sand in the right eye –' he pretended to strew a pinch of it into her eye – 'sand in the left eye . . .' She relaxed and grinned up at him, becoming a child. 'Shed a little tear –' he drew a finger lightly down her cheek and then, chucking her gently under the nose – 'here's mud in your eye.' He bent low and kissed her lightly on the brow. The remnant of the fart was aphrodisiac. Hastily he skipped the six feet back to his bed, turning out the wall light on the way.

Now at last he knew she was, beyond all shadow of a doubt, the most precious, the most wonderful person in the entire universe. She made the very air in this room special. She made everything special. She seemed to carry an aura of . . .

something indescribable . . . some kind of exceptional light that bore a hint of gold. It transformed everything around her, making it radiant and extra-real. He could also dare to acknowledge, at last, that his real purpose in making this visit was to be with her – away from England . . . away from the Dower House . . . away from . . . Manutius . . . just to be with her, blessed with a new sense of life and hope in that magical nearness of her.

Hope? Could two people who had suffered as they had suffered hope to make a normal life together? He *felt* normal enough. He had not shut out the horrors of the past but nor did he dwell on them – though, to be honest, everyday life was filled with sly reminders. Faith doling out the porridge could recall the sound of a stodgy heap of beans being thwacked onto a tin plate . . . the 'barbecue' thing that Willard had used in the summer evoked the crematorium . . . young Sam getting a bramble thorn in the palm of his hand revived an image of the capo pinning a thief's hand to the table with a dagger . . . but it *was* porridge, not beans . . . a succulent T-bone steak, not a cadaver . . . an accidental thorn not a deliberate barbarity.

And so he sank into a pleasant fantasy in which he lay at ease in the back of a light, clinker-built rowing boat while she rowed them, once again, at the gentlest, most leisurely pace round the Wannsee. She had the most powerful and yet the most feminine arms he had ever admired.

And at the precise moment when she rested on her oars and the boat glided under the shade of a mighty weeping willow overhanging the water's edge, she – the real Angela in her bed a few hundred miles away – gave that sort of double-intake of breath that people make after tears.

Jolted back from his fantasy, he listened acutely for more. But no – he must have been mistaken. It was just the sort of double-inhalation people make in their sleep when their bodies have forgotten to breathe a while.

He would not – could not – speak tomorrow. He would write something for them instead.

Tuesday, 30 September 1947

I have lived two lives. [Felix wrote] One was in a Koncentrationslager called Mauthausen. It lasted less than a year and a half but if I live to a hundred, it will still be the longer. On every one of those days we woke up <u>knowing</u> it would be our last. Every new day was also a new lifetime. Why? Because we were in the clutches of people who felt physically sick at the very <u>thought</u> of a Jew, a homosexual, a Romany. Of course, they had elaborate intellectual and metaphysical arguments that lent apparent respectability to this visceral emotion, but my greatest fear is that you good people − <u>all</u> good people − all who want to build a Europe where it can never happen again − will try to disprove those arguments when the real target lurks far below the level of words.

So I urge you to go for the guts of it. As Christians, you could start by wondering what made Catholics and Protestants burn with such ardour that they gleefully slaughtered one another only a few centuries ago. What in the teaching and practice of Rome filled Protestant souls with such gut-hatred as that − and vice versa, of course? What allowed the Inquisition to throw sacred human life back in God's face and yet feel certain of His approval? Why is it no longer so? What changed people's perceptions on both sides? Reason? The law? Or something that lies deeper in each one of us?

If you can answer that and apply it in post-war Europe, you will have made a good start.

Angela spoke in German. 'The reason I am here at all,' she said, 'is that I am on my way to Hamburg to meet an old comrade in the German underground to whom I gave the transcript of a conference held at Interpol Headquarters in January, nineteen forty-two − for which act of "treason" I was sent to Ravensbrück until the Liberation. You may not have heard of that meeting but the whole world knows now what was decided there − the

Vernichtung of Jews, homosexuals, and Romanies. I had intended to describe it to you in some detail but – having read what my friend Felix Breit has submitted for you to consider – I will focus on just one aspect.

'Remember – that conference was called for one sole purpose: to allow the Schutzstaffel to inform the wider Nazi party that it, the SS, had perfected the means to massacre up to ten thousand people per day, seven days a week.'

There were gasps all around the room.

'Yes – the true scale of what happened still hasn't sunk in. I wonder how long it will take, in fact. But the one thing I want to tell you about is that, despite all the boasting on the part of the SS, even the most hardened of them had to concede the awfulness of it all. One of them told the meeting that Himmler himself, head of the SS, was physically sick when he was present at one of the gassing experiments on children that went wrong. Another, after describing early experiments in forcing Slavic Jews to dig mass graves and then stand beside them to be shot, said that "good decent Germans" could only bear it for about two months before they became "burnt out". They could not forget that they belonged to the race that produced Goethe and Schiller and Beethoven. Their Slav collaborators, he said, made much more efficient killers because they were of a lower order of humanity.

'There were several other instances of their recognition that what they were doing was bestial and unworthy of the highest standards of the German soul, but I think those two are enough to make my point – which is this: Even there, in the highest echelon of the vilest part of the nightmare that was Naziism, they felt compelled to acknowledge the regrettable – to them – necessity of the *Vernichtung*.

'But was it *German* culture that pricked their consciences? No! The culture was European – the values bequeathed to Europe by the son of a carpenter in Galilee two thousand years ago – values now shared even by those who (like me, I'm afraid) admire his message but do not think him divine. European values – which now hold the key to the European disease. And so it is to *Europe* that we must turn for a cure. We must all think European first before we add German, French, Italian . . . English . . . Spanish . . . and so on. And you – Germans and French – can make a start today. Imagine the new Europe – a

Europe at peace after how many thousand years of war? It may yet trace its very beginnings to *this* room on *this* very day, the thirtieth of September, nineteen forty-seven!'

After an awestricken pause the German delegates banged the table with open hands, palms down; the French, who had started with conventional applause, joined in somewhat sheepishly.

Felix passed her a piece of paper on which he had written: '*Hervorragend! Magnifique!* Not bad!'

'I'll bet we have separate rooms by the time we get back there tonight,' Angela said when they were on the bus to Paris.

'Damn! We missed our chance!' he joked.

She did not join his laughter. After a long, awkward silence she said, 'Perhaps you really mean that, Felix?' And when he did not respond: 'Do you?' And then there was a further, almost intolerable silence before she added, 'Because I wouldn't mind. You know?' She swallowed so heavily that he heard it over the boneshaking rattle of the bus.

'Oh God!' He grasped her hands — which let him feel that she was shivering as much as he — and said, 'I lay awake a long time last night because . . . when I kissed you on the forehead like that, I suddenly knew that you were the most . . . the most *precious* thing in my life. God! The most precious in all the universe. What are we going to do?'

The question jolted her. 'What d'you mean — what are we going to do?'

'I mean I actually had that feeling about you from the first moment I saw you — in Schmidt's, when I was sitting there with Fogel, before Fritz told me anything about you. But I thought I couldn't trust it.'

'Why?' She was more aggrieved than curious.

He shrugged. 'I suppose I believed nothing so wonderful could be real . . . or be really happening to *me*.'

Two words popped into her mind: 'Jewish fatalism'. She had seen plenty of it in Ravensbrück. But could someone brought up in complete ignorance of his Jewishness still 'catch' it?

'Even so,' he continued, 'I knew it was no passing fantasy that day when we walked in Regent's Park . . .'

'When you picked that rose?' Now there was relief in her laughter, but she still wondered about that question: *What are we going to do*? 'Why did you . . . No – it's all right.' She had actually started asking him why he had picked that rose and held it beside her and declared her the winner; but he misunderstood. 'You mean why did I take up with Faith?'

'Oh . . . I . . .'

'No – you have every right to ask. It's truer to say that Faith took up with me . . . but I found it convenient not to resist. She's very good company. She's a good shield against the office politics at Manutius. A good guide to the subtleties of English life.'

Angela could not help asking, 'Good in bed?'

'*Y-e-s*. Or yes and no. I mean she's not passionate. It's just jolly good fun to her. She enjoys horse-riding more, I think. And dancing. We both know we're not in love – and we've never even pretended. We're good for each other's careers.'

'Does she know how you feel about me? Did you ever tell her . . . what you've just told me?'

'As I said – I hardly dared tell myself until last night, when it became so overpowering. I don't *think* she knows – and I've certainly never told her.'

'But? I can hear a *but* in your voice.'

He sighed. 'But she's very . . . I mean she's almost a mind-reader. She can know lots of things about people without ever asking or being told. So I expect she does know. In her bones.'

'In which case,' Angela spoke carefully, 'don't you find it odd that she *encouraged* you to make this trip with me?'

What Felix ought to have replied was: 'Did I tell you she encouraged me?' for, indeed, he had never told Angela any such thing and, until now, she had been just as careful not to ask. Instead he said, 'I suppose – if she *does* know how I feel about you – she's baffled as to why I've not done anything about it.'

'Well, Felix, my darling,' Angela exploded in frustration, 'she's not the *only* one! Why *have* you been doing nothing about it? You've had lots of chances – and never a better one than last night!'

'I know! I know!' he said wretchedly.

'While you were lying there, two metres and a million kilometres away from me, I was lying there with tears running down my face.'

'Oh . . . oh . . .' He rolled his head in savage anguish on her shoulder until she put up a hand to cushion his weight.

'Why?' she whispered. 'Why?'

'Trocadéro!' the conductor called out.

'Oh! Let's get off here!' Suddenly animated, she grabbed his hand and dragged him along to the exit.

The conductor reminded them that they had bought tickets to the Place de la Concorde but Felix just shrugged and, tilting his head toward Angela, said, '*C'est la femme eternelle!*'

No argument there.

'Here!' Still tugging him by the arm she dragged him across the open space to the balustrade from which you get the most famous view of the Eiffel Tower. 'Does this remind you of anything?' She went right up to the balustrade, threw back her head, squared her shoulders, and clasped her hands in front of her, arms straight down in a V.

Seeing her from behind, a commanding silhouette against the Eiffel Tower, he felt the hair rise on the back of his neck. 'Hitler!' he whispered. 'Here. Right here!'

She turned round, grinning joyfully. 'The only time he ever visited Paris. He stood exactly here and did a little jig of pleasure.'

Felix gazed down at the flagstones beneath their feet, trying to comprehend that the jackboots which had figuratively crushed the life out of so many millions and plunged the world into a crisis that might yet precipitate a further war – *those* jackboots had literally danced a little jig of childish joy right here, on these very stones. *That* stone, perhaps . . . or *that* one. He felt nauseous.

'Don't you see!' Angela exclaimed, her eyes shining, her whole body a-quiver. 'He thought he'd finished us off, both of us. Our deaths were among the millions in his mind when he stood here and danced his little jig. With France in his grasp he had secured the last escape routes out of Europe. From that moment on, we were in the trap and he could hunt us all down at his leisure. But where is *he* now? He's dust and ashes and we're here instead. And we're alive and it's our turn to dance!' At which she grabbed him and whirled him off in a mad polka, round and round on the spot where that man had once dared to suppose he could lift his sights from Europe to take on the world.

At the top of the Eiffel Tower he said, 'I don't really know Paris at all. There's Sacré Coeur – I never went inside. All those times

I went to Montmartre I never went inside Sacré Coeur. And the Panthéon . . . Napoleon's tomb . . . never went there. Never went inside Nôtre Dame. That's the Pont de la Concorde – the bridge with the famous Marly horses – I never walked across that one.'

'The Louvre?' she suggested. 'You never went inside there?'

He laughed and, bending his head to hers until they touched, said, 'Sorry. I was just preparing you not to expect too much in the way of a tour.'

'This is a good tour – *un tour d'horizon!*' She swept a hand across the panorama. 'But the tour I really want is one around the inside of your head. Paris can wait.'

'What d'you expect to find?'

'What I'd love to find is the reason why you thought you couldn't trust your own feelings and why you thought something wonderful could never happen to *you*.'

'You've never doubted such things in yourself?' he asked.

'Never. I can doubt my memory, my judgement, my reasoning, but never my feelings. How can you doubt *feelings*? Doubt itself is a feeling. It's like saying doubt can doubt itself.'

'But – more *personally*,' he replied. 'You were twice as long in Ravensbrück as I was in Mauthausen, and yet . . .'

'You think that has made it impossible to have true feelings? Or to trust them?'

He gazed down at cars that were smaller than the smallest Dinky Toys, at huge apartment blocks no larger than sugar cubes, at trees like moss. Somewhere down there, he thought, there must be hundreds of people who could explain this so much more clearly than I can. 'You see . . . with Faith—'

'To hell with Faith! Tell me about you, about me and you.'

'No. The thing is . . . I thought, you see . . . that if I can find life so comfortable and congenial with her . . . stimulating ideas . . . laughs . . . trust . . . I mean, there may not be any love between us but there's lots of emotional trust . . . but then, of course, I could never live a single hour without also thinking of you . . . and . . .'

'What does "thinking of" me mean, Felix?'

The sun emerged from behind a cloud, low in the sky and a fiery orange; it was as if a warm spotlight had suddenly been trained upon him. 'I thought the worst thing for me would be to tell you I love you and then be rejected. But—'

'You could at least—'

'No – wait! There was something even worse – because, of course, I could feel that you were not indifferent to me.'

She drew breath to say something bitter-sweet . . . and then thought better of it.

'And,' he continued, 'it would have been even worse if I had been honest about my feelings and you had responded and . . . you know . . . got engaged . . . got married . . . and then found we are too emotionally damaged to . . . I mean, I couldn't face the risk. What d'you think? D'you think we can?'

She leaned out over the rail and watched people moving like ants, casting long shadows in the lowering sun. 'You can see why bomber pilots have such easy consciences,' she murmured.

'Perhaps it's possible?' he prompted. 'You and me?'

'It will be a tender plant,' she said. 'And it won't prosper if one of us keeps digging it up to see how the roots are getting along.'

He stared past her, toward the sun; his gaze put her in mind of some raptorial bird – intense, bright-eyed, and yet chillingly expressionless. That, more than anything, gave her an intimation of the trouble he feared. She shrugged it aside; she, at least, was made of stronger, more optimistic mettle. 'And you *would* be doing that – wouldn't you!' she insisted.

'Words!' he said scornfully as he took her face in his hands and moved close enough for their noses to touch. Staring deep into her eyes he saw them melt and liquefy; when she blinked, the tears overran her lower lids and sprouted on her cheeks. She tilted her face upward until her lips brushed his. He planted a tiny kiss at the more distant corner of her mouth . . . another in the centre . . . another at the nearer corner . . . and then the universe closed around them and it was as if they slaked a thousand-year hunger in one long, sustained kiss of immobilized passion. To a casual observer – and there were several up there on the topmost level – they were no more than a pair of lovers yielding to some trivial stimulus. Outwardly there was nothing to reveal that *this* kiss, at *this* moment, in *this* place, was the kind that changes the entire course of two people's lives.

And when it was over, they both felt an enormous sense of calm. Still too close to focus her clearly, Felix peered into the dark, misty pools of her eyes and thought, A lifetime will not be long enough.

And Angela . . . well, to be honest, she was thinking, Must get him a better razor.

Hand in hand they returned to earth in easy silence. They recrossed the Seine by the Pont de l'Alma and walked up the right bank, along the Quai de la Conférence, saying things like '*Liebe dich!*' and '*Je t'aime!*' as they strolled, because the things they really wanted to say were all too momentous and too ill-formed and, anyway, they didn't need to be put into words just yet.

They hugged so tightly into each other that their steps became clumsy and they had to relax a little. And then everything was funny – ducks, fishermen, the *bateaux mouches*, the floating swimming baths where intrepid Parisians could swim in filtered Seine water . . . they smiled or giggled or laughed aloud at each until they came back at last to earth.

'Talking of the Dower House . . .' she said

'Were we?'

'Well – we are now . . . what to do about it? Do you move in with me in Robert Street and travel out of town to work each day at the Dower House, in the studio part of what will be Faith's cottage? Or what?'

'I thought we'd just – you know – talk it over with Faith. She will certainly have her own ideas.'

'She won't give up the stabling for Jupiter too easily.'

'Exactly,' he said. 'I'm glad you see the problem. D'you think we could buy your flat in Robert Street and keep it as a pied-à-terre? It would be nice to have a little place in Town. We could go to the opera . . . the theatre . . . concerts . . . without having to trek all the way out to Hertfordshire when it's over.'

She dragged him to a halt and jerked his arm to make him face her. 'You're serious!'

'Well, I am doing quite well – largely thanks to Fogel . . . which really means largely thanks to Faith. I've been invited to become a sculpture tutor at the Slade – two days a week – and I have a commission from the BBC at Ally Pally and another from the LCC for a large piece in Battersea Park – and there's a convent in Chelsea where they want—'

'All right!' Angela laughed. 'I had no idea.'

'And since I can't buy the cottage . . . I mean, the gravel company is never going to sell the Dower House – it would make sense to buy a property somewhere. Your flat seems ideal. Or should we look around Primrose Hill? That's also within walking distance of the West End and there are some lovely places there, starting at under five thousand.'

'Five *thousand*? Whew! Could you afford that much?'

'We.'

She stopped and faced him. 'We! Is that a proposal, Felix?'

He took up both her hands and kissed them, first the right, then the left. 'I suppose it is. Of course, you'll need time to think it over.'

She gazed skyward for about five seconds. 'OK. I've thought it over and I accept. You did say five *thousand*? What about Faith – if you and I are living at the cottage . . . ?'

'I'm sure we could reach some accommodation,' he said vaguely.

'You mean . . . *no*! She could stay on?'

'It's quite a big cottage – and there's an unused one-up-one-down at the end. She could have that. And we could knock a doorway through to it so she could use the bathroom and kitchen.' He laughed. 'Just think! Back in 'forty-four – if anyone had told us then "Three years from now Hitler will be two years dead and you'll be walking by the Seine, in a Paris free of Nazis, arm-in-arm with the one you love, discussing living in an English stately home and buying a pied-à-terre in London" . . . we'd have said he was delirious.' After a pause he added, 'I suppose that's why I find it impossible to plan too far ahead.'

'Or at all,' she murmured.

That night they did, indeed, have separate rooms.

'Shall I come night-crawling?' Felix asked at the parting of their ways.

After a brief hesitation she said, 'A bit treacherous? To our host and hostess, I mean? We have the sleepers tomorrow night.'

When they kissed goodnight she felt him harden. She pushed him away. 'Can you wait?' she asked.

'Sure.' He set off for his room, adding over his shoulder, 'It's just hooked up to the wrong parts of the nervous system. The bits we can't reach.'

The dangerous bits, she thought.

Wednesday, 1 October 1947

They left their bags in a locker at the Gare du Nord and then, at her pleading, he rather reluctantly showed Angela his old apartment – or the exterior of the building, at least – in the Rue d'Argenteuil. 'They took three Jewish families from that building over there,' he said. 'And I stood up there and wondered what I could do to help. Give them a character reference? Protest? Being German, I thought my protests might carry some weight!' He gave a single harsh laugh that turned a few nearby heads.

'Where had you been living for the previous *nine years*?' she asked.

He nodded ruefully. 'Not in the real world. Being German, I hadn't paid too much heed to the situation of the Jews. And then the police crossed the street and entered my building. I thought, *Hello! I wonder who's Jewish here?*' He sighed. 'Oh – enough of this!'

They set off for the Avenue de l'Opéra but had gone only a few paces when a man came running out, hatless, crying, 'Monsieur Breit? Herr Breit? *C'est vraiment vous-même?*'

Felix turned and after a shocked moment of non-recognition, cried, '*Monsieur Tesnière! Vraiment?*' Then to Angela: 'This is the gentleman who got word to Dufy. *Oh Pierre . . . mon chèr ami!*' And he pumped the man's arm fit to break its bones.

It was a pleasant shock for Angela to hear herself introduced as his fiancée – the first public acknowledgement.

'You must look after this gentleman, mam'selle,' Tesnière told her solemnly. 'He is a great artist.'

'Ah, Pierre, you have no idea how important this young lady is!' Felix slipped his arm around her. 'And how precious.'

Tesnière made an expansive Parisian gesture. 'You must come up to the apartment. Hélène will be so pleased! I saved some of your smaller sculptures.'

Felix's jaw dropped.

'It's true. I have kept them for you. I knew you would be back.'

The concierge was new; the introduction was brief. With the merest shake of his head, Tesnière nipped in the bud Felix's questions about Mme Réage, the concierge of his day.

Steps. These familiar – and safe again.

'La Réage informed for the Gestapo,' he explained when they were out of earshot . . . and he drew a finger across his throat. 'In the Seine.' Without a pause he continued, 'You recall that it was just one *flic* and one Gestapo man who arrested you? Well, in the four or five minutes your apartment was empty and unguarded . . . *pffft!* Out came six little sculptures. I had to leave two or they would have been angry enough to search the entire building. They were angry anyway – but they had more important business that day.'

Angela was surprised. 'So when they released you that day – you didn't come back here at all?'

'Certainly not! I sat in a café – *La vache qui rit* – and sent light-hearted *pneumatiques* to my friends – because I knew the Gestapo would intercept them and it would make them relax. And meanwhile the best forger in Paris was producing the necessary papers – and so, by midnight, I was out of the city and on the road to Vichy France.' He grinned at Tesnière. 'Only five years ago, eh!'

'We heard this,' Tesnière said. 'We knew you got away safely because they offered rewards for your capture. You joined the Resistance, I suppose?'

Madame T. was waiting for them at the head of the last flight of stairs.

'Hélène!' Unusually for him, Felix took them two at a time.

Moments later both had tears running down their cheeks. Angela realized she had never seen him cry. In the apartment Felix said, 'But nothing has changed!'

'What should we change?' Hélène asked. 'There is nothing in the shops half so good as this. Aiee, it will be *years* before Paris becomes again the city *we* all knew.'

It was an upper-middle-class apartment, instantly recognizable from dozens of French movies – polished wooden floors, silk-brocade wall hangings, and a mixture of Louis XVI and Art Nouveau furniture. Angela guessed it was mostly inherited and that their true taste was displayed in the pictures and sculpture and bric-a-brac, which were all uncompromisingly twentieth century, from Expressionist to abstract to *objèts trouvés.* Including . . .

'Ah!' Felix cried out in delight as his eyes fell on the six rescued masterpieces – not a difficult achievement, since they were all assembled on a low table near the porcelain stove. 'I had forgotten these – truly.' He picked them up, restlessly, one by one . . . put them down . . . picked them up again. 'I mean, I knew I had abandoned *some* sculptures here, but I couldn't remember which ones.' He handed one to Angela. 'I wasn't bad in those days, eh!'

She would have taken it for a rather artistic dumb-bell. 'It feels beautiful,' she said. 'Granite?'

He nodded. 'Black . . . African – from Nigeria, I think. Ha – the egg I did for Fogel was not the first, after all! I had completely forgotten this one. Cararra marble, too! But actually, it's just any old spheroid . . . Fogel's is a real *egg.*'

True? Angela wondered, or was he preserving the memory that the egg idea had come to him when he and she were lunching at Schmidt's?

She became aware that Mme T. was surveying – indeed scrutinizing – her. She and her husband were much of an age with Felix but their relationship was clearly protective toward him. 'We have a friend who works on *Le Figaro,*' she said. 'He told us you survived the Nazi camp and had landed on your feet in England. I wanted to let you know about the sculptures but Pierre said no, you would surely come back one day and he wanted to see your face when he told you.'

Pierre laughed. 'And it was worth it!'

'But our journalist friend said nothing of a fiancée?'

Angela said, 'That's because he wasn't at the top of the Eiffel Tower yesterday afternoon.'

'Oh!' Mme T gave a cry of delight and clapped her hands. 'How perfect – Paris, the Eiffel Tower! It's why you have no ring – yet.'

Angela could not help laughing at this acute juxtaposition of Gallic romanticism and practicality.

Felix explained that they were on their way to Germany, to Kiel, to see his aunt-by-courtesy, who might have all his mother's rings still. And for that reason he begged that they would retain the sculptures until their return in a week or so's time – and in any case he would be delighted if they would choose two of them to keep.

Mme T prepared a light lunch, after which the four of them spent the afternoon walking to Père Lachaise to see the Epstein sculpture at the tomb of Oscar Wilde and the mausoleum of Abélard and Héloïse. It was there that Felix suddenly dodged behind one of the columns, saying, 'Go on talking, act innocent!'

After a full minute he relaxed and said, 'That was close!' Then, to Angela: 'We should gently make our way toward the station.'

'What was close?' she asked.

'I'm sure that was André Breton.'

'Ah!' The Tesnières were disappointed.

'You know him?' Felix asked.

'No, but he's a great man.'

'He was. But surrealism is dead – aesthetic monkey-gland stuff kept alive by clowns like Dali.'

At the cemetery gates Felix pointed out that the first tomb was for a family named Adam and he wondered if Breton's fertile mind had ever made anything of that.

They wandered back toward the centre until they reached that parting of their ways – a low-key parting since they'd be together again in a week or so. As he and Angela continued toward the station, Felix said, 'I wonder if it really was Breton back there – or did I imagine him because he was in my mind the night before last?'

When he explained the circumstances she asked what the two of them were doing in the countryside around Fontainebleau at night, anyway?

'I don't know why he chose Fontainebleau,' Felix replied. 'Maybe some association with *François premier* or maybe Leonardo, who designed the great staircase there? Anyway, he wanted to show me surrealism in action – that it was an entire politico-cultural *process* not just a wayward style of painting and poetry and stuff. So what we did was knock on people's doors and offer to sell them a cow – or he'd offer to buy a cow if they said they already had one. And it had to be done in that total darkness you get in French villages at night.'

'Why?'

'Well, he had a point in a way. He thought the world had become too organized, too bureaucratic – too predictable. People needed to get back to the irrational – which, of course, comes at you out of the darkness of the mind.'

'By buying and selling cows? The Führer had a much darker way than that.'

Felix laughed grimly. 'There was a lawyer who got the better of him that night, though. Breton introduced himself as Mister Corpse-Divine and offered to sell the man a cow and the lawyer said, "What shall I do with it then?" "Sell it back to me," Breton explained, "at a profit, of course. Then I can sell it back to you for an even greater profit . . . and so on. And in no time at all our combined profits will be in the milliards and we can take all our promissory notes to the banks and take out loans for at least a couple of million." And the lawyer asked why should the banks do that? And Breton said, "Because it's no different from what they're doing anyway – all day, every day!" So this lawyer promised to think it over. And when Breton and I were halfway back to the gate, he called after us, "We don't even need a real cow." And when we reached the gate, the fellow added, "*Enchanté, Monsieur Breton!*" He knew all along, you see. But even then, Breton had the last word: "I lied to you," he called back. "It wasn't a cow – it was an ambulance!"'

The sleeping and dining cars were Pullmans and the standard was almost back to pre-war levels. Dinner was cordon bleu and the table wine – as always on France's railways – was Châteauneuf du Pape, because, at its peak it never throws a deposit. They dined slowly and downed rather more wine than they might have done on any other night.

Felix told her about the nuns at the convent in Manresa Road, Chelsea, who had commissioned a sculpture by him. 'They want a Madonna and Child,' he said. 'We discussed something in stone, a pale, fine-textured granite with no obvious grain, but now I'm thinking more of doing something very fluid, very plastic, in bronze.'

'When did you change your mind?' Angela asked.

'At the top of the Eiffel Tower.'

'Because of what happened there?'

'It must be. That was a liberation of . . . so much more

than . . . I mean of my whole spirit. To be able to say "I love you" and—'

'You can say that as often as you like!'

'I love you. Everything around you is so . . . alive. And special. Stone can be rather static and *pure* – only someone like Bernini can persuade it to look like butter frozen after melting. Anyway – that's marble as nature never intended it to look. If *I* want something as vibrant as that, it'll have to be bronze. I know my limitations.'

'That's the second time you've mentioned Bernini to me, d'you realize?'

His eyes narrowed. 'When was the first?'

'At the midsummer party, or the day after, when we went for a walk in the walled garden and . . . did you ever put pigs in that comfrey?'

'Oh – *that* day!'

'Yes – *that* day! When I saw you stroking the apple-tree wood like that I wanted you to stroke me instead. I longed to throw my arms around you and say, "Let's . . ." you know.'

'Well, I'll say it for you now: "Let's . . . you know!"'

They kissed and caressed and undressed each other without embarrassment, languorously at first and finally with hasty abandon, so that they fell awkwardly between the sheets, which were tucked in so firmly that he could not rise above her without an angry struggle.

'Here!' As he was about to settle upon her she fished up his underpants from the floor.

'What . . . why . . . ?' he asked.

'For when you finish like a gentleman.'

'Oh.'

'What were you going to . . . have you got a . . . an FL?'

'Don't you want a baby?'

After a silence she said, 'Do you?'

'Yes. I think you'd make a wonderful mother – the best any child could ask for.'

'Whew!' She pulled a little away from him and lay back into the pillow, hands interwoven behind her head. 'But I have a career.'

'It wouldn't interfere too much with that. You can work up

to the eighth month – and go back to the job as soon as you like afterwards.'

'And the baby?'

'We can find a German girl who wants to learn English – or a French girl – during this visit. Maybe Tante Uschi knows of one. The French have this custom they call *au pair*—'

She started to laugh. 'Pasha Breit with his Anglo-German-French harem!'

'Marianne's getting a Swedish girl to live *au pair* and look after Siri so that she can go back to the drawing board. And Sally's thinking of doing the same. There's an unmarried mother in the village – a jilted GI bride-without-a-wedding-ring. She could look after both . . .'

'Well! They'd have a fit in Germany but maybe it's possible. But still I'd like to be in our own home and our own bed – and preferably with rings on our fingers – before we even think of starting babies.' She groped down into the bed and giggled. 'You won't be starting many babies with *that*!'

'I know . . . but if you just . . . yes, leave your hand there.'

'Oo-ooh!'

'Miraculous, eh? Oh! That's fantastic . . . yes! Yes!' He levered himself over her and she spread her thighs and let out a long, low moan . . . and . . .

A sudden shiver passed over her.

'What's wrong?' he asked.

'We just crossed the border into Germany. I know it.'

He gave a baffled laugh. 'So? We're not going to stop. They already checked our—'

'No! I just *know* it. I felt it.' She shivered again.

He lay beside her. 'You'd rather not?'

For a moment she was silent, breathing forcefully, panting.

'It's all right,' he assured her. 'I'm the insensitive one. I should have realized . . .'

'What's *wrong* with me?'

'Nothing. Is this your first time?'

'No! Well . . . yes . . . I suppose it is . . . in a way.'

'Oh, Angela!' He lay tight against her side, folding her in his arms. 'Angela! Dear sweet darling love. You should have said.'

She burst into tears, folding her face into his chest, sobbing with great, almost silent heavings of her body.

'It's going to be all right,' he murmured. 'Just don't take it to heart.'

When her crying had run its course she gave a huge, glutinous sniff and whispered, 'Sorry!'

'Nothing to be sorry for.'

'I thought it would all be just . . . so natural.'

'And it will be.' He began planting little kisses all over her face.

'Do "Sand in the right eye . . ." that thing Willard . . .'

'Sand in the right eye,' he said, raising himself on one elbow to perform the ritual. 'Sand in the left eye. Shed a little tear – here's mud in your eye! She sniffed heavily a couple of times and – at last – relaxed.

Thursday, 2 October 1947

At Hamburg Hauptbahnhof they saw a man standing by the ticket barrier, holding up a placard saying: Wirth/Breit.

He introduced himself: 'Hermann Treite.'

Angela was taken aback. 'Oh, but when I phoned you this morning . . . I didn't mean you to . . .' She held out her hand to shake his. But he raised it to within an inch of his lips and made a kiss, murmuring, '*Ich küsse ihren Hand, gnädiges Fraülein.*'

She laughed. 'Not exactly the greeting of a communist!'

'And Herr Breit?'

They shook hands. Felix took an immediate liking to him – a man at ease with himself and not above a little self-mockery. The New German, perhaps?

'You had to ring off, Miss Wirth, before I could—'

'The train was just leaving.'

'I know. But I wanted to tell you . . . that is, to invite you to stay with me while you're in Hamburg. I hope you haven't booked a hotel?'

Angela said that Felix knew a pension in St-Pauli and—

'Good!' he interrupted. 'Then you can stay with me. I don't know how the British government expects its people to survive abroad on just five pounds. I have a villa on the Elbchaussée.'

He mentioned the name nonchalantly but they both knew that was the most elite quarter of the city, an area of stately villas each in its own parkland. They thanked him kindly enough – although at a pension they could have shared a bed.

He picked up her suitcase and led the way out to a drophead Mercedes Sedanca de Ville of the kind favoured by the Führer for his triumphal cavalcades through conquered cities. He piled their cases on the front passenger seat and ushered them into the back. 'I must say,' Angela told him as they set off, 'Marianne von Ritter's description did not lead me to expect anything like this. She said you work in the docks. Are you still a communist?'

'That was true when she knew me – I did work in the docks. And still do. The day after the British army drove into Hamburg I saw my chance. I was a civilian clerk in the military docks – the old U-boat pens. So I just walked away from that and I bought a horse and cart and started carrying rubble from the docks. I thought if I'm doing something useful, they won't move me away from it.'

'But almost the whole city was rubble,' Felix said. 'Where did you dump it?'

He laughed. 'I didn't dump it – I graded it properly and sold it! Mostly to the city, for filling craters . . . mending roads . . . Within a year I had a dozen trucks – British army surplus. And also three fuel tankers. I was still carrying rubble but now also goods and fuel. And so it went on. I had unemployed boys carrying messages around the city on bicycles. Now they have Vespas.'

'And it's all legal?' Angela asked.

He was surprised. 'Why not?'

'Well . . . rationing for one thing.'

'Rationing?' He shrugged. 'It's not severe. Next year they say it will end completely, anyway.'

'Next *year*?' Felix exclaimed. '*You'll* be sending *us* food parcels next!'

'You think that's a joke? What about those Americans, eh – our enemies of three years ago? They're giving us hundreds of millions of dollars to get back on our feet and stand up against the Russians. And to the British – their *allies* of three years ago? To them they say, "Now you can pay us back our war loans!" We're lucky they weren't *our* allies!'

He had driven straight down to the northern bank of the

Elbe, to Neumühle and Övelgönne, avoiding the Elbchaussée until forced to join it; the route also avoided the Reeperbahn area where Willard and Marianne had been reunited.

'By the way,' he said, 'what is the ration in England now?' Angela answered, 'A quarter-kilo of meat, ditto fat, ditto sugar, ninety grams of bacon, sixty of cheese, sixty of tea, two litres of milk, a pound of bread, and a hundred-twenty grams of bon-bons. And that's it!'

He looked at her askance in the mirror. 'Well, that doesn't sound too bad. It's more than most Germans eat in a day.'

They laughed. 'That's the ration for a *week!*'

He whistled. 'We *must* organize those food parcels!'

They drove on past Klein Flottbeck and through Othmarschen.

'All the trees!' Felix sighed. 'Gone!'

'Blame last winter. We got as warm sawing them down as we did when burning them. A lot of land round here is owned by English merchants. The RAF never bombed it much, not even in 1942.'

'Gomorrah.'

'Yes. Even though the great Blohm and Voss armaments factories were just across the Elbe. And the Luftwaffe HQ just up the road here. Property is sacred to the English, *Gott sei dank!* Ah – that's Jacob's Restaurant. I have a table booked there for us this evening.'

A few hundred yards farther up the Elbchaussée they turned into a once-imposing gateway, now stripped of all its ornamental ironwork, and started along a newly gravelled drive that led up to a large stucco villa, classical in style and dating, Felix guessed, from the mid-nineteenth century.

'By the way,' Treite said, 'Birgit, whom you're about to meet, likes to be known as Frau Treite. I *will* marry her one day, when there's time, but I swear – if you take even a few days off in Hamburg nowadays someone else has stolen a contract from right under your nose. You are not married, eh? May I ask . . . that is . . . do you . . . what would your preference be for . . . ?'

'We can share a room,' Felix said.

'Even a bed,' Angela added.

'Good.' He relaxed, killed the motor, and stretched luxuriously. 'Life is good. We don't deserve it, but life is good.'

'Our house never had a bathroom,' Angela said after he had

showed them their room. She felt the mattress and approved. The décor reminded her of Kitty's, the Gestapo brothel in Giesebrechtstrasse – lots of pink, lots of silk, lots of smoky-grey glass, and carpets that swallowed your feet.

'Our bath hung on a nail.' Felix stripped to his waist and went to wash.

'Ours too, but there was no special room. That remark of his – "we don't deserve it, but life is good" – that was a sort of apology, you realize? I could feel all the way that he wanted to say *something* about us both having been in the KLs and also that he *didn't* want to say anything, either. I think that's the nearest he'll get.'

'Good thing, too.' He spoke through the towel as he scrubbed his face dry. 'One of my fears was that people would dwell on it.' He inspected the towel. 'God, that train was dirtier than I thought.'

'D'you suppose he's completely legitimate? He's certainly not the person Marianne remembers.'

She took his towel, after a brief tussle. 'We might as well get just the one dirty. We can share a clean one tomorrow.'

'In England he'd certainly be classed as some kind of posh spiv – but that's because there are so many thousands of rules and restrictions on everything there. I know we've only been in Germany less than a day but I already get the feeling that there's a lot more enterprise and . . . I don't know – freedom to *do* things here.'

'I can't wait to see what sort of woman Birgit is.'

In fact, 'Frau' Treite was a surprise to them both. They half-expected a bubbleheaded showgirl, ignorant but self-assured, ten years his junior and pneumatic of build; but she was, if anything, slightly older than him, dark, reserved, and lissom in a little black dress. She wore small diamond earrings and an intaglio brooch depicting a lady in profile, in ivory on a brown enamel ground; that, too, was ringed in diamonds. Everything about her was tasteful and understated. Angela suspected that Treite would not marry her until he felt he was good enough to *deserve* her.

But when the introductions were over and Manhattans poured out she said, 'And it's true you both survived the KLs?'

'*Katze!*' Treite gave an embarrassed laugh.

'What?'

He shrugged awkwardly. 'Anyway, the people who put them

in the KLs are either hanged or in jail or being hunted like rats. It's over.'

'The Ravensbrück trials have been held in Hamburg,' Birgit said. 'At the Curio House. They say there will be at least three more. They've already hanged quite a few.'

Angela drew breath to name a few of her favourites but Felix cut her short: 'Did Marianne tell you much about us?' he asked Treite.

But it was Birgit who answered with, 'How *is* Marianne?'

'You know her, too?' Felix said.

She glanced uncertainly at her man, who said, 'You don't know?'

'What?'

'I don't know if I should tell you.' After a pause he continued, 'Well, why not. It's nothing shameful.'

Birgit took over. 'She stayed with us – not in this house – where we were before. But she went through a bad time when Willard threw her over and went back to America . . . didn't eat . . . drank too much. But Hermann knew just what to say.' She grinned at him.

Like one confessing to a mean trick he said, 'I told her we were sure Willard would come back. And he'd look for her – he'd go straight to her old lodgings. Of course, I didn't believe it. But *she* did. She pulled herself together and went back there. But instead of living on her father's allowance she started this pavement-artist thing, which just about kept body and soul together. Then she wrote to us from London – thankyou-thankyou-thankyou! So my lie was the truth.' He shook his head at the strangeness of life. 'I don't think she touched her allowance since 'forty-three. It must have been a tidy sum by 'forty-seven – a wonderful dowry for Willard!'

'Willard has just opened an office in Mayfair,' Felix said quickly – for he had seen Angela draw breath, presumably to say that they knew nothing of this 'dowry' (and doubted Willard knew about it, either).

'Willard always fell on his feet,' Hermann said admiringly.

'He's not the only one,' Birgit said. Then, glancing at her watch – a primly elegant Philippe Patek – she added, 'Our table is waiting. We can walk – it's just down the road.'

*　　*　　*

Jacob's in 1947 was like Jacob's in 1937 except that the few uniforms on display were 'best blues' or khaki rather than *Feldgrau*. An elderly trio played selections from Johan Strauss, Millöcker, von Suppé, and Lehár . . . with an occasional soaring up to Mozart. And a booking in the name of Treite evidently commanded a table at the centre of the enormous bow window, with a view through the linden terrace to the Elbe. And a bottle of Sekt on ice in a silver cooler.

'Hard to believe there's a war on,' Angela said as they took their seats.

The Treites looked at her in surprise.

'It's a joke in England.'

The sommelier filled their glasses and it was *Prosit* all round.

The maître-d' took their orders − or, rather, recommended the turbot, which they all accepted. Angela and Felix wanted *Aalsuppe,* Birgit and Hermann melon.

When the man withdrew, Hermann said, 'We have Erhard, who says, "Let the people make the choices and make the money." You have Attlee, who says, "We'll take your money and spend it on making all your choices for you." Can it be true that they're forcing industry to go where unemployment is high?'

'What's wrong with that?' Angela asked.

Hermann glanced at Birgit and spread his hands in a gesture of jocular hopelessness. 'What's *right* with it?' he countered as four commis waiters brought their entrées. 'Do they ask *why* there's high unemployment there? Perhaps the factory site is on the far side of some mountain in Wales? Or the telephone exchange is the same as it was in nineteen twenty-seven? Or all the people with technical training have gone to Coventry, where business is booming *despite* Mister Attlee? Or the workers are split among thirty different trade unions and negotiations are a nightmare?' He grinned. 'I read the English papers, you see. England spent eighteen million pounds *a day* throughout the war and now they're so deep in the hole they can't see the way out. Also . . .' He hesitated.

'What?' Angela asked. 'And this is not the Hermann Treite that Marianne once knew.'

'War destroys more than the *physical* world. I was going to say − Germany has so many advantages, not just American aid.

We will never try to develop atomic weapons. Big saving. We have had our illusions of empire taken away. More big savings. Poor France. Poor Britain. Old-fashioned industries mostly intact. Old-fashioned thinking . . . *absolutely* intact! Give us ten years and we'll be the powerhouse of Europe.'

The empty Sekt bottle was replaced by a Mosel from the Bruderschaft vineyard in Klüsserath – not chilled, as it would have been in London, but cool. Deliciously cool.

'Did Hermann mention your papers?' Birgit asked Angela.

She, in turn, glanced at Felix and then let out a brief, explosive sigh at the impossibility of explaining – or justifying – what she was about to say. 'The thing is . . . the thing is . . . Felix and I . . . I mean, when we started this journey at Victoria Station –' she glanced at him – 'how many months ago?'

He shook his head. 'I don't remember. I think it was in another lifetime.'

Birgit cottoned on before her man, who seemed bewildered. 'You fell in love!' she cried, clapping her hands and then resting them in an attitude of prayer below her open mouth; her eyes begged them to go on.

'We fell in love . . . oh . . . lo-o-ong ago . . .'

'The first day we met,' Felix said. 'We only found the courage . . . *I* only found the courage to admit it when we were in Paris.'

'Nowhere better,' Hermann put in.

'Meanwhile he's started living with another woman.'

Birgit made a strange little indrawn scream and turned great searching eyes on Felix. He laid a demonstrative hand over Angela's wine glass and said, 'With a woman who has never said she loves me – which she doesn't – and whom I've never told I love – which I don't. It is an arrangement that suited her career and my career at a particular time.'

'And the sex is good,' Angela assured Birgit with all the wide-eyed enthusiasm of an ingénue.

'To sex – *prosit!*' Hermann said with all the shifty-eyed enthusiasm of the embarrassed. 'All sex is good.'

'You asked Angela about those papers,' Felix reminded Birgit.

Angela cut in: 'The thing I was going to say was that . . . well, life is very different now from the way it was. Even from the way it was last week.' She smiled at Felix. 'I did what I could back in 'forty-five. I gave it to the British, who say they can't now find it.'

'But they found what they *say* is the true protocol of that same meeting,' Hermann said. 'A fake, in my opinion.'

'Not entirely,' Birgit said with quiet insistence.

'You've read it?' Felix asked.

'I've read them both – the protocol they dug up for the von Weizsäcker trial—'

'He wasn't even *at* the Wannsee meeting,' Angela said.

'But Luther, who reported to him, was,' Hermann pointed out.

One waiter removed their dishes, four others served their turbot.

'None of your fancy Frenchified sauces,' Hermann pointed out.

'Anyway,' Birgit continued after an interval of appreciative chewing, 'when Hermann showed me the British protocol, at first I agreed with him that it was a fake – especially the covering letter, which is in very poor German. But when I read your transcript of what was actually said that day, I changed my mind.'

'This is *her* theory,' Hermann said dismissively.

'You think the protocol the British found is *genuine*?' Angela asked.

'I think it's a genuine Nazi document,' she replied, 'but it was written – or, rather, *concocted* – sometime in 'forty-four and then backdated . . . and for very good reasons.'

'What she thinks happened . . .' Hermann said impatiently.

'I can tell it,' she insisted, turning to Angela. 'Did anyone at that meeting – apart from you, of course – make any kind of record of what was said?'

She shook her head. 'Heydrich said Eichmann would circulate a summary but I don't know if he ever did. I *do* know that he collected every bit of paper on which anyone had scribbled any sort of note. And burned them. They were certainly determined *at that time* to make sure there was *nothing* on paper. He even came back that evening to break up all the ashes. Caught me dismantling the equipment! I told him I was *assembling* it for an Interpol conference the next week but he knew I was lying, even though Heydrich backed me up. And when Heydrich was gone . . . *pffft* – *wiedersehen Angela!*' She turned to Birgit. 'But what is your theory about this fake protocol?'

'Not fake. Concocted.' She leaped in ahead of Hermann. '*I* think that at some point in 'forty-four, when it became clear even to the blindest Nazi that we were going to lose the war, some of the people at that conference, and dozens more to whom they had reported, suddenly realized that the absence of a proper protocol would look highly suspicious – as if what was said and decided there was just *too* shocking to record, which, of course, it was. So they concocted a protocol that was much milder in tone. They knew they couldn't deny the *Vernichtung,* but even so, no prosecutor could rely on that protocol to prove that *those present* – that's all they were worried about "those present" – knew or were told anything about the actual workings of the *Vernichtung.* The worst they heard, according to that so-called "official" protocol, was that the Jews would be marched around eastern Europe building roads and factories and railways and a lot of them would die under harsh conditions. But the same was true of German soldiers on the Eastern Front . . . so what? It was very clever.'

'But why did they then fake a covering letter in such poor German?' Hermann asked, as if it were his trump card.

'Because,' she replied with weary patience, 'the British and the Yanks are too lazy to learn any foreign language. They wouldn't recognize how poor it is. And that makes it possible for *surviving* Nazis to discredit the made-up protocol itself. Not every Nazi will be hanged or imprisoned. There are thousands of true believers out there who will pounce on that letter and show it is an obvious forgery, which isn't difficult. And, as I say, that will discredit the protocol itself, as well. The Nazis were thorough. They thought of everything from every angle, you see. I'm sure Eichmann was one of those who concocted the fake Wannsee protocol, because the population figures for Jews in various European countries – as you recorded them on the actual day, Angela – are repeated precisely in the *ersatz* protocol. So that's why I say it's the work of a fiendishly clever Nazi, or group of Nazis, who realized the trap was closing around them. It gives the Allies the faintest hint that the *Vernichtung* was planned from 'forty-one onwards and it allows true believers to deny there ever was a *Vernichtung* at all. And by the way – it's not just poor German language that gives it away as a fake. In fact, the biggest giveaway is the typewriter they used for the covering letter. It doesn't use the *Runenschrift* SS – you know, like two lightning strokes.' She drew ⚡ on the tablecloth with her finger.

Felix laughed. 'I think we can just about remember what it looked like!'

'Of course!' She grinned guiltily. 'Anyway, the covering letter uses the ordinary, standard double S throughout.'

Angela was shocked. 'But that's unthinkable in any Nazi document. Every official typewriter was modified to be able to type the SS in *Runenschrift*.'

'So you see why I call it fiendishly clever! To the Allies it says "genuine" because they have no idea how significant the *Runenschrift*-SS was – and to those in the know it shouts "fake"!' Angela turned to Hermann. 'And why don't you believe this?'

'I believe half of it – why the alleged protocol was concocted in 'forty-four or even later. But I think the covering letter was a hasty and badly executed forgery *by the British*, who needed some sort of document to "give it provenance", as the art dealers say. It's the simplest theory that fits all the known facts. But from your point of view it doesn't really matter whether Birgit is right or I am right. That conference – where you recorded every word, every nuance of speech, right down to that spine-chilling "funny story" Lange tells Heydrich at the end – when they're standing outside the villa and watching everybody go . . .'

'What's that?' Felix asked. 'You've never mentioned—'

Angela shook her head violently. 'You'll have to read it. I couldn't possibly tell it without being sick. Again. If there was one single moment when I became anti-Nazi, that was it – when I heard Lange say that.'

'Anyway,' Hermann insisted, 'you are the one person now alive and free with incontrovertible *proof* of what was actually revealed at that conference. If you don't speak out, then a concocted protocol and its fake covering letter are what history will record as what happened there that day. And it may be convenient for the Allies to rely on them today, but they won't stand the scrutiny of time. So I don't think you have any choice.'

'Aren't you angry with me?' Angela asked Felix when they were alone in their room again.

'Because of Faith – what you said about her and me? No.

You have every right. I should never have let her move in. Or I should have insisted on separate rooms.'

She folded her dress neatly over the back of her chair and stood facing him, uncertain and awkward, reaching behind her for her bra hook but not slipping it loose. 'How long would that have lasted?' she asked.

'You have beautiful breasts.' He turned out the light as he crossed the room to her. On the way he shed the last of his underclothes.

A dim orange light seeped out from the bathroom; she stood like a rabbit caught in a distant headlamp, alert but not yet anxious.

When he took her in his arms, pressing her hard against the wall beside their bed, she slipped the catch of her bra. But he stopped her shrugging it off, insinuating his fingers up underneath the material and playing upon her nipples. His erection found its goal but he did not press home just yet. Passionate kiss followed passionate kiss as his hands strayed all over her nakedness, raking the long muscles of her back and the firmness of her buttocks, feeling every curve with a sculptor's relish, which was masterful, and a lover's passion, which was soon impossible to contain. They broke their kiss for breath and her muscles yielded; she would have slid to the floor if he had not forced his broad, strong hands beneath her buttocks and lifted her up and – finally – onto him. She let out a gasp and then clung to him, shivering. Two or three thrusts and he came, not copiously. She bit his shoulder. Tears, reflecting orange light, wet her cheeks.

'Let's go to bed and do it properly,' he suggested. 'Oh – and let's get married as soon as possible after we get back home?'

'Home,' she murmured, kissing his face all over, sharing her tears. 'Yes.'

Friday, 3 October 1947

As Felix had explained, Tante Uschi lived not in Kiel but in Laboe, a village at the mouth of Kiel Bay. 'It's the smallest house in Rosenstrasse,' she told Felix on the phone that morning. 'And it's a very short street, so we're easy to find. You should be with us in time for lunch.'

'We?' he queried.

'Me and . . . Max.' There was an awkward pause, broken by her laugh. 'My dog!'

Felix decided he wanted to walk the last hundred metres, so the taxi dropped them at the end of the street – or, rather, at the beginning, for the end was a cul-de-sac. After no more than ten paces he halted. 'There's no doubt which is the smallest house,' he said. 'But . . . well, maybe Max *isn't* a dog.' He pointed out the man standing at the gate.

She clutched at his arm. 'Oh . . . Felix . . .'

'What now?'

'D'you think that could be . . . oh, my God . . .'

Felix looked again at the man and whispered, '*Ach, du liebe Zeit!*'

'I had a feeling when I read . . .' Angela began, and then, looking at Felix, thought better of it.

He dropped their suitcases and broke into a run, not halting until he was a few paces short of the man at the gate, at which he stopped dead.

'Felix!' The man smiled and stretched out his arms.

'Why?' Felix asked.

'Those letters . . . they *were* genuine.'

Felix shook his head, in bewilderment rather than denial.

'Otherwise . . .'

'Otherwise what?'

'I was afraid you wouldn't come.'

'Oh . . . Vati!'

With tears brimming at her eyelids Angela watched as a suddenly awkward Felix lumbered forward and drowned his father in a tight embrace – a gesture made even more awkward by the gate between them.

She hefted the suitcases and set out to join them, knowing he would welcome the intrusion. A ragged lilac tree obscured all but the roof of the house until she was almost there; she took her eyes off the two men long enough to see . . .

'Tante Uschi!' she murmured, and waved at the woman who was watching them from an upstairs window.

'It's not her fault.' Vati broke from his son and turned toward

Angela. 'Blame me. I asked her to write those letters. She was against it.' Then, to Felix: 'And she's no longer Tante, by the way. She's Mutti – your new stepmother.' Then, with a nod toward Angela: 'Am I not to be introduced?'

'May I present my father, Herr Willi Breit. Late of the grave. Also known as Max the dog. Vati, this is Angela Worth, soon to be yet another Mrs Breit.'

'*Ach so-o-o!*' He shook her hand and then raised it to kiss.

Angela could see no resemblance whatever between father and son. The old man was slightly built, wiry, fair-haired, restless; his son – tall, stocky, powerful, dark, and, at times, infuriatingly taciturn. Neither looked remotely like the Jewish stereotypes Goebbels had propagandized.

Tante – now Mutti – Uschi appeared in the doorway.

Vati offered Angela his arm and they strolled side by side up the path. Felix now hefted the bags and followed them. 'Were you going to say you suspected something like this?' he asked Angela.

'"Suspected" is a bit strong. But I did wonder why – in the second letter – she said she hoped you reached Sweden safely but didn't exactly describe how and when you left here. Actually, I suspected that might have been because you really intended going back to Berlin and that Sweden via Denmark was a bluff.'

Vati gave her a swift, penetrating glance and then turned to Felix. 'Always listen to this lady,' he said. 'She's no fool. When I wrote that letter I did intend returning to Berlin, but then I thought if the letter ever got intercepted, the Gestapo might see through it. So I did exactly what it said. And yes, I did escape. And I did reach Sweden.'

When the further introductions were over and Felix and Mutti had mopped their eyes, she held out her arms to bar the door. 'Stay here a moment,' she said. 'Some of our neighbours are watching and I want two of them in particular to have a good long look at this reunion.'

'Who?' Felix asked.

'Sanders down there on the corner, for one. And Bachmann, with the new red tiles on his roof – they have five children, for which she got the Hitler Cross. Two years ago, both those fine families would have gladly denounced the four of us to the Gestapo. We must all go for a walk after lunch and I hope we meet them.' She sniffed deeply on the air and concluded, 'Just smell the freedom now!'

After lunch, Angela excused herself and left for a walk on the beach; the others protested – she was part of the family now, inside the perimeter of their privacy, and so forth . . . but hers was the wiser head just then. An hour or so later Felix set out to join her. But at the edge of the beach, where the tarmac ended and the sand began, he paused. She stood, statuesque and statue-still, gazing out to sea – the sea where his mother and grandfather, old Billy Breit, had drowned, eleven years ago. For a moment he was overcome by his love for her – a love like no other, at least not in his experience, for it was a mixture of desire, not just to possess but to protect as well, and to know all those unknowable things about her as a separate human being . . . of desire and . . . fear. Beneath that mature and reconciled exterior, who could know what unresolved conflicts and guilts still lay in ambush?

And not just the obvious guilts, either, but the treacheries they had both committed (and tolerated in others) simply to survive in a KL. From the theft of a crust to the substitution of an unknown name for that of a friend on a list of prisoners destined not to survive . . . these acts were survival's stock-in-trade. In the imperative of the moment they scored no mark, left no outward scar; but there must be internal bruises – healed or bruises still?

The broken waves rushed at her, hissing over the sand in tongues; she stood, watching, as if daring them to lap her ankles.

'It's not very tidal here,' he called out as he drew near. 'All the water has to come in and out through the Kattegat.' He folded her in his arms and luxuriated in that magical presence which seemed always to surround her, and only her.

'Here,' he said when they broke.

'What?'

He fumbled in his pocket. 'My mother's engagement ring – now yours. Hand!'

The moment it was on her finger she flung her arms around him and hugged herself tight into his chest. 'So precious,' she whispered.

'Nothing like so precious as you.'

She broke from him and held her hands up to his face, palms to his nostrils. 'Smell that,' she said – then immediately plucked them away and, bunching them into a tight fist, said, 'No! I'm sorry.'

'What?' he asked.

'Nothing.'

But he had already caught a whiff of what she had wanted him to smell. Gently he took her wrists between thumb and one finger and raised them again to his face. As in a trance, she watched him unfold them, finger by finger, and press them to him. He sniffed deeply, then closed his eyes and murmured, 'My God! That's it! That's it!' He opened his eyes again. 'What is it?'

'Wild geranium.' She let her hands fall to her side and gestured vaguely to a clump growing above the tideline. 'A mad woman once told me that if I ever needed to remind myself how the KL smelled, just crush geranium leaves. At least I thought she was mad then . . . now . . . I'm not so sure.'

'It's exact,' he said. 'Wash it off.'

They went down to the water's edge, where she slipped off the ring and handed it for him to hold while she used wet sand to scour her hands clean again.

They kissed and he replaced the ring on her finger. 'It looks a bit loose to me.'

'It's fine. Food parcels from Germany will take care of that.'

They took a few aimless steps while she held her hand splayed before them, admiring the simple gold band. 'I met Herr Sanders,' she said.

'And?'

'He asked if you were the son they thought had died in a KL – the famous artist. I said you were and he said thank God you survived. So they never told him you survived! Anyway, I asked what he thought about the others – the *millions* who didn't survive. He just shook his head. He was too choked to speak.'

Felix sensed she had not finished but he did not press her. At length she continued, 'I told him I was an SS-*Führerin* . . .'

'You didn't!'

'I wanted to see if he'd change his tune. But he didn't. He actually backed away from me. So then I said I protested at the *Vernichtung* and they put me in Ravensbrück, and d'you know what he said?'

'What?'

'He shook my hand and said, "So you spoke out in time!" I just laughed and said my little gesture didn't save a single life, and he said, "That's not what speaking out in time means. It's when you *suffer* for speaking out — that's what matters. You spoke out in time to suffer. And now the rest of us must suffer for *not* speaking out." D'you think he's right?'

Felix gave the easy answer: 'In your case, yes.'

'I told him something Nicole once said to me, which was . . . we were talking about resistance to the Nazis and she said it was like standing at the edge of a vast marsh, a horizon-to-horizon marsh, and shooting arrows into it at random. In the dark. The pleasure . . . no, the *reward* was simply in firing off the arrows. It didn't really matter whether they hit anything or not. You just had to keep firing. And hoping.'

'Let's walk — or d'you want to go back to . . . ?' He nodded toward the house he could not quite call home.

'Walk. I want to hear what happened.'

'Then you should have stayed!'

She dug him sharply with her elbow. 'Why d'you say Sanders was right "in my case"? Don't you think he was right in your case, too?'

'I never spoke out — not in any situation where I'd suffer for it. I took great care not to. So I was like any other German — and a good many French and Poles and Dutchmen. And Italians, too.'

She swept a hand vaguely out toward the sea, much as to say, *What's the point?* 'Anyway,' she went on, 'tell me all about it — this unexpected reunion.'

After a pause he said, 'Vati didn't know we are Jewish. Were Jewish.'

'Until they arrested *him*?'

'No. He got warning from someone in the Brown House. Anyway — we both got away. When I first read those letters, it intrigued me to think that while I'd been on the run in the south of France — after the Nazis occupied the whole country and we couldn't rely on the corruption of the Vichy authorities — Vati had been undergoing a similar ordeal in occupied Denmark. But it's more amazing still. Listen! We both had false papers in the name of Brandt!'

'Someone you know?'

'No! *That's* the extraordinary thing. We each chose it out of the blue. It held no special significance for either of us.'

'Apart from being close enough to Breit for you to answer to it – without much hesitation, that is.'

'Well . . . yes,' he conceded. 'There is that.'

She giggled. 'Sorry. Am I spoiling it? I won't say another word.'

'My father has learned – this was only last year – he's learned how old Billy Breit – born Solomon Breit – became Christianized. My great-grandparents, about whom we know nothing, were wealthy Orthodox Jews living in Berlin and, because they couldn't even turn on a light switch on the Sabbath, they employed Christian servants, who could break all those old laws for them. And so baby Solomon had a young Catholic nursemaid. And when he got whooping cough or measles or something, the girl got in a panic at the thought that this little baby whom she loved was going to spend all eternity in hell if he died. So she asked her priest what to do and he told her how to baptize the baby. Which she did. He lived, of course, but the priest then invoked the law, which said that a baptized Christian child could not be brought up by Jews. And they seized him. The priest came with a squad of police and they seized him. And they put him for adoption with a violently evangelical Protestant couple – childless . . .'

'Protestant?'

'I'm sure money changed hands. Anyway, they brought him up as Billy Breit, the famous artist and anti-Semite. It took half a dozen words and a splash of water to make him Christian but it took five kilos of the Nuremberg Laws and the most ruthless bureaucracy in history to turn us back into Jews again. Funny old world.'

They had reached the northern end of the beach, where municipal sand gave way to heathland; there they turned and strolled slowly back again. She was silent so long that he was at last forced to say, 'Well?'

'I don't want to come back to Germany for quite a while,' she said. 'Certainly not to live.'

He gave a baffled laugh. 'Was that ever on the cards?'

'It was at the back of my mind before we set out from

London – and still just about possible in Paris, even after . . .
you know – the Eiffel Tower.'

'We both have a much brighter future in England. In London
– don't you think?'

'Yes, of course, but apart from that . . . I mean, seeing the
way Germany is recovering now . . . when I left, they were
defeated. Now they're realizing that actually it wasn't defeat but
liberation. The Allies liberated us just like they liberated France
and Holland and so on. And it seems obvious to me that liberated France and liberated Germany, or half-Germany, are going
to dominate the rest of Europe. The English have no idea. At
the BBC I can listen to the news from anywhere, not just what
they distil for British ears. But even I had no idea how things
really were until this trip. You heard how young Treite speaks.
That's the voice of the new Germany. It shocked me. I thought
it would be decades before any German would speak like that
again. But the English don't listen to foreign news at all. They
have absolutely no idea of what's going to happen here in Europe.
They *must* wake up! They must join in. They must make a
balance between France and Germany in the new Europe or it
will all go wrong again. The state will triumph over the
individual.'

Felix stared out across the sea, to the horizon that hid
Denmark. Was this going to be their first serious quarrel?

She pressed him for an answer . . . some word of
agreement.

'Include me out!' he said, aping Willard. 'The English will
never belong in Europe.'

'Not immediately. But eventually they must.'

'They *ought* to, but they won't. Ever. The mentality of a
nation that has only ever been the conqueror has no place among
nations whose history has alternated between victory and defeat.'
He laughed drily. 'If we try to convert them, we'll just be known
as The Breit Bores!'

She shook her head. 'Only if we go about it crudely. Not
go for conversions – just . . . bearing witness.'

Friday, 10 October 1947

A week later, on the train back to Cologne, and thence to Paris, Felix took out the Wannsee transcript and said, 'You came all the way to collect this, and you haven't even looked at it.'

'I know what's in it,' she said. 'Of course, I always did know – in general . . . a fading memory. But seeing it again, exactly as I typed it, has brought it all back. And now I don't think I can.'

'Because?'

She sighed and it was a long time before she answered. 'Because . . . because one day, when I was delivering some tapes from Giesebrechtstrasse to B-IV, I went to the Ladies and there was a Jewess there – part of some liaison or welfare committee. You know how the Nazis liked the Jews to administer as much of the resettlement programme as possible – because it gave confidence to the proceedings. I assume she was on one of those committees. She had an escort, of course, but that woman was in one of the toilets. I could just have whispered, "Don't believe in *Resettlement* – it's a cover-name for *Vernichtung*." I could.'

'And risk her shouting, "What? What are you saying?" . . . Or just the give-away look on her face when her escort came out? Or her telling everyone on the committee and word of it getting back to the Gestapo, who would trace it back to you? Or—'

'Felix!'

'What?'

'Darling! Of course *all* those objections raced through my mind at the time, but whenever I thought about it afterwards, I could never be sure that I didn't simply fail to overcome a decade of Nazi indoctrination . . . that I could not risk my life for a bloody *Jew!*' After a pause she added, 'And that suspicion would haunt me through every single page of this transcript. Anyway – just holding it in my hand . . . smelling the paper . . . official German paper had a particular smell in the war. Have a sniff. That takes me right back, so I don't actually *need* to read it again.'

He sniffed the paper and said, 'God, you're right.'

He settled back and opened the package.

A verbatim protocol of a meeting held at Interpol Headquarters,
Am Großen Wannsee 56/58 on January 20, 1942, secretly recorded
on tape and wax by me, ∯-Führerin Angela Wirth, on the orders of
∯-Obergruppenführer Reinhard Heydrich. This transcription from
that tape was made without his knowledge and the tape itself was
made without the knowledge of any of the participants.

It is now my intention to convey it, through certain channels,
to a neutral embassy, so that it may become known to the world.
Angela Wirth
1 March, 1942

[In the anteroom – a meeting exclusively of the ss]

HEYDRICH: I've decided to change the seating plan I circulated
   among you. We were – you remember – going to be seated
   with an ss officer between each civilian – to inhibit them from
   writing damaging notes. But Gutterer can't come, Greifelt can't
   come, our own Krüger can't come, and Freisler will be
   standing in for Schlegelberger, so . . .

MÜLLER: Cold feet?

HEYDRICH: If so, they'll never forgive themselves. Today is one of
   the truly great days in the history of the Third Reich. Anyway,
   seeing that we are now seven civilians and eight ss, I believe
   we'll make a stronger impression if we sit in one solid rank, all
   along one side of the table – with our backs to the windows –
   facing them.

LANGE: And they can write notes?

HEYDRICH: They can write whatever they want. Comrade
   Eichmann will collect every last scrap of paper at the end and
   burn it.

MÜLLER: After reading them!

HEYDRICH: No! What they write, what they think, what they feel
   – it's of no consequence. They're only messenger boys, deliberately chosen from the second-tier of the party and government
   (and I include myself here) to carry the message of the Final
   Solution back to their masters. And the message comes from
   my master – our master – the Reichsprotektor himself.

MEYER: And ultimately from his master – the Führer.

HEYDRICH: Of course. And for that reason, there may not even be
   a protocol. [*surprise*] Think about it. What we're going to do
   will, in the eyes of many, even of many good Germans . . . I

mean – put it another way. Do any of you think the Führer
should go on the radio and announce that we are starting a
programme of annihilation of every last Jew in Europe – and
ultimately the world?

SEVERAL: No!

HEYDRICH: Precisely. And for the very same reason, we will probably have no protocol. Or we may produce a general or
summary version. We'll make that decision later. First I want to
gauge the reaction of senior party members like the ones who
are here today. But we already know that a literal protocol
would be a time-bomb waiting to explode in our faces if
certain milk-and-water party-members had their way. Comrade
Müller, I just want one assurance from you – we are ready, are
we not, to go ahead with the annihilation of Jews and other
undesirables at the rates we discussed?

MÜLLER: When Höss has put the Auschwitz facility in place –
which will be before the autumn – we can process them at the
highest rate of all. Ten thousand on a good day. But – as I
noted in my report – the 'Brack solution' is not the answer.
Carbon monoxide is too slow and the killing rate too variable.
We will continue to perfect it at some of the camps but our
main agent at the big camps of last resort will be Zyklon-B –
the gas that was so effective with those gypsy children last year.
When the remaining camps are fully in action – Belzec,
Sobibor, Treblinka, and Majdanek . . .

EICHMANN: The problem will shift to the railways!

HEYDRICH: Speaking of Höss, the Reichsführer-∦ wants direct
communication with him. Cutting out Glück. Make sure Höss
understands that. Good! Excellent! We're so far ahead that now
no one can volunteer to take the honour out of our hands. Let
us join our colleagues . . .

MÜLLER: And show them who's master!

HEYDRICH: The order is unchanged. I'll open the proceedings,
then I'll ask you, Comrade Schöngarth to cover the history.
Then you, Comrade Eichmann, will reveal the sheer size of the
problem – in case anybody there still thinks they could share in
the glory. Then Comrade Lange will show why the Action
Groups – despite amazing achievements – are not the Final
Solution. Then Comrade Müller will tell them what that Final
Solution really is.

KLOPFER: And us?

HEYDRICH: You and Comrade Hofmann have the most important task of all, which is to answer objections from the bureaucrats. Treat Kritzinger with respect. Be firm but not belligerent with Neumann, who will want to keep his privileged Jews and high-level workers. Remember he is a brother officer. Be as scornful as you like with Stuckart with his pleas for half-Jews and quarter-Jews. But be sympathetic with Gauleiter Meyer and Doctor Liebbrandt and Doctor Bühler of the Generalgouvernement, who will all want their Jews to have priority for liquidation – for very understandable reasons – but promise them nothing unless we have to.

EICHMANN: Liquidating the eastern Jews first would ease the strain on the railways.

HEYDRICH: Politics may dictate otherwise. Think what a birthday present it would make for the Führer to announce to him that the whole of Germany was Jew-cleansed! A birthday present exclusively from the ss! Come! We've kept them waiting long enough. [to Schöngarth, on their way to the chamber] Can you find some occasion this morning to let either Meyer or Liebbrandt know that there will be no detailed protocol and that their report to Frank will be either verbal – and minuted there in the Reich Ministry for the Occupied Eastern Territories – or in their words over their own signatures? Frank must understand he is a fully committed party to the Final Solution, not sitting on the fence. You understand?

SCHÖNGARTH: Perfectly, Herr Obergruppenführer! [They enter the conference room]

HEYDRICH: Good morning, gentlemen. Heil Hitler!

ALL: Heil Hitler!

HEYDRICH: Doktor Kritzinger, may I invite you to sit at the head of the table? We need a wise and experienced head to keep an eye on all these eager civilians! [laughter] The rest of you, please take whatever seat is nearest you, without ceremony. Today we are all on one niveau, united – I trust – in one single task.

Here Angela had inserted the seating order, with all the top men in the ss (except Himmler himself, of course) ranged down one side and all the second rankers from the civilian ministries

and the bureaucracy governing the occupied East facing them
on the other, with the veteran Kritzinger at the head of the
table. The real powers – Goebbels, Göring, von Ribbentrop,
Speer, Bormann, and, of course, the Führer himself – were
taking care to be absent.

KRITZINGER: Am I in the chair? I hope not. It should surely be
    you, Herr Deputy Reichsprotektor?
HEYDRICH: It should be, and it is. But our purpose today is for
    us, of the Schutzstaffel, to tell you, representing all the impor-
    tant ministries and branches of the party and government, what
    progress we have made in the Jewish Question – specifically,
    the Final Solution to that question. So . . . to our duties! Herr
    Gauleiter, State Secretaries, Herr Reichsamtsleiter, Herr
    Ministerialdirektor, ss comrades – you may remember this
    meeting was first convened by Reichsmarschall Göring in July
    last year, but it had to be postponed for various strategic
    reasons – not least our declaration of war against America last
    autumn. However, we have not been idle in the intervening
    months. Last autumn we could only have told you of various
    promising experiments we were then conducting. Now we can
    assure you that we have the perfect means to fulfil the Führer's
    dream of a Jew-cleansed Europe within a reasonable number of
    years! [sensation] But I'm getting ahead of myself. A copy of
    the Reichsmarschall's letter was enclosed with your invitations
    today, so I needn't read it fully now. 'Berlin, July the thirty-
    first, nineteen forty-one . . . Reichsmarschall of Greater
    Germany, Chairman of the Defence Council, to . . . myself
    . . . Further to . . . etcetera . . . I instruct you to make all
    expedient preparations of the complete solution to the Jewish
    Question in Europe . . . produce for me a detailed plan for
    carrying out the Final Solution . . . as for the other depart-
    ments of the party and state . . . these should be involved to
    the fullest extent necessary . . . etcetera, etcetera.' In other
    words, gentlemen – you!
KRITZINGER: Is there to be no protocol of this meeting?
HEYDRICH: Oberstürmbannführer Eichmann will circulate a
    general protocol next week – a summary of the main points,
    only. In half an hour from now, I'm sure you'll not simply
    understand this caution – you'll applaud it. So! I will now ask

the Chief of Security Police and the SD in the Generalgouvernement to provide a brief outline of the problem.

Felix let his eye wander down over Schöngarth's politically sanctioned version of the Jewish diaspora and Eichmann's interminable country-by-country listing of Jewish populations – they were, in any case, familiar to him from the 'official' transcript. He picked it up again several pages later:

EICHMANN: Over eleven million Jews! Of which over four and a half million are already under our control.

FREISLER: Dear God! They breed like lice. The Romans kick a few hundred-thousand out of Israel – and end up making us a gift of eleven million!

KRITZINGER: How can we resettle even four and a half million? And where?

LANGE: Some in the earth, some in the sky. [laughter]

KRITZINGER: Kill them?

HEYDRICH: What else?

KRITZINGER: That's a lot of bullets. My son is serving on the Russian front and has written to me of a shortage of many things – including, at times, ammunition.

HEYDRICH: Yes, we agree entirely. Bullets are not the answer – as Sturmbannführer Doctor Lange will describe next. First, I must explain that we have since 1939 liquidated hundreds of thousands of Russian, Baltic, and Polish Jews – often with the enthusiastic support of their fellow non-Jewish citizens. [applause] This has been achieved by using mobile Action Groups [Einsatzgruppen], sweeping across the country in a systematic way, leaving the land cleansed of Jews behind them. The Führer told me he sees himself as a political Robert Koch, killing off harmful germs to save the body politic. And Comrade Lange has been the Führer's medicine – the silver bullet. His part has been truly heroic. [applause]

LANGE: It is not difficult if we apply ourselves with true German thoroughness. There are four Action Groups. I command one of them. Each has a thousand men, or, I should say, a thousand personnel, of whom about two dozen are women. They are drawn from the SS-Reserve, the Waffen-SS, the Gestapo,

Security, and the Criminal Police. But they are all united in
one purpose. An Action Group works from day to day, splitting
up into Commandos whose size depends on the terrain, the
cooperation we receive from the local population, the density
of the population, and so on. Rounding up the Jews is almost
always the easiest part. They live among people who covet
their houses and whatever small bits of property we are careful
to leave behind. If they are reluctant to cooperate, we can
usually find a priest who will remind them that when the Jews
chose to crucify Christ and set Barabbas free, they said, 'On
our head be it, and on the heads of our children for ever.' In
one case we even found a rabbi who made the same point for
us! [laughter] We then send the able-bodied men and boys out
to dig a mass grave. When they've finished, they strip naked
and jump into it – after some encouragement – and are shot.
We then make the remainder – the women and children, the
old ones, the sick, and so on – we make them run out to the
graveside, strip off their clothes . . . and then they join
their menfolk in the grave. We try to make it with a hundred
bullets to every hundred Jews.

KRITZINGER: So you do use bullets, after all!

LANGE: No. It is true that we have rid the world of tens of thousands of Jews in this way, but all—

KLOPFER: But how do you make sure that all of them are dead?
People survive shootings every day.

LANGE: We pile the earth back on top of them. One way or
another they die.

FREISLER: And they never try to run away?

LANGE: Only if they'd prefer to have their throats ripped out by a
dog. But I was going to say that despite all our efforts – and
successes – all we have proved is that this can never be the way
to liquidate Jews by the million. Apart from the fact that it's
wasteful of ammunition that belongs in Russian flesh, it is sadly
the case that even the most ardent Jew-hater is affected by
having to look thousands of Jews in the face – especially the
women and children, and the old ones – and then shoot them.
Day after day after day. I assure you, it is no easy matter to
force a mother and two screaming children into a pit full of
corpses and then machine gun them. We would not be a civilized people if we could remain unaffected by such things. You

can tell yourself a thousand times that today's sweet little Jewish child is tomorrow's full-grown filthy Jew, but it doesn't make it any easier for our people. What all-too-often happens is that they drown their finer feelings in vodka and schnapps. Even so, many are burned out after just eight weeks. In fact, we have found that Slav collaborators – and Slavs, as we know, are racially backward compared to us Aryans – they can stand it much better than most Aryan Germans. It's not a pleasant thing to confess but it's a fact. We do it out of duty, determination, and the iron will of the Führer. They do it because they don't think it's any different from shooting pigeons or hares.

MÜLLER: I think I can reveal – in this company – that the Reichsprotektor himself was physically ill when he witnessed an experimental gassing of only forty prisoners at Chiemnitz, a gassing that went wrong and left almost a dozen still clinging on to life. But he is adamant that our finer feeling should not compromise our duty. He said it proved that we are human beings with all our civilized feelings intact despite the unpleasant things we have to do. He also said that we must keep this extermination campaign secret – to avoid panic among the victims and to avoid a hypocritical outcry from other nations, who will secretly applaud and thank us even while they publicly condemn us in the same breath.

KRITZINGER: I'm glad to hear that bullets are ruled out because, as I said—

HEYDRICH: Except in small-scale mopping-up operations, where it is unreasonable to spare transport to move the Jews to the facilities we're about to describe. Their development has been led by Gruppenführer Müller – assisted by many of the others you see on this side of the table. Comrade.

MÜLLER: Our valuable experience with the Action Groups persuaded us that we had to find another way. We needed to be able to liquidate Jews at the rate of not hundreds a day but thousands a day. Perhaps even tens of thousands. To handle four and a half million Jews even at the rate of five thousand a day would still take three years. Everything flows from that – and from one key sentence in *Mein Kampf*! It's on page 772 if – like me – you have the first edition. There – after describing the treason of the Jews – the Führer writes that it would be better to take the entire Hebrew nation and poison them with

gas. Poison them with gas, gentlemen! His precise words! The
Jews of Europe are about to learn to their cost that it does not
pay to ignore the words of the Führer – he means them! Every
single one! Literally!

NEUMANN: What gas? Is this going to demand a diversion of
industry into manufacturing large volumes of—

MÜLLER: No, not at all. But what if it did?

NEUMANN: The Reichsmarschall charged me specifically today to
object to anything that might divert industry from the war
effort.

MEYER: Is this the same Reichsmarschall who has convened this
meeting and charged us to approve a Final Solution? He pats
us on the back and then trips us up!

MÜLLER: Fortunately, it's not an issue here. One small canister of
gas can liquidate four-thousand people at a single time – at
least, it will be able to when we have finished building the
necessary facilities. Let me describe what will happen from the
point of view of Abraham and Sarah and young Aaron and
Little Hymie and Baby Rebecca – because that way you'll see
it isn't a simple matter of putting them in a railway wagon and
killing them when they arrive at the end of the line.

The next few pages brought it home to Felix that the extermination system was already old by the time he was thrown into its
maw; vicious dogs and whips had greeted him at the railhead but
here was Müller describing arrivals in an apparent resettlement
camp whose cheerfully bright walls were decorated with soothing
posters of faraway places, all suggesting an imminent departure to
a place of one's choice . . . the Ukraine, the Black Sea, Turkey-
in-Asia. Was anyone ever really fooled by it?

What followed the idyll was also detailed by Müller: the ten-
thousand-a-day target, the selection for immediate 'processing'
or for slave labour; the quick and the slow death; the commercial
value of human hair, false teeth, gold teeth, spectacles, shoes,
clothing. (At one point Heydrich said, 'My next birthday present
to my wife will be a doormat made from shaved-off Jewish hair
no longer required by its original owner.')

The entire process was described in detail . . . the arrival, the
undressing ('Tie your shoes together by their laces and note the
number above your peg for when you come back.'), the

head-shaving, the 'showers' where they were gassed 4,000 at a time, and the crematorium ovens – all performed by a *Sonderkommando* of Jews, who, as Lange said, 'will do anything to snatch just one more day on earth. Sell you his own grandparents.'

Heydrich suggested a short break to toast the success of the Final Solution. 'You will find the brandy served in this establishment has improved enormously since we have consolidated our hold on France,' he said.

There followed fragments of conversation picked up by the microphones while the waiters served the brandy. Stuckart thought they were losing the important distinction between quarter- and half-Jews, which he had defined in the Nuremberg race laws. Meyer wondered how he could get his east-European Jews at the head of the extermination queue. Kritzinger told Neumann their Blitzkrieg success in the East had led to a bureaucratic nightmare; they were nowhere near ready for such a bold and visionary scheme as this. Neumann thought it all a terrible waste of potential slave labour. Some of his words were dignified with an exclamation mark, no doubt added by Marianne when this document had been in her possession:

NEUMANN: The trouble with them all – from my point of view – is that they can never decide between using the Jews as unpaid workers and liquidating them. I was talking with Speer the other week. He thinks that a man who lets a Jewish worker die of disease or starvation or overwork is in the same class as a driver who never maintains his vehicle and has a breakdown in the middle of a battle. Both of them should be shot. Unpaid Jewish workers – and Polish and Russian . . . any of them – they're an incredibly valuable resource when you think that we're now fighting the two biggest empires and the single richest country in the world. It's sheer lunacy.

HEYDRICH: Prosit, gentlemen! To the Final Solution of the Jewish Question!

ALL: The Final Solution!

The conference resumed. The next section was already familiar to Felix from the 'official' protocol – an explanation by Eichmann of how they would clear the Fatherland of all its Jews first, as a birthday present to the Führer, followed by the Atlantic seaboard

– which brought objections from the delegates from the east, who wanted their territory judenrein first. But Eichmann pointed out that when the Allies invaded France, as they inevitably would some day, no one wanted guerrilla bands of Jews there ready to help them, stabbing the Wehrmacht in the back.

He pointed out that the goods wagons that brought food and requisitioned machinery from the occupied land to the Fatherland would return to the east filled with Jews who had no more need of either.

The meeting dissolved in happy laughter. It was by no means the end of the conference but they were now to enjoy a buffet. But Felix was riveted by what he read next.

[Fragments of simultaneous conversations during this interval]

FREISLER [to LUTHER]: I've been admiring this painting. It's the Wannsee as seen from the lawns outside, I imagine . . . somewhere near here, anyway.

LUTHER: It's by Billy Breit. Admiring it, you say?

FREISLER: Very much. It's surely in the approved style?

LUTHER: You should be careful. It shouldn't be hanging here at all, especially in the German headquarters of Interpol! Our dearly beloved Obergruppenführer obviously doesn't know that old Billy Breit was a Jew!

FREISLER: Really? No – surely you're mistaken? He was a famous anti-Semite.

LUTHER: Of a Jewish mother and a Jewish father – Hannah and Benjamin Breit. He was baptized Solomon.

FREISLER: Du liebe Zeit! I never heard that.

LUTHER: Nor had I – until Gestapo D4 sent a list of French Jews and decadent intellectuals, communists, and so on that they intended rounding up on the twentieth of . . . my God! Today! That's what Müller was talking about of course. Anyway, there were some German émigrés among the decadents and they were asking the Reich Main Security Office to run a check on their racial history. I was kept informed because there will certainly be international repercussions.

FREISLER: But . . . Billy Breit? I mean, he's not still alive, surely?

LUTHER: No, but his grandson is. [laughs] I wonder if he even knows he's quarter-Jewish? Almost certainly not, I'd say. Well! He's in for a big shock today!

FREISLER: You mean Felix Breit? The sculptor? There'll be quite
an outcry if they arrest him.

LUTHER: I certainly hope so! My advice to D4 was to let the
protest run for twenty-four . . . forty-eight hours and then
release him with a great fanfare as a gesture of goodwill – him
and a couple of other scribblers – the French love their scribblers. Meanwhile it will have taken the limelight off the arrest
of the others, rich nonentities, mostly. The usual parasites.

FREISLER: We can always pick him up later, I suppose.

LUTHER: From the Foreign Ministry's perspective, I'd prefer it if
someone helped him escape to Switzerland. He's less than a
half-Jew and these highly publicized arrests of distinguished
people do not help the cause of the Reich among neutral
nations and the churches. Some of our best people never
raise their eyes to look beyond their own immediate occupa-
tions. This pâté is superb.

He set himself to read the rest of the protocol but again and again
it dissolved into a blur as his mind kept returning to that exchange.
They had played god with his life! Of course, they had played
god with every single life in Europe – and he had been part of
that, too – but they had done it with him in particular, by name,
ordaining his release even before his arrest! He could not explain,
even to himself, why it rankled so much but it made him impatient with the rest of the protocol, with Stuckart banging on
about half-Jews and Kritzinger tut-tutting about the lack of bureaucratic rigour and Hofmann pointing out that the Jews were no
longer useful as bargaining tools now that America had joined
the war at last, and everyone worried about the Red Cross and
Eichmann assuring them that Theresienstadt – the 'holiday camp'
KL – would take care of them . . . and Liebbrandt teasing the SS,
pointing out that once the whole of Europe was judenrein, it
might be expedient for the rest of the Reich to make them
scapegoats and have them all liquidated, too, to appease foreign
criticism . . . and – good heavens! – here were the first inklings
of a rift between Luther and his boss, von Ribbentrop, which
ended in Luther being sentenced to a KL himself!

This surely had to be the genuine protocol of that meeting?
Either that or Angela was an unsung giant of German
literature.

The most interesting part – especially for a quarter-Jew like Felix – was where Stuckart defended the rights of the *Mischlinge*. The SS tried to suggest he was only half-hearted in his support of the Final Solution but he pointed out that if Germany lost the military war, it would automatically fail to achieve the Final Solution, too – so it was the SS who were risking both failures, by their insistence on diverting resources and men to promote their own glory. It did not go down well. Heydrich's only answer was that the Führer had decreed it – at which Kritzinger leaped in with a demand to see that in writing in the Führer's own hand. Heydrich answered that adroitly:

HEYDRICH: I'd like to quote from a speech he made as long ago as the twelfth of April, 1922. 'My feeling as a Christian,' the Führer says, 'points me to my Lord and Saviour as a fighter. It points me to a man who once in loneliness, surrounded by a handful of followers, recognized these Jews for what they were and deputized men to fight them.' Remember, Adolf Hitler himself had only a 'handful of followers' at that time, so the parallel does not escape us. He goes on: 'In God's truth, He was greatest not as suffering Jesus but as warrior Jesus. It filled me with boundless love, both as a man and as a Christian, to read how He at last rose in all His might and, whip in hand, drove that race of vipers out of God's Temple. How inspiring is His struggle against that Jewish poison, a struggle on behalf of us all! Today, two thousand years later, I am most profoundly moved to recognize that it was for this God-ordained struggle that He had to shed His blood at Calvary.' And so on. There is much more in the same vein – all of which proves, if anyone here still needs such proof, that the Führer has not cooled in his desire to drive out this race of vipers. On the contrary – if he wants to hear no more about the Jewish Question, it is because he trusts us to get on with it. And let me assure you that I heard as much from his own lips only last year.

After that, Neumann flexed his muscles and demanded that all his Privileged Jews should be exempt from the Final Solution. 'This is not a request,' he said. 'Reichsmarschall Göring has authorized me to make clear that this is a condition of our cooperation.'

Heydrich and Eichmann caved in at once, which gave Stuckart the chance, once again, to make the case for partial Jews.

STUCKART: The half-Jew is also a half-German. He has as many
  Aryan relations as Jewish ones. The quarter-Jew is a three-
  quarters-German. He has three times as many Aryan relations
  as Jewish ones. It is one thing to arrest a Jewish family. No
  German will worry about that. Other Jews will worry, of
  course, but they will soon take the same road east. But if you
  were to arrest all of the Mischlinge and deport them and
  process them, you will leave behind several million Aryan
  Germans who have lost a relative – a husband, wife, son-in-
  law, daughter-in-law, aunt, uncle, cousin. They will talk to
  other Germans . . . who will talk to others . . . and soon the
  whole country will know what we have been told here today.
  Is that the will of the Führer, too – that all the world should
  know what 'Resettlement in the east' really means? If so, why
  not simplify matters and just publish a verbatim transcript of
  this meeting?

And it all turned to farce when Heydrich mused that if two half-Jews marry, they produce a full Jew.

STUCKART: Not necessarily.
HEYDRICH: I beg your pardon?
STUCKART: They have only a twenty-five percent chance of
  producing a full Jew – and, equally, a twenty-five percent
  chance of producing a full Aryan.
KLOPFER: Impossible!
STUCKART: Not at all. It's simple science. Genetics.
HOFMANN: It is impossible . . . it is repugnant for a pair of half-
  Jews to produce a full Aryan.
STUCKART: Nonetheless it is the case, believe me.

From that point the discussion veered back to the well known arguments for sterilization of the *Mischlinge* by radiation – which was also a feature of the 'official' protocol. Mixed-race Jews could be invited into a special room to fill out a form that would keep them busy for twenty minutes or so, during which time a secret dose of gamma-rays would do the trick. They might have tummy upsets for a day or two but Stuckart put it all into its historical context:

STUCKART: Ha! So we go right back to Athens and the birth of democracy!
HEYDRICH: Really? How?
STUCKART: Slaves. They castrated all their male slaves. They were afraid they would breed and outnumber the Athenians. Democracy was only for them, not for the slaves.
HEYDRICH: So! A noble precedent. [to Eichmann] Make a note of that. It sounds feasible.

Then, after Neumann yet again staked the claim for his Privileged Jews and all their relations, Heydrich brought the conference to a rousing conclusion:

HEYDRICH: Thank you Herr State Secretary. It is clear that we have started as we mean to continue – united in purpose, strong in our determination, and steadfast in our desire to see Europe cleansed of this filth once and for all. It has been our Führer's most heartfelt desire ever since he returned from the battlefield to a Fatherland defeated and bankrupted by home-grown Jewish traitors and the international Jewish conspiracy. And now – working together with the will, the vision, and the spirit that only National Socialism can supply – and only German National Socialism, at that – working together under the cloak of war, we can turn that long-held desire of his into a reality. We on this side of the table are merely the agents of that transformation. The driving force lies elsewhere – on your side of this same table, gentlemen, for you represent every important branch of the party, the government, and the Reich. If you falter, if you take your eye off this great objective, then we cannot make up the difference. So I ask you all now to stand – and take the man on either side of you by the hand – and say with me that one word our great Führer most longs to hear in all this world: judenrein!
ALL: Judenrein!
HEYDRICH: And again!

ALL: Judenrein!

HEYDRICH: And again!

ALL: Judenrein!

HEYDRICH: One more time!

ALL: Judenrein!

[applause]

HEYDRICH: ⚡-Obersturmbannführer Eichmann will now collect up all the notes you have been taking during this meeting. [protests] In the next week or so his office will circulate a very partial version of our discussions to all departments that request it. But in general we think you will agree – when you think about it – that a verbal report by you to your various departments and ministries (or, in fact, to those who wish to know) is far preferable to a verbatim protocol. Heil Hitler!

ALL: Heil Hitler!

But Angela's transcript did not end there for she had also recorded some conversations among the delegates as they dispersed – one of which almost made him vomit:

KRITZINGER [to STUCKART]: I didn't want to point this out at the meeting but when you spoke of the 'bar-mitzvah Jew' and the 'circumcised Jew' you were straying from strictly racial criteria into religious ones – despite the fact that you and your office have always said that the Jew's crime is racial not religious.

STUCKART: It's a little bit more subtle than that, Herr Ministerialdirektor. The Mischling is a fundamentally ambiguous creature, half pulling toward the Aryan, half toward the Semite. So the question becomes, 'Which half is pulling the harder?' This Mischling is an atheist . . . loves Wagner . . . so the Aryan is pulling harder. But this Mischling loves Mendelssohn and won't light a fire on Saturdays . . . well – he selects himself as a Jew. And the consequences follow as night follows day. He is not being liquidated for practising religion but because his practice reveals which side, Jew or Aryan, is the stronger in him.

KRITZINGER: Elegant!

★　　★　　★

HEYDRICH [to MEYER, LIEBBRANDT, and BÜHLER]: Gentlemen! You cannot come all this way, here, to the very heart of the Reich, without taking back some happy memories.

MEYER: Today's decisions have been the happiest of my—

HEYDRICH: I mean happy in a more personal sense.

BÜHLER: The house in Giesebrechtstrasse!

HEYDRICH: Just so! Unfortunately I have to return to Prague this afternoon, but I'm sure ϟϟ-Gruppenführer Müller will be happy to take you to dinner and then onward to that delightful rendezvous!

LIEBBRANDT: Talking of which – I didn't think it correct to bring this up in the meeting – but many young Jewesses are extremely . . . what shall I say . . .

MEYER: Voluptuous.

LIEBBRANDT: Yes. So, just as fit young Jewish males can be temporarily spared for unpaid work in our factories, surely voluptuous young Jewesses could be put to unpaid work in brothels for . . .

HEYDRICH: It's already happening.

LIEBBRANDT: Ah!

MEYER: Men in uniform needn't pay, I presume?

EICHMANN: A token. To cover the running costs. And there will be no Mischlinge as a result. The girls are sterilized first.

HEYDRICH: Before taking up their positions, one might say.
[laughter]

LANGE [to Heydrich, on the doorstep]: Maybe I ought to have told Kritzinger we don't waste bullets on the children – or maybe not?

HEYDRICH: How do you process them, then?

LANGE: So! [makes some gesture] Up to about eight, one good shake just snaps their necks. Older than that, strangling is easier – with bare hands or a garrotte. But we don't waste bullets on them until they're thirteen . . . fourteen.

[A dog barks]

HEYDRICH: You actually brought your dog!

LANGE: Max. Here boy! Let him loose. Here! Catch! This is the sort of meat they have in the kitchens here.

HEYDRICH: What teeth!

LANGE: Wasn't there some sort of decoration for dogs in the last war? I thought I read that. If not, we should start one. I tell you – this dog's hatred of Jews is even stronger than the Führer's.

HEYDRICH: Careful!

LANGE: It's true, though. I can give you an example. About ten days ago we were processing the Jews in a little village in . . . no matter. It was well below zero – below minus thirty – and the ground was almost impossible to dig and everything got out of synchronization and the women and the children had to be kept waiting back in the forest a bit. They were already naked so they huddled together really tight and did their pathetic best to keep the little children warm. But some of the children's feet froze to the ground so that when we drove them on . . . well, you know how frozen flesh just comes away? Bits of their feet were left behind, frozen to the ground. But that didn't please my Max! He ate every last bit of that flesh. He couldn't stand the thought that even those small morsels had escaped justice! Good boy! Good boy!

HEYDRICH: [undecipherable]

'What d'you think?' Angela asked.

Felix told her.

'I'm still shocked,' she said, 'that I didn't really *hear* what they were saying until I typed out that transcript. You know how you can sometimes see the world through a window all running with condensation and you can't make out a single thing? Then suddenly you realize that one of the blobs is . . . I don't know, a car . . . or the branch of a tree. And suddenly everything else starts to make sense. It was like that. All that fog of Nazi . . . *stuff* . . . that endless stream of propaganda on the wireless – it all fell into place. I saw it for what it actually was. Where it was going. All those things they didn't dare say . . . talking instead of the Jewish *question* . . . the final *solution.*'

Something Felix had not realized until now: for months after her eyes were opened, she had worked against them while she continued to act the loyal Nazi, the steadfast SS officer, the confidante of Reinhard Heydrich. And when he died, and they took their revenge on her, even under torture she had admitted no more than what they already knew – that, yes, she had, indeed, made tape recordings of that conference.

And now he knew how she had survived when so many in Ravensbrück had not. 'When we get back to the Dower House . . .' he said.

'What?'

'It will be the start of a new life. For both of us. A wonderful new life. You'll see.'

Is Felix right? You can follow the continuing lives, adventures, and misadventures of Felix, Angela, and the other Dower House families in *Strange Music,* to be published soon.